THE KEEPERS' CHRONICLES

THE SKYLIGHTER

THE KEEPERS' CHRONICLES

THE SKY

Also by Becky Wallace

The Storyspinner

LIGHTER

BECKY WALLACE

MARGARET K. McELDERRY BOOKS
NEW YORK LONDON TORONTO SYDNEY NEW DELHI

MARGARET K. McELDERRY BOOKS
An imprint of Simon & Schuster Children's Publishing Division
1230 Avenue of the Americas, New York, New York 10020
This book is a work of fiction. Any references to historical events, real people, or real places are used fictitiously. Other names, characters, places, and events are products of the author's imagination, and any resemblance to actual events or places or persons, living or dead, is entirely coincidental.

The text for this book is set in Kepler Std.
Manufactured in the United States of America
2 4 6 8 10 9 7 5 3 1
Library of Congress Cataloging-in-Publication Data
Wallace, Becky.
The skylighter / Becky Wallace.—First edition.
p. cm.—(The Keepers' chronicles)
Summary: Joanna and Rafi are on the run, trying to protect the kingdom of Santarem from rogue Keepers.
ISBN 978-1-4814-0568-3 (hardcover)
ISBN 978-1-4814-0570-6 (eBook)
[1. Fantasy. 2. Magic—Fiction.] I. Title.
PZ7.W15472Sk 2016
[Fic]—dc23
2015007088

FIRST EDITION

For my grandma,
Edie Winkelman, with
love and gratitude

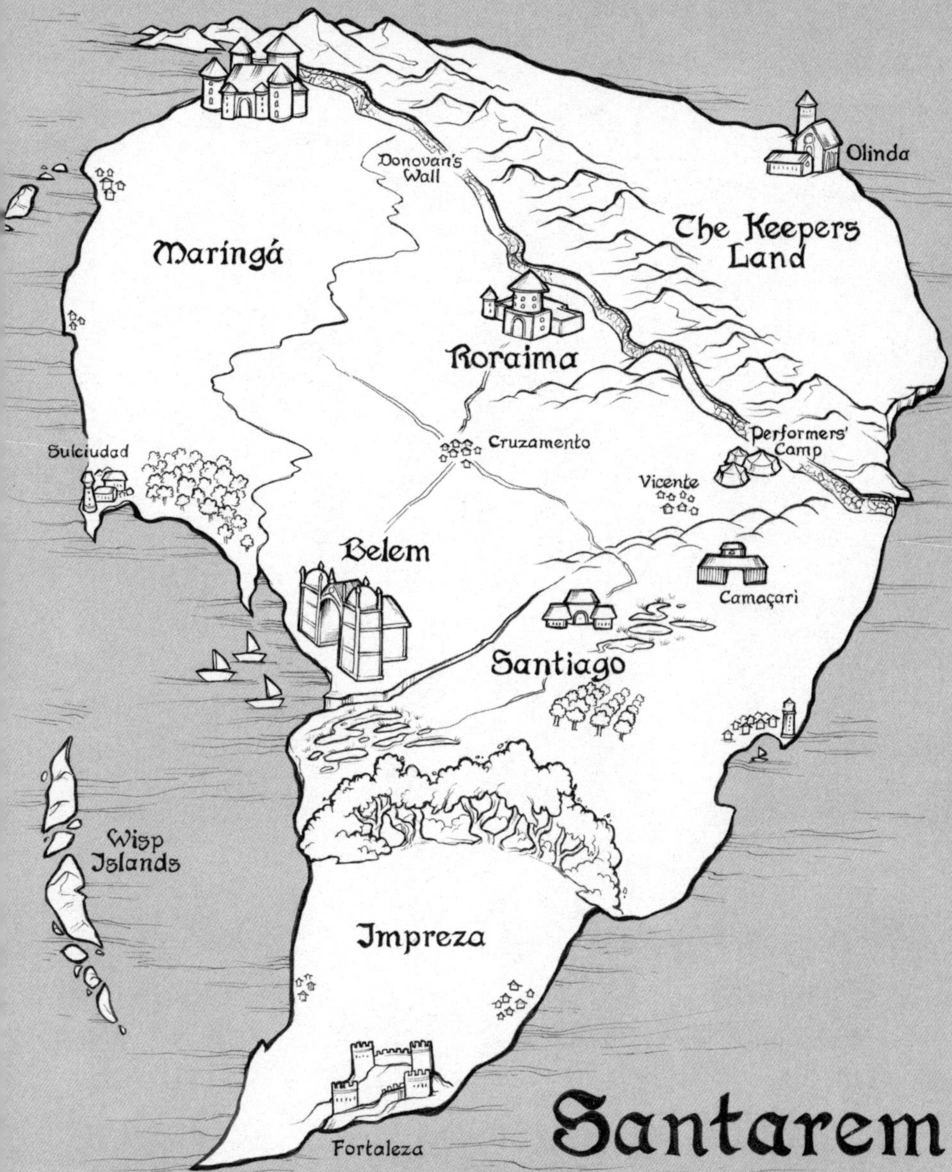
Donovan's Wall
Olinda
Maringá
The Keepers Land
Roraima
Sulciudad
Cruzamento
Performers' Camp
Vicente
Belem
Camaçari
Santiago
Wisp Islands
Impreza
Fortaleza
Santarem

Chapter 1

Pira

Millions of tiny feet stampeded over Pira's skin, under her shirt, through her hair, into her nose. Leather strips bound her wrists and ankles together, making it impossible for her to dislodge the nasty little creatures. She thrashed, rolling across the gravel-strewn campsite, trying to crush the *paraponeras* under her weight, but nothing deterred them from reaching her flesh.

As if responding to a silent command, the ants sank their needle-sharp pincers into her body, injecting a venom that burned and throbbed. She bit her tongue to keep from crying out, and letting the ants crawl *in*.

"You will answer my questions," a voice whispered from somewhere both near and far. Coming from both within her mind and without.

Pira couldn't see the speaker, couldn't see anything with her eyes shut tight against the agony. Sweat dripped from her forehead as her body shuddered and rocks dug into older wounds. Those injuries gave a different sort of hurt, dull and achy, the bruises from an earlier battle.

She clutched that ache like a lifeline to reality. *It's magic,* she realized. *These ants aren't eating me alive. It's all in my head.* Knowing didn't stop the phantom pain, but it gave her the strength to hold on a little longer.

"Tell me about your companions. Tell me their affinities. Tell me about Jacaré, and I will make this all go away." The voice had a sibilant quality, stretching out the words with a hiss.

Vibora. The viper.

Pira tried not to think about the events that led to her capture, afraid the collar around her neck would somehow relay the information, but the sensations flooded her mind unbidden. She saw the ambush and Tex burning in a column of flame; she felt the marsh, stagnant and thick against her ankles as she led Johanna toward Santiago; she heard the hail of pebbles thunk against Vibora's flesh and the sound of the horse galloping away with Johanna tucked close to Rafi's back; she tasted the acrid words she'd shouted at Leão the last time they spoke—words she'd never be able to recant while living as another Keeper's slave.

Rolling to her side, Pira tucked her knees tight to her stomach, as if she were protecting herself from the magical barrage. The position also hid her efforts to remove the collar. She could feel metal pressing somewhere between her chin and her collarbones, but she couldn't *feel* it.

Metal was Pira's specialized affinity, but her gift failed her.

Jacaré had warned that someday she'd have to fight against a weapon she couldn't sense. She never imagined the battlefield would be inside her own head.

"Your *essência* is draining away," Vibora said with a laugh, a sound like scales slithering over dry leaves. "The collar will suck away every drop, and when you recover, I'll drain you again. I will use your own power to torture you until you tell me Jacaré's location and his plan."

Pira's muscles began to spasm, a late reaction to the *paraponeras'* bites. Her body believed the magic, even if her mind recognized the truth.

"Tell me."

The ants bit again.

"Tell. Me."

Pira opened her mouth.

And screamed.

Chapter 2

Johanna

Dawn, pale as fresh butter, melted through the tangle of branches above Johanna's and Rafi's heads. The light nibbled away the mist that hung over the marsh and revealed a strange sort of beauty in the twisted limbs of their temporary haven.

The light did not, however, expose a safe route to escape from the caimans that had chased them into the tree. At some point during the night the lizards had stopped hissing and snapping their teeth. Disappearing into the black water, they were content to wait for their prey under the knotted roots of the mangrove trees. She couldn't see them but knew they were out there lurking. Hidden. Hungry.

And they weren't the only cold-blooded monsters stalking her.

Keepers, the heroes of so many of Johanna's stories, were real and nothing like she'd been trained to believe. She'd sold so many lies as a Storyspinner, unwittingly building up the Keepers as magical saviors. As soon as she had the chance, she'd correct those misconceptions, recounting her own adventure as their captive.

Would people still idolize the Keepers who had kidnapped Johanna as she was weeping over her brother's dead body?

Probably, she realized with annoyance. Jacaré and his group did have a noble purpose; an audience might approve of any tactics that would save Santarem, especially given the real villains they'd been pitted against.

Vibora. Thoughts of that magic-wielding witch and her mindless slaves made Johanna shiver. She'd spent only a few moments in that woman's clutches, but it had been a few moments too many.

If Vibora had her way, the story would conclude with all the people of Santarem serving as her slaves. It was the only fate worse than having Duke Inimigo, the failed usurper and the tyrant of the Ten Years' War, on the throne.

Unfortunately for Johanna—*and everyone else, really*—the country's future rested on her very unprepared shoulders. She'd been raised as a Performer, instead of as a princess, and was unsuited to rule anything greater than a few wagonloads of acrobats and Fireswords. But a princess she was, albeit a reluctant one. And Santarem's tale would come to a very unpleasant end if she failed to reach Donovan's Wall and secure the magical barrier that kept her country protected from the Keepers' land beyond.

Thinking about it all—the deaths of her family members, the truth of her heritage, and her duty to the people—made her lightheaded with anxiety. A dangerous thing to be, considering her precarious perch.

We have to reach Donovan's Wall.

She took a deep breath, trying to calm her racing heart, and Rafi's arms tightened around her waist in response. His touch sent her pulse sprinting for a different reason.

Even though they'd spent several hours nested together, her back to his chest and his back against the tree, the closeness between them was a new thing. It made her feel timid and green; it was a new high-wire routine she hadn't quite mastered, and there was real danger if she fell.

"Are you awake?" Rafi asked in a hoarse whisper.

"Of course I'm awake. I couldn't possibly sleep with you snoring in my ear."

"At least I don't drool."

Rafi's tone was dry, but she felt his chest bounce with a barely restrained laugh.

Johanna frowned, feigning offense she didn't feel. They had spent weeks circling each other like snarling animals, taking every opportunity to nip at the other's confidence and pounce on the other's flaws. It was easier for her to slip into the familiar role of prickly Performer than to think of the night they had spent together.

It was the wrong turn of phrase, and her whole body blushed with the implied meaning. They had kissed—*More like you threw yourself at him*—and it had been perfect and delicious, and then horrifically interrupted by Vibora, intent on Johanna's capture.

Rafi laced his fingers around Johanna's middle, as if sensing she needed comfort. During the night, when she'd mourned for her family, she'd sobbed brokenly in his arms, but now she shrugged out of his embrace. Instead of soothing away her pain, his touch made her keenly aware of every loss.

Johanna maneuvered around on the branch to face him. "Pira should have been here by now. I hope she escaped. I hope . . ."

There was so much sympathy in Rafi's expression that Jo had to look away. Instead she studied the water below and added Pira's name to the tally of casualties. The list had gotten very long, very quickly. *Joshua, Thomas, Mama, Captain Alouette, Snout, two of Rafi's guardsmen, and now Pira.*

The loss of life made Johanna sick to her already empty stomach.

"The caimans probably moved to the banks to sun themselves at daybreak." Rafi snapped a handful of twigs off the branch over his head and threw them into the water. Nothing rose to the bait. "This is the best time for us to make a run for it."

The safest, maybe, but there was no guarantee that either of them would make it out of the swamp alive. They had no food or water and only one weapon, and Rafi had lost a boot and his sword in their frantic flight from the caimans.

"It'll be easier to find our way out with the daylight," Johanna agreed, trying to reassure both of them that they weren't about to face death at the jaws of a hungry beast.

"I'll go first," he said, sliding his dagger free of its sheath. "If anything happens, then you can still escape and continue on."

"You couldn't get into the tree without my help. And if the caimans do attack, then it will be much easier for you to pull me back up." Johanna didn't give him the chance to argue. She smacked his elbow with the top of her fist, and the knife popped out of his grasp.

"Jo—" He reached for the weapon, but she clenched the blade between her teeth and scurried away. "What are you doing?"

She smiled around the dagger and fell backward, hooking her knees around the branch.

It wasn't much different from swinging on a trapeze. She flipped, catching the lowest limb. It bowed under her weight, dislodging a spray of leaves. They floated on the water's black surface, flecks of green on a tar pit.

"Stop, Johanna." His voice broke on her name. "Please."

Nothing stirred. Nothing lunged out of the water. It didn't mean the animals were gone, but it did give her a bit of hope. She looked up once more, catching Rafi's wide eyes. Her heart gave a painful thump at the distress on his face, but sitting in the tree was certain death—from starvation or *when* the evil Keepers found them.

Praying her instinct was correct, she dropped onto the clump of roots that arched out of the murk.

Chapter 3

Rafi

Dread made Rafi's palms slick with sweat. He gripped the trunk tightly and shimmied down behind Johanna, keeping one eye on his path and one on her. Any moment a caiman would lurch out of the water and snatch her away. She would disappear forever in a flash of blood and screams.

But as he worked his way out of the branches—his stocking foot snagging on twigs—nothing happened. The swamp's mirrored surface remained perfectly flat, not even a jumping fish or large bug created ripples in the water.

"I think they're gone." She leaned forward a bit, peering beyond the tree's roots, as if she could see the creatures through the blackness.

"Stay back. They're faster than you can imagine." His arm still ached from the vicious attacks he'd fended off with his sword. Caimans had thrown themselves against the blade, nearly knocking it from his grip a half dozen times. Even if he hadn't dropped the weapon while climbing into the tree, he wasn't sure he'd be able to heft it now.

He had no way to defend Johanna, besides throwing himself into the teeth of the beasts.

"Get behind me, please." He slid in front of her, boxing her between his torso and the tree trunk. "And give me back my knife."

She frowned at him but slapped the blade against his palm.

"Let's agree on one thing," he said as he returned the knife to his belt. "You are more important than I am."

"Rafi—"

"No," he said sharply. "Last night you said you wanted to go to Donovan's Wall. You said you wanted to save Santarem from people like Vibora."

"Of course I do," she said, raising her chin defiantly. "But you can't put yourself in danger to protect me."

"That's where you're wrong, Johanna. Protecting you is exactly what I *must* do." He ignored the hard set of her jaw and continued, "I know how it wounds your pride to feel indebted to anyone. But please, just this once, will you allow me to go first?"

With a flourish she held her arm out to the side. "Be my guest."

"Thank you ever so much," he said with equal acerbity.

"Certainly, *my lord*."

Her tone made his hackles rise, but he forced himself to ignore the irritation.

There were two islands of weeds within leaping distance. He studied the water around both, in case he missed, and decided that the one on the north side looked like it was more likely to support his weight. From there it would be a quick hop to a dead mangrove tree that lay on its side, half out of the water.

"Rafi?" Johanna's fingers touched his forearm gently, and he found real worry pinching her features. "Be careful, won't you?"

Her concern matched his growing trepidation, but he hid it with a smile he hoped looked confident. “Of course.”

Trying not to think about the caimans and their vicious teeth, Rafi swung his arms and landed squarely on the center of the island. His feet punched through the bracken, and the tangle of weeds sucked him under. He gasped, spluttering as water closed over his head, cutting off Johanna’s frantic screams.

CHAPTER 4

JOHANNA

Johanna didn't think. She leaped, landing on the island's closest edge. It held her much lighter weight, and she immediately dropped to her belly and slithered close to the Rafi-size hole. Broken stalks of weeds bent downward, pointing into a warren of roots. She could see nothing in the black water except bubbles breaking at the surface.

"Rafi!" she screamed, and reached into the opening, never considering what else could be lurking below. Flailing for anything that felt human, her hand encountered the feathery texture of weeds and the sharp bite of twisted roots and raking thorns. Something bumped into her arm, then snatched it, yanking her toward the hole.

A terrified shriek escaped her lips as she dug in her toes and tried to scuttle backward, but the weight was too heavy, dragging her toward the water.

She grabbed at the weeds with her free hand, a weak anchor, and dug her toes into the mud, certain her shoulder would tear out of the socket.

Something flashed above the water level, slimy and muck covered, but identifiable as a hand. The top of a head followed, fronds tangled into black curls.

Jo gave one more violent tug, feeling her joint pop in protest, and Rafi's face appeared. He sucked in a huge lungful of air and heaved himself out of the water, mimicking her pose, dispersing his weight over the island.

"The roots," he said between wheezing breaths. "I couldn't get free—couldn't tell which way to the surface."

She gulped, breathing as if she, too, had been underwater for too long. "Well then, you should probably thank me."

"I don't know if I should thank you . . . or strangle you."

"What?" She lifted her head. "I saved your life."

"You stuck your arm into a hole where a caiman could have been waiting to eat you." He wiped the dirty water away from his eyes and gave Jo a hard stare. "Next time will you please *think* before you act impulsively?"

It was so ridiculous that she laughed. She laughed loud enough to startle the birds out of the trees, and after a few moments Rafi joined in.

Hours later when they finally emerged from the swamp, neither of them was laughing. They were too tired, too hungry, too tense to talk. Crossing the swamp had been grueling. The trees had trapped the heat and humidity close to the water, sapping their energy and creating a breeding ground for swarms of biting bugs.

They were grateful to be on a solid road, but miserable and itchy. And Rafi was in far worse shape than Johanna. His fall had resulted in a dozen deep scrapes on his side, and his stocking foot was bruised and bleeding. While they both had been wet, his clothes had dried stiff and stinking.

The only good news was that Rafi had a general idea of where they were, and was certain a fishing village was only a few miles north. There they could barter for fresh clothing and shelter.

At sunset they caught sight of a few small homes and a tiny inn, all built on raised platforms. The thatch roofs mingled with the lowest branches of the ironwood trees, making the houses seem as if they were built right into the trunks. Clumps of hydrangea, blooming in bright greens and blues, hugged the stilts below the inn and climbed up the staircase to the covered porch.

It would have been picturesque without the dried monkey heads dangling from the eaves.

Johanna arched away as a light breeze stirred the gruesome garland. The animals' eyes had been stitched shut, but their gaping mouths revealed shriveled black tongues between sharp yellow teeth.

"They're for protection," Rafi said as he held open the door for her to pass through. "It's a local custom."

Johanna pulled a disgusted face. "Not one you practice in Santiago."

"Well . . ." He offered her the grin that she always thought was just a smidgen arrogant. "You haven't seen the inside of my closet."

"Ah. That explains your odor."

He barked a short laugh and followed her into the common room.

Johanna's hair was clean, and her stomach ached with fullness. It was her first real meal since the Keepers had captured her and dragged her away from Santiago, leaving the wreckage of her family in their wake.

Her brothers would have loved the food. She could imagine Thomas devouring bowl after bowl of *feijoada*, and Michael eating so fast he'd dribble some on his shirt. And Joshua . . .

Pressing her hand to her mouth, she forced down the sob that threatened to rise with thoughts of her brothers. She could still feel Joshua's blood on her skin and hear his rasping final words. *Safe,* he'd said, using his last breath to reassure her that Michael was alive and hidden.

In four months' time she'd lost her father, mother, and two of her brothers, and watched a handful of other people die trying to protect her. Her career and identity had been snatched away and replaced with something ephemeral.

And all for what? Because I'm apparently the heir to the throne of a broken kingdom and responsible for a barrier I don't know how to fix?

Jacaré had sworn that as the magical barrier weakened, it created an elemental vacuum, siphoning power from Santarem and throwing the environment out of balance. Panthers crept out of the mountains to harass farmers, snakes infested the ruins of the capital city, and a vicious drought stretched on, killing crops and leaving many of Rafi's people without enough food for the winter. And that was only the beginning of the danger. The Nata, as Jacaré had called them, were Keepers motivated by greed and power. They would flood Santarem and control its people if the wall fell.

Tears burned in Jo's tired eyes, but she refused to let them drop. Rafi had gone down to bathe and bandage the gashes he'd gotten when he fell, but he would be back soon. Johanna would not fall apart in front of him. Not again.

A voice broke through her dark thoughts, its tone soothing and familiar.

Think of Beta, her father would have said, retelling one of

Santarem's oldest stories. *She lost her hand to the* dragão, *but did she give up the fight? Did she let that monster raze the countryside and destroy Santarem? No! She walked into its lair and fired the killing bolt with one hand and her teeth!*

Get up, Johanna. Get up and fight.

After a few deep breaths she did. She and Rafi had worked out a plan as they made their slow progress through the swamp. The magical barrier had to be repaired. But without Jacaré's help, Johanna had no idea how to make that happen. There was only one place that might have the answers she sought: the Great Maringa Library.

It housed the greatest collection of Keeper lore, some of which was rumored to have been looted from the Citadel after it had fallen and Johanna's birth parents, King Wilhelm and Queen Christiana, had been slaughtered by Duke Inimigo's troops.

"We cannot go to Maringa. Inimigo will have our heads," Rafi had said when she initially made the suggestion. "It isn't worth the risk, no matter what those books can tell us."

"Can you think of another way?" Johanna had challenged.

Neither of them would consider going to Duke Belem for help. The fat menace had attacked Johanna and stolen her necklace, King Wilhelm's sigil. He had been untrustworthy before he had the necklace, but now he was a dangerous foe with the means to consolidate power and make a play for Santarem's throne. They couldn't afford to let him get close to Johanna again.

All other arguments had dissolved, and Rafi and Jo had agreed to continue traveling north to Cruzamento before turning west to Maringa. They hoped that any pursuers would expect Rafi to return to the DeSilva estate, and be thrown off their trail.

At least that's what they wanted to happen. They had no idea how many Keepers had sided with Vibora or how many subjugates might be helping her.

If they could get to Maringa. If they could find the information. If they could figure out how to stabilize the wall. If they could stand against power-hungry dukes and powerful Keepers . . .

If. If. If. No guarantees. No assurances.

She swiped away the doubts and determined to hold on to whatever shreds of hope she could grasp, knowing too well the consequences of succumbing to despair. After her father's death, Johanna's mother had fallen into an awful, crippling depression, and the rest of her family had been casualties.

For now, Johanna would have to find some pocket in the back of her mind to stuff her own hurts and woes into. Someday, when this whole tangle was unraveled, she'd allow herself the time to grieve for her family properly.

Footsteps approached from the common room, and she forced a smile onto her face. It trembled, but held.

Rafi knocked lightly before pushing the door open. "Johanna?" He edged into their shared room, as if he were invading her private space. He'd purchased a new shirt, a garish woven thing with a wide V at the neck, a large pocket across his belly, and a hood that hung to his waist. It wasn't quite long enough, looking like something that might have shrunk in too-hot wash water.

Johanna wanted to laugh, but she couldn't look away from the lines of muscle the shirt exposed. She'd always been attracted to

Rafi, even when she refused to admit it. She had spent weeks ignoring his good looks, branding him a conceited noble, and taking every opportunity to wound his pride. But now heat crept up her cheeks when she realized that neither of them had spoken, that they both waited, frozen, staring at each other.

"That shirt is absolutely hideous," she said, finally breaking the silence.

"Wait till you see the dress I got you." He flung a package in her direction. "I thought it was a good disguise."

She unrolled the bundle and fingered the purple, brown, and yellow material. "Are we blind beggars?"

"No, we're wool merchants."

"Who specialize in selling the ugliest fabric possible?" She held the dress up to her neck and saw that it was meant for a much larger woman. She'd have to hack off the bottom and find a way to cinch the neckline, but it was far better than the shirt she'd rinsed out in the bathtub. "What is this pattern? Clouds with legs? Trees with too many trunks?"

"I believe they're sheep." Though from the look on his face, it seemed he, too, was struggling to decipher the picture. "Wool merchants dye their cloth in the brightest colors possible as showpieces when they travel to larger towns."

"This one has five legs."

"I think that's a tail." He reached across the small space to touch the animal in question, his hand lingering on her arm.

The contact sparked a fuse, lines of heat raced across her skin, spiraling inward, making her stomach clench.

Breathe, Johanna. No need to get ninny-headed every time he walks into a room.

She wanted to turn away, to pretend she felt nothing, but his fingers slid past the bend of her elbow and landed on the dip of her waist.

Rafi pressed her closer. The ugly dress was crushed between them, her hands fisted against his ribs, his heart pounding against her knuckles.

There was a moment of hesitation, when he gave her the chance to back away.

She didn't.

Chapter 5

Rafi

Their first kiss had been a gift; sweet and innocent, new and hesitant. This kiss was stolen; bold, daring, and a little wicked. Johanna's hands relaxed, slipping down his body, fingers splaying over his abdomen. The dress forgotten.

Rafi's lips slid to Johanna's jaw, then her neck, as his hands quested up her back, tracing over the small bones of her spine. She twined one hand into his hair and held him tighter.

He wasn't quite sure when he'd moved, but his forearm was pressed against the room's rear wall, his weight pinning Johanna to the rough wooden planks. Her fingertips had crept under the hem of his too-short shirt, and he was painfully aware of her skin against his.

That was the moment when a chaperone, or an angry father, or his irritating younger brother, Dom, would have burst through the door—at least, that's how the stories went. Kissing was always interrupted when it was still just kissing, before lines were crossed, before one of them had to be brave enough to stop.

Before rules were broken.

Where's your honor now, Rafael DeSilva?

He ignored the thought for a moment longer, before pulling away with a groan. Even if Performers' rules were different, his behavior wasn't in line with his own sense of right and wrong.

He pressed his forehead against hers, neither of them speaking until their breathing had calmed a bit.

"I'm sorry. I should have . . . I shouldn't have . . ." He pinched his eyes shut. "Do Performers have betrothal contracts like nobles do? I mean, I thought that since you'd been raised a Performer, maybe those would be the standards you would want to follow, but since you're not actually a Performer—"

"Betrothal contract?" she asked, with a wide grin and a laugh in her voice. "Rafi, what in Mother Lua's name are you talking about?"

"I just . . ." He stepped away, needing the space, needing to breathe air that wasn't scented with the sweet smell of Johanna. It would have been so easy to pick up where he left off. "If there's a right way to do things, I want to know. I want our betrothal to be a success. I want you to feel comfortable and happy and—"

She held up a hand, stopping him, and for that he was grateful. He was babbling like an idiot.

"Last night you said that this would be a story to tell our grandchildren about," she said slowly, the happiness fading from her face. "You meant *our* grandchildren."

A tickle of trepidation, like an unseen spider, raced across Rafi's shoulders. "Well . . . of course. You know our fathers arranged our betrothal after you were born."

"Your father and King Wilhelm arranged it. My father was Arlo Von Arlo."

"Your *real* father was the king. You are Princess Adriana."

Jo turned slightly to the side, not facing him directly, almost as if she was avoiding the truth. "I don't have to be."

"Of course you do. You're the heir to this kingdom." They'd discussed her identity; he'd shared the letter his father had written. Even if she was afraid or didn't understand her duties, there was no reason to deny them completely. Unless . . .

He ignored the bite of rejection and pressed on. "With my help and with my uncle Fernando's, you could put Belem and Inimigo in their rightful places." He stepped closer to her and softened his tone. "After the barrier is repaired, we could do so much good."

"Oh, we should *definitely* get married for the sake of Santarem." Her words nipped, sharp with teeth of sarcasm. "Or, here's another idea, once I repair this magical barrier, I could remain an anonymous Performer and live my life without constant threats from people who want to kill me and everyone I love."

The words he was going to say dried up on his tongue, and he swallowed a few times, forcing away the hurt. This wasn't about him. At least, not entirely. "You're scared. I understand that—"

"This isn't *only* about being afraid, Rafi. Marriage? Thrones? This isn't something two dead men should decide for us."

"Those two dead men were our fathers," he said, his temper flaring. "They'd want us to put our selfish concerns aside and think about our people."

That was the wrong thing to say. He knew it as soon as the words left his mouth, and he watched the instant effect they had on Johanna's posture.

She faced him squarely, spine straight as a sword. He'd seen her do this before, making herself seem bigger and more threatening, like a hunted beast facing down a predator.

"Selfish concerns," she said, her words clipped. "Michael, my little brother, is a *selfish* concern?"

"You know that's not what I meant—"

"You're asking me to put Santarem over what's left of my family—and I'm already doing that by going to the wall. He is the only thing I have left. What else is this country going to ask from me?"

Everything. Rafi had been raised to serve the people, and while it was a burden, he also felt honored to bear it. Maybe it was unfair to ask Johanna to carry the same weight, but he'd harbored a humble hope that she'd be willing to share it as his partner. His wife. Working together toward the same goal.

He never anticipated how much that commonality would mean to him, and he had to look away, afraid she'd see something vulnerable and disappointed in his expression. There was a blanket on the bedside table, and he made a bed on the floor while Johanna turned her back and slipped the ugly dress over her head.

The silence between them stretched cold and uncomfortable, neither of them warming the small room with words. Eventually Johanna cleared her throat. "Were there any horses to buy?"

"No," he said as he stepped out of his boots and lay down fully dressed. "We can ride out with the peddler who is staying downstairs. His cart is crowded, but I can spend most of the time jogging alongside."

"We can take turns."

"Jo—" He cut himself off before he started another argument. "Fine. We'll take turns."

Chapter 6

Dom

A shaft of sunlight shone through the open hatch that led to the manor's roof. Dom jogged up the narrow stairway and shouldered through the opening.

"Michael?" he shouted as he stepped onto the flat space. "Are you up here?"

The roof was cluttered with chimneys, stacks of terra-cotta repair tiles, and the roost that housed the DeSilvas' messenger pigeons. Plenty of places for a child to hide.

"If you're up here, please come out."

The little boy tried to keep his emotions hidden, but when he was too sad, he hid himself instead. The maids found him under tables, beneath the stairs, and once, sound asleep in a pile of clean laundry. This time he'd been missing for hours, and Brynn, the head maid, was pulling her hair out with worry. She'd enlisted every household member, the off-duty guardsmen, and even the few remaining visitors to help search for the boy.

"Michael!"

Only the pigeons responded to Dom's call. He checked the cage for any new arrivals, any message from his brother or the other group who'd gone in search of Johanna.

But there was nothing. Not a message. Not a sad, lonely little boy.

Dom crossed to the half wall that wrapped around the landing, and leaned his elbows against the railing, feeling tired and frustrated. The past week had been hellish, even without worrying about his young charge. People kept coming to him with questions he didn't know how to answer.

Lord Dom, a representative from the Farmers' Guild is here. Would you like to speak to him?

Lord Dom, would you prefer to have the guest situated in the east wing or the west?

Lord Dom, where should I put the cartload of pickled beets? In the cellar or the pantry?

At first he redirected everyone to his mother, but when he realized how overwhelmed she was in Rafi's absence, Dom tried to handle the requests himself. And was certain he'd done everything wrong.

Come back soon, Rafi. I'm not capable of taking care of anyone but myself. He looked toward the Milners' mango orchard, where a bare patch marked the spot where the Von Arlos' wagons once stood. At this distance he couldn't see anything besides a black smudge in the green canopy, but he knew the bones of the wagons were still there.

Perhaps Michael had tried to go home?

Dom turned toward the stairs and saw a hint of purple fabric sticking out from behind one of the chimneys. He wasn't particularly observant, but that precise shade had been stretched over a body that was difficult to ignore.

"You may as well come out, Lady Maribelle." Dom stepped between the chimney and the roof's exit, blocking off any escape attempt. "I know you're hiding."

"I'm not hiding." She straightened from a crouch, shaking out her silky black hair. "You seemed to be having a private moment, and I didn't want to interrupt."

"Hmm." Dom folded his arms across his chest and spread his feet wide. "For some reason I'm hesitant to believe you."

"Like you, I enjoy the view of Santiago," she said as she stepped out of the narrow space, dragging several feet of skirt behind her. Her fashion selections were a topic of much conversation among the staff and nobles. Today her dress was decidedly bottom heavy, baring her clavicles and arms despite the slight chill in the air.

Maribelle moved with a sway, shifting her hips from side to side as she circled toward the hatch.

Dom wasn't distracted by her curves or her ploy to slip past him, and kept himself between the lady and her escape. "I could take you to a few places that have excellent scenery."

"That would be lovely, my lord," she said with a coy shrug.

Neither of them moved, each waiting for the other to make an excuse to leave or to stay on the roof.

I can play this game all day. Dom grinned at Maribelle without showing his teeth. "Since you were up here enjoying the view, you didn't by chance notice Michael out on the grounds anywhere?"

"I didn't." She moved one hand to her waist. "I've always found that haylofts are a perfect place to hide. Perhaps we should check there?"

Brazen. I like that. "Sounds like an excellent plan."

"I'll follow you down."

Dom held out his arm. "Let me escort you."

Maribelle's smile faded. "Perhaps after lunch? I promised my ladies I'd join them."

Dom withheld one of a dozen caustic remarks about Maribelle and her two attendants. The women spent all their time strutting around the estate or fluttering to the township to gossip with every highborn and—if the rumors were true—some significantly less savory fellows.

"Shall I call a maid and have the kitchen bring something up?"

"I'm fine on my own." She softened the edge to her words with a quick, "Thank you."

Dom knew he'd won. "How about you give me the message you're so desperately trying to send to your father?"

"I don't know what you're talking about, my lord." She looked away, but her left hand twitched on her skirt. "Please excuse me."

He stepped to one side, nodding toward the stairway. Maribelle hesitated for a moment, her eyes flicking to the roost and back, then hurried toward the exit.

As she passed, Dom snatched her wrist. She twisted away, hunching as if expecting a blow.

"Please . . ." She raised her free arm to protect her head.

Guilt nipped, and Dom loosened his grip. "I'm not going to hit you, Lady Maribelle," he said in the gentlest voice he could muster.

The girl had certainly faced her father's anger a time or two, most recently as Inimigo had rushed to depart Santiago a few days earlier. It had been an ugly scene, starting at the dinner table, where the duke received an urgent message from one of his underlings that described problems rising in Maringa, and then continuing into the courtyard.

Inimigo dragged Maribelle by the arm out to his waiting carriage, whispering fiercely. Dom wasn't able to hear the words they exchanged, but their body language was clear. She kept her head down, waiting for a blow to fall. The audience of DeSilvas and staff on the stairs might have been the only thing that saved her from a beating.

"Is everything well, Maribelle?" Lady DeSilva asked as Inimigo's carriage bumped down the road.

"Yes, my lady," Maribelle said, folding her arms to cover the red marks her father had left behind. "My father cannot abide disobedience, and one of his closest advisors has gone against his word. With that and the peasants' rebellion, he's quite discomfited."

"Is that what he was reminding you of?" Lady DeSilva's tone was kind, concerned, but the question was worded so as not to pry.

"As always," Maribelle said with a dramatic sigh. It would have been a believable act, but Dom caught the quick grin she exchanged with one of her attendants—a bit too pleased, considering the circumstances.

Now, standing on the manor roof, and knowing the stories of Inimigo and his gift for treachery, Dom was certain something nefarious was afoot. Leaving Maribelle behind had supposedly been an effort to foster a good relationship between families and to allow her to seek Rafi as a suitor. But with Rafi on the hunt to find Johanna and her kidnappers, Maribelle had every opportunity to gather information about the DeSilvas and stir up trouble in the household.

Dom was determined to stand in her way at every turn.

"What've you got?" He took her hand.

"Nothing." She kept her face down and wouldn't open her fist.

"This doesn't look like nothing." The edges of a crumpled paper stuck out from between her fingers.

Gently he pried it free. The paper was rolled into a tight scroll, ready to be attached to a pigeon's foot. He released her so he could slide off the twine that held it shut.

She snatched the roll and lunged toward the nearby chimney, where a hint of smoke was rising.

Dom reacted instantly, grabbing the girl around the waist, tripping on her skirts, and landing them both in a heap on the rooftop. He scrambled up her body and knelt over her, snatching the paper before she could shred it to oblivion.

"What is this?" He picked up the scattered pieces of paper and tried to fit them together.

She answered him with a glare sharp enough to gut a rabbit. "It's not what you think it is."

Lindo,
Remember the night in Cruzamento? I think of it often. You must be more careful when approaching me in public. . . .

He read the words once, twice, a third time, before turning over the scraps and studying the back. "Is this . . . a love letter?" It could have been written in code—and probably was—but to the casual eye it appeared innocuous. "Who's Lindo? Is that a real name or a code name?"

Maribelle pushed him away and rolled to a sitting position. "I'm not answering any of your questions. My personal correspondence is none of your affair."

"You're a guest on my family's estate. Any secret message that will bring trouble—"

"It won't!" Tears glistened in her dark eyes, and her cheeks had gone splotchy. "It's a love letter, just as you deduced."

He didn't believe her. Ladies like Maribelle used tears as tools, shedding a few salty droplets when they needed a little leverage. They'd cry and sniffle, and expect a man to bend to their will. But Dom wasn't falling for it.

"You're in Santiago to gain my brother's affections, and you're sending a message to a lover on the sly?" Dom held the paper up to the sunlight. It didn't reveal anything new. "I don't think you're that stupid."

"Just a fool for love," she said with a little hiccup.

Dom grimaced at the continued dramatics. "I'll take this down to my mother. She'll know what to do with you."

"Wait!" Maribelle lurched to her feet. "Please, if she sees that . . ."

"She'll figure out the code and stop whatever your father has planned?"

"No." Her voice cracked and she covered her mouth with her hand. "If she knows I'm in love with someone else, she'll never let Rafi consider me for a bride."

Rafi and Duke Inimigo had discussed uniting their states through marriage, but the conversation had been another play in a very long game of intrigue. The consolidation of houses meant one less opponent for Inimigo if he tried to take the throne—something the DeSilvas would never consider.

"I know your brother is in love with that Performer girl," Maribelle said, putting both her hands on Dom's arm. "But I *need* my father to think I have a chance at marrying a DeSilva. As long as he remains convinced I have a future in Santiago, then I can stay here." She leaned close. "Please, Dominic. Please don't send me back to my father."

Dom refused to be swayed by her big, glistening eyes and the desperation in her voice. This was the daughter of Inimigo, a man notorious for his machinations. Surely Maribelle was part of his scheme.

But the way she flinched away from me was real, and so are the fading bruises on her arm.

"Fine," he said with a groan, and stuffed the letter into one of his pockets. "If you need to send a message, for any reason, bring it to me. If I catch you up here again, you'll be on the first carriage back to Maringa, no questions asked."

"On your honor?"

"For all it's worth, yes." Dom rolled his eyes skyward. "I'll swear on my honor."

She flung her arms around his waist, murmuring her thanks into his shoulder. Dom accepted the embrace. She was beautiful, after all.

Feet pounded up the stairs, and Brynn stepped onto the roof. "Michael . . . oh. Lord Dom." She blinked a few times rapidly, realization dawning on her face. "Excuse me. I didn't mean to . . . I thought Michael might come up here to hide."

With an unexpected twinge of guilt, Dom extracted himself from Maribelle's still-lingering touch. "You haven't found him yet?"

"No. I . . ." She backed up slowly, cheeks growing pinker with every step. "I was hoping, maybe . . ."

Maribelle shot Brynn a dark look, then wiped at the tears streaking her face.

Brynn rushed back to the stairs. "I'll find someone else to help me look. Please excuse me, my lord."

"Lady Maribelle and I were going to check the barns," he said, following Brynn to the hatch.

She whirled on the last step, her face as red as the curls escaping her bun. "You may as well check that shady little nook in the garden while you're at it. I know that's where you go when you have something, or *someone*, to hide."

Dom's mouth worked as he tried to come up with a response. "Brynn . . ."

But she'd already disappeared down the hall.

Chapter 7

Jacaré

A sense of wrongness pulsed along Jacaré's skin, setting all senses on high alert. The swamp was a dangerous place, that was certain, but something else made his fingers twitch for the blade over his shoulder.

He scanned the clearing where they had discovered the bodies of Rafi's men—Johanna's would-be rescuers. Besides the rustling of a hungry tamandua as it snuffled for ants on the forest floor, nothing stirred. And yet Jacaré couldn't ignore the feeling of being watched.

"Leão?" The young Keeper moved with sharp, jerky actions as he used his Earth affinity to dig graves for four corpses. Three wore the DeSilva insignia above their heart, and the last wore a silvery collar around his neck. "Do you sense anything out there?"

"No. That's your conscience, Jacaré," he said without looking up from his task. "It's trying to tell you that leaving Pira in the hands of our enemies is wrong."

Leão had been able to follow Johanna's and Pira's tracks from the site of their ambush to the edge of the marsh. He had made an attempt to lead Jacaré through the dark water, but then their remaining horse was attacked and eventually eaten by caimans. Without Tex, their tracker and Jacaré's mentor, to guide them through the swamp, they could only guess which direction the women had gone.

Forced to rest their tired, injured bodies, and even more exhausted spirits, they had camped on the roadside till daybreak. Neither had spent much time sleeping, too preoccupied mourning their dead comrade, fearing for their missing companions, and half-certain they'd failed their mission.

Once the sky started to lighten, they had made slow progress around the swamp till they crossed another set of tracks that entered the marsh at a different location. They followed the marks to an abandoned campsite where another magically aided battle had occurred. Broken trees, upturned stones, and pebble shrapnel littered the area. Blood smeared the ground, both around the bodies and where another had been dragged to a waiting horse.

It was a sight far too familiar to Jacaré.

"We know Johanna and one other person rode north. And that Pira has been captured or killed." The words tasted vile as Jacaré's tongue slipped over them. "We need to focus on finding Jo—"

"How can you say that?" The mound of dirt Leão had been moving with his Earth affinity shot skyward, filling the small clearing with dust. He didn't seem to notice that he'd lost control of his magic along with his temper. "How can you brush this off like it means nothing? Pira's not just another soldier, Jacaré. She's your *sister*."

"She's not our mission. We always knew there could be casualties."

"Pira is *not* a casualty," Leão said through gritted teeth. Dirt streaked his face from brow to jawline, striping him like some sort of feral creature.

"Neither is Johanna, and unless you enjoy burying dead bodies, then we need to find her before anyone else does." Jacaré grasped a fistful of the younger man's shirt. "Don't forget, Pira is trained. She'll give her captors hell. Johanna is a young girl, lost in the woods, aided by one other person whose skills we know nothing about."

He followed his words with a little shove, making Leão stumble back a few steps. "I didn't ask you to join this crew so I could be your nursemaid." He pushed Leão again, punctuating his words. "Step up. Do your duty. That's what Pira would expect you to do."

Leão deflated before Jacaré's eyes, his emotions shifting from livid to exhausted. "How do you do it? How can you act like Tex and Pira mean—*meant*—nothing to you? You're moving forward like they didn't matter."

The question was honest; it wasn't insinuating anything. Poor Leão wanted to understand.

Pacing away, Jacaré surveyed the wreckage of the clearing, the bugs humming above the bodies and the half-dug grave. "I want you to imagine carnage like this stretching for miles around you. Men, women, and children torn apart, their blood filling every depression in the ground, and their screams echoing in your ears." He pointed into the distance. "And right there, out of your power's reach, is someone you love. You watch them suffer, but you can do nothing to save them because it will cost hundreds of other lives. Can you imagine that, Leão?"

With sagging shoulders, Leão turned back to the pit. "I already have."

Chapter 8

Pira

Pira couldn't say for sure what woke her. Maybe a log had fallen in the fire. Maybe a creature had stirred in the woods. Maybe it was her own horrible nightmares shocking her awake.

She rolled to her side, racked with a deep ache, and swallowed a whimper. Between the punishing ride and intermittent rounds of torture, Pira was certain she'd never been more miserable in her entire life.

"Oh good. You'll live," said a voice from the far side of the fire. "I thought perhaps I'd taken things too far. You were breathing when I stopped, but I wasn't sure you would regain consciousness. That would be a terrible waste of *essência*."

Vibora sat cross-legged on her bedroll, her fingers plaiting a braid around her head. It was difficult to imagine someone so calm and composed had spent the better part of two days making Pira scream.

"You're welcome to try again." The words were out of Pira's mouth before she could stop them—her most common failing. She didn't really want to have ants and then a jaguar eating her alive. Her abdomen was still tender where the hallucinated cat had raked her open.

The woman tilted her head to the side, studying Pira's prone form with intense interest. "You're so much like him," she said in a whisper. "The way you talk, the color of your eyes, even the curve of your mouth when you taunt me. I could almost imagine . . ."

Standing suddenly, Vibora walked around the fire. Pira's body went rigid, preparing for another round of punishment. Her limbs were pinned to the ground with bands of air, and what little *essência* she'd recovered drained out of her and disappeared.

Vibora's hand touched Pira's cheek and turned her face toward the firelight. "I used to love to watch him sleep. It was the only time he wasn't dangerous." She stroked the top of Pira's head with cold fingers, dragging them down to the base of her neck. "Close your eyes."

"You are insane."

A blast of wind carrying bits of sand blew across Pira's face. She instinctively blinked to protect her sight from the stinging grains.

"What did your mother look like? What was her name?"

Pira didn't answer, cringing when the collar around her throat seemed to tighten. It pressed against the gouges she'd inflicted in her effort to break free, sending new waves of pain.

"Was it Pavao? She always wanted him."

"What are you talking about?" Pira mumbled.

"Jacaré!" The collar constricted with Vibora's anger, digging into Pira's voice box. "Who did he marry—" Her words cut off abruptly and she whirled to the north. She cupped her hands around her mouth and shouted, "Barrata! I know you're out there. You may as well come out."

The pressure on Pira's throat disappeared. Over the sound of her own gasps she heard a strange noise, a scratching of tiny feet on a rocky surface. She turned her head toward the sound and saw a fleck of red in the forest, then dozens of them, all rushing toward her.

Rats.

She whipped her head to Vibora, wondering if this was some new type of torture, but the woman's interest was focused into the woods.

"Send them away, Barrata!" Vibora's command was answered with a high-pitched cackle.

A wave of rodents broke into the camp. Their paws trod over Pira's body, careless of her squeals and efforts to wriggle away. One fat little monster stopped on the middle of her chest, regarding her with a verminous glare, before nuzzling its pink nose into the top of her shirt.

Then it bit.

Its horrible yellow teeth broke the skin below her collarbone, and Pira shrieked. She screamed louder than she had during the worst of her torture, her voice breaking as more of the creature's friends followed suit. Blood welled across her body. Abrasive tongues lapped against her skin. The ant bites had been awful, the jaguar horrific, but she had withstood the anguish because her mind recognized it wasn't quite real. There was always something a little off—the number of ants, the precision of their movement, the too-green shade of the jaguar's eyes—but her imagination couldn't have conjured up rats with such perfection. Their fur was coarse and slightly damp as it brushed against her flesh. An odor of rot clung to their twitching whiskers.

They were eating her alive.

"Barrata! I need her." Vibora's shout went ignored. She seized a rat by its tail and flung it into the woods, but two more clambered into its place.

Knives, irons, pliers, were all things Pira was prepared to face, but having hunks of her flesh torn away and consumed was the worst torture she could imagine. "Please," she moaned. "Make them stop."

A sharp-tipped paw clung stubbornly to her cheek as she whipped her head from side to side, trying to dislodge its owner.

A tongue clicked. "No, no, no," said a male voice. The animal was plucked from Pira's face. "She has to be able to see. All of you, off."

One by one the rats slid off her body and disappeared into the trees, leaving a trail of bloody prints.

Pira tried to still her shuddering, to take deep breaths, but her flesh burned with a hundred open wounds, then Vibora crouched over her.

"Damn it, Barrata." She pressed a hand against Pira's chest, and the bleeding began to slow. "I don't want to waste *essência* healing her."

"You weren't getting anywhere. All this 'Tell me about Jacaré' nonsense," the man said, imitating Vibora's pitch. "Good Goddess, no one cares if he waited five minutes or fifty years before he moved on. He's here. He's powerful. And he's keeping us from capturing the heir and taking down the wall."

A face appeared in Pira's line of sight. He wasn't particularly handsome, but like Vibora, there was something striking in his uneven features. Dark hair, darker than most Keepers', was held down by a braided *cadarço*. He had a long nose that hooked to one side. His eyes were narrow, but even in the half-light she could tell they were a light color.

Under one arm he held an enormous rat and stroked its blood-mottled fur like it was a beloved tabby. A flash of silver ringed its tiny ankle. "Though I can see why you were asking." He leaned closer to Pira and studied her. "She does bear a remarkable resemblance. Prettier, certainly."

Vibora finished the healing and leaned back. "Why are you here?" She sounded weary, though the power she used had been stolen. "We were supposed to meet in Cruzamento."

"You were *supposed* to trap the heir in Santiago. I was *supposed* to make sure she couldn't escape. There weren't *supposed* to be other Keepers in Santarem." He dusted off a log before he sat down, spreading his tunic wide and crossing his ankles. "There are many, many things that were *supposed* to happen, and we failed on every count."

"We've been searching for sixteen years. There was no guarantee we were going to find her now. Or ever."

Barrata sighed, his whole body slumping dramatically. "Sapo will know we got close, and that's just going to make him angry, and then I'm going to lose fingers and maybe some toes—"

"Enough," Vibora snapped. "Sapo's not going to injure either of us. He can't do everything on his own."

Pira's head rang with blood loss, but she tried to hang on to consciousness and focus on their conversation.

Who's Sapo? Why are they so afraid of him?

"He gets a little closer every day."

"He loves me too much to hurt me." Vibora raised a trembling hand to her throat, belying her claim.

Barrata laughed at her words. The laugh rolled, continuing on and on until tears dripped from the man's chin. "He doesn't love anything like he loves his ideas. What's worse is that you're continually making yourself inconsequential. Every time you give him a collar, every time you bring him a new slave, you are bringing yourself one step closer to your grave." Barrata wiped away his tears with a flick.

"He's had years to figure it out," Vibora said, her posture small. "He hasn't done it yet."

"Why would he?" Barrata whistled and a horse trotted into the camp, its reins dangling on the ground. Four more riders followed it, with collars around their throats. They got to work setting up a tent and cooking a meal without a command. "You've always done all the hard work, and if you continue to help him, then he'll have no need to keep you around. He will rule Santarem unimpeded, and once he has everyone here collared, he'll move beyond the wall."

Chapter 9

Dom

Dom smacked away the advancing sword with a quick flick of his wrist. The owner grunted, threw his weapon down, and followed it to the ground.

"Michael," Dom said with barely contained exasperation. "We've talked about this. You can't quit every time I score a point. You'll never learn anything if you keep giving up."

The child's behavior was understandable. With the days stretching on, and no sign of Johanna and no word from Rafi or the other search party, the eight-year-old's bright personality had become overshadowed with despair. Dom had hoped that teaching Michael swordplay would serve as a distraction and give him something to do besides stew, pout, and watch for riders to come in—all things Dom would have done if the choice had been his.

"Do you want to quit?" Dom flicked Michael's sword into the air and offered the wooden blade to the child. "Or do you want to show me that you're not a big baby?"

"I am *not* a baby." Michael lunged for the weapon, but Dom raised it above his head.

"You're sure?"

"Give it to me," the little boy said, his blue eyes narrowing. "And I'll show you."

The victory was small, but Dom warmed with the success.

After a few moments of sparring, sweat beaded Dom's brow, but it wasn't from fending off Michael's wild attacks. Dom had retreated into a dark corner of his brain where he kept his own worries. The rumors coming out of Belem and Maringa were disturbing. Threats that Lord Belem was going to close his borders to Santiago, forbidding any trade, if Johanna wasn't delivered to him. And then the continued civil upheaval in Inimigo's home state.

Neither of those events surprised Dom too greatly—Belem had left Santiago under ugly circumstances, and Inimigo was practically a demon in the flesh. It was about time his people finally recognized their oppression and did something about it. What shocked Dom the most was that his mother had learned the information from her *spies*. She had a whole network of them.

His *mother*.

She apparently received reports daily, shared the information with Rafi, cultivated responses, and took action. Dom had never known, never even guessed. Learning about it now, even though he was only a figurehead, terrified him.

Were there other important things he didn't know? If something happened, and he was actually left in control of Santiago, would he be fit to rule?

He knew the answer, and he didn't like it.

The flat of a blade slapped against his knuckles.

"Hey!" Michael sounded more chipper than he had in days. "I got you!"

Dom forced a smile to his face and ruffled the boy's blond curls, while mentally berating himself for his lack of attention.

"Lord Dom!" One of the guardsmen dressed in his on-duty gear, a boiled leather vest over a long cotton tunic and knee-high boots, jogged across the training ground. "Riders." He eyed Michael and didn't say another word.

"Take Michael to the kitchens, please." Barbs of worry ran down Dom's spine, leaving a hint of nausea in their wake. He handed the practice sword to the guardsman with a few mumbled words about a promised treat, but his mind had already moved on.

Someone's dead. Someone's dead. What'll I do if it's Rafi?

Dom rested his chin on his knuckles, trying to sort through the accumulating emotions. Fear, anger, and confusion stacked one after the other as Raul Ortiz, the estate's weaponsmaster and the leader of the second party that had gone looking for Johanna and her family's killers, reported what he'd found.

"The trail looped east around the marsh. At first I thought it would turn north along one of the smaller trails, but it continued in a circle till it headed back to Santiago." He paced across the room that had always been Duke DeSilva's office, hands clenched behind his back, sword whisking against his leg as he moved. He took four steps, then pivoted and took four more. "We came across the site of a bandit attack. We found several bodies. They each carried military-style weapons, but they didn't wear a uniform from any particular state. After that the tracks were muddled, and they all seemed to turn south."

He stopped in front of the cold hearth and pressed one hand against the mantel, seeming to gather strength from the stone. Lady DeSilva didn't make note of the pause in his story. She faced the citrine-colored windows, watching the rain that was quickly turning the training ground into a muddy mess.

Raul continued. "We followed them and found signs of a second skirmish . . . and a large grave site."

Dom lowered his head to the table.

"Is my son dead, Raul?" Lady DeSilva's voice was low and cool, devoid of emotion, as it had been when she heard of her husband's sudden death.

"We don't know, my lady. The bodies were . . ." Raul trailed off, reliving the moment. "We dug and dug, but they were so far down. We unearthed only one. It was Snout."

There was a swish of skirts and Dom felt the weight of a familiar hand between his shoulder blades. "So you're saying that someone took the time to bury our dead?"

"Yes, my lady."

"Bandits don't bury their own, let alone their victims. Am I correct?"

Dom raised his head, feeling a crease from the table's edge across his brow. His mother brushed the spot with her thumb.

"And I'm assuming you found tracks away from the site?"

Raul sagged with relief. "Yes, two sets. One going north; the other to the west."

"Then as far as I'm concerned, my son is alive. And until we *know* otherwise, we will continue to operate under that assumption." She rubbed Dom's neck gently. "Only my son, bound to his honor, would continue such a hunt and leave his mother to worry."

It was a positive way to look at things. There was no guarantee that Rafi was alive, but the knot of anxiety binding Dom's lungs loosened.

Until his mother said, "While we wait for Rafi to return, we'll prepare for war."

Chapter 10

Johanna

Only lovers and troublemakers visited Camaçari's turrets. The wooden watchtowers stretched above the stockade walls, crowning the city with eight pinnacles, and offered an unhindered view of the surrounding countryside.

Strands of tattered garland dangled between the barbicans, fluttering under the gentle rain as the peddler's cart rolled through the guarded gate. Raucous music and laughter mixed with the smells of cooking food and moderately good ale.

Camaçari was a town famous for parties and gambling. It was a place people came to get lost and forget.

Without her training as a Storyspinner, Johanna would never have guessed that the walls, splattered with vibrant murals and lines of crass poetry, surrounded what had once been a major stronghold of the Ten Years' War.

The bones were there, she supposed. The iron-wrapped gate, the guardhouses at both entrances, the soldiers who nodded to cart drivers as they passed. But otherwise, the people were loud, their laws lax, and their morality questionable.

To put it nicely, she couldn't imagine why any DeSilva—except perhaps Dom—wouldn't have straightened out such a crooked town long ago.

"You didn't tell me we were coming to Camaçari." Johanna and Rafi sat side by side in the peddler's cart. It was nearly empty now that the peddler was done with his route, and there was enough room for them both. "I love it here."

He wrinkled his nose as if he'd stepped in horse dung. "Why?"

"It's a fun place to visit. There is a lot to do."

"It has the highest level of poverty of all the townships under my control, and a resultant amount of crime. But the inns, gambling halls, and entertainment houses are incredibly lucrative." He nodded to a man lying on the front porch of a pub, passed out drunk. "Underlord Ceara is . . . he has . . . a very different style of administration. We don't see things the same way."

Neither do we.

Two days with the peddler had worn away some of the friction between them, but it hadn't smoothed out the ruts caused by their disagreement. Rafi hadn't brought up their supposed betrothal again, *thank Mother Lua*, but he was clearly frustrated with her unwillingness to accept the future their fathers had laid out. And she was equally exasperated with his inability to see her as a person, instead of some uncompleted contract.

It forced a physical distance between them, making Johanna wonder if what she felt for Rafi—a sort of anxious longing—was what she *should* feel.

Since the kiss at the inn, *and oh what a kiss it had been*, and the argument that followed, their conversations had become strained, their interactions too polite. But then there were moments of awareness, when she caught him looking at her from across the fire or as they bedded down under the peddler's cart, and she found it impossible to break his gaze.

There was something hungry in his eyes. The girlish part of her hoped that his interest went beyond duty, but the world-weary part of her feared it might be something else. Maybe that desire was an unspoken longing to take the throne, instead of reciprocated emotion? Did he look at her and see an avenue to power or a girl he could fall in love with?

"Are we headed to Ceara's manor?" she asked as they bounced over a particularly bad pothole, which made them both wince. Rafi clamped his elbow against his wounded side. Johanna hadn't seen the scrapes, but she could tell the injury was plaguing him more than he'd like her to believe.

"Not unannounced. We'll have to stop at an inn first and clean up." Rafi brushed at his now-dusty but still-hideous shirt. "And even if Ceara lets us in, he won't necessarily welcome my company."

Though Santiago seemed like a quiet, content state, there was apparently a great deal of subterfuge and maneuvering beneath the surface. Two of Rafi's underlords had planned to send underlings to his naming ceremony, instead of coming in person. Not attending and swearing fealty was a blatant act of protest, a show of no confidence, and a personal slight. In the end, one underlord had been convinced to change his position, agreeing to support Rafi in return for someone from his township being appointed to the Merchants' Guild.

The other underlord held to his opinion that Rafi was too young to be duke, and wanted to head a council of underlords to fill the seat until Rafi was deemed "mature" enough.

Johanna felt guilty for having judged Rafi so harshly, assuming he was quiet and aloof out of arrogance. The honor gifts he'd sent as part of his Punishment hadn't been an attempt to buy her forgiveness; he'd been overwhelmed with all his other duties.

"We don't have very much money left, but we'll need new clothes before we approach Ceara," he said, and plucked a leaf from Johanna's dress. "I can't go to his house looking like a beggar."

"Wait . . . Ceara was the underlord who refused to stand for you. Wasn't he?"

Rafi didn't respond, but she could tell by the set of his jaw that she'd guessed correctly.

"You're willing to go to him for help?"

"I promised to get you to the wall, and if that means asking Ceara for help, I'll do it." He reached for Johanna's hand. "When I make a promise—"

Johanna leaned forward and gave him a quick kiss midsentence. "I know. When you make a promise, you're honor-bound to keep it." His lips had been so hot under hers it was amazing they didn't steam in the rain. She was tempted to kiss him again and taste that heat; instead she pulled back and grinned at the sudden blush that stained his cheeks. "The good news is that I know a place where we might be able to get baths and beds for the night for a *very* reasonable price."

"Fine, but let's stay anonymous. It'll be safer if no one realizes we're here. You never know who could be watching for us in a town this size."

I don't know if a song or two would be your definition of anonymous, but I'll try not to make a spectacle of myself. She hopped off the back of the cart and motioned for him to follow.

They paid the peddler, collected their small bundle of possessions, and headed into the city's lower streets.

Camaçari reminded her of a Performers' tent city, except the buildings were permanent. Even so, the atmosphere, the *energy*, was the same. For the first time in days Johanna had a bounce in her step despite her wet clothes. Her mind was full of good times, long nights of dancing and even longer laughs.

Rafi followed close behind, occasionally touching her elbow when groups of people pressed too close. His concern for her was as sweet as it was irritating.

All the buildings were jammed together cheek-and-jowl, with only a narrow, sometimes impassable alley between. The bright stucco storefronts changed to larger, more solemn-toned inns. Johanna passed several before turning onto a busy common, her footsteps quickening as she saw the familiar sign in the distance.

The Bean and Barley wasn't the fanciest inn in Camaçari, but it was the biggest. It had an enormous eating area, far larger than any duke's hall, and a raised stage—the site of her first public performance.

And my last one. At least for a little while.

Chapter 11

Rafi

Rafi wished Johanna didn't have to smile at every single person she passed. She was pretty enough to attract attention without her grinning at every cross-eyed beggar and swaggering mercenary.

Yes, they were somewhat safer in Camaçari than on the road, but he hoped to get in and out of the town without lighting a signal fire for their enemies to follow.

A sense of uneasiness thrummed in his fingertips, and he checked behind him, searching for eyes watching them too intently.

The moment he looked away from Johanna, she quickstepped up three short stairs to a questionable-looking inn. Men and women lined the wooden walkway at either side of the door, waiting for entrance, but she ignored them and pushed past the crowd.

A huge man, as tall as Rafi but twice as wide, followed her in. As the door began to swing shut, the man grabbed Jo around the waist and tossed her over his shoulder. She screamed, legs flailing wildly.

"Johanna!" Rafi shouted, hurtling up the stairs and forcing the door open. His mind raced in time with his pulse.

They've found us. They're taking her away.

"Hey there." A heavy palm slammed Rafi in the chest, knocking him back a step. "Watch where you're going."

Rafi shouldered past, ignoring the warning. Johanna's purple-and-brown-covered rump was in the air but disappearing deeper into the cavernous room.

Something snagged the hood of Rafi's shirt, pulling him up short.

"My friend said to watch where you're going." A man with horrendous breath and rotten teeth stepped in front of Rafi.

He barely heard the words over the wild thumping of his heart. Who had her? Who had found them? Rafi threw an elbow at the man holding his hood and rushed forward, only to be attacked from behind. A fist smashed hard and fast into his kidney, while a boot caught him in the knees. He stumbled into a waitress's back, catching her around the waist to stay on his feet. She shrieked, dumping her tray of drinks onto the nearest patrons.

Another blow glanced off his shoulder, and then he was fending off an uncoordinated attack on three fronts. Fists, feet, knees, and elbows flew at him. He dodged some, blocked others, and broke both a hand that reached for his throat and the nose of an undefended face.

"Johanna!" He turned, trying to catch sight of her, but left himself open for a ringing blow to his ear. Over the cacophony of grunts and shouts, he heard the high-pitched whistles used by the garrison soldiers.

His forearm connected with a throat, his heel with an instep. The initial attackers were down but had been replaced by other patrons, who were fighting him and one another. He couldn't see Johanna anywhere.

Glass crunched, a bench overturned. Leaping onto a table, Rafi slid in the remnants of someone's meal.

"Jo—" Something swept out his feet and he fell hard, pain raging across his ribs.

A punch crossed his jaw and stars burst in his vision. The whistles seemed to fade in and out, replaced by a vibrating buzz.

Don't stay down. Down is dead.

He rolled off the table, taking an attacker with him. A bone crunched and the man screamed.

"Rafi!" Johanna's voice cut through the ringing in his head.

He fought harder, moved faster. Striking again and again, he tried to shift in the direction of her shout. There was no finesse in his action. It was blunt and brutal, survival over strategy. The pain in his jaw and head and side were fleabites compared with the fear brought on by Johanna's scream.

A weight bore him to the ground, pressing his face against the sawdust-covered floor. More piled onto his legs, though he bucked and flailed. One of his arms was yanked behind his back.

"Rafi, stop!"

The words didn't register until his other arm was pinned. Hands pushed his head down, making it impossible to move. His breath whistled through his nose, and the nutshells that littered the floor dug into his cheeks.

"Please!" A body thumped down beside him. Knees covered in a pattern of five-legged sheep appeared next to his face.

He could hear Johanna talking quickly, pleading.

"You don't understand," she said. A hand, small and familiar, touched his neck. It was cool, forcing some of the violence out of his head. The scene around him slowly shifted into focus.

A group of matching boots—garrison-issue, no doubt—surrounded them.

"He thought I was being attacked."

"Look around! Look at this destruction, Johanna."

Rafi's wrists were bound together, none too gently, despite her protest.

"I'm sorry, Bartlett. He'll pay for the damage."

A laugh rang out, hearty and deep, but it lacked humor. "Oh, and I suppose he's a duke in disguise?"

"Well . . ." She hesitated. "Can we talk about this in your cellar?"

A hand gripped Rafi's curls and twisted his head away from the floor. He looked into a man's fat, florid face.

"Monkey balls," the stranger cursed, then let Rafi's head drop. "Johanna, you have a lot of explaining to do."

Chapter 12

Johanna

The cellar of the Bean and Barley hadn't changed in all the years that Johanna had visited. Casks of Bartlett's home-brewed ale lined one entire wall, while the other boasted an enormous wine collection. Bottles gleamed faintly in the flickering torchlight, tossing squares of maroon and green on the slate floor.

Bartlett sat behind his desk. A weathered door, worn smooth under years of ale glasses and liquor decanters, made for the desktop. His massive hands gripped a tiny porcelain teapot. It was an odd contrast, sausage-thick fingers deftly pouring tea from the fragile object.

He was nothing if not a man of contrast. Bartlett looked like a blacksmith, sold every sort of alcohol, but preferred to sip the Wisp Islands' finest brew. A wormlike scar, puckered and pink, stretched from where his left ear should have been and down into his shirt, yet he loved good music. And he was as quick with a kind word as he was with a weapon.

Usually.

Today his face was set in hard lines, a frown tugging down his mouth, as he studied Johanna and Rafi.

"I know you learned from your father how to twist a story onto its head. Arlo was the most potent liar I've ever met, but as his friend and as yours, I expect the truth." Bartlett set the teapot down with an aggressive clink. "You brought trouble to my doorstep. I want to know why and how much more I should expect."

He had sent away the men from the garrison with a few whispered words, and Johanna was grateful he hadn't revealed their identities. The soldiers respected either Bartlett or the Bean and Barley's ale, and they didn't spare Rafi or Johanna an extra glance.

She'd never had reason to pay attention to military discipline, but she knew that a brawl in any Santiago township should be reported to the authorities. In this case, she was thankful the laws were a little more relaxed in Camaçari.

"We . . . I . . ." She shot a nervous glance at Rafi, but he lounged in the chair beside hers, one arm thrown over the ladder back, not quite around her. He met Bartlett's eyes, the purpling bruise that stretched from his cheekbone to his chin adding something malevolent to his handsome features.

"Don't look at him. I want the explanation from *you*." Bartlett returned Rafi's stare. "I know a DeSilva when I see one. They like to sugar hard truths so you think you're getting cake when they're really serving you stones. And by the Light . . . with the two of you here together . . ." His words faded off as he shook his head.

The story she'd planned to knit dissolved into a heap of unconnected threads.

Bartlett was someone she could trust. Her father always had. There had been some scrape before Johanna was born, and Bartlett had lost his ear coming to Arlo's rescue. The details of that particular escapade were a little thin—and her father had always been specific unless he had something to hide—but the Von Arlos had stopped at Bartlett's inn every year and stayed for a few weeks. Longer than anywhere except Performers' Camp.

He was closer than any of her extended family and deserved better than a glittery falsehood about young lovers and a grand misadventure. Johanna took a deep breath and told the truth. "My family is dead."

His gray brows jumped and the rosiness faded from his face. "Your mother? Thomas—"

"All but Michael," she clarified. Rafi's hand closed around her shoulder for a moment, his fingers warming her through the weave of her dress. It was a small action, but typical of Rafi.

"Oh, Johanna. I'm so sorry." Bartlett's eyes gleamed, and he blinked away the sheen of tears. "An accident? The wagons?"

The words were pebbles in her mouth, grinding against her gums with sharp edges. She wanted to spit the story out, to let each nugget plink to the floor, roll away, and disappear forever.

"They were murdered, Master Bartlett," Rafi said, filling the void in conversation. His voice was unusually low. "They were murdered and Johanna was kidnapped."

"So the truth is out, then." Bartlett brought his fist down on the table, rattling the tea set. "How many people know your identity?"

Johanna jumped, her hand fanning over her breastbone. "*You* knew?"

"We all have secrets," Bartlett said, eyeing Rafi darkly. "Arlo had more than most men, but I was privy to a good number."

"My mother thinks Arlo was once a spy for King Wilhelm," Rafi said, his voice gravelly. "That may be—"

"Something Lady DeSilva should have kept to herself." Every time Bartlett's gaze landed on Rafi, the scar on the side of his face grew more livid in color. Johanna wasn't sure what had turned Bartlett against the DeSilvas, but she didn't like what this anger did to her normally placid friend.

"Bartlett, please listen—"

He continued talking right over Johanna's plea. "I've heard the rumors about you, boy. I should have guessed, with both Arlo and Camilio dead before their time. I don't suppose you've heard from Duke Fernando in a while, have you, young DeSilva? Or did you find a way to get rid of him as well?"

"What?" Rafi asked on a gasp. "I had *nothing* to do with my father's—"

"So you say." He pointed at Rafi, condemnation in the action. "Simple poisons, dismissible proof. I should have let the garrison drag you to jail on suspicion of murder."

"What are you talking about?" Johanna stood, knocking over her chair. "Rafi would never—"

"Which one are you working for? Belem? Inimigo?" Bartlett swept the tea set aside, porcelain shattering, hot liquid splashing. "Don't you see it? Someone is killing all those who stood with Wilhelm. Anyone who could rally others to support his heir."

"My father died of natural causes," Rafi said, rising slowly to stand beside Jo. "I would never have done anything to hurt him."

The door to the cellar flew open. Two of the inn's bouncers hurried through, taking stock of the situation with a glance.

"Take him to the garrison," Bartlett commanded, coming around his desk.

"Please, Master Bartlett, this is unnecessary," Rafi said as the first man through the door grasped his arm. "Johanna and I will find someplace else to stay."

"*You* will. That's for certain. Johanna is staying with me."

She stepped between Rafi and the second bouncer. "There's been a misunderstanding. You can't take him. Do you know who he—"

"Johanna." Rafi's voice cut over her words, and he gave a minimal shake of his head, then took an unsteady step to the side.

She thought perhaps it was a ploy, a show of weakness that would lure the bouncers closer. Rafi had given better than he'd gotten in the barroom brawl. *He could certainly break free of these two. . . .*

Red blotches marred the side of his ugly shirt, and the floor next to his chair featured wine-colored drops that weren't from anything in Bartlett's collection.

"You're hurt. Why didn't you say anything?" Her fingers brushed Rafi's ribs, and he flinched away from her touch. Even over the thick material, she could feel heat radiating from his skin. The color on his cheeks, the heat of his lips, the gravel in his voice . . . how had she not realized? The wounds he'd gotten in the swamp were infected. "Bartlett, this is ridiculous. He's sick."

"Let Ceara handle it. Nobles can take care of their own."

"No." She eyed the dagger hanging from Rafi's belt. She lunged toward him and was clotheslined by Bartlett's cask-size forearm.

"Let me go, Bartlett. Let *him* go." She kicked backward, aiming for his shins, but he deftly avoided the blow.

"Stay safe," Rafi mumbled as he was half dragged, half carried away. "I'll be back for you soon."

"He fought to protect me, Bartlett." She struggled harder, whipping her head from side to side. "That has to mean something to you."

"There are only two things a man fights for: power and love," Bartlett said, his voice gentle in her ear. "I've never met a noble who followed his heart."

Chapter 13

Dom

Lightning flashed outside the library window, drawing Dom's attention away from his pile of books. Usually it didn't take much to distract him—a sound in the courtyard, a pebble from his pocket, a stray whisker on his tutor's chin—but he'd honestly tried to stay focused and he'd succeeded for . . .

He looked out the window, realizing that night had long ago fallen and the moonlight was blotted out by roiling storm clouds.

Hours. Standing, he stretched his arms above his head. *I've been working for hours.* Frustration forced out a sigh. *I still don't know anything.*

What do you expect? You can't make up for years of laziness with a few days of intense studying.

Dom had always gotten by with natural ability and a good memory, but he'd never excelled at his studies like Rafi had. Second sons didn't need to be well rounded and well versed in history, military tactics, crop rotation, politics, or science. Second sons represented the family at parties and danced with pretty girls. Second sons were never expected to do anything meaningful.

Until now.

His mother was handling most of the preparations: food storage, weapons and armor purchasing, and contacting and conferencing with the underlords. She'd tasked Dom with looking through his father's journals for the physical plans they'd used to defend the estate during the Ten Years' War. The fighting had never come as far south as the manor, but his father had fortified their residence, their outlying garrisons, and portions of their border that he felt were particularly susceptible to attack.

It was an assignment that actually mattered, and Dom was failing miserably. He slammed the cover of a book shut, scattering the torn pieces of Maribelle's letter and the sheets with his scribbled attempts at decoding it. Another failure.

One of the hounds that had been sleeping near his feet raised its head and regarded Dom with sad brown eyes.

"Don't look at me like that. Go back to sleep, you ugly mutt."

Instead of turning away offended, the animal sought Dom's attention. It padded across the room and pressed close to Dom's leg, its tail thumping the floor in anticipation.

He stroked the hound's silky red-gold ears and scratched beneath its chin. "If only everyone were so easy to please—"

"Hello?" a voice called from the library's doorway. "Is someone in here?" Brynn peeked around a bookshelf, looking a little nervous. "Oh, Lord Dom. I heard a crash and worried."

She pinched closed the collar of her light-green dressing robe.

"I'm trying to figure a few things out." Dom knelt and gathered his papers, though his eyes kept drifting to her face. Brynn's red hair was tied back in a loose braid, a few curls escaping in a way that suggested she'd just woken up.

Her cheeks flushed, and Dom realized that he was kneeling at her feet among the papers. And staring.

Brynn had always been pretty, with fair coloring, green eyes, and a nicely rounded figure, but seeing her in the sputtering candlelight long after they both should have been in bed made her even more appealing. There was something clean about her appearance, something that made it more honest than Maribelle's obvious beauty.

"Is . . . um . . ." Dom cleared his throat. "Is Michael in his own room, or has he escaped again?"

"I just came from there. I read him to sleep." The color in her face deepened. "And must have nodded off myself."

Dom squared the edges of his notes and stood. "He is exhausting."

"I'll say." Her smile was sweet, and Dom could see that she had grown attached to their little charge. "I best be off. Mother Lua knows he'll run me into the ground tomorrow."

She turned to leave, but Dom stopped her. "May I ask you something?" It was an oddly formal way for him to phrase a question. Their relationship had always been more like equals or age-mates than noble and servant. She'd helped him sneak treats from the kitchen, and mended holes in pants so he didn't have to explain how he'd ruined another pair. Lately something had shifted between them, and Dom didn't feel like he could go to her with his flights of folly anymore.

"Of course," she said softly.

He took a step closer, close enough that he could have reached out and touched her, but he didn't. "I need you to do me a favor. Something I trust only you to do."

"Anything," she said, her tone dropping to match his.

Alone, on a stormy night, in a dimly lit room—Dom had a difficult time remembering what he meant to ask her. The situation seemed perfectly suited to so many other, more enjoyable things.

The moment stretched before he forced out the words, "I hate knowing there is a spy in our house and doing nothing about it."

She gasped, her eyes growing round. "Wh-what do you mean?"

"I'm certain Maribelle is here for one of Inimigo's wicked schemes. Reporting our every action back to her father."

Brynn blinked a few times, her eyelashes fluttering against her creamy skin. "Well, of course she is."

"You have access to her room," he continued. "You can search through her things and read her notes. You're just a maid. She'll never suspect you."

"Just a maid," she said, and took a quick breath. "Yes, of course."

Dom offered her a bright grin. "You can report what you find when you bring Michael to his fencing lessons."

"That won't work." She returned his smile, but it lacked all its typical warmth. "Lady Maribelle is extremely wary of all the servants. She doesn't let anyone into her room for any reason. The two ladies she brought with her do all the work, cleaning the space, taking care of her wardrobe."

"Oh."

"You might be able to get into her room, though." She took a step away, her voice returning to normal volume. "She'd never guess you were there for *information*."

"I suppose I could do that." Dom knew her words were true, but the way she said them made him feel guilty—like he was doing something wrong.

Brynn retreated to the doorway. "Getting into ladies' rooms is the one thing you truly excel at."

It took a moment for her message to sink in, to strike the tender spot that he had already been nursing.

He called after her, but she was already gone.

Chapter 14

Pira

Rain pelted Pira, dripping down her face and running under the collar. The rivulets of water made the raw skin underneath sting and burn.

Her horse tossed its head, as impatient and uncomfortable as its rider. They'd come to a crossroads, the small forest trail opening onto a broader, well-traveled road. "Is there a reason we're sitting in the rain?"

As soon as the words were out of her mouth, a ball of air was forced between her teeth, her jaw cracking as it stretched around the invisible gag.

"You were told not to speak," Vibora said without looking at Pira. "If you can't learn to obey, I will make you."

Pira growled in frustration, bringing her fist down on her thigh. It did nothing to make her feel better. She'd already learned a few hard lessons about obedience.

The evening Barrata arrived, she had tried to run when her captors had fallen asleep. She made it beyond the perimeter of their camp, when the collar yanked her off her feet. Pira fell flat on her back, cursing the sky, as stinging, hot prickles raced along her skin.

Barrata stood above her and giggled. "Make her crawl," he said to Vibora, clapping his hands excitedly. "It's always best when they know they're nothing better than pets."

Without her consent, Pira's limbs flailed. She groaned, trying to lock her joints and keep her muscles tight. Vibora's face contorted in concentration, and a dull ache started in the back of Pira's head. At first it felt like a hand pressed against her skull, but the pain grew in intensity. In response, her muscles began to loosen, then move.

It was an uncoordinated slither, but eventually Pira followed her master back to the blanket they'd given her by the fire.

"Make her beg," Barrata said.

With a tired sigh Vibora complied. "Ask me for a drink of water."

"I don't want a drink," Pira managed through gritted teeth. The fist of control closed around her brain and squeezed. Tears sprang to her eyes as she tried to assert herself.

Get out of my head. Get out of my head. Get out of my head.

"Ask me for a drink of water," Vibora repeated.

"No," Pira managed with a moan as the pain spread to her spine.

"Sapo's going to love this one," Barrata said, chafing his palms together. "She's full of vinegar and violence."

"It'll be easier for everyone, especially you, if you simply obey." Vibora had dropped onto a log, stretching her feet toward the fire.

Pira shook her head, failing to dislodge the invader inside her mind. *I will not do what you want.*

"You will do what I tell you."

The fist clenched. Sparks flashed across Pira's vision, and she collapsed into the dirt. Something hooked around her vocal cords, and the words were yanked out of her mouth. "I want a drink of water," Pira heard herself say, followed by a mumbled, "Please."

After that it had seemed that Vibora's control came easier. It didn't matter how hard Pira fought, eventually after a round of torture and a headache that left her functionally blind, she gave in. As her *essência* drained away, Pira found that her ability to fight grew weaker.

She understood why Barrata's minions seemed mindless. They hadn't had as much *essência* to start with, and as Pira sat in the rain, she wondered how much longer it would be until she, too, lost her will.

"We're a few hours outside of Cruzamento," Vibora said, finally turning to look at Pira, a horse length away. "If Sapo had already arrived in the city, a rider would have met us here. As I neither hear nor sense anyone, we can ride on." She held up one threatening finger. "If you're going to cause any problems, I'll leave you here in the forest. In the rain. With a command not to move no matter the situation. I can do that, you know."

The ball of air in Pira's mouth dissolved. She took a moment to rub her jaw but didn't respond to Vibora's threat.

The Keeper tilted her head to the side, studying Pira. "Jacaré made the same face when he was being stupid and stubborn. It must have aggravated him to have his child use the same tricks—"

"You loved him once," Pira interrupted. "Did he break your heart? Was that what made you abandon your people and join this . . . this Sapo?"

A blast of power knocked Pira off her horse. She managed to

catch herself before any bones snapped, but the fall forced the wind out of her lungs.

Vibora trotted her horse close and leaned over in the saddle. "Do not presume to talk to me about who abandoned whom." An electric shock jolted through Pira's body, and she bit her tongue as her muscles went rigid. "You know *nothing*."

Panting, aching, but dauntless, Pira pressed on. "You don't know much either." She wiped a trickle of blood from her mouth. As part of her training to become an Elite Guard, she had been taught never to engage the enemy in a verbal confrontation. It gave too much away and left openings for secrets to leak out, but she couldn't stop the words from rolling off her tongue. "Jacaré is my half *brother*. He never married. He lived alone until he was named as my caregiver when my parents died."

It felt so good to have something to hold over Vibora, to know something she didn't. Pira wanted to see her captor splutter, look shocked, or incensed, or surprised, but she was sadly disappointed.

"The forest or Cruzamento? Can you behave, or should I leave you here?"

Not a word about Jacaré, about their relationship, whatever it had been, or the information Pira had shared. Invisible bonds wove around her body, trapping her to the ground, staking her out for any hungry predator. Or rodent.

Pira cleared the images from her head.

Fool. She's at least three hundred years old. She's using a metal that the Mage Council doesn't know about or has kept an incredible secret. She drains me of my essência *and beats me with my own power.*

You are overmatched, Pira.

For the first time since she'd been captured, Pira felt afraid. "Cruzamento."

"Ask me nicely."

Pira bowed her head. "Cruzamento, please."

Cruzamento had been occupied before. The remnants of war were evident on the buildings' faces and poorly concealed by slapdash construction. A doorframe boarded over, a wall that ended abruptly, leaving too large a gap between buildings, a weathered foundation with nothing on it—all signs of a city that had stood against Inimigo during the Ten Years' War and been punished for it.

The people showed their scars with furtive, hurried movements, dashing past the Glorious Gander as if expecting to be snatched inside. The inn was, as its name suggested, glorious. With a columned portico, a curving driveway, and more greenery than the rest of the city combined, it looked more like a country manor than a place of lodging in a bustling merchant town.

Behind the fountain—which featured an enormous, water-spewing goose—a lacquered carriage was parked. The door had been gilded with a clenched fist, similar to the one on Vibora's cloak.

"Were you expecting someone?" Pira asked as Vibora handed her reins to a waiting groom.

She didn't respond but didn't punish Pira for speaking out of turn, either.

Pira guessed that was a no.

They walked through a marble-floored entryway into a well-appointed sitting room full of polished tables and padded chairs—atypical for any inn Pira had ever visited. Even the clean establishments didn't have rugs that could be spilled on or dirtied by muddy boots.

A man sat in a chair in the room's rear corner. His feet rested on a tufted ottoman, and while he looked relaxed, in a silk jacket and lightweight canvas pants, his eyes took in the entire room. He was in a prime position to monitor entrances and exits, close enough to the window to bolt, but out of a bowman's range.

His black hair was pressed flat under a band of woven gold, a metal version of a *cadarço*. Pira didn't remember much from her history lessons of Santarem, but a crown meant royalty, and she knew this man had no claim to the country's throne.

A second man, dressed in well-cut traveling attire, sat perpendicular to the duke. His face was chapped, his cheeks and forehead sunburned.

"Inimigo." Vibora stopped in front of his footrest and offered a stiff bow.

She bowed *to him. What in Mother Lua's great name does Inimigo have that can command Vibora's allegiance?*

"That," he said, pointing to Pira, "is the wrong girl."

"Yes. I know, sir." Vibora snapped her fingers, and the muscles in Pira's knees turned to water. She tumbled to the floor with a graceless thump. "Barrata has gone after the princess."

The duke considered this information for a moment, one finger tapping the side of his face. "That is upsetting," he said in a monotone that defied the anger in his eyes. "Perhaps, then, I won't be able to uphold my end of the bargain, since you've failed to uphold yours."

Pira's head was bowed, but from the corner of her eye she saw Vibora's lips thin. Why didn't she burn Inimigo where he sat?

"I don't think that would be wise, my lord. Sapo would be vastly disappointed."

Inimigo grunted, but the sound was vexed instead of fearful. Barrata was afraid of Sapo. As was Vibora. Was Inimigo stupid—a pawn in some game he didn't understand—or was he truly that powerful?

"I, too, am disappointed, and I know that Duke Belem will feel similarly." He turned to the man whom he hadn't bothered to introduce, and said, "Well, Underlord, you've heard the information firsthand from my miserably incompetent steward. Please relay the message to your master. Our plans must go forward with all due haste."

What plans? Pira wondered.

"It will be done," the underlord said as he rose from his chair. "Be certain that my duke will remain forever your ally."

"As long as he's dependent on Maringa's steel, he will be."

The underlord's mouth opened, but he held his tongue.

Inimigo flicked his hand, and the underlord fled from the room with steps that got quicker as he drew nearer the door.

Once the man was gone, Inimigo reached for a small bag that rested at the base of a crystal lantern. "So many people need me, or at least what I can offer." He tossed the bag to Vibora. It hit her palm with a wet smack. She opened the drawstring and looked inside.

A wicked grin split Inimigo's face. "You'll never find it. Waste as many of your servants as you wish, but without my help, you, Sapo, and Barrata will never amount to anything more than side-show Performers. You can't conquer a country without me. You can't muster an army without me. You can't rule without me. And I won't let you."

He stood and smoothed the wrinkles in his jacket. "I'll see you in Cruzamento in two weeks, Vibora. Do not consider defying my orders."

When the door to the inn closed and Vibora dropped the leather bag, Pira had a clearer idea of how to regard the duke. The contents spilled onto the woven rug and spread into a macabre circle.

Eyes, at least six pairs, irises glazed, stared up at Pira. Their owners had seen something forbidden and paid the price.

Inimigo might not have *essência*, but there was no question that he had some sort of power.

Chapter 15

Rafi

His mother called them fever dreams—hallucinations based loosely on truth, but mixed with fantastical elements of his imagination.

Rafi knew, as he sweated and shivered, that the things he was seeing weren't quite right. Johanna wrestling a bear. A giant drinking tea out of a thimble. A familiar laugh ringing in his ears.

Icy water splashed onto his face, and he surfaced from the nightmare with a gasp and a cough.

"Mighty Keepers." The laugh rolled again. "It is Lord DeSilva. I can't believe such greatness is quivering on my prison floor."

Raising a shaking hand, Rafi wiped the water from his eyes. It was dark in the jail, and he'd been asleep on the molding pile of hay for what felt like an eternity. His muscles throbbed and his head pounded as he looked around the room's stone walls.

Against the floor-to-ceiling bars that created the cell's door leaned a man with a bucket. He gave it a second toss, thoroughly drenching Rafi with its chilled contents.

Cold rivulets dripped down his face, but none managed to wash away the rancid flavor in his mouth. A hint of moonlight somewhere down the hall backlit the man's body, but Rafi recognized the build and arrogant slouch.

"Ceara," Rafi managed. He'd never liked the underlord and neither had his father, but they couldn't force an underlord out of his position without cause. Smugness and poor taste weren't quite enough, and Camilio DeSilva had never found legitimate reason to strip the man of his title.

No matter the history between Ceara and the DeSilva family, Rafi was grateful the underlord had arrived to free him from incarceration. "I think I have blood poisoning. Please call your physician and get your men to let me out."

Rafi tried to roll over, but the agony that tore up his side made him stop with a low groan. The gashes from the weeds hadn't been terribly deep—he'd survived worse wounds—and he had cleaned and bound them as best he could without assistance. They weren't healing very neatly, having seeped green as he and Johanna traveled on the peddler's cart, but it wasn't until they arrived in Camaçari that Rafi realized he might need medical attention. The brawl had certainly done the injuries no good, tearing them open afresh.

"My men?" Ceara said, stepping closer and grabbing the bars with both hands. "Do you see anyone else around here?"

The narrow hallway beyond the cell appeared to be empty. Rafi remembered Bartlett's men handing him off to the garrison soldiers, who deposited him none too gently on the prison floor. After that everything slipped into darkness. He was still struggling to clear the haze from his mind. Something was off, something was wrong, but he couldn't quite figure what it was.

"All the prisoners in this wing have been moved," Ceara continued. "Apparently, the guards brought in a common tavern brawler who was sick with marsh fever. They had to isolate him for fear it would spread to the rest of the prisoners and the garrison. You know how contagious it is, especially with the fall rainstorms finally starting."

Common tavern brawler. "Ceara, you know who I am. You know I don't have marsh fever."

"One of my men, who was raised in Santiago, mistakenly identified a commoner as the young Lord DeSilva." Ceara clicked his tongue. "That soldier is going to face an unfortunate accident tomorrow morning, and no one else will remember that a man matching your description was thrown into my prison. In a few days a corpse will be carted out of this cell and burned so that the marsh fever won't continue to spread."

A tremor shook Rafi's body that had nothing to do with his illness. "This isn't funny, Ceara. People know where I am."

"That's true." Ceara's shadow nodded. "Old Bartlett, who has no love for you or any of the DeSilvas, turned you in. Did you know his family was in Roraima when it fell? He always blamed your father for not going to King Wilhelm's aid sooner. Not that anyone would believe anything Bartlett said about you. He's taken one too many blows to the head." Ceara chuckled and raised his hand to his left ear. "You may have noticed."

Sweat broke out along Rafi's brow. He reached for his belt dagger, though he knew instinctively that it wasn't there, and that even if it had been, he was in no condition to use it.

"What I'm really interested in is the little beauty who accompanied you to Bartlett's inn. What kind of girl could have drawn an honorable DeSilva away from his estate and his duties?"

"She's no one." Rafi wished he could take the words back the instant they were out of his mouth. He sounded too defensive, too desperate.

"Really? That is disappointing." Ceara stepped back from the bars, almost disappearing from sight. "I'm afraid you're alone in that estimation. I received a very interesting letter from the Duke of Belem. He asked me to send one of my . . . assistants . . . to Santiago to kidnap this girl, but you so kindly saved me the effort. When I deliver her to Belem's estate, he's promised me a little something in return."

Rafi knew the answer; it was the one thing that Ceara couldn't simply take for himself. Still, he asked, "What did he promise you?"

"All of Santiago."

Closing his eyes, Rafi wished he could slip into a nightmare. Bears and giants were preferable to the ringing echo of Ceara's laugh.

"It would be silly of me not to test the veracity of Belem's claim. So I'm asking you one more time: Who is the girl you brought to Camaçari, and why does Belem want her?" Ceara reached his arm through the bars and held out a small glass vile. "In return for the information I'll offer you a way to expedite your suffering. It's a simple poison. Colorless. Tasteless. It takes about thirty minutes to stop a strong man's heart." He snapped his fingers, the sound reverberating off the stone walls. "And you drop dead. No one will ever guess how you died."

"Poison is a coward's tool. Come slit my throat and be done with it."

Ceara snorted. "I'm certain your father would have said the same thing had he been given the chance."

A rush of anger lent strength to Rafi's limbs. He lurched to his feet and took two steps before crashing against the bars. The material of

Ceara's tunic slipped through his fingers as the underlord skipped away.

"Did you poison my father?" Rafi asked with a growl.

"No. I wasn't anywhere nearby when Camilio died."

Rafi's legs buckled and he crumbled to the floor, his ears buzzing with untruth.

"It's so much cleaner to pay someone else to commit crimes in your name," Ceara said, and laughed as Rafi attempted a weak swat through the bars.

"Bastard." He leaned against the cold iron, too dizzy and weak to move.

Glass shattered above Rafi, shards raining down onto his unprotected head. A small wooden plug fell onto his lap.

"I hope you die slowly, then," Ceara said as he marched out of the prison, leaving Rafi to suffer alone.

Chapter 16

Johanna

Johanna's fists were bruised, but the wooden door she'd punched and kicked and screamed at was no worse for wear. Like the rest of the inn and its owner, the door was solid. She'd tried picking the lock, but the splinters she'd stripped off the bed frame snapped when she jammed them between the tumblers.

The windows were sealed tight—she'd checked. She could have broken one and tried to climb down the three-story building, but the room Bartlett had locked her in faced the street. Patrons and soldiers milled in the city square, certain to notice a girl climbing out of the bridal suite in a hideously bright dress. She'd be returned to Bartlett's care or worse.

Ceara.

Outwardly there was nothing wrong with the underlord. But Johanna had performed for him the year before and had gotten a sense that there was nothing particularly *right* with him either.

Camaçari was a fine place to visit, complete with a large assortment of inns and a plethora of entertainment options, many of them illegal. She'd heard that Ceara ignored that kind of activity because it brought revenue to his township and lined his pockets with gold.

As a Storyspinner, Johanna knew that rumors were embellished for the sake of the tale, but worry had burrowed under her skin and nested in her bones. Rafi had been reticent to face Ceara on uneven footing, and he'd been delivered bloody, broken, and ill. Would Ceara press this advantage? Would he hurt Rafi or . . . do something worse out of his desire to see someone else in charge of Santiago?

Hours passed and the common room below began to quiet, but Johanna's unease didn't fade. The dinner crowd had come and gone. Most of the late-night drinkers had stumbled home, and though the inn likely had occupants, no one seemed to hear her pleas for help or the obscenities she directed at Bartlett.

When the moon set, she decided to break things. If nothing else, destroying some of Bartlett's property kept her thoughts from sinking to her darker fears for Rafi's safety. She started with an ivory water pitcher, throwing it and its contents against a wall. It shattered and no one came.

The bedside table was solid and awkward. She couldn't pick it up, so she settled for knocking it over. It thumped against the rug on the floor with a hefty thud, the sound mimicking the heavy beats of her heart.

"Bartlett, let me out!" she yelled for the thousandth time. "Why have you locked me up?" Her voice was jagged with his betrayal. *Why? Why would he do this to me? Why won't he listen?*

All the throwing, kicking, and screaming had made her sweat, but as night drew on, her damp clothing chilled her. She shivered, turning to the empty hearth.

The chimney.

She stuck her head into the fireplace; only a trickle of smoke drifted up from the kitchen two floors below. A navy square of night sky brightened the end of the otherwise black tunnel. She couldn't quite judge the distance to the roof; it was perhaps twenty feet up, but she was a Performer. An acrobat. She could climb the brick chimney without difficulty.

"Good-bye, Bartlett," she said as she slithered into the narrow opening.

The chimney was wider than she'd guessed, making it a little harder to use both hands and feet to propel herself upward. The bricks were set tight, too close for her to wedge her toes in the seams, so she relied on her fingers to pull herself up. Ash lodged under her nails and slicked her palms. Loose bits of residue mixed with the smoke and made her choke and her eyes run.

Not quite as easy as I thought. Still, the opening drew closer.

Five feet from the top her fingers slipped off a soot-covered block, tearing back her fingernails. She flailed for another hold, sliding down and scraping her forearm, until she snagged a crevice with her right hand.

For a moment she considered giving up, returning to the room, finding another avenue of escape. Bartlett wouldn't keep her locked up forever.

Then she heard the scratch and click of a key in the lock.

"I assure you, Lord Ceara, I'm only holding this girl for her own safety," Bartlett said as the door creaked open. "I care for her as if she were my own. I know her father wouldn't have wanted her to run off with that DeSilva boy, no matter the circumstances."

"I believe you, Bartlett. I do. But my hands are tied. When a duke suggests that his lover is being held against her will by one of Camaçari's most prominent innkeepers, I have a duty to see to his request."

"She's not his *lover*, no matter what DeSilva says. She's a sixteen-year-old girl who has been swept away by a smarmy noble." Feet crunched over glass. "Johanna? I know you're upset, sweetheart, but please come out."

"Where is she?" Ceara asked, his tone razor edged.

The bed curtains rustled. A tin tray gonged. Johanna's fingers pulsed, the torn nails shooting bolts of pain into her cramping hands. She could have slid down, making her presence known, but something in Ceara's voice made her ignore the pain. Rafi would *never* have called her his lover.

"I don't understand. . . . The windows are locked from the outside," Bartlett said, sounding baffled as he drew closer to the chimney. "A drunk groom took a header from this room last year."

"She couldn't have disappeared. Are you sure none of your staff let her out?"

"I'm positive. I've got the only key."

Boots stomped back and forth, as if the men were looking for some place where she could have secreted herself.

"There's no other way out of this room?"

"None."

Johanna's arms shook with the effort to hold on; her feet scrabbled against the wall for anything that would help relieve the strain on her shoulder. She found a tiny lip, enough for her left hand to grip.

"Damn it." Ceara grunted, then cursed again. "Winston, run to the wall. Send the signal to close the gates. I don't want anyone leaving the city. Maxim, knock on every door. Drag everyone out of their beds—"

"That's not necessary. There's no one staying on the second floor, and someone would surely have seen her come down the stairs."

Ceara's men ignored Bartlett, and footsteps rushed out of the room.

"If she's truly in love with DeSilva, she'll come back to him," Bartlett continued. "There's no need to scare the girl with such drastic measures."

"Drastic . . . measures," Ceara growled.

A grunt. A gasp. Two thuds. Both heavier than the sound the table had made when it hit the floor. She knew what made that sort of noise.

A body.

Johanna's muscles spasmed; her fingers slipped. Years of training saved her and she landed lightly. The charcoal remnants that littered the fireplace barely crunched as she backed to the chimney's farthest corner. Waiting, holding her breath, her entire body tense, she prepared for someone to notice the soot hanging in the air and the toes of her stained boots.

Footsteps returned. A new voice spoke. "No one's seen her, my lord. But . . ."

"What is it, Don Diego?" Ceara asked with a snarl.

Boots, scratched with wear but well cared for, stopped in front of her hiding spot.

Injuries forgotten, Johanna reached for the bricks but was too slow. An iron grip snagged her ankle and yanked her out of the chimney.

Chapter 17

Dom

Dom gave the palisade pole a hard shake and was pleased when it didn't shift under his weight. It was the tenth he'd laid that afternoon, and his body ached with the effort. Blisters marked his palms, and the muscles in his arms throbbed, but there was something pleasant about the feeling.

Don't get used to this. You're much better at being lazy than you'll ever be at working. Once Rafi comes back, you'll never have to be useful again.

He'd put his father's defense plans into action—clearing the land, digging an eight-by-eight foot trench around the wall, and filling that trench with sharpened stakes. It formed an impossible obstacle for both men and horses to cross.

Stonemasons sealed all but the estate's main gate, and craftsmen built shutters for all the windows. Blacksmiths filled barrels and boxes with pike points, mace heads, and arrows.

A steady stream of carts delivered foodstuffs that had been held in warehouses nearer the wharf.

All the underlords had been apprised, and their various townships put similar plans into place. The townspeople and farmers were given points for escape if Belem attacked.

If, Dom assured himself as he wiped a droplet of sweat off his brow. *Not when.*

His mother was using all her diplomatic channels, friends on either side of the border, to encourage Belem to recall his threats and reopen trade. A few of her more clandestine contacts reported that the duke was preparing for action, but it appeared he was alone in his exploits.

Inimigo hadn't outwardly picked a side in this argument, reportedly too busy crushing the rebellion that had risen in Maringa during his visit to Santiago.

And at the estate rumors blazed. Everyone, from soldiers to washerwomen, speculated as to the reasons behind Belem's actions. Lady DeSilva issued a message to be read in every town square, hoping to squash the conjecture: "We are uncertain of Duke Belem's motivations and the reasons for his actions. We are working to achieve a quick and peaceful resolution to this situation."

The words were true to a point. Belem wanted Johanna. A fact Lady DeSilva chose to keep secret from her people, because no matter the duke's intentions—whether he wanted to kill her or control the throne through her—they didn't *have* Johanna. Even if they did, they would never use her as a bargaining chip, so they prepared for war.

Dom wasn't sure if defense was enough. He'd studied his father's notes, maps of Santiago, its hills, valleys, and marshes. With the walled city of Camaçari and its powerful garrison guarding the state's northern border, Dom worried only about Belem making a direct attack from the west.

And he had a few ideas that would make that difficult.

The dinner cart rolled past, and Dom's empty stomach reminded him that he'd missed lunch, but he was much too filthy to eat. He'd take a quick break to wash, then grab a meal and get back to work.

The road between the estate and the township was littered with age-old walnut trees, too wide and rooted to be chopped down easily. The shade from the trees was a welcome reprieve from the sun that baked the now-barren land around the trenches. A few birds flitted through the canopy, adding flecks of color to the rich gray-green leaves that shivered overhead.

Tucked off the road and hidden by the trees was the Keeper's Fountain. It was one of his favorite places to visit—not because it was sacred, but because it was usually forgotten.

A stark white pillar, humanoid in shape, rose from the center of an onyx pool. Time had worn down the statue's features, rubbing away the sharp lines where its arms had broken off and flattening the nose into a small lump at the center of the head. Water lapped quietly around the figure's pockmarked feet.

Dom eyed his filthy shirt and dirt-encrusted fingernails, and the cool, clear water beckoned. He whipped his shirt over his head and dropped it into the pool. Leaning over the edge, he scooped handfuls of liquid onto his dusty hair before dragging the sodden linen out of the water and using it to wipe off his face.

"Hello, Dominic."

He groaned at the voice before opening his eyes.

Maribelle stood with one hip against the onyx and eyed Dom's torso with undisguised approval.

He straightened, and snapped his shirt, spraying water droplets in her direction. "Why are you here?"

"You've been busy, and I thought perhaps we could share a meal." She set a picnic basket on the fountain's edge. "Why do you let people believe you're weak?"

"What makes you think I'm not?" He smiled, though her perusal made him uncomfortable. Dom hadn't inherited his mother's height or preternatural leanness. He was all DeSilva. Thick shouldered, thick armed, thick chested. Where Rafi was quick and calculated grace, Dom was raw, brute force. He'd always felt heavy and slow when he and his brother squared off on the training yard. It wasn't until Dom began digging the trenches and working on the palisade that he really appreciated the benefits of his build. "Aren't you here to gain my brother's favor, anyway?"

She waved to the empty woods. "Do you see your brother around?"

"Did you have something to do with that?"

"Are we only allowed to talk to each other in questions?"

He gave an irritated cough. "Why do I have to talk to you at all?"

With a tilt of her chin and a raised eyebrow, she answered him directly. "Your brother, and now you, are my only avenues to escape my father's house. Until Rafi returns—and let's be honest, the prospects are not promising—*you* are the heir to Santiago. Even if by some miracle Rafi does return, you're set to inherit your uncle's dukedom."

The words made goose bumps rise along Dom's exposed flesh. He had learned a few days before that his uncle Fernando planned to name Rafi as heir to Impreza. Should something happen to Rafi, both states would be left to Dom. No one had been in his mother's office when she relayed that awful news. "Where did you hear that?"

"I know lots of things. I know you love caramel and hate red peppers. You don't like white flowers because they remind you of your father's funeral. Your birthday was two days ago, and you had a small cake in the kitchen with only your mother and Cook for company." A satisfied grin spread across Maribelle's face, and she stepped closer to him. "And right now I know you're thinking about how easy it would be to kiss me."

He wasn't. Not until she mentioned it. His eyes dropped to her mouth, and he felt the press of her palm at his waist.

It would be easy. She's beautiful and smells so good. Why not?

Why not? Because you don't trust her. You don't even like her.

But she is *attractive. And I've kissed a lot of girls I don't like.*

This is wrong.

I don't care.

Yes, you do.

He wrapped his arm around her, pulling her against him. She gasped, arching under his touch, closing the whisper of space between their bodies. He lowered his head, feathering his lips along the line of her jaw, breathing in the floral scent that rose off her skin.

"Maribelle," he murmured, against the corner of her mouth. "Who told you about Fernando?"

Her fingers spread over his back, dragging slowly from waist to neck. "Do you think you can kiss information out of me?"

The thought had crossed his mind, and the twist of her lips told him she knew it.

Dom straightened, looking down into her dark eyes. "I know you're spying for your father."

"You're wrong, but I'm certain someone else is selling information to Lord Belem." She gave a great sigh. "The problem for both of us is that I haven't been able to locate the spy and convince them to serve me instead."

That day on the roof—he had *known* the message she'd tried to destroy was more than a love letter. He disentangled himself from her grip and wrung the remaining water out of his shirt. "Why are you telling me?"

"Because the spy may reveal your defensive plans to Belem, helping him prepare an attack against your estate."

"May?" He yanked the material over his head. Whereas the water had at first felt refreshing, now with Maribelle's words and the chill of the setting sun, it felt dank and uncomfortable against his tired muscles.

She reached for a red-tipped lily that had been pressed against the fountain's wall by the wind. Instead of answering, she twisted the petals sharply.

"Maribelle?" Dom's voice was sharp, but she didn't look up. "What do you mean, 'may'?"

With an angry toss she threw the flower into the fountain and wiped her stained fingers on her skirt. "The information the spy has shared has been carefully vague thus far. I ignored the first few letters because they were nothing more than idle gossip, but this most recent message . . . the details were too specific for someone trying to ingratiate themselves with another noble house."

"Explain yourself."

"Spies sell information. It's much easier to bribe one to sell to you rather than place a spy of your own," she said, her tone changing from intimate to instructive. "Spy rings have a series of relays that pass information. I managed to . . . *sway* one of Belem's relays to pass me the information as well."

Dom had suspected that there was something conniving behind Maribelle's good looks. She was Inimigo's daughter, after all. "That's where you learned about Fernando naming Rafi heir? From one of these relays?"

"Yes."

He paced to the basket and flipped off the napkin covering the food inside. *Pão de queijo*, dried salami, and some late-season grapes sat nestled on top of a bottle of wine that Belem had delivered for Rafi's naming . . . a naming that never happened.

"It could have been a guess," Dom said, holding up the wine and receiving an unabashed shrug in return. He yanked the cork out with his teeth and drank directly from the bottle.

"The informant said that upon Fernando's death you would be named steward until Rafi or one of his children could fill the role. It would have made more sense to will the state to you outright—properly dividing the power and whatnot."

"No, Fernando knew what he was doing." Dom snorted. "I'd be a puppet while someone like . . ."

Mortimer? He's served as our secretary for decades. He wouldn't sell my family's secrets. Would he?

"Someone like?" she pressed, but he ignored her, trying to comb through the estate's staff for possible culprits.

What about Raul? He's been serving as weaponsmaster for only a few months. I've been trusting him with so much. With defense plans and training the men till Mother names the next captain.

What do I even know about him?

"Lord Dominic." She was standing close again, her hand covering his on the neck of the bottle. "I told you about the spy in good faith and hope I can ask for a favor in return."

"No."

"You don't even know what I was going to ask."

"I don't particularly care, Maribelle. You just admitted to buying information about my household from spies."

"I need you to pretend that you care for me."

His mouth went dry with her nearness, but he mustered a quick, "No."

"Would it really be so awful?" She leaned close, her lips curving in a tempting grin. "I'll share every bit of information I discover that pertains to Santiago."

"No."

"And," she said as she pulled the bottle from his hand and took a swig of her own. "I'll help you catch your spy."

CHAPTER 18

PIRA

A hum startled Pira from a dead sleep. It throbbed on the air, making the hairs on her arms stand at attention. Her heart faltered, then raced to march in time with the beat.

"What is that?" She sat up in her small pallet on the inn's floor, and pressed her hand to her chest.

Across the room Vibora burst into motion, flying out of bed, reaching for the blouse she'd laid across the chair the night before. Her fingers sailed through the buttons, closing them all, then loosening the top few.

"Get up. Get dressed." Vibora stepped into a skirt. It was sleek and fitted, and completely unsuited for any type of activity beyond standing.

The pulsing thrum moved into Pira's head, making her feel clumsy and disoriented. She struggled to tie the laces on her pants.

"Didn't I tell you to hurry?" Vibora sent a little zip of power through the collar that cleared Pira's mind enough that she could function.

"What's going on?" Pira asked as she stamped her feet into her boots. "What is that?"

In response Vibora shocked her twice more, and Pira staggered.

"You are not to ask questions. You are not to *talk*." Her face had grown dark with rage. The muscles in her thin neck stood out as she stepped closer to Pira. "He will cut out your tongue and feed it to you if you speak out of turn."

Weakness made Pira stupid with anger. "Who? Inimigo again?" she growled, thinking of the bag of eyes on the floor downstairs.

With hard fingers Vibora clenched Pira's chin. "That pulse you feel is *essência*—so much *essência* that he could burn Cruzamento to rubble in a blink and leave nothing but the dirt behind."

Through the collar Pira's power was sucked out of her body and flowed into Vibora. Dizzy, Pira barely caught herself from crashing to the floor.

"Be afraid, Pira," Vibora cautioned as she turned to the small mirror above the washstand. "You're about to meet someone who makes Inimigo seem like a rabbit in comparison. Someday that rotten little duke will kneel and lick the dirt off Sapo's boots."

Pira expected anyone with the power to make her physically sick to have a presence to match. She imagined Sapo as an imposing figure, tall and broad, with a warrior's body. Someone like her brother or Leão.

As she reached the midpoint of the stairs, she stopped and surveyed the scene, looking—as always—for an avenue of escape and anyone with the capacity to stand in her way.

She must have passed over Sapo twice, placing him with the servants that fluttered around the night-darkened room. She realized the one person at the center of all the activity, who lazily unpinned his cloak and draped it over a padded chair, was the only person not hurrying to complete a task. Still, it wasn't until Vibora threw herself into the man's arms that Pira knew for certain.

And almost laughed.

He was a few fingers shorter than Vibora, short for a Keeper, with a slight build and plain, regular features. The only remarkable thing about him was the sandy-blond hair that curled around his ears like a child with an overgrown haircut.

Then he opened his mouth.

"Vibora, my love," he said in a rich baritone. His voice commanded as much attention as the energy that pulsed around him. Honey tones drew Pira in as he spoke. She couldn't hear the rest of his words clearly, but the sound of his voice made her want to be close to him, to please him.

She straightened, realizing that she was leaning toward Sapo, and a strange ache settling deep in the pit of her stomach.

Spirit. He's using his affinity to compel everyone—maybe even Vibora—to do his will.

His servants, perhaps ten in all, returned from their tasks and settled at the long mahogany table or on the rug near his feet. They wore thick silver collars around their necks, all watching him with rapt attention. It may have been Pira's imagination, but they seemed to shiver like good hounds waiting to heed his next command.

Vibora stepped back a bit, and Sapo gave her a quick, tactical kiss on the lips before he caught Pira peeping from the stairs.

"What did you bring me?" he asked, his dulcet voice urging Pira's feet down another stair. His gaze was a physical pressure, rounding her back; his words, a heavy hand forcing her to bow.

She fought the weight of his power, struggling to break free of the swirling force, but it pulled her under and held her there till she stopped thrashing.

"This is Pira," Vibora said, with a gesture toward the stairs. The movement was slightly timid; perhaps she wasn't as excited to see Sapo as she seemed. "She's a full-blooded Keeper, Earth affinity."

Sapo's eyebrows rose as he studied Pira. "You found her on this side of the wall?"

"There were four Keepers total, all on an unsanctioned mission to check the stability of the barrier. It's why I came immediately to meet you and sent Barrata to complete our assignment."

Vibora relayed the story she'd tortured out of Pira: the Mage Council's inaction, the four-member crew's escape beyond Olinda's borders, and their hunt for the princess. At the end of the retelling Pira wished she'd been able to hold more back. But every time Barrata had called for his rats, Pira had spilled new information. She'd been able to keep quiet on only one subject, and that was more because Barrata and Vibora didn't know to ask than because of any great act of will.

She'd kept Leão's identity a secret. Vibora knew Leão was strong, that he was a full Mage, but Pira hadn't told them he was one of the strongest Mages among all the Keepers in Olinda, that he'd been earmarked to head the Council someday, and that his grandmother Amelia—a name that Vibora would certainly recognize—was the leader of the Keepers.

For now they'd see him as a tool, as one more person with *essência* they could use. If they realized who he was, that he had ties to the

Council, he could become a bargaining chip. Or worse, a weapon.

Leão was a warrior, trained to kill when necessary, but his soul was gentle. It was one of the qualities Pira loved best about him. If Leão's power was used against his will to harm others, it would destroy him.

She'd hurt him enough already—the harsh words they had exchanged haunted her almost as much as the kiss they'd shared—but she would protect him from a distance.

"One Keeper is weak, he'll serve as no great threat," Vibora continued. "The other is young. He won't make it far on his own."

Something caught Pira's attention, something wholly unexpected. In Vibora's entire retelling *she* never once mentioned *Jacaré's* name.

The question was why.

Perhaps Sapo sensed something missing in the tale. The plain lines of his face changed. His jaw took on a sharp edge, his hazel eyes flashed with anger. The hand that had so gently rested on Vibora's lower back turned to a claw, bunching the material of the dress she'd donned to impress him.

"And the princess? What of our plans?" All his collared companions flinched—dogs cringing after a sharp kick. Neither Vibora nor Pira felt the direct result of his anger, but a pulse of *essência* rocked Pira back onto her heels.

"I . . . I had her for a little while, but Barrata is after her now." Her poise melted as Sapo's face hardened. "He'll catch her long before she reaches the wall."

"He's had sixteen years to find her, and she's evaded him at every turn." His hounds cowered, some sinking to the floor. "Yes, you did a little better but ultimately failed. How hard is it to bring me one girl?"

When yelling, his beautiful voice turned harsh, making Pira's knees weak. She leaned against the wall, supporting her weight with one hand.

"Because they had the glass." It was a new voice, so soft compared with Sapo's shouts. "They've watched her for all this time."

Pira couldn't quite see the speaker; she was hidden by the table and its benches, but the words rang with defiance.

Sapo marched around the table and hefted a thin blond woman to her feet. "Why didn't you say anything about this before?"

Her body convulsed, taking the full force of his anger and power. He shook her, and the shawl slid off her shoulders, revealing the severe jut of bones under an ill-fitting dress. "I didn't *know* before."

"You're supposed to *know* everything."

The woman raised shaking fingers to her throat, where a fat band of silver hung loosely above her collarbones. The band, the same color as those around the others' necks, seemed a little oddly shaped. The edges weren't quite straight. It looked less like jewelry and more like the harsh tool a jailer snapped around his prisoners' throats before dragging them to meet the executioner. Whereas Pira's was smooth and symmetrical with an invisible clasp, this band was hinged and locked with a large, awkward mechanism. "How am I supposed to *see* anything when I have no *essência* to use?"

She said "see" the same way Elma—the old Keeper who'd hidden among the Performers—had. Seeing, as if to discern the future. Like Pira's Earth affinity was specifically attuned to metal, a very small group of Spirit users could discern murky versions of the future. Sharing what they saw affected the outcome, and though some had learned to talk around their visions, their riddles were often too convoluted for any real use.

If Sapo continually drained the woman's *essência* to keep his own at a powerful blaze, then it would be practically impossible for her to see the future at all. "You didn't even foresee the destruction of your beloved home. I don't know why I ever expected anything useful out of you." He gave her a hard shove. She tumbled into a chair and her elbow clacked loudly against its wooden back. She fell to the floor and remained lying there, unmoving.

Pira rushed to help the injured woman, but her body halted a few steps short of her goal, frozen by the collar. Vibora eyed her like a pet with poor impulse control.

The woman on the floor jerked, tears pooling in her gray eyes, as she suffered some sort of torture that Pira was incapable of stopping.

Struggling against Vibora's hold siphoned away Pira's energy, and though her will held, her strength didn't. The inability to act was almost as daunting and frustrating as feeling her power drift away.

After a few moments the woman on the floor relaxed. She rolled onto her side, pulling her long blond braid over one shoulder.

She met Pira's gaze. And smiled.

Chapter 19

Johanna

Ceara learned from Bartlett's mistake. The windowless cell had only one exit: a door of slatted iron. There was no use beating her fists against it or screaming herself hoarse once they'd whisked her away from the public. No one in the courtyard that separated the prison from the garrison barracks paid any attention to one more shrieking inmate.

Still, she had fought and bitten and kicked till they forced her across the threshold and slammed the lock in place.

"She's practically rabid," Ceara said to his guard. He covered a bleeding spot on his forearm where her teeth had removed a hunk of flesh and torn his shirt. "I personally prefer my women with a milder temperament, but to each his own, I suppose."

His guard didn't respond, stepping away from the cell door and leaning against the opposite wall, arms folded tightly.

Johanna spat in their direction, though it fell well short.

"I don't care what you do to her, Don Diego, but she has to be alive when Duke Belem comes to claim her." Ceara leaned closer to the bars, tempting her to try again. He studied her for a moment, tilting his head from one side to the other as if the angle might reveal the secret that eluded him. "On second thought, the duke might be upset if we damage his little prize, so if she's naughty or refuses to eat or gives you trouble, punish the boy instead."

"What boy?" Fear collapsed Johanna's lungs. She said it again, louder. "What boy?"

Ceara's teeth gleamed in the gray predawn light. "Did you actually believe what I told old Bartlett? That I'd come to rescue you on DeSilva's behalf?"

"Of course not. Rafi—"

"Is in the next cell. Where he'll stay until he *dies*. Unless, of course, you have some information to give me? What do you have that Duke Belem wants so badly?"

Her identity was her only bargaining chip, and even that wasn't going to be enough to save Rafi. Ceara had already killed Bartlett, burned down the Bean and Barley, and betrayed his liege lord. "I have nothing," she said, and the words struck her deeply. "I'm just a girl who caught Lord Belem's fancy."

"Ha! Do you think I'm new to this game, child? Dukes don't maintain their lands for long when guided by their heart or other organs." He nodded to the next cell. "And young Lord DeSilva will be a perfect illustration for this lesson."

She closed her eyes, drained by her climb up the chimney, her fight against Ceara and his guard, and an overwhelming sense of desperation. All her worldly possessions, her family, and her identity had been stripped from her. The only thing she had left was her Performer skills. What could Storyspinning and acrobatics do for her now?

With a chuckle Ceara slapped his guard on the shoulder. As he walked away, he yelled, "Keep an eye on her. If DeSilva starts to stink, come get someone to drag what's left of him away."

Think. Think. Think. The cell was well constructed, the barred door was iron. She couldn't break out, but could she appeal to the guard's humanity? She'd done it before—talking her younger brothers out of trouble more times than she could count.

Johanna listened till she heard the outer door of the prison shut, then waited a little longer. She wanted to give Don Diego enough time to feel relaxed, complacent. Eventually he leaned against the wall across from her cell, resting his back against the stone column.

"Don Diego," she said, in her meekest voice—the one that she used when she was performing the role of a child. Most men, even the meanest and ugliest, like this guard, had a soft spot for the innocent. "Why are you doing this? Why do you serve Ceara?"

He straightened a little and his arms dropped to his sides, but he didn't answer.

She inched toward the bars, keeping her hands folded at her waist. "Please, let us out."

Don Diego's top lip curled and he shook his head.

Innocent isn't working. Bribery perhaps?

"Is Rafael DeSilva really in the next cell?" She saw Don Diego's eyes slide to her right, but he made no other movement. "You know he'll soon be the Duke of Santiago. Letting him go, getting him help, it would be worth a fortune."

Not a twitch or a shift or a blink. He was listening. Johanna knew she had his attention.

"If you don't believe me, ask around," she said, wrapping her hands around the bars and leaning as close to the soldier as possible. "Go get a drink. Listen to the gossip. His mother will have sent birds by now, seeking assistance in finding her son. She'll reward you." She eyed the boots on his feet, old and broken in, but cared for. The leather breastplate he wore over his short-sleeved tunic showed similar maintenance. "She'd treat you far better than Ceara. You could have ten pairs of boot—"

Don Diego's arm shot between the bars, his hand clenching around her throat. "Shut up."

She gripped his wrist and tried to pry free.

"Ceara chose me to stay with you because he knows where my loyalties lie." He shook her to emphasize his words. "Do you want me to make DeSilva scream? Lord or not, all men cry if pushed hard enough."

Spots floated across her vision, and her hands slipped away from his.

"Let her go." The voice was rough, barely loud enough to make out the words. "She bruises easily. Ceara will notice."

Rafi. Her heart cartwheeled, spinning with the dark blotches in her eyes.

Don Diego's fingers tightened another notch, and Johanna went up on her toes to try to relieve the pain. Then he released her with a quick shove.

She stumbled into the wall that divided the cells, sinking to the floor and struggling for breath.

"Are you worried that I'm touching your pretty things?" Don Diego kicked the cell door, making it vibrate.

Rafi laughed and it turned to a hacking cough. When it subsided, he managed to say, "No, but Belem doesn't pay for damaged goods, and you really don't want to make Ceara angry. He'll slip a little poison into your rations if you're not careful."

Don Diego's eyebrows rose for an instant before his face settled into a sneer. "Ceara would never hurt one of his own."

"He killed his own liege lord. He'd have no problem dispatching a common soldier in the same way."

Chapter 20

Rafi

Don Diego was a man who enjoyed hurting the defenseless, who took pride in destroying the weak.

The way he looked at Johanna made Rafi's skin crawl.

Ignoring the pain, Rafi forced himself to scuttle across the floor. It was a slow, tedious process, with his arm pressed against his infected side and his pulse thrashing in his ears, but being closer to her—even with a stone wall between them—made him feel better.

"Johanna." He tried to clear his throat, but he couldn't muster much saliva. "Johanna, are you all right?"

There was a beat before she answered. "Of course. I'm fine."

Rafi imagined her sticking out her chin stubbornly and giving their guard an evil glare. She never liked to appear weak. That gumption was one of her most attractive qualities.

He heard a rustle of fabric, and when she spoke again, her voice was closer. "How are you? I've been so worried—"

"Just a fever," he said, wincing at the lie. From the smell rising from his wounds, he was fairly certain his time was short. Blood poisoning was fatal unless treated quickly, and Rafi feared his chance had passed. He was going to die from a simple infection. It certainly wasn't the glorious exit he'd imagined for himself. And it was happening much too soon. He had plans, hopes to right the wrongs of Santarem, see his family. . . .

He pressed his fist to his mouth, holding it there until he was sure his words would be steady. "Will you do something for me?"

Don Diego repositioned his feet, frowning at them alternately.

"Now?" she asked, and Rafi wished he could see her face. Would she look surprised or would there be humor beneath it?

"Yes, *now*."

"What do you want, *my lord*?"

There it was, the irritation he was hoping for. She'd need to hang on to that fire in the days to come, especially since she'd have to face them alone.

"Will you . . . will you sing for me?"

"Sing."

Despite the tears pooling in the corners of his eyes, he smiled. "Did you have some other pressing engagement?"

A snort. "Yes, actually. The highest lord in the land was expecting me at his table any moment."

"I am one of the highest lords in the land, and I'm asking you to sing for me. Please."

Don Diego grunted and folded his arms. Rafi doubted their guard was overly fond of music, and hoped it would send him scurrying for an early breakfast. A drink. Anything that would leave Rafi alone with Johanna for a few moments.

She let out a long sigh, as if she was so put out to use her talents. "What would you have me sing?"

"Sing 'Lamento de Amantes.'"

Her answer was immediate. "No."

"Johanna, please."

"I know what you're thinking, Rafael DeSilva, and you're wrong." The last word came out as two wavering syllables. "The Lovers' Lament" was the song his mother had sung at his father's funeral. It was low and haunting, telling the story of a love that reached beyond the grave.

Rafi wasn't sure he understood a love like that, but he imagined that the protectiveness he felt, the concern, the sweet heat when he touched Johanna, was the beginning. He wished they'd have more time together to find out what it could become.

He crawled as close as he could to the wall and stretched out along its length, wanting to be wrapped around her instead.

"You sang it so beautifully back home. Just this once. Sing it for me."

She took a breath, and Rafi was afraid she'd deny him again. Instead, when she opened her mouth, she filled the entire prison with sound.

Halfway through the first verse, Don Diego left, stomping away and slamming the door behind him, but Rafi didn't care. Over her song he heard the rustle of her moving closer, then saw the flicker of a pale hand in a narrow shaft of the dawn's light.

Lying on his side, he reached through the bars so he could brush her fingers. They were cold and small against his fever-flushed skin, but already so familiar. He cushioned his head against his outstretched arm, relieved by her touch.

The pull of sleep overpowered him, and his eyes drifted shut. He tried to listen to every word, afraid that if he gave in before the song ended, he'd never hear her voice again.

Chapter 21

Johanna

As Johanna sang, a pall fell over the prison. The moans and screams from the floors above were replaced with the quiet shuffle of feet and the occasional muffled cough.

She didn't realize it at first, too focused on Rafi's overly hot fingers clenched around her own to recognize that her private performance had many more listeners. And when Rafi's hand relaxed, her chest spasmed with fear. She searched for his pulse and found the slow thump against her fingertips, and left her hand there.

Over the sound of her relieved sigh she heard a voice through the thin layer of planking that divided the floors of the prison. "Please, I haven't heard anything like that in so long. Don't stop."

That plea was echoed by one, then a dozen other voices. "Angel! Angel! Sing again."

Music had always been a gift, an outlet for her feelings. With nothing to do besides hold Rafi's hand through the cell bars, she sang. Songs of heartbreak, songs of rage, and songs of vengeance and despair. The stone walls of her cell reverberated the sound, and she sang louder, stretching her voice to its furthest range.

She poured every ounce of her own tattered emotions into her music, giving a performance she'd never be able to replicate for its authenticity. And failed to notice the creak of the door and the tread of heavy boots till the heel stomped down on her hand.

Her song turned to a startled inhale.

"Stop," Don Diego said, grinding his foot. "Stop singing."

In the sudden silence she heard her bones crack. Pain flared and she screamed.

"Make another noise and I'll break your other hand."

He lifted his boot, and she scuttled to the farthest corner of her cell.

"Not another whisper," he said, kicking the barred door to imply his threat.

Johanna clutched her arm to her chest.

"Angel?" a voice yelled from above. "Sing, angel!"

Don Diego moved toward Rafi's cell.

"Please! I won't make a sound," she promised, and the guard halted.

Angry shouts started on the upper floor. Feet stomped, metal ground. And then the rioting began.

Chapter 22

Leão

Something about Camaçari made Leão feel claustrophobic.

It wasn't the walls, exactly. Roraima was a walled city, but the ruins, even in their tumbledown state, had a sense of pattern—as if the generations of builders had followed some master plan, allotting a specific amount of space between buildings and an equal distance to the road.

There wasn't a straight road in all of Camaçari. In the older sections the homes and businesses were centered on a well or fountain. Those on the immediate square all faced toward the water source, but beyond that the streets branched every which way, winding and twisting till they dead-ended at hovels built right against the barbican walls. The walkways and turrets above, which no guard patrolled, seemed to tilt inward, dangling precariously over the inhabitants.

Maybe that's what it is, he thought as he shifted the sword on his back. *There's nowhere in the city that lets you see beyond the walls.*

The people didn't seem to notice that they were sheep corralled in a butcher's pen. They went about their business, heedless to the world beyond.

Jacaré and Leão had arrived late in the day and immediately parted company, each with a specific task and agreeing to return the following afternoon. Jacaré was going to check the inns, asking after girls who matched Johanna's description, and listening to gossip.

Leão scouted along the city's perimeter, looking for any sign of Johanna, listening to conversations, and testing the air for any lingering *essência.*

He found it.

Occasional threads of magic pulled at his attention. At first he chased them, expecting to find a Keeper manipulating slaves, but instead he found a bricklayer with excellent balance, using the merest breath of Air to keep him on a steeply pitched roof. And later, as the sun was beginning to set, a woman haggling with a street vendor used Spirit to get her way. Neither of them realized what they were doing—their gifts were innate and untrained—but it added to Leão's discomfort.

Ever since Leão had led their party into the ambush that left Tex dead and separated them from Pira and Johanna, he'd tried to stay sharply attuned to the energy of the people and animals around him. He wasn't going to be caught unaware and let his crew down again.

Guilt coated him like the mud around the city—thick and deep and nearly impossible to avoid. He tried to push past the feeling, but it churned around him, dragging him into a pit of misery. Leão knew he couldn't do anything about Tex now—the old man's death would always stain his conscience—but Pira was out there. Somewhere.

Once Johanna was found, and safely in Jacaré's care, Leão was going to find Pira. No matter what commands he had to defy. He'd find her, and they'd talk about that night at Performer's Camp. She could deny it, but there had been something between them besides exhaustion-driven folly. It had been too real and too intense for it to have simply been a lapse in their judgment. He knew it. Just like he knew she was out there, alive, waiting.

Leão took a room in a small inn and rested uneasily until dawn. He ventured out with the earliest risers, the street cleaners and delivery boys, moving through the city as if they owned it.

A bell sounded on the north side of the city. One on the south side answered. A baker dropped an entire pan of bread in surprise. Shop owners stopped their daily preparations and exchanged interested looks. Boys whooped and dashed past Leão, headed toward the northern bell.

He caught one by the back of his vest and hauled him to a stop. "What is it? Why are you all running?"

The child took a swing at Leão's arm. "Lemme go! I gotta get a seat!"

"For *what*?"

"Prison riot."

Leão let him drop and joined the throng.

As Leão neared the prison, he felt a tickle against his consciousness. It wasn't *essência* precisely, too faint and too fleeting to be of any real power.

He followed the boy up a rickety ladder to the walkway that was suspended above the prison and gave a clear view of the quad.

The prison stood across a walled-in courtyard from the Camaçari garrison's barracks. Dozens of windows, filled with bars instead of glass, checkered its stone-and-wood face at regular intervals.

"What's happening?" the boy asked as he sat beside a friend on the walkway, dangling his legs over the edge.

"Prisoners went crazy," answered another boy.

"Why?"

The other boy shrugged and watched the scene.

Farther down, a child of about twelve answered, "A girl was singing, and someone made her stop."

"Singing?" Leão asked, hope zipping into his chest.

"Yep," the boy answered. He pointed to a greasy cloth sack at his side. "I was delivering breakfast to the soldiers. One minute she was singing and the prisoners went scary-quiet listening. Then she stopped and they all went crazy." He leaned toward Leão and the other boys like he was sharing something confidential. "They were pounding on the bars and walls. When a guard went in to see what was happening, they snatched him and stole his keys, then captured the rest of the guards on duty. They aren't gonna let them go until Ceara releases all the prisoners."

"Is it common to sing in prison?"

The group eyed Leão askance, and he guessed that it wasn't. "Are there lots of women in there?"

The boy who had guided Leão to the walkway answered, "The whole top floor is for women."

"That's not where this one was," the delivery boy replied, pulling a slightly mashed meat pie out of his bag. "I heard her, and her voice was coming from the Crypt."

All the boys oohed like this was important information. It

probably was, and judging from the name, it wasn't a good place to be. Leão said, "So, the Crypt . . ."

"You're not from here, are you?" the delivery boy asked around a mouthful of food.

"No, I'm not."

"No one who goes down into the Crypt comes back alive. You only get sent there if you're gonna die."

Soldiers milled about the garrison quad, waiting for a command for action. Some figured they'd just wait until the prisoners ran out of food and water. Others expected an order to burn them out, and damn the consequences to their captured comrades.

The thick layer of fog that draped the square between the barracks and the prison had nothing to do with the overcast sky. From the walkway above, someone might have noticed that the low-hanging cloud didn't extend beyond the courtyard and stopped abruptly at the gate. But the walls of Camaçari were, as usual, unattended.

Fog wasn't like rain or ice. It was too ephemeral, too easily disturbed, for Leão to blanket a larger area without straining, and he knew with a creeping sense of unease that before the day was over, he'd probably need every shred of his power.

The soldiers pacing around the perimeter called out every few minutes, but even their voices seemed stifled by the mist. They drifted closer to one another, leaving a large portion of the yard unchecked.

As the watch switched positions, Leão descended from the barrack's roof where he'd spent an impatient half hour waiting for clouds to drift in front of the sun and cast a myriad of shadows onto the foggy prison yard. He moved with all the silence his training supplied, staying low. Leaping down the stairs to the Crypt, he landed silently on the balls of his feet and slid two picks from his pocket.

One minute passed. Two. The tumblers in the lock wouldn't shift, even when he urged them with a hint of Air. Frustrated, and feeling his hold on the mist begin to wane, he resorted to a less delicate tactic.

Using his body as a shield, Leão sent a concentrated blast of fire into the lock. The heavy piece of metal melted, running down the door's face like tears of mercury. The stones beyond were slick beneath Leão's feet. Above his head the murmurs of the prisoners planning their revolt were muted.

The corridor didn't run in a perfectly straight line, but drifted off slightly to his right. A few more steps and he felt it again—the flickering *essência*, spotty and incomplete, and wholly different from anything he'd ever come in contact with.

Distracted, he didn't sense the guard till it was almost too late. A dagger lashed out; Leão raised his arm to block it, taking a nasty gash on his forearm. A blast of air slammed the guard against the nearest cell with a skull-smashing crack.

Leão pressed forward, releasing his magical hold and letting the dead man slump to the ground. The cells on either side of the guard's body were empty. The barred doors were open, revealing piles of moldy hay and lumps that might be old blankets, scraps of clothing, or worse.

Then he caught a whiff of rotting flesh.

He cringed but rushed on. Needing to know, for sure, that it wasn't Johanna moldering in this hellhole.

The second-to-last cell was windowless, but foggy white light revealed a huddled lump too large to be a pile of blankets.

This lock fell away easily, clicking open in less than five seconds, but the barred door whined as he pushed it open. The body didn't move.

From the next cell he heard a whisper of movement and tensed.

"Hello? Is someone out there?"

He knew that voice. "Johanna? It's me, Leão."

"Leão—"

The rest of her words were cut off when an explosion rang out overhead.

Chapter 23

Jacaré

Jacaré followed the leads he had received from various barmaids and street-corner gossips, and with no results, he sat at the city's central fountain, waiting for Leão to report back. After two hours, and with an increasing sense of irritation and impatience, Jacaré went to look for his companion.

He hadn't gone far when there was a blast of *essência* and an equally loud eruption. Leão wouldn't have done anything to draw attention to himself, but someone else with enough power for Jacaré to feel halfway across the township had just blown something up.

Turning north, he ran.

CHAPTER 24

JOHANNA

The explosion was immense—stones churned against one another, and dust showered down on her head. Flames flickered through the plank ceiling, and men screamed.

"Jo!" The lock on her cell clinked to the floor, and Leão filled the doorway. "Are you hurt?"

She threw herself into his arms, sobbing with relief that the one person who could save Rafi had arrived. "In the next cell," she said. "You've got to help him."

"No, Johanna. There are other Keepers here. I didn't cause that explosion—"

Ignoring his words, she brushed past him and into the adjoining cell. "Rafi." She fell to her knees next to his crumpled form, one of his arms still stretched between the cell bars as if reaching for her. "No. No. No. No," fell from her mouth in a broken refrain.

Her heart hadn't had time to heal. The pain from her family's deaths had been hastily bandaged, still raw and festering, something she could survive till she slowed down enough to inspect the wounds. But seeing Rafi, vulnerable and unmoving, with sunken cheeks and cracked lips, was *severing.*

"We have to leave," Leão said gently.

Johanna didn't hear him and didn't feel his hand on her shoulder. She reached forward with nerveless fingers to brush the tangled curls off Rafi's forehead, tracing the line of his brow, the slant of his cheekbone.

His face was hot, practically broiling with fever. "He's alive," she whispered, leaning over Rafi's body.

"Jo." Leão's tone was half plea and half command.

"He's alive, Leão, and you will heal him, or I will not move from this spot." It was a weak threat and she knew it. Rafi had carried her away from her brother's body. Leão could most certainly haul her away from Rafi, but she wouldn't make it easy. He'd be fighting a battle on two fronts, against her and whoever else was out there. "He's the Duke of Santiago and my . . . my betrothed." She could see the conflict on Leão's face. "Please. He's my Pira."

The young Keeper took a quick, surprised breath and knelt down beside her. He pressed a hand against Rafi's chest. "I can't heal all of this. Not if I have to fight."

"Fix him. He'll fight beside you. He's good."

"Against magic?"

She opened her mouth to counter, but Leão shook his head. "I'll clean and close the wounds, but I can't do any more without risking our survival."

It was already a risk, she could tell by the stiffness of Leão's movements, but he pressed one hand to Rafi's chest while Johanna prayed to Mother Lua for a miracle.

Rafi shuddered as the magic poured into him; he gulped air and his eyelashes quivered.

"Please, please, please," she said aloud, clasping her broken hand over her shattered heart.

His eyes opened slowly. "Johanna? What's going on—"

She smothered his words with a kiss, then said, "We have to go."

Another explosion blasted overhead, and she threw her body over his.

"I'm pleased to see you, too," he whispered against her neck, his voice scratchy.

A glistening bubble surrounded them, and Johanna looked up, seeing Leão's expression shift from concern to concentration.

"We run *now*," Leão commanded.

With Rafi's arm draped around her, Johanna followed Leão up the stairs and onto the small square of stones beyond the door.

A bell pealed wildly. Soldiers struggled out of the garrison, stepping into boots and pulling shirts over their heads. Simultaneously, a head peeked out the hole in the prison's side. Limbs bound in ragged fabric followed. One barefoot man, then a dozen, streamed through the opening. Some wore random pieces of armor and carried handmade weapons—a table leg, the back of a chair for a shield, chunks of rock from the tumbledown wall. Shouts rang. Fights broke out. The flood of prisoners overran the men at the burning gate.

Weapons were raised against the unarmed, knocking some back, forcing others to the ground. A crack. A stab. A wheeze, groan, and splatter.

A gust of air blew the gates open, crushing those who stood nearest to them. Five men stood silhouetted in the opening. The man in the center was significantly taller than the rest; the other four held crossbows.

"It's been so long since I've had another Keeper to fight face-to-face. This is shaping up to be a very pleasant day." The voice was male, a tenor with a slight vibrato. He raised his hands chest-high and pushed outward. Everyone in his direct path tumbled over. "Or you could bring the girl to me and I could kill you speedily, but that wouldn't be nearly as much fun."

Johanna knew who "the girl" was, and from the arms tightening around her, she guessed Rafi knew too.

Leão pressed them both back into the stairwell. "I'll create a hole in the city wall behind us. It will open onto the jungle. You run. You don't look back. I'll send Jacaré after you." He handed Rafi a short sword. "Protect her. Get her to the wall."

"I will." Rafi took the blade without hesitation.

"Leão—"

He hushed Johanna with a touch, his fingers firm. "Be safe. I'll come when I can."

She hadn't liked the Keepers much, even once she understood their mission, but Leão had always been sweet to her. "Be safe."

Raising one hand toward the wall and one hand toward the approaching group, Leão counted down.

The earth lurched under their feet, a violent wrenching that knocked five of the barbicans out of the wall. Rafi and Johanna clung to each other, lumbering over obstacles, till they were through the hole.

Johanna stopped to see if Leão was following. He stood, tall and fearsome, protecting their escape with a shimmering barrier of light. Bolts of lightning struck on the far side. Crossbow bolts flew, thumping into chests and limbs. Some men died instantly and others slowly.

Leão stood firm, never flinching against the cataclysm that threatened to overwhelm him. Johanna turned away, ignoring the weight of guilt. More people were going to die, and it would be on no one's head but her own.

Chapter 25

Jacaré

Jacaré moved through Camaçari as only a Keeper could. His speed and agility drew the attention of the people standing on the street, and they moved out of his way.

The garrison courtyard was a nightmare relived. Soldiers cut down untrained men. The dying screamed, clutching at gaping wounds as if they could keep their blood from escaping between their fingers. Fire licked the bodies of the unmoving.

For a moment recollection was superimposed over reality. Jacaré could see the hazy image of a girl kneeling at the feet of a sword-wielding Mage. Her blond hair ruffled in the wind, the delicate wing of a shoulder blade exposed by her torn and bloodied dress, the soft curve of her spine as she waited for the death stroke.

The earth rolled under Jacaré's feet, and the sharp bite of a stone against his palm shocked him to the present scene. A Mage was there, taller and darker than the one who haunted his nightmares, but he was surrounded by collar-wearing minions for protection. No girl was hunched at his feet, but it was little relief. Johanna would soon be at his mercy unless someone could guide her to safety.

Jacaré took a deep breath, forcing away the horror of the memory, and he rushed forward with his weapon drawn. He could approach from behind, take down some of the Mage's men, and provide enough distraction for Leão to get Johanna away.

But would Leão know how to fix the barrier?

Across the courtyard, blocking a narrow gap in the picket wall, Jacaré spotted Leão casting a broad iridescent shield and fending off the lightning assault. He didn't need such a large shield to protect himself. If he had made it smaller, he could have reserved power for a stronger offensive attack.

The shield shuddered under a fireball, wavering for a moment before stabilizing. It changed color to a deep green and flashed three times, then returned to normal, then switched to the flashing green again.

The pattern of lights sent a code that only another member of the Elite Guard would recognize, telling a distant crew to pursue. It was simple and brilliant, but obeying it meant that Jacaré would be leaving his companion behind to face this Mage alone—a Mage with unknown ability and power.

It was the right thing to do to ensure Johanna's survival, but it was a wicked slice. Tex had predicted that this mission would result in casualties, but neither of them had anticipated losing the entire crew.

Except me. Always the lone survivor.

The pattern of lights flickered faster, urgency in the flash. Pride filled Jacaré's chest at the boy's bravery, but it was tempered with grief. He hesitated for one long moment, questioning himself, his decisions, the value of many lives over the life of one so valiant and true.

He pressed his closed fist to his heart and raised it in Leão's direction in a farewell salute, then dove through the hole in the wall.

With a crackle that shook the trees in the forest, the shield disintegrated and blasts of molten fire blazed against the prison's remaining walls.

Chapter 26

Leão

Jacaré took the opening Leão provided, and sprinted past with the speed only an Elite Guard could muster. They shared a glance, a moment of unspoken agreement. Jacaré would follow after Johanna, and Leão would do whatever it took to stop their pursuers.

Leão's throat was dry from breathing so hard for so long. He was winded, worn down, but he pushed on to give his friends a chance to escape. There was no room for trepidation in this turmoil, only action and reaction. Attack, defend, or die.

After a count of one hundred, giving Jacaré ample time to get into the jungle, Leão tore down the city's side wall. The barbicans fell like a giant's pile of kindling, making that exit impassable.

"You're going to make this difficult, are you?" It was that same high-pitched voice, magically magnified so that Leão could hear it over the melee. "You're welcome to try."

Instead of responding, Leão sent a blast of air to slam shut the garrison complex's gate and cut off the other Keeper's last avenue of retreat.

Six lightning bolts hit his shield at once, and the earth cracked beneath his feet. If he wanted to live, he couldn't make many mistakes. Before his shield could unravel, he leaped to the side, sprinting for cover behind the still-standing walls of the prison.

Before he got far, a rope of liquid fire smashed into the place where he'd been standing. He dove, feeling his skin tighten from the scalding heat, and rolled until he fetched up against the prison's stone foundation.

He was shaky, inside and out. His arms quaked, and exhaustion cramped the space between his shoulder blades, but his mind was racing through and disregarding possible scenarios.

I could try this. . . . No, this . . .

"I know you're out there," came a singsong shout. "It won't take me long to find you!"

Leão worked his way behind the prison, using the remaining walls as a barrier, drawing closer to his attacker's position. A wind tunnel appeared a dozen feet ahead, tearing at his clothes and sucking him toward the whipping gusts. He grasped for Air, desperate to establish a shield that would protect him, but the element wouldn't stabilize.

This! His mind latched on to one of Pira's tricks and pulled on the metal flecks in the fallen pile of stone. A portion of the prison wall sailed toward him, creating a head-high barrier, a perfect crescent of protection. The pieces fit together seamlessly, cocooning around him in a barrier shorter than he was tall.

He ducked down and hoped the guards and escapees would follow his lead and find someplace safe to hide. A few dashed inside his alcove, but too many others were struck by battle lust, trapped in the moment of kill or be killed.

And they would die, struck down by lightning or burned by flame. Nothing held out for long against the elements.

Leão did his best to protect them, narrowing his blasts of fire to long, vaporizing ropes, but the pinpointed attacks were sapping his strength, and his opponent wasn't making the same effort to avoid casualties. Swaths of flame burned the field and anything that stood in their way.

Pressing his back to the wall, he took a deep breath, trying to steady his breathing and slow the pounding of his heart. He had enough energy for one final assault, but it needed to be brilliant. It needed to be unexpected.

"This has been entertaining. Really it has, but I've got princesses to catch, people to kill, pastries to eat." The Keeper gave a little giggle.

Then there was a new sound, the tinkle of glass shattering against the stone. The man nearest Leão screamed, clutching the icicle that had stabbed through his stomach. Thousands of shards fell from the sky; some were as slim and pointed as stilettos and others were bludgeons, knocking men from their feet. One sliced a frozen line down the side of Leão's face. The chill of the ice and the heat of his own blood redirected his thoughts to something else, something totally inappropriate for the moment.

Pira. She was also hot and cold, lethal and beautiful. She could cut you with her words or cudgel you with her fists. And she was the perfect inspiration Leão needed.

Even though he was close to blackout, his energy tapped, a small smile played at his lips.

He remembered one particular day when he was a greenling—

a trainee for the Elite Guard—and couldn't seem to stay on his feet. Mud had slipped him up when he tried to use a bow, engage a peer, and even mount his horse. Pira had used her Earth affinity to make the ground slide under his feet. She'd done it as a simple prank meant to test his mettle, but today it would be a weapon.

Leão dug his fingers into the dirt and held his other hand aloft. With the last dregs of his power, he tore a hole in the earth beneath the Keeper's feet and slammed a fireball over the top like a burning lid.

Then he, too, fell . . . unconscious.

Chapter 27

Leão

A bell rang, a steady gong filling Leão's skull with an endless reverberation. He raised a hand and pressed it to his ear, but the sound didn't fade. The ringing was *inside* his head, and it wouldn't stop.

He blinked a few times, hoping to regain his vision, and slowly colors replaced the blackness. Fleshy, dancing shapes, edged with lines too dark to be shadows, appeared first. The blurring image became two distinct shapes before dissolving into one . . .

Arm.

It was draped lifelessly over a stone wall, and its owner was missing. Or more accurately, its owner was missing an arm.

Struggling to his feet, legs as wobbly as a newborn fawn's, Leão pushed himself to stand against the stacked stones. Once he was upright, once he saw what was beyond, his knees buckled and only his grip on the top kept him from toppling again.

Oh Light. Did I do this?

He couldn't remember. He didn't want to remember. And then, like the opening of a door onto a room of memory, he did.

The scorch marks on the ground were wide as a carriage but round, with narrowed tails pointing in his direction—arrows identifying the culprit of the destruction. In the center of the field, not far from where the gates stood, a crater smoked. Bits and pieces of *people* littered the ground like overlarge confetti, with streamers of blood stretching from each portion.

The man nearest Leão, blessedly intact, began to stir. A whimper rose from his lips, then cut off as if it had never existed. He rolled to his side, covering his ears. Perhaps also hearing the gong in his head.

At least the movement was a good sign. At least one person had survived.

Despite his horror at the wreckage he'd caused, Leão couldn't stay. He'd exposed his gifts; there was no disguising what had occurred. Rumors of Keepers, living magic-users, would soon have people searching for anyone that met his description.

One step, then another, careful to avoid the bodies of the dead—and a handful of living—he stumbled past his burning crater. The hole was deep, but he could see crumpled bodies at the bottom. Rats were already sniffing along the edge, looking for a meal from the corpses.

It was a sick sort of relief, knowing that the Keeper wouldn't be able to follow Jacaré, Johanna, and Rafi. They could proceed to the wall unhindered and reestablish the barrier.

It also meant that this particular threat to Johanna had been eliminated, but there were other hazards out there. The Keeper who'd captured Pira had gone west. A soldier would follow up on a perceived danger and eliminate it. It was his duty.

At least that's what he convinced himself.

The gates to the prison were open wide enough for Leão to squeeze through. Weary and exhausted, he didn't wonder who had pried them open.

Chapter 28

Dom

The palisade was complete; the cellars of the estate were stocked. The townspeople had been drilling on proper procedures to get inside the estate's walls in a reasonable amount of time—too slow, in Dom's opinion.

There was only one thing left to do, and it wasn't something in his father's plans. It was something Dom had discovered while studying the maps of the roads that led into and out of Santiago. He wasn't sure if it was going to work, and with a spy around (and because he didn't want to look like a fool if his idea failed), he didn't mention his plan to anyone.

Instead he gave all the villagers a day off and told Cook to pack him a lunch. He invited Michael along, thinking the ride would tire the boy out and give Brynn a break, but his plan backfired.

"Ask Brynn to come with us," Michael demanded, his cherubic face set in a pout. "I don't want to go without her."

Dom sat at the downsized table in the nursery that had been aired out for Michael's use. Some of the toys were too young, even for him, but the table and its battalion of hand-carved soldiers had become one of the child's favorite sources of entertainment.

Brynn sat in the rocking chair, stitching a patch on another pair of Michael's pants.

"I'm sure she has other things to do," Dom said, trying to draw her gaze, but she refused to acknowledge him. "Like fixing your clothes, which, by the way, you need to stop destroying."

He didn't have a clear view of Brynn's face, but from the way she jammed the needle through the material, he guessed she was upset. Likely at him. For something he couldn't name.

"She's not *fixing* them. She's adding pockets like yours." The boy reached into the pocket on Dom's right knee and pulled out a wrapped *doce de leite*. "And she wants to come. Don't you, Brynn?"

"Oh, I wouldn't want to invite myself along, Michael." She stayed intent on her work, snapping off the thread with her teeth and holding the pants out in front of her. "I'm sure Lord Dom's right. I've got plenty of things to clean, and sew, and straighten up."

Dom held out his hands, palms up, but Michael didn't get the point.

"I know she wants to go." Michael left the table and stood next to the rocking chair. "You want to go, don't you, Brynn?"

"Well . . ."

Tired of fighting, Dom groaned. "Do you want to come, Brynn? It'll be a long ride, but if it sounds like a pleasant afternoon, you're welcome to join us."

Michael beamed; Brynn sighed.

"If you insist, my lord."

I didn't insist. Michael did, but if it will get us out of the house before dark, then fine.

The ride *was* long, and Michael enjoyed the first hour, talking and telling tales like a tiny Storyspinner. Once the second hour began to stretch, his stories turned into complaints and then into whining.

When they finally reached their destination, Dom led the horses down a steep incline to drink from the bottom of a ravine. The drop from the twisting trail was at least fourteen feet, and the path to the bottom was barely wide enough to allow one horse to pass. There were two bridges that crossed the ravine: one closer to the marsh that marked the boundary between Santiago and Belem, and another where the flat meadowlands turned into a scrub forest.

By the time Dom returned from watering the horses, Brynn had laid out lunch on a trampled-down patch of weeds. Michael was curled up on one corner of the blanket, well on his way to sleep.

"I knew it would wear him out, but I didn't think it would be this bad," Dom said as he sat across from Brynn.

"He doesn't sleep well. He's up half the night every night afraid to go to sleep, and once I can finally calm him down, he doesn't rest." She passed Dom a loaf of bread to slice, worry bowing her mouth. "He's troubled by nightmares."

Dom studied Brynn and noticed that she, too, looked worn. "And how are you, Brynn? Are you getting enough rest?"

Her green eyes flashed, her cheeks burned pink. "How I sleep is none of your business."

The sharp words, the cold disdain, the odd tension between them, made Dom edgy. "Brynn . . . what's wrong? You've been so angry lately."

"I've been worried a bit for my brother. That's all." She wouldn't meet his eyes. "Gavin's sailing with Guildmaster Tolapia for the autumn spawn. You know how treacherous the northern sea can be this time of year."

"*Is* that all?"

She gave a quick nod and busied herself with the lunch.

"I just . . . I feel like something is wrong between us," Dom said, struggling to put words to the awkwardness. "You and I . . . we . . ." *Have always been friends. I've always felt close to you, and lately I've wanted to be close to you.*

With a raised brow she waited, not saying anything.

"You've always been my favorite," he said eventually.

"Your favorite *what*?"

There it was again, the bite in her voice that he didn't understand. Dom wasn't used to having people upset with him. For anything. Sometimes girls pouted to draw his attention, but Brynn wasn't that kind of girl.

She picked the seeds off her bread crust and tossed them into the grass. Her red curls, escaping her bun as always, gleamed against her alabaster skin. The spray of freckles across her nose and cheekbones nearly disappeared under her blush.

"You didn't answer my question." She turned, finally making eye contact. "I'm your favorite what?"

He didn't know exactly how to answer. She wasn't just hired help; she wasn't a girl he knew; she was Brynn. She was special and beautiful and funny and capable and kind.

None of that was new information, but he'd never put all those pieces together.

Her neck grew red, her lips pressed into a tight line. "Don't look at me like that, Dominic DeSilva. I'm not one of your throwaways. I'm surely not Maribelle."

"Don't look at you like what? How am I looking at you?" he asked. "And what does Maribelle have to do with anything?"

The bread fell from her fingers, uneaten. "Nothing." Her tongue slipped out to moisten her bottom lip. "Why are we here? This was a long ride for a picnic, and there were a dozen prettier meadows to stop in along to way."

He hesitated, fearful to speak, though he knew neither Brynn nor Michael would expose his plans.

"If Belem were to attack and make it all the way to Santiago, even with all our planning and preparation, we wouldn't last long." He eyed the ravine, knowing that if he blew the bridge that crossed the marsh, this stretch of land would be a significantly easier approach for enemy cavalry than the winding road through the forest farther to the north. "If he's going to attack, I'd rather meet him here. Use the hill behind us to our advantage and force his troops to cross the ravine. Even with fewer men, we'd be able to hold them for a while. Then we could spread our soldiers more evenly, blockade the road coming south from Cruzamento in case he decided to try to flank us."

She nodded, following his line of thought. "Then you could always fall back to the estate if things got bad. Smart."

He smiled, a small thrill that she was impressed.

"How will you stop them from crossing the ravine?"

His plans were simple, stolen directly from one of the tactics books among his father's personal things, but he was sure their strength was in their simplicity. Still, he shrugged. Getting all the elements together would be hard, and he didn't want to say anything till he knew it would work. "Oh, I've got something in mind."

"I'm sure you do." She reached for the picnic basket and searched through the remaining contents. "Would you like some linguica?"

"No. I'm not hungry."

Brynn looked up, her face surprised. Dom felt a little surprised as well, not because of his lack of appetite, but because he wasn't sure what to say. He usually had a list of phrases that were certain to smooth over any little disagreement. But with Brynn he felt tongue-tied and unsure of himself.

"Do you remember when we were twelve, right after you came to work at the house, and Underlord Braulio came to visit?"

Her face broke into a smile, the first he'd seen all day. "And you kept asking me to sneak you more pudding, and I did because I was new and nervous?"

"Yes, and then I threw up under the table and Braulio stepped in it?"

They both laughed, remembering the man's disgusted face, and his attempt to use the tablecloth to wipe away the evidence without drawing anyone's notice.

"You've been my favorite ever since then."

The happiness left her face. "Your favorite *maid*. The one you could always get to do your bidding."

She stood and Dom followed, touching her wrist to stop her from turning away. "Never just a maid, Brynn." One of her flyaway curls was stretched across her face, stuck to the corner of her mouth. He freed it, sliding it between his fingers. "You've always been more than that. You're my coconspirator."

"Aren't we a little too old for mischief?"

Finally, the opening he'd been waiting for. "Are we?" Dom trailed his fingers down the side of her neck, across her shoulder, and over her back. She was soft, rounded and comfortable, in all the right ways.

He raised his other hand, cupping her jaw, and she titled her face into his touch.

"Dom . . ." Her lip quivered, and it hurt him to watch.

He stilled it with a brush of his mouth. She listed toward him, and he accepted the invitation, holding her closer.

With anyone else he would have rushed to a shady spot beneath the trees where they'd be out of Michael's sight. But this was Brynn. He kissed her slowly, leisurely enjoying the now rather than focusing on what could come next.

"No," she said suddenly, backing out of his reach. "This cannot happen."

"Brynn—"

"Please, let's go." She turned to the blanket, throwing the food and flatware into the basket with none of her usual attentiveness. "Michael, wake up. You need to eat something before I pack it all away."

Dom stood with his feet on the blanket's edge, his mouth half-open. He didn't know if he should apologize, or joke, or smooth the moment over like it hadn't happened. But he didn't want to cheapen the way he felt.

He'd kissed dozens of girls, but that had been all lips and hands, sensations instead of emotions. Kissing Brynn made him *feel.* His heart rushed, seeming to grow too large for his chest, expanding till it pressed down on his stomach, filling his body with a mellow warmth, instead of a hungry heat.

It was something he wanted to experience again. Immediately. But the hunch in Brynn's shoulders made it clear that she would not be receptive.

He stood silently, watching her, his hands hanging idle, till birds in a nearby tree squawked and took to the sky. Dom watched them fly overhead and disappear across Belem's border. When he heard the hoofbeats an instant later, he knew what had sent them fleeing. One horse, possibly two, approached.

Brynn straightened, looking toward Santiago, and the hurt on her face morphed into fury as Maribelle rode into the meadow.

The lady's dark hair flew out behind her as she galloped her horse down the hill. She jumped out of the saddle before the horse came to a stop. One attendant, a wiry girl perhaps a year older than Dom, followed but didn't dismount. Her animal pranced nervously, reflecting its rider's emotions.

"Dominic." Maribelle was breathless, sweating, her riding dress open at the throat, as if she'd hurried to don it.

Apprehension crept on clawed feet across his skin. "What is it? What's wrong?"

She reached out to him with both hands, grabbing hold of his forearms. Her muscles trembled, strained from the hard ride. "I have information about your brother."

From the corner of his eye he saw Brynn's mouth work.

"Please." Maribelle tried to pull him toward the clump of red-flowering trees that lined the ravine. "This is for your ears only."

"Brynn can hear anything you have to say." He said the words hoping that his demonstration of trust would fix things between them.

"No. She can't."

He shot an apologetic look at Brynn, but if the information really had something to do with Rafi, then it *was* important. Hurt feelings would have to be soothed another time.

Maribelle dragged him a dozen steps away and angled her body so she could watch the trail, and Brynn and Michael. Brynn did not look in their direction, while Michael, still sleepy, seemed thoroughly confused, darting glances between the groups.

"Rafi's alive," Maribelle said in a near whisper. "He was seen in Camaçari two days ago at an inn called the Bean and Barley."

Dom sagged with relief as a million pounds of worry dropped off his back. "So he's with Ceara. He's safe."

"He's not. There's been some sort of violence in Camaçari. An explosion at the prison. My contacts gave conflicting details—"

"Contacts. As in more than one?"

"One said it was a man throwing balls of flame. The other thought it was the cannon powder. Either way, most of the prisoners escaped or were killed."

Prison? Balls of flame? Why was Rafi in Camaçari? And news of the cannon powder was bad. They had only a small storage of powder at the estate. The majority was kept at Camaçari because it had the most cannons. "I don't understand. What does Rafi have to do with the prison?"

She took a deep breath and blew it out in a narrow column. "Ceara had Rafi imprisoned, but it appears your brother escaped after the explosion."

"What . . ."

"Ceara's declared for Belem. If there's going to be a war, Camaçari will side against Santiago."

The words slammed into Dom, and his knees wanted to buckle under the burden. Maribelle touched his elbow, offering him support.

"We'll be hemmed in on two sides," he said, sounding like he was the one who'd just galloped into the meadow instead of Maribelle.

"There's more. . . ." She studied his eyes, and Dom felt like he was being evaluated. "My father's certain he'll be able to put down the rebellion in Maringa in the next few weeks. When it's finished, he plans to march to Belem's aid."

Chapter 29

Rafi

Johanna found a game trail and stuck to the meandering path. It was the obvious choice, and pursuers would have an easy time following them, but they were able to put a greater distance between themselves and Camaçari by sticking to it instead of fighting their way through the densely packed trees.

Rafi thought they were heading north, which was neither good nor bad. Eventually they'd cross a larger road or river and follow it to a town. After ten grueling hours, and on the verge of blackout, he hoped he'd find civilization sooner rather than later.

The wounds on his side were closed and his fever was gone, but he was altogether wasted.

Johanna wasn't doing much better, trudging along beside him at a pace much slower than her usual clip. Her pale face, the circles beneath her eyes, the quiet rasp of her breath, all concerned him.

They didn't waste energy speaking, moving forward as silently as possible, till the sun drooped in the sky and Rafi knew they needed food. And soon.

"Look," she said, raising a quivering finger. Ahead, right off the trail, hung a very green bunch of bananas.

Rafi sent a silent prayer skyward and hurried forward to rip down a few. They were hard and would taste horrid, but they were food. He passed one to Johanna and peeled his own. It was full of bitter seeds and coated his tongue with a thick layer of starch, but it was edible.

He opened a second and realized Johanna wasn't eating. "What's wrong? Do you hate bananas so badly . . ."

Then he saw her fingers. The first two knuckles on her left hand resembled overripe plums. The skin had grown taut and shiny with swelling, and the black-blue color seemed to drip down her palm before disappearing into her wrist.

"What happened?"

"The guard stepped on my hand to make me stop singing." She offered him a wan smile. "I bet he never expected it to start a riot."

"Why didn't you say something sooner?" He took her good arm and guided her to a tree trunk.

"While we were running for our lives or when we were lost in the forest?"

She sat down on the ground and ate the banana he peeled for her, while he looked for something he could use to splint her hand.

Two flat, straight sticks would work, but he needed something to secure it with. "What are you wearing underneath that dress?"

Johanna gave a half laugh. "I hardly think that's an appropriate question for our situation."

Rafi actually blushed. "I wanted . . . wondered . . . can we use part of your dress for a sling?"

"I have on my hunting breeches. I was hoping to get rid of this ugly sack at some point, but it has proved unfortunately sturdy." With a wave, she gave him permission.

Kneeling, Rafi reached for the hem and drew the material up over her knees. Even though he knew her legs would be covered, his hands shook as he found the dress's seam.

I'm hungry and exhausted. There's nothing interesting about tearing Johanna's clothes off. . . . I mean tearing her clothes.

He sliced a fat strip, leaving her dress a knee-length tunic. Then he tore it into several long pieces. Tying the ends together, he made a makeshift sling and looped it over her head.

Settling her arm into the pocket made her breath rush out in a hiss.

"I'm sorry," he said as he tightened the fabric so that her arm hung at an angle across her body.

"That's twice that you've apologized for something that isn't your fault." She ran her finger along the thin scar that marked the underside of his chin, as if seeing it for the first time. "Why is it so much easier to say you're sorry for something out of your control than for something you're responsible for?"

"I think apologizing is like admitting you're wrong—it's easier to do when you're not at fault."

"I'm sure," she said with a teasing grin, "that you aren't at fault all *that* often."

"We both know that's not true," he said with a humorless laugh. "It's just . . . the more I travel, and the more I see of my own countryside, the more I realize that even the way I *think* is wrong."

"Rafi, that's not what I meant."

"But it is true. Look at Camaçari, if you don't believe me. I always thought that because the township was part of my state, the people would be loyal to the DeSilvas. Yet the soldiers—men I'm supposed to be able to call on to protect our borders—didn't even recognize me."

"When have they ever had a chance to meet you?"

"That's just it. I should have made time to meet them."

"You're not even duke yet."

"I know, but . . ." He let the thought hang, and fiddled with the fraying hem of her dress. "Every day feels like a reminder of all the ways I've fallen short of my father's memory."

"No, Rafi. That's not fair. Memory is an impossible thing to compare yourself with," she said, covering his hand with her good one. "We roll it around in our minds until we've buffed away all the flaws. Memories, especially when they are of someone we love, are an unblemished version of the things we'd *like* to remember."

He felt an overwhelming surge of protectiveness, a need to hold her close and block out the rest of the world. Instead he raised her good hand to his lips and kissed the inside of her wrist.

She gave a coy sort of smile in response. "That was a very Performer thing to do."

"What was?"

"So many nobles thrust their fist toward your face, expecting you to kiss it as a sign of obeisance." She pressed her lips across his knuckles to demonstrate. "It's quick and cold and thoughtless." With a gentle twist she exposed the underside of his arm to the sunlight. The skin was smoother there, clean and pale. She touched the spot lightly with the pad of her thumb. "Turning your palm upward leaves you exposed. A kiss here is given only between Performers who are willing to share that vulnerability."

"I'm sorry," he said. "I didn't mean any offense."

Moving slowly, gaze locked on his, Johanna raised his wrist to her mouth. It was a simple brush, a contact so subtle, but it burned through his chest, forcing his breath out with a sudden rush.

It took all of Rafi's self-control not to tackle her into the weeds and repeat the kiss they'd shared at the inn. And the sly little quirk of her lips told him she knew exactly what he was thinking.

"Is there . . ." He stopped and reconsidered his words. "Is there anything else I should know about Performers? I wouldn't want to make any other missteps."

She looked away then, studying her swollen knuckles. "Performers don't have betrothals. There are no contracts. No dowries."

"Oh," he said, crestfallen. If she'd been raised without the concept of betrothals, it would be very difficult for her to accept something she never imagined for herself.

"To show interest in a Performer, you usually exchange token gifts. Flowers, favorite foods, little things. And there are, of course, actual performances." She worried her bottom lip between her teeth. "A singer, for instance, would sing her intended's favorite ballad. Like 'Lamento de Amantes.'"

"Is that . . ." He hesitated, unsure he wanted the answer to his question. "Is that why you didn't want to sing it for me in the prison? Because you were afraid of misleading me?"

"No, Rafi. No! I'm explaining this all wrong." She blew a strand of hair out of her eyes. "Leão was certain you were too far gone to save, but then I told him you were my betrothed, that I cared for you the same way he cares for Pira, and he healed you."

"You told him we were betrothed? Did you say it only to save my life? Or because you felt . . ."

"Our betrothal is complicated. It's so much more than two people who care for each other. It's kingdoms and dukedoms and enemies." She brushed the spot on his wrist as she considered her next words. "I don't want to rule. I don't want to be afraid for my life or for my family. But that doesn't mean I'm saying no to *you*."

He nodded slowly, trying to keep the growing sense of hope from showing on his face. "So . . . no promises?"

"At least not yet."

Rafi could accept and respect that, but it wouldn't stop him from making a few promises of his own. He would see her to safety, no matter what it cost him. He'd protect Johanna, and by doing that, protect Santarem.

Then, later, once their problems had been solved, he'd try to change her mind about taking the throne.

When he felt the prick of cold steel against his back, he wondered if there would be a later.

Chapter 30

Johanna

Jacaré's sword point pressed into Rafi's neck, not cutting the flesh but denting it.

"Stop!" Johanna scrambled to her feet. The movement was clumsy, and it jarred her broken hand. "Put down your sword."

Like an animal, Jacaré froze as if hearing some whisper of prey in the distance. "Say it again."

"What?" Johanna's eyes darted between the kneeling Rafi and the towering figure behind him.

"Tell me to put down my sword." His gaze was intense, focused.

Rafi, on the other hand, looked one moment from detonation.

"P-put down your swor—"

Rafi ducked under the blade, spinning on his knee, and threw an elbow into Jacaré's forearm. The Keeper's fingers loosened, but the blade didn't fall. Lunging forward, Rafi tried to tackle Jacaré around the knees but somehow missed.

Johanna had seen the swirl of Jacaré's movement, sidestepping the attack with incredible speed. He lowered the blade again, pressing the point into the middle of Rafi's back.

"That wasn't bad," he said as he prodded Rafi with his boot. "You're more agile than I expected."

There was a ring of compliment in the words, but it was negated by an overarching air of superiority. He stared down at Rafi with lowered brows, studying him intently. "You're very dark. I doubt there's any Keeper in your bloodline. Yet . . ."

He didn't finish his sentence, but sheathed his sword and offered Rafi a hand up. Rafi didn't take it, coming to stand on his own. He tried to hide it, standing straight and proud, but the attack had cost him. A sheen of sweat coated his forehead, and he held his right arm a little too closely to his side, protecting the still-healing wounds there.

"What was that all about, Jacaré?" Her good fist clenched, and Johanna wished her fingers were gripping her dagger. She'd managed to stab him once, on the night her family was killed, and right now she'd be willing to do it again. "It was quite obvious that Rafi was helping me, not hurting me."

"A lesson," Jacaré said, eyeing them like an unhappy taskmaster. "You both let your guard down, too busy being romantic to be sensible. We don't know who our enemies are. We don't know where they are. They could be a half day or half mile away. Or they could be hiding in the bushes, waiting for the opportunity to knife you in the back or shoot you full of arrows."

He turned his attention to Rafi. "If you care for her, you must do a better job taking care of her."

Johanna huffed. "I take care of my—"

Jacaré held up a hand, forestalling Johanna's words. "I know you try, but right now the entire world is looking for you. You need someone to watch out for you. A lot of someones, actually."

"Right now I don't have a lot of *someones*, I have you two." *Two of the world's most obstinate, single-minded people—like sides of the same coin.* Both were tall, with lean frames and stubborn chins. Though she realized as she looked at them side by side that she was afraid of one and afraid *for* the other.

Though Jacaré looked young, his experience showed in the down-turned corners of his mouth and the wariness in his eyes. Rafi's face was animated, full of undisguised anger.

She'd feared for a while, when he'd been so close to death, that the flame of his life was fading before her eyes. Johanna knew that if Rafi's life was snuffed out, she'd never be the same. She'd changed in the last year, even more so in the last two months. Scars of loss marred her heart; those would fade over time, but Rafi was like a brand. He'd seared his way into her soul.

Her father would have laughed, asking her if she'd learned nothing from the tales they told, about the fallacy and inconsistency of first love.

Yet Father's final wish was for our family to go to Santiago. Was that because of the betrothal? Did he expect me to fall for Rafi?

No matter her father's intentions, no matter the whims of fate or twists of destiny or power of Keepers, her feelings for Rafi had grown. He was good and honorable, and always put other people's needs before his own . . . even to his own detriment.

"What was your plan?" Jacaré asked, shading his eyes from the sunlight and facing north.

"To get away from Camaçari." Rafi looped the pouch he'd made with another portion of Johanna's skirt over his shoulder and slung the short sword through it.

Jacaré raised an eyebrow. "And then?"

"We'd planned to go to the Great Maringa Library and research Keeper lore," Johanna said, and felt awash with gratitude that they wouldn't have to make the journey. "Without your help, we had no idea what our next steps should be. We had no other options."

"You were willing to go into your enemy's lair to save Santarem?"

It could have been Johanna's imagination, but she thought she detected a grudging note of respect in his voice. "If it had to be done, we were going to do it."

"I suggest we go to Performers' Camp instead," Jacaré said. "They'll welcome you home and provide us with some supplies, and the location will give us ready access to the wall."

Home. The word was almost thrilling. *Someplace safe. Someplace normal.* The feeling spluttered. "That will be leading the danger directly to them. I can't do that."

There was no amusement in Jacaré's smile. "You have no other option."

Chapter 31

Dom

Dom sat on the windowsill in Lady DeSilva's office, one foot planted on the floor, the other tapping against the baseboard. He tried to stop after his mother tossed him a furiously irritated glance, but his knee would not quit bouncing as he listened to the information Maribelle relayed regarding his brother and Camaçari.

"This can't be right," Lady DeSilva said for perhaps the third time. "May I see your correspondence with your source?"

"You know I can't share it with you. I won't do anything that will endanger the few people who are loyal to me." Maribelle folded and unfolded her hands in her lap, more nervous now than Dom had ever seen her. "I'm sure you, of all people, would understand."

"What makes you think so?" Lady DeSilva's voice had a keen edge.

Maribelle tilted her head, not missing the sharpness in the sentence. "Every noblewoman needs a network of informants. You wouldn't strip me of mine."

"I'd strip you of everything, including your shift, if it meant getting the information I need to find my son and protect our state."

Dom's leg froze. He'd made a lot of mischief; a few times he'd been in real trouble with real consequences. Usually when he hadn't considered the results of his decisions. His mother's tone was the one that meant a punishment was going to be delivered.

"I understand your position, my lady."

But Dom was fairly certain Maribelle didn't. Lady DeSilva did not make idle threats. He cleared his throat, drawing their attention. "Mother, perhaps we should thank Maribelle for the information and excuse her to join her ladies?"

Lady DeSilva drummed her fingers on the arm of her chair, eyes narrowed slightly in Maribelle's direction.

There was some sort of communication happening between the women, neither of them moving or speaking, staring at the other, their faces revealing nothing besides cool calculation.

Finally his mother spoke. "Thank you, Maribelle."

"Of course, my lady." Maribelle stood, sensing her dismissal. She offered a brief nod to the duchess, not quite a curtsy but a gesture of esteem between adversaries.

She made it almost to the door before Lady DeSilva stopped her.

"One thing."

Turning slowly, an inmate whose reprieve has been rescinded, Maribelle faced the duchess. "Yes, my lady?"

"If you happen to hear more information—about my son, Camaçari, Ceara, or anything else that will affect Santiago—you *will* share it with me." The ultimatum hung unspoken.

"I'll share what I know about Rafi, Camaçari, Ceara, and things that affect Santiago."

And not one word otherwise. Her specificity made Dom's ears burn, as did the smile she gave him as she walked out the door.

Neither Dom nor his mother said a word till the footfalls had faded away completely and silence had filled the room.

Lady DeSilva's gaze was distant, focused to the north, where her eldest child had last been seen. Her fingers resumed their drumming, and Dom stood, waiting for her to voice her plan.

"I have a spy placed high in Ceara's household, and I've heard nothing—*nothing*—about an alliance with Belem." She opened one of the large ledgers on her desk and turned to the center of the book. All the pages looked identical to Dom's eyes, but she ran her fingers over what appeared to be a bill of sale, lips moving with words that weren't on the page. "He said Ceara received a huge shipment of high-quality wine from Belem, but I didn't think . . ."

Dom's mind was less concerned with the spies than with the potential of Belem attacking from the north. It would mean a long march for Belem's troops, a longer supply line, and dividing his army, but it would also mean Santiago was hemmed in in every direction except the south.

"I know you met Maribelle at the Keeper's Fountain."

The words were not at all what he had expected his mother to say. "Excuse me?"

"I have informants *almost* everywhere, Dom." Her tone was bitter; her anger at Belem and Ceara dribbling into her voice.

"You have me watched?"

"You left a work site in the middle of the day and met the daughter of a powerful duke at a community fountain. Did you honestly think that your actions would go unnoticed?"

"Maybe it was stupid of me, but yes. I thought we were hidden from view."

She shook her head, and her laugh was cold. "I'm afraid not. Rumors of you half-naked in public will always reach my ears."

"Mother—"

"I don't care." She raised a hand, as if warding off his explanations. "And I certainly don't want to know any more."

"Mother." Dom shifted, uncomfortable. *Nothing happened. Not really. It could have. It would have been so easy, but for once I was actually thinking ahead. Well . . . somewhat.*

For some reason he couldn't explain, he didn't want Brynn to know. She used to tease him about all the hearts he'd broken, and promised that at some point all his "conquests" would return to haunt him.

Like right now, for instance.

"Twist this to our advantage," Lady DeSilva continued. "Maribelle is sharing information with us, information we'll need until I can get verification from my contact in Camaçari."

"I don't think I'm the best person—"

"Don't be obtuse. Maribelle brought this information to *you*, not me. There's a reason, but I'm not certain if it's part of her end game or something more simple. . . . She could fancy you, I suppose."

"Many ladies do," Dom said as he stepped away from the window, using humor to hide the crumb of hurt. He brushed it off, as he preferred to do with emotions that made him uncomfortable.

"It is true. You have more than your father's fair share of charm. Put it to work. I've let you coast for far too long. I've been too focused on your father's death and preparing Rafi to take his place." She faced him and held his gaze. "I'm sorry for that. I'm sorry I didn't divide my attention evenly."

"I didn't need more attention," he said, feeling that sliver sink a little deeper. He'd always tried to be endearing, entertaining even, to balance out his brother's intensity. And he felt a little stab of something—guilt or hurt, he wasn't sure which—that his mother held him in such low esteem. "I just like getting into trouble."

She ran a hand down her tired face. "Well, then . . . feel free to get into trouble with Maribelle. As long as that trouble gets us the answers we need."

Chapter 32

Pira

Pira slid down the wall, her feet toward the forge at the room's center. Tendrils of smoke drifted though the chimney, obliterating the scent of her sweat.

She hadn't slept in two days. Not since Sapo arrived with two hundred of Inimigo's soldiers. It was only half the amount the men had agreed on—the other half would be sent when the princess had been delivered to Maringa.

The duke had also shorted the leader of the Nata on something else: beryllium. As none of the Keepers could sense the metal, Inimigo was in the prime position to manipulate Sapo and Vibora into doing his will for as long as they needed the beryllium for collars. It was a distinct bargaining chip, but Pira knew that soon the Keepers would be free of that particular dependence.

A fractured piece of something they hadn't smelted yet stuck to her leathers. She plucked it away and held it to the stream of light peeking through the door that opened onto the yard. It glimmered with a faint silver whiteness. She could see the beryllium, but she still couldn't *feel* it.

Vibora came into the shop just long enough to direct the fire to melt the metal down, and teach Pira how to shape it into the curved band that would snap closed around a neck. Pira did the heavy labor, and Vibora finished the process.

That was where the secret lay, Pira realized. The metal absorbed power, but Vibora had figured out some way to manipulate it. An idea sat at the edges of Pira's mind, tickling like a memory she couldn't quite grasp.

The door to the shop swung open, and Pira expected Vibora to walk in and command her to get back to work, but instead it was someone shorter. The woman Sapo had tortured. The Seer.

She wore her pale-blond hair in a loose braid and carried a basket under one arm. There was something in her face, the set of her cheekbones or the width of her eyes, that reminded Pira of someone else.

Someone from Olinda perhaps? She's taller than most of the women of Cruzamento, but shorter than Sapo. That might not mean anything, but her coloring is all Keeper.

"Who are you?" Pira asked without preamble.

"No one of consequence." She smiled, the hollows in her face sinking skeletally.

"That's not an answer."

She shrugged a bony shoulder, and the movement made the collar around her throat shift. The skin beneath was smooth and shiny, scarred after years of friction.

Pira looked away, sickened at the sight and what it meant. The skin beneath her own collar was raw and irritated, from tugging on it and searching for the latch that kept it shut. Her fingers simply slid off the metal. How long would she have to be a slave for the collar to stop grating against her skin?

"I have had and lost many names, and I have no way to get them back."

And there it was. Proof that the woman was unbalanced, as Seers tended to be. Instead of providing helpful information in a clear, concise way, they dropped clues like pieces of a shredded painting. Pira had never been one for games or puzzles. If she couldn't see the whole picture, she couldn't be bothered to figure it out.

"What's in the basket?" Pira asked, hoping it was lunch, and that if she accepted it and got back to the smithing—a job she could do almost as well without *essência* as she could with it—the woman would leave without imparting some senseless phrase that was meant to make Pira second-guess every decision.

The woman pulled back the cloth, revealing two hard rolls and a tiny clump of cheese. Crumbs littered the basket's bottom, and Pira got the sense that she was the last in a long line of slaves to be fed.

"All right, thank you." She hoped the woman would go, but she just stood there staring, mouth open a little. "Vibora will be back soon," Pira said, shooing the woman to the door. "She'll expect me to have some work done."

"No, she won't. She's counseling with Sapo."

"Are you going to tell me what they're counseling about? Or are you going to act like a typical Seer and make me guess?"

The woman gave a confused half smile and said, "You can call me Críquete, if you wish."

"I only wish to eat my lunch in peace." Anger at her situation made Pira's tongue sharper than she intended. "Please."

The smile disappeared off Críquete's face, and something sad and empathetic replaced it. "He's out there, you know. Worrying about you."

"Who?"

"The warrior," Críquete said simply, as if that clarified anything. "Make sure you tell him how much you care when you see him. It'll be the last chance you get."

Pira's heart contracted, feeling as if she'd caught the butt end of a staff to her chest. "I don't really want to know."

"I know you don't." She patted Pira's hand, though the action was undeserved. "But you need to be prepared. As we leave for the wall in a few days, it will be much sooner than you'd like."

"What . . ." Pira let the word hang, uncertain if she wanted any more convoluted revelations.

"Finish the collars." Críquete turned toward the door. "Don't try to trick Vibora. She'll notice the flaw you've built into that one the moment she touches it. She is a *natural* Earth affinity, you know."

Pira frowned at the collar she'd set on the worktable. The latch closed but would slip open with a slight tug. She'd hoped to give one person a chance at freedom.

"Fix it before she comes," Críquete advised. "And be ready for the opportunity when it arrives."

Chapter 33

Rafi

The list of people Rafi hated seemed to grow every day.

At first it was short, with a roughly scrawled "Inimigo" filling a mental page. The man was responsible for so much death and heartache across Santarem that sometimes it seemed impossible for Rafi to hate anyone else with such vehemence.

Ceara's name, a new tally, splattered the page with blood. The hate Rafi felt for his underlord was fresh and fierce, and would be managed only when Rafi could authorize a warrant for capture, then Trial and Punishment. Though in this case a beating wouldn't be enough. Rafi wanted Ceara's head mounted on one of the pointed pickets over Camaçari's main gate.

As they marched through the jungle, Jacaré had earned a mark too. It wasn't because of the way the Keeper carried himself, all arrogance and aggression, or even the way he'd thwarted Rafi's attack, but that he had the power to heal Johanna's hand and he'd refused. He'd given some thin explanation about energy and power and wasting it.

Healing Johanna would be a waste. Thinking the words added a new layer of ink to Jacaré's name on the list. If Rafi had actually been writing it, the nib of his pen would have bitten through the paper.

Jacaré's orders chafed, but Rafi swallowed the sharp words on his tongue. They needed the man—and his knowledge, supplies, and weapons. Still, Rafi would have chosen to face a regiment of Inimigo's troops rather than travel anywhere with the Keeper.

"We'll stop here for a few hours," Jacaré said, waving to a flatish spot near a small cluster of jaboticabas. "Rest. Eat. I'd like to push through till full dark. We could reach Performers' Camp by tomorrow evening."

The trees' globular fruit would supplement their meager rations of bananas and water. Johanna plucked one of the purple-black balls that grew on the tree's trunk instead of on its branches, and took a bite. A line of juice dripped down her chin. Rafi felt a grin tug at his lips, till he realized the knuckles of her injured hand were nearly as dark and glossy as the fruit.

Anger flared anew. "You can't do anything to help her?"

Jacaré turned slowly. "No. Especially not if it hinders me from saving her life later."

"You're a Keeper. Can't you do both?"

Rafi knew a Keeper's power was limited, but surely Jacaré could do *something*.

"It's fine, Rafi," Johanna interjected. "It's not bothering me that much anymore."

He could see the lie plainly on her face, and in the protective way she held her hand over her heart. It made him sick to know that she was suffering, again, and he could do nothing to fix it.

"When Leão catches up to us, he can heal it." Her voice was light, optimistic, but she was also oblivious.

She hadn't noticed all the times Jacaré had looked behind them, checking their back trail. It wasn't merely for protection; he was hoping to see his companion lope up behind them, but as the day stretched on and Leão didn't appear, Jacaré's face grew grimmer.

Leão wasn't coming.

Rafi didn't know exactly what that meant, but he knew what it was like to expect something and be disappointed. He even knew what it was like to look constantly for someone and never have him appear. One passing hint of sympathy and then Rafi's anger resurfaced.

"There's a stream nearby," Jacaré said, holding out their communal water bag. "Fill this. If it's cold, Johanna can hold it against her hand. It will help a little."

"Fine." Rafi snatched the bag and strode toward the sound of the stream, tracing Jacaré's name permanently on the list.

Chapter 34

Jacaré

King Wilhelm's necklace had been magically connected with a glass that allowed Jacaré to monitor Johanna's actions all her life. He'd seen her as a bright-eyed baby taking her first steps, and as an adventurous child facing new challenges. At first she'd been another element of his command, another task to be completed, but now that he knew her as a person—not simply an image—he'd grown to like her. She was tough and cagey, but still young and pliable.

Which made what he was about to do feel underhanded and despicable, and was something that would surely make her unhappy.

Johanna sat against a tree trunk, knees tucked to her chest, completing the picture of youthful vulnerability.

He squatted at her side, trying to appear idle as he peeled away the fruit's skin. "DeSilva is going to have to make a choice soon."

"A choice?"

"Of course," Jacaré said, as if he expected the thought to be obvious to Johanna. "You'll need to stay near the wall so the barrier remains stable. And he'll have to choose whether he'll stay with you or return to his people in Santiago."

She reeled, the words as stunning as a blow to the head. "But what about my brother? He's in Santiago."

"Rafi will arrange for someone to deliver Michael to you."

"I thought you could do something to reestablish the barrier. I didn't think . . ."

Guilt tingled at the back of Jacaré's throat before sliding down to his stomach. "Magic has limits, Johanna. You should have realized that by now." He waved to her wounded hand. "Distance puts a strain on it. If we restore the barrier but you continue to stretch the magic's boundaries, then we'll be back in the same predicament again and you'll put all the people you care about in danger."

"You're saying I'll have to stay by the wall forever."

"You could return to Roraima, though it isn't a very pleasant place to live. And without my crew . . ." Thoughts of Tex, Pira, and Leão dried his throat, and he had to swallow to continue. "Without my crew and an army of supporters, there's no way for you take the throne."

"I don't want it anyway," she said quickly.

"That's good. Once the Nata are taken care of and you renounce any interest in ruling, you'll be safer. With a dedicated guard, someday you might even be able to live at Performers' Camp. It's close enough to the wall."

"Someday. When people stop looking for me, you mean." Her tone was sour.

"And that makes your relationship with Rafi difficult. He has a duty to Santiago, and being betrothed to you will put his people in danger. The other dukes will always wonder if either of you has aspirations toward the crown."

It was like watching a dragonfly die. The paired wings of hope and optimism were pinned down under his words.

"I don't know Rafi well, but he seems honorable," Jacaré continued. "Would you ask him to give up his seat as Duke of Santiago to stay with you at the wall, or wage a war for you to take the throne?"

"No. Of course not," she whispered, her eyes looking suspiciously glossy.

Her words were exactly what Jacaré hoped to hear, especially as Rafi's footfalls were drawing closer.

"His goals are different from yours. He wants to help you *now*, while it serves his purpose and while he's accomplishing something that will protect his state, but that will change soon enough. You need to prepare yourself to let him go, Johanna." Handing her another jaboticaba, he added, "Don't make him choose between his duty and yours. It will be a hard decision. Make it as easy for him as possible."

Jacaré took her broken hand gently and healed the worst break. He couldn't do much else to make her feel better.

CHAPTER 35

DOM

Dom had done as his mother asked, finding an excuse to pull Maribelle aside nearly every day, pretending to flirt as she shared slivers of information. She had no new word on Rafi or Ceara, but the spy within Dom's household had sent out another message.

In those quick, private discussions he learned that Maribelle's eye-catching appearance and vapid air were a carefully cultivated act. And while he hated to admit it, even to himself, Maribelle was growing on him. She was smart and complicated, like her coded notes, a puzzle he couldn't quite figure or walk away from.

He leaned back in his chair, staring out the library window onto the night-darkened yard beyond, and considered the girl and her games. The room had a fairly good view over two sides of the estate. It also offered him a sense of privacy. The high ceilings and wide windows meant no one could come close enough to listen to a whispered conversation without being noticed. There was nothing between the oversize table and the bookshelf-lined walls except a few padded chairs and a rug.

The dog asleep near the hearth raised its head, and a moment later the double doors swung open, surprising Dom out of his chair.

It was Brynn. And she was crying.

She startled when she saw him and backed toward the hallway. "I'm sorry. I wasn't thinking." Raising her arm, she hastily wiped her tears on her sleeve. "I didn't realize you'd be here. I'll just—"

"No, please. Don't go." He hurried to her side, unsure of himself, of where to put his hands. It had been only a few days since their kiss, but every interaction since—even when they passed in the hall—had been charged. "What's wrong? Is he missing again?"

Her eyes, always a bright and lustrous green, gleamed with unshed tears. She shook her head in confusion.

"Michael. Is he hiding again?"

"No. No, Michael's fine," she said, her voice a shade above a whisper. "Michael's fine. I'm fine. It's silly. I'm . . . tired. That's all."

He did touch her then, fingertips lingering on her shoulder. She didn't turn away, so he left his hand where it was. "I understand. We're all worn to the bone. But are you sure that's all that's worrying you?"

"Yes. Of course."

Dom waited, knowing that his silence would force her to talk. She wasn't the kind of person who could stand an awkward pause, and she always tried to fill it with bubbly conversation.

"It's just . . ." She straightened, tucking a few wayward strands behind her ears. "Renato, the butcher's son who makes all the deliveries? You've met him before. He asked me to marry him, and it isn't a bad offer, really. He'll take over his father's business someday. Their home is quite lovely. It's nothing like the estate, of course . . ."

She kept talking, unaware that Dom had stopped listening as soon as she mentioned the proposal.

Brynn can't get married. She's not . . . is she even seventeen yet? Why don't I know when her birthday is? How do I not know this? But even if she is, she can't get married. She belongs in this house. She belongs here . . . with me.

"You can't marry him," Dom said, cutting her off midsentence. "You don't even know him."

"Of course I *know* him." Her face had gone a little pink, but Dom wasn't sure if she was angry or embarrassed or something else entirely. "I've known Renato since Gavin and I moved to Santiago when our parents died. And even if I didn't know him, it wouldn't be up to you to decide who I get to marry. You might be the lord of this house, but you don't get to make those decisions for me."

Dom opened his mouth, but he couldn't find the appropriate response. Brynn was actually considering marrying the butcher's son, who, if Dom remembered correctly, was too pretty for any man to be. Which somehow made this all worse. "Is this what was bothering you the other day?"

She answered with a noncommittal shrug.

"Do you love him?" he asked.

"I . . . does it matter?"

The color on her cheeks deepened. It wasn't a yes, but it wasn't a no, either. Imagining Brynn with anyone else, caring about anyone else, made something inside Dom's chest give a twist. The pain was too sharp for something as simple as petty jealousy; it wasn't the childish possessiveness of a boy whose favorite plaything had been snatched away. He cared *deeply* for Brynn—it was a surprising realization—and the feelings were more profound than simple friendship.

"I think it matters," he said, his voice low. "I think you should be with someone you love." *Someone like me.*

She gave a humorless laugh. "I will never, ever be with the person I love."

He stepped forward and nervously, hesitantly, touched her cheek. "Why not?"

A slow blink and the tears spilled down her face. Dom raised his other hand and wiped the droplets away with his thumbs. "Please don't," she said, but didn't pull away. "You're making this too hard."

"I'm sorry," he said, but wasn't sure what the apology was for. His eyes dropped to her lips, and he pulled her closer.

She put a hand on his chest, keeping him at bay. "Sometimes it's too late for apologies." Straightening, she turned for the library doors and never looked back.

Chapter 36

Pira

The burlap bags were scratchy and smelled like rotten potatoes, but Pira was too exhausted to care. She fell onto the pile on the smithy floor and tucked her arms, heavy with two days of overuse, close to her body. Flexing the fingers of her right hand didn't alleviate the ache in her knuckles and tendons.

She'd always been proud of her rough hands and muscular arms, but for the first time in her life Pira wished she'd trained in a softer, less useful art. An entire row of collars, nearly fifty in all, lay spread across the smithy's workbench. Hinges open, gaping like jaws of some frightful leech, ready to parasite the energy off some poor, unsuspecting creature.

Turning her back to the glinting, silvery metal didn't put her creations out of her mind, but she managed to doze off, napping lightly till arguing voices drew her out of sleep's clutches.

"You don't need her and I do," Vibora said as she walked into the shop. "She's not that powerful anyway. She's weak, really, and there will be so many others to draw from when we reach Performers' Camp."

"Don't presume to tell me what I need." Sapo pushed past the other Keeper and kicked Pira in the thigh. "Up, girl."

"Sapo, please." Vibora's voice wobbled. "Won't the wall be enough? What's one more Keeper in the face of all that power?"

"There are no guarantees. What if the heir is successful? What if she solidifies the barrier before we get there?" He kicked Pira, hard this time, and held a hand out to Vibora as if she could literally hand over control.

Too focused on the interaction, Pira didn't feel the kick. She knew there was something here, some clue as to how the collars functioned and what their plans were for the future.

"Then we'll still have all the collars that Pira is creating, and we kill Johanna," Vibora said, sliding needy fingers down Sapo's arm. "The barrier will snap and—"

"And all that power evaporates. I'm left no better than I started."

"You're the most powerful Mage alive. You've got more power than any ten Mages." Vibora's voice was gentle, calming.

A thick tube of air wrapped around Pira's torso and forced her to her feet, holding her against the wall. She didn't struggle, trying not to draw Sapo's focus and to glean their plan from the argument.

Sapo couldn't possibly use all the power from the wall. That was crazy. Wasn't it?

If they'd discovered a metal that defied her affinity, could they harvest the stored *essência* of one hundred Keepers? And if so, who could possibly stand against that force? No one on this side of the wall, and even Olinda would be in danger.

Sapo gripped Vibora's upper arm hard enough that she cringed. "Give her to me."

"No." Vibora said the word softly, battling the compulsion in his voice. "In less than a week you'll have all the power you can ever imagine, and an entire country of people worshipping at your feet. You don't need this one."

He grabbed the front of Vibora's shirt with his free hand. With a shove he slammed her to the ground, and stepped onto her throat. Vibora gripped his ankle, no collar protecting her from his bruising weight.

"If you're wrong," he said, bending close to Vibora's face, "then I will take you both."

He pressed down on Vibora, forcing a strangled half cry, before walking out of the smithy.

The air ropes around Pira dissolved and she sagged to the floor next to her master, both women gasping.

"Why . . ." Pira took a halting breath before continuing her sentence. "Why do you let him do that to you? Why don't you fight back?"

Vibora didn't answer immediately, pushing herself upright. "He's not always like this. The power—you've felt the constant pulsing—it does this to him."

"You want to give him more? You think that's going to make him treat you better?"

A brief spasm of pain ran through Pira's body, but it wasn't the worst she'd felt. Almost as if Vibora had shocked her simply because it was the expected outcome of her disobedience.

"I know my brother would never have treated you like that," Pira said.

Vibora recoiled as if Pira had slapped her, then shook her head. "Your brother left me to die, Pira. Sapo saved me. He healed my wounds and killed the Mage who hurt me." She struggled to her feet. "Jacaré left me to die."

Chapter 37

Leão

Leão wanted to doubt his senses. The first pulse of energy danced along his skin like a mosquito, the barest hint of awareness. When it became a perpetual hum, Leão dismounted from his stolen horse and led the animal off the road.

He found a quiet spot, near enough to hear the traffic that passed down Cruzamento's main road, but relatively out of sight. It was almost impossible to ignore the thrum of *essência* once he recognized what it was. The force tugged at him like a string tied through his navel, and he fought the instinct to run to its source. Instead he built a small fire and sat cross-legged, with his hands resting palms up on his knees.

With his body oriented toward the town, Leão listened. What he found both did and did not surprise him. The pulse was many layered, a discordant melody of high and low tones held by a clumsy musician. One person was ill suited to maintain so many notes at once. It was a poor opus compared with the perfect symphony of blended power that created the barrier.

Leão tried to pick out one thread, one alto note that rang like a stone dropped in a cavern—the tone he associated with Pira's Earth affinity.

He didn't find it.

Instead he was able to pluck one high, clear note, almost a descant to the rest. He didn't *know* it, but there was something about it that felt familiar, like he'd heard an echo of it somewhere before.

Focused on that bell-high chime, he tried to match it to his memories. It wasn't anyone from Olinda, he knew that for certain.

Which meant he could only have heard it on this side of the wall.

His eyes snapped open with realization. It wasn't the exact pitch he'd heard in Camaçari, but the texture and timbre were the same. Just like Pira's and Jacaré's had the same grainy, familial roughness that exposed their relationship. There was a tie between one of the people enslaved in Cruzamento and that spotty power he'd felt outside the prison.

There was something more there. Something he was missing. He listened again, hoping to find the connection between the two different *essências* in two different places.

The pulse of power revealed one other thing he didn't want to face: He was incredibly overmatched. With that much energy under a Keeper's control, Leão didn't stand a chance against whoever was waiting in Cruzamento.

He racked his mind for some of the lessons he'd learned from his grandmother—like how to defeat a Mage who was significantly stronger than you.

Chapter 38

Dom

Dom dunked his hands into the Keeper's Fountain, watching as white dust swirled into the flower-laden water. It turned milky, clouds twisting away from his palms as it washed away the evidence of his day's work.

Working side by side with the masons, mixing cement to shore up weak places of the estate's wall, had left his hands dry and coated with a layer of mortar he was certain would be ingrained in his skin for decades.

Physical labor was hard but surprisingly rewarding.

He leaned back against the onyx, feeling the afternoon's heat burn through his trousers, relaxing his fatigued muscles. Dom toiled all day, working himself to exhaustion, so that when he fell into bed at night, he was too tired to think of the impending war, Rafi's absence, his inability to protect their people, and Brynn and her potential engagement.

"So," Maribelle said as she entered the clearing, a basket over one arm. "I've crossed a few names off my list. I know for certain who our spy is not."

Standing, he snatched the basket off her arm without an invitation and searched for anything fast and simple to eat. His mother had recently learned that two units of Belem's men were moving north, and with the daylight failing, he needed to get back to the house to work through the details with Raul. The problem was that no one seemed to be sure whether Belem would be crossing into Santiago via Camaçari, or if he'd cut through the countryside and come from the west. Either way, Dom didn't want to be caught unprepared.

"Who's left on your list?"

"I have a few suspects," Maribelle answered as she sat in the spot he'd vacated. She tilted her chin back, letting the sun shine on her upturned face, as if posing for a portrait.

For a moment Dom just looked at her, studying the clean lines of her profile and her full lips. There was something different about her in that moment—nothing sensuous or sly—and it made her almost likable. Almost.

He reached into the basket for a second meat-and-cheese-filled *pastelzinho*, but Maribelle slapped his hand away and took one for herself, bouncing the hot pie from palm to palm.

"I saw you talking to Raul in the barn. Which list is he on?"

Maribelle regarded him over the top of her pastry. She took a bite, and melted cheese dribbled across her chin. She wiped it away with the back of her hand, but it seemed to stretch and spread. "I haven't eliminated him as a possibility. He could be the spy."

"How are you *eliminating* people at all? Where are you getting your information? I see you every day. You're rarely alone. When do you have time to ask questions and find answers?"

"A girl needs her secrets."

"Then tell me who's *not* on your list, Maribelle," he said as he jammed his hands through his hair.

"Oh, poor boy." Maribelle smirked. "Are you upset about the spy or about that little conversation you had with Brynn in the library? Must be awful to think that a servant girl might choose a butcher's son over you."

"How do you know about that? The library was empty."

She sucked the grease off her fingertips one at a time. "People talk."

"Which people? Give me *something*, Maribelle, or I swear on Mother Lua's name, I'll personally escort you to the border and leave you there."

"Don't threaten me, Dominic," she said, dropping the crust of her pie at his feet and idly brushing the crumbs off her hands. "You need me a lot more than you know."

"Prove it."

"Fine." She hesitated, closing the basket's lid before she spoke again. "Three nights ago I received some information from one of my sources. Your spy passed information—specific details about your food storage, well locations, and estate defenses—through one of my relays."

The *pastelzinho* Dom had so quickly devoured threatened to make a reappearance.

"Don't worry, I was able to stop it from spreading beyond my source. A coded message was tucked under a table leg at the Duke's Dagger. The inn was crowded, as always, so my relay wasn't able to see who left it behind, or who wanted to make off with it."

"Which means any number of people could have put the message there."

"True," she conceded with a nod. "But it was in a code specific to Belem's spies, and only a few people who serve at your estate were at the inn that night."

"Who?" Dom's fingers twitched; he wished she'd stop dragging out this game and get to the point.

"One groom from the stable, two maids, Raul, and one other soldier."

Raul. Raul who we've all trusted so fully. He'd be a perfect person for Belem to use.

"The other names?"

"I'll get them to you, but I need something in return."

Dom snorted and dropped onto the fountain's edge. "I'm not surprised."

"It's nothing painful," she said, biting her bottom lip but failing to hide a smile. "Send a letter to your uncle Fernando, asking him to pick up a package for me the next time he has a ship in the Wisp Islands. I'll write out the details for you later."

"There's a trick in this. I can feel it."

She moved in front of him, wedging herself between his knees and smoothing her fingers up his chest, then interlacing them behind his head. "Sometimes tricks can be fun, Dominic."

"Maribelle . . ."

Her voice was low, her breath fanning across his cheek. "You should kiss me now. Put on a show for whichever spy your mother has watching us."

He wasn't surprised that she knew, or at least guessed at, his mother's plan, but still he hesitated.

"What's wrong? Are you worried your precious Brynn will hear about this little tryst?" She pressed a slow kiss below his ear.

It shouldn't have mattered to him what Brynn thought. She was practically engaged to someone else.

But she hasn't said yes. Yet. There has to be a reason for that.

"Send a message to Fernando," Maribelle continued. "I promise the package will only benefit Santiago and your uncle." She must have sensed his inattention, and pecked him quickly on the lips.

He jerked away. "Fine," he said, knowing his uncle wouldn't take aboard a package that would cause any harm. "I'll do it."

Chapter 39

Johanna

Four men stood across the road that led to Performers' Camp. Bright sashes tied around their hips held their swords loosely, never getting in the way of a quick draw. Matching bands wrapped around their brows. Hands loose at their sides, faces stoic. They would have seemed dangerous to anyone but Johanna.

She knew those guard dogs for what they were, playful beasts more likely to slobber on you than bite. Fireswords, all of them, and her friends.

At the sight of the men Rafi took her arm. She jumped at the contact. They hadn't done much touching during their march—or talking, for that matter. Jacaré had discouraged any sort of conversation, constantly hassling them to move faster and quieter.

The silence had been nearly as heavy as Jacaré's words, and she'd spent the majority of their hike weighing the truth and its consequences.

The Storyspinner in her screamed to follow her heart and fight for love, finding some sort of compromise that would allow Rafi to continue ruling Santiago and her to stay near the wall. But too many tales were doomed from the opening lines, especially when the lovers were working at cross-purposes.

It might be better for everyone if Princess Adriana went back to being dead.

Stepping away from Rafi's touch, she broke into a light jog. "Didsbury!" She aimed for the man in the middle of the line.

His stance loosened; his head bobbed forward in surprise. "Johanna?" Then his face broke into a wide smile and he threw open his arms.

Johanna leaped into them; bands of lean muscle pressed her close and lifted her off the ground.

The other men's voices broke into excited welcomes and questions.

"Light, it's good to see you!"

"Where have you been?"

"Give me a hug."

She was passed from one embrace to another, lips planting hard kisses on her cheeks. They were all warmth and homecoming, till they remembered she hadn't come alone.

"Who'd you bring?" Didsbury asked, edging in front of Johanna, his body creating a physical barrier between her and Rafi. "Is that . . ." His voice trailed off, his hand dropping to the pommel of his sword. It wasn't a threat exactly, but it certainly wasn't a welcome.

"Rafael DeSilva," Rafi said, nodding at the men.

"The future Duke of Santiago," she said, finishing for him.

Didsbury's brow creased with concern. "Why's he here, Jo? Why'd you bring him *here*?"

He's my betrothed. While it was technically true, she wasn't sure the legalities had any hold on either of them. Santiago was Rafi's home and his heritage. Staying with her in Roraima would cost him both, as well as his family, and Johanna knew too well that price of that particular sacrifice. She'd never ask him to make that choice.

"It's a long story," she said, feeling Rafi's eyes on her. "And it's not one to be told on a trail."

"It better be a good one." His voice was limned with concern rather than interest. "I'm surprised he'd leave his home with war on the horizon."

"What? War?" Johanna's words were a snap, and both Rafi and Jacaré jerked to attention.

"Duke Belem's planning to attack Santiago. He's closed his borders. How did you *not* know?"

Rafi's mouth worked, but it was Jacaré who spoke. "May we enter Performers' Camp? It seems we have a lot to discuss."

The other guards sidled closer to Didsbury, and Johanna noticed that the band around his sleeve was red instead of yellow. She touched it with a questioning finger. "You're the head of the guard now?"

He nodded; his lips, which tended toward smiling, curved sharply in the other direction. "Ask your other friend about Benton," he said, nodding toward Jacaré. "We're a little short on the details."

Jacaré had told her that he and his crew had visited Performers' Camp in search of information about her whereabouts, but that was it.

Johanna edged out of the box the guards had made around her. "May we come down to camp? Please. We need information."

"You need more than that," Didsbury said, his mouth ticking toward a grin. "You need a hot meal and a bath." He nodded for Rafi and Jacaré to follow. "We can offer you, all of you, that hospitality at least."

Wagons speckled the valley floor like bright beads in a palm. Fingers of green, studded with black knuckles of rock, cupped Performers' Camp and sheltered it from the winds that blew out of the north, and hid the ocean to the east.

Johanna drank in the sight. Her eyes passed over the Council House at the center of camp, unconsciously searching for a red-and-yellow wagon.

It wasn't there, of course. Its bones lay in a crumbled heap in a mango orchard, far to the south.

"We heard about your family." Didsbury seemed to know what she was looking for and gave her arm a light squeeze. "Mother Lua will see their souls home."

She nodded, grateful that it wasn't a tale she'd have to tell. They walked past the bell pole, and her gratitude spread. Instead of announcing their arrival with three peals, Didsbury led them into camp like family instead of visitors.

Jacaré carried himself as always, watchful and wary. Rafi seemed to mirror the Keeper's attitude, but nothing could hide the emotions in his dark eyes. He caught her gaze for a moment, then it dropped to the arm draped around her waist.

She almost stepped away, moving to his side instead, but she stayed with Didsbury. *Distance,* she counseled herself. *Don't make this harder than it has to be.*

"You three can clean up at the springs, and we'll gather Elma and the Council at the House." Didsbury sent one of the Fireswords as a runner and the other two to watch the trail. "She's been asking for you. Seemed to know you'd be here soon."

"Hmm." Johanna couldn't muster much enthusiasm for the old hedgewitch. If it weren't for Elma and her supposed ability to see the future, Johanna's family would have stayed safely in Performers' Camp.

Had Elma sent them away knowing that it would result in their deaths?

Johanna didn't like the answer to that question, no matter what it meant.

Chapter 40

Rafi

War. Belem. Home. Mother. Dom. War.

Rafi didn't want to believe what the guard had said. It was only a rumor, and rumors got blown out of proportion.

But what if it's not? Oh Light. Mother will manage the food, but Captain Alouette's dead, so preparing the state for attack will fall to . . . Dom?

So lost in his thoughts, Rafi didn't notice when their guide, a blond boy of about ten, stopped. Rafi trod right on the boy's heel and earned a dirty look in return.

"I'm sorry," Rafi said, finally taking in his surroundings.

"This way," the boy said, waving them into a series of caverns tucked under the mountain's feet at the northern edge of the valley. They entered through a natural cave and went down a half dozen man-made steps. The rock was dark and porous, light peeking through crevices above and pocking the ground beneath.

Two benches, each built into the tunnel's wall, held mounds of neatly folded towels and a stone bowl full of soap shavings. Water lapped a few paces away, a hint of steam rising in the distance.

"Leave your boots and stuff here. No one will steal it," the boy said with a growl in his voice. "The pools are down that way. Didsbury said to have you wash up and give you some clothes from the castoff pile. I'll be back in a minute."

Jacaré clapped Rafi on the shoulder as he walked past. "I know you've got a lot on your mind, but you're not going to be able to go anywhere now or in the next few hours. Clean up and rest."

Anger flashed through Rafi, replacing his fears instantly. "Don't give me advice. We're *not* on the same side." He gave the Keeper a shove that forced him back onto his heels. "I heard what you said to Johanna. You can't possibly expect her to stay *here* now that the world knows who she is. Everyone, everywhere, will be after her for their own gains."

"Does that include you, Rafi? Or are you willing to give up your dukedom to live the quiet, powerless life she wants?"

"That's not—"

"You've had half a day to tell her that I was wrong. Why didn't you take her aside and promise to give up Santiago?" Jacaré smirked and stepped out of his boots. "Because it wasn't a promise you could make. You won't give up your dukedom, and you want her to take the throne. Then you can manipulate her every decision, turning Santarem into the happy kingdom you always imagined."

"No!" Rafi's voice echoed in the narrow cavern. "I mean . . . I don't want to *control* Johanna. I just want her to take her rightful place."

"Even though she wants nothing to do with politics and birthrights."

"She *should*." Rafi stood still, staring at the water eddying a few feet away, trying to ignore the whirlpool of his own emotions. His mother had once asked him if he wanted to be king, and his answer had been an instant no. But as the other dukes had fought for power and control, sacrificing Santarem's best interests for their greed, and as his own underlords had betrayed him, taking the throne had become a more and more attractive idea. Being king meant he would have the power to pull down the other dukes and replace them with better men.

The ambition, however, made him feel guilty. He couldn't simply take the throne; he needed Johanna for that, and she had no desire to rule. Rafi wouldn't force her to do anything against her will, or he'd be no better than Belem and Inimigo.

But if she could only see . . .

There was no clear way out of this maelstrom. The thoughts circled around and around, tugging at him one way and then another with no clear escape.

Jacaré shrugged out of his shirt and folded it neatly before he spoke again. "I see something in you I once saw in myself—a compulsive need to fix the ills of Santarem. That's a worthy goal." The Keeper strode toward the pool. "Just make sure you're not using Johanna to get what you want."

"I am *not* using her. I want to protect her."

"And the best way to do that is to let her disappear."

Chapter 41

Johanna

Johanna slipped the jade-colored gown over her head. It was a typical Performer style with a corseted bodice and full skirt. Hints of eyelet lace traced beneath the bust and along the elbow-length sleeves.

The material was lightweight and smelled of the lime soap they produced at Performers' Camp. She closed her eyes, breathing in the familiar scent. The quiet trickle of the water in the women's bathing cavern, the metallic tang of damp stone under her feet, the texture of the ribbons as she struggled to tie the bodice with her still-healing hand: All of it gave her the sense of home, of belonging. This place, this sheltered little valley, with its boisterous people and loud wagons, would always call to her.

And yet the thought filled her with a trembling sense of sadness. Her hands stopped fumbling at the laces. She leaned against the stone wall, and closed her eyes, trapping the tears that tried to form

This is my forever. No more traveling with friends. No more wagons stuck in the mud or performing by the beach. No more hesitant kisses under balsa trees, or hungry kisses in tiny inns.

Once this is over, once the barrier is stabilized, there will be no more Rafi.

She told tales of miracles, of love reaching across distances, of happy endings, but this story, *her* story, would be the other kind. It would be the allegory—one that taught about sacrifice, and the good of the many over the desires of the one.

Oh stop it, Johanna. This isn't martyrdom, for Light's sake. So you don't find true love. You get to live *and help others and save a kingdom.*

Raise your chin. Be Johanna the Brave, Johanna the Bold. Never, never Johanna the Heartbroken.

A crunch of wood over stone drew her attention, and one tear escaped down her face. Silhouetted against the bright daylight at the cavern's mouth stood a stooped shape Johanna knew. It belonged to perhaps the last person in all of Performers' Camp she wanted to see.

"Oh, my dear girl." Elma's voice sounded like Johanna's heart felt—raw, wounded, sorry. "I wish there was some way to have prevented all of this and all that is to come."

If it were possible, the tear trail on Johanna's cheek would have evaporated from her sudden flash of anger. "There wasn't any way to protect us? You turned us away. You sent my family to their deaths! You—"

"Did exactly what needed to be done to save Performers' Camp." Elma straightened, and for the first time in her life Johanna realized how tall the woman would have been without the weight of years on her back. "Trouble follows you. I wanted to let your family stay, but that would have been the end of all of us. And even after sending you all away . . ."

"What then?" Johanna clutched the hedgewitch's arm, not to steady, but to shock.

"I . . . I don't know. I'm not sure." Elma dropped heavily onto the bench, sending the small bowl of soap skittering to the rocky floor.

Her wrinkled eyes were pale, nearly white in the dim cavern light, but under the pockets of sagging flesh Johanna saw the fine almond shape.

Erase the years, add a healthy flush to her skin, shave away the white hair . . .

"You're like them. You're a Keeper," Johanna said as she pinched the bridge of her nose. "How did I not see this before? I always thought your gift was wisdom and an uncanny ability to read people. A trick like the rest of us Performers have, but you can see the future. Can't you?"

Elma reached for Johanna's hand and finished the healing Jacaré had started. It erased the pain, but it didn't piece together her broken heart. "The future is too fluid to be able to tell too much too far in advance. If you look beyond a few days, there's no guarantee that the circumstances won't have changed by a breath of wind or the death of a giant."

"And yet you forced my family to leave."

"That was one thing I was certain of. If you stayed at Performers' Camp, all the rest would suffer."

"Well, I'm back now. Does that change what you see, *witch*?"

Elma closed her eyes. Time ticked away with the water that dripped into the bathing pool. A prickle of discomfort made Johanna fidget as she waited for Elma to complete whatever it was she was doing.

"I see an end or a beginning. I see the demise of all you've ever loved or a rebirth of those you *will* love but do not know. I see misery and chaos and murder," Elma said finally. Her voice was flat, brushing against Johanna's senses and making her shiver.

"What else?"

Elma pulled up her hood. "No matter what happens now, what decisions are made, I see death, death, death. And you are at the middle of it all."

Johanna's heart thudded rapidly in her ears; her panicked breaths matched it. "Is there nothing I can do to stop this? Nothing to save us all?"

Elma used her stick to heft herself to her feet. She paused, looking down at Johanna, her expression shadowed by her cowl. "Remember one thing: No matter what I tell you, Johanna Von Arlo . . . Princess Adriana Veado Von Wilhelm . . . you will determine who has the power. Choose well."

Didsbury sat on a fallen log outside the bathing cavern, elbows on knees, sword dangling at his side. Johanna could see it now, the hint of Keeper heritage that marked the faces of so many of her friends—light eyes, fair hair, and sun-kissed skin. Unlike their distant relatives, however, the Performers were always quick to flash a smile and show emotion.

He met Johanna's eyes as she left the tunnel, and Johanna schooled her features, but it was too late. Didsbury's bright grin faded with the last of the day's light.

"And here I'd hoped you'd be happy to see me." He waved to the ribbons of Johanna's bodice, hanging loose at her waist. "May I?"

She nodded but felt strangely unhinged at his nearness. Performers weren't shy when it came to helping one another with a quick change between acts. Didsbury's troupe had performed with hers a half dozen times over the past two years. Johanna knew she'd helped him into a vest once or twice, and he'd laced her shoes when she'd switched from an acrobatic costume into a Storyspinner's dress.

His fingers were sure and quick as he tied the bow, yet his hands lingered at her waist longer than necessary.

There had never been anything between Johanna and Didsbury—her father wouldn't have allowed that—but he was a well-known flirt, quick to kiss with the merest hint of encouragement.

Johanna took a step away.

"Elma said to bring you and your . . . *friends* . . . to the Council House when you're all cleaned up." There was a question in his words, but it wasn't one Johanna even knew how to answer. And when she didn't, Didsbury pressed.

"You're a pretty girl, Jo. Always have been." His tone was light. "Pretty enough to attract a duke for sure."

"Oh stop, Didsbury." She tried to play along, though really she didn't feel like playing at anything. "It's not what you think it is."

"Really? I suppose Duke Rafael DeSilva escorts girls across the country on foot, when his state is on the brink of war, out of a sense of . . . what would you call it? Chivalry, maybe?"

"Actually, yes. He's perfectly gallant." *Decent, moral, noble, wonderful. And never, never, never going to be mine.* "And when we left Santiago, there weren't any threats."

Didsbury laughed, unaware of Johanna's heartache. "That may be true. He is from Santiago. Those DeSilvas would bite off their own tongues to avoid offense."

It was an old joke, and one that wasn't completely untrue. Johanna felt an unwilling smirk tug at her mouth. Didsbury's laugh was unburdened and infectious. It was a lifeline to an easier time, and she was tempted to snatch it, letting him reel her closer to something more comfortable and familiar.

He reached for her freshly healed hand. "I'm glad you're home, Jo. No matter the circumstances."

It felt good to be welcomed by someone, and she gave his fingers a squeeze in response.

"Johanna."

Rafi's voice was a terrible jolt of reality. She released Didsbury's hand too quickly, guiltily.

The young duke's face was free of the dark stubble that had dusted his chin, and she remembered its rough texture against the delicate skin of her throat. His expression, however, was as forbidding as a fortress gate.

"When you're done here," he said, and the gate creaked open for a moment, revealing the awful hurt that hid beyond it. His jaw clenched, and he stared at a point just beyond Johanna. "When you're *through*, can we please move to the Council House? Apparently, Santiago is in danger, and my first duty should be to my people."

Should be. Will be. He didn't say it, but he might as well have. Rafi would be returning to Santiago with or without her, and that knowledge left her with a tangle of happy disappointment. He would be doing his duty, and she'd be left alone—giving her exactly what she thought she wanted.

Jacaré missed none of it, standing behind Rafi and taking in the scene. His face, as always, was unreadable, but Johanna imagined that behind all his stoicism was a malicious sense of triumph.

"Of course," she said, ignoring her own hurts. "Didsbury, please take us to the Council House."

Chapter 42

Pira

"Wake up, Pira."

A hand jostled her shoulder, making her arm throb. Without opening her eyes, Pira grabbed the wrist of the person shaking her and twisted it to the side. The bones ground and the owner gasped in surprise.

Something hard cracked Pira across the ribs, and her grip on the assailant slackened.

"What the . . . what was that?" Pira peeled open her too-dry eyes to find Críquete standing over her with a stout hammer handle.

Críquete regarded Pira for a moment before dropping the handle with a dull thump. "You might find that useful."

"Did you have to hit me with it?" Pira said, rubbing the injured spot.

"Did you have to try to break my arm?" Críquete rolled her wrist, testing the joint.

"I'm tired of being woken up when I've barely fallen asleep."

Críquete made a disgusted face. "Are you a member of the Elite Guard or not?"

"What could you possibly know about the Elite Guard?"

The woman was too young to have lived on the Santarem side of the barrier before the Mage Wars. It wasn't that Vibora and

Sapo looked hundreds of years old, but there was something about their presence that felt ancient. Críquete was older than Pira, but Keepers aged at less than half the rate of the people of Santarem, and Pira wasn't sure if or how that affected people who shared Keeper blood.

"Probably more than you do. I had a very thorough teacher."

With a grunt Pira pushed herself up to sitting. "I wouldn't trust anything Vibora or Sapo told you, and nothing Barrata said. Ever."

"Not them." Críquete's smile was sad. "Tex."

Pira tried to block the memory, not wanting to hear the scream of the horses or feel the heat on her skin as the column of flame struck. Tex had been in front of her and had taken the blast straight on. It was shocking to see someone's life extinguished so suddenly.

"Ah." Críquete nodded, reading the look on Pira's face. "He's dead now. Alas, it is how it was intended to be."

Oh Light. There it was again, crazy Seerspeak. *But she knows Tex's name,* Pira thought. *Seers' visions aren't usually that specific. General, hazy details, faded landmarks, whispered voices, but names?*

"How did you hear about Tex?"

"Pira, I *knew* him. I slept on the floor of his cabin on the border of Olinda. I know the color of the curtains in his windows because I sewed them. I know his children's names and how keenly he felt their loss, even though he never showed it." She leaned against the forge and wrapped her arms around her body, trying to keep some warmth in her too-thin frame. "I even know why he was cast out."

Speculation about Tex's exile was widespread. He'd murdered someone in cold blood. He'd lost his temper and beaten a recruit.

He'd killed a young woman who may or may not have been his mistress. He'd publicly ridiculed the Mage Council.

None of the rumors made any sense, but Pira knew that one day he'd lived on a small piece of property not far from her and Jacaré's cottage, and the next he was gone, banished beyond the borders of the city, forbidden from entering on pain of death. No one had enforced the threat—he'd been an honored member of their community and a legend among the Guard—but she'd seen Tex only a handful of times after his supposed banishment. To an inquisitive little girl, Tex had been a white-haired phantom who occasionally appeared at their fireside and spoke to Jacaré in hushed whispers.

"He was exiled because of me," Críquete said, her wide eyes haunted. "He gave up his prestige and his reputation because of me."

"Well . . . he obviously didn't kill you. So what got him in trouble?"

Her smile was a bit vague. "He helped me commit suicide."

If Pira could have kicked herself, she would have done it. Obviously, Críquete was insane. "See, here's the thing: You're not dead," she said in her most patient voice. "You're breathing. And that indicates the opposite of death."

"Didn't you wonder as you left Olinda how he knew the valleys and passes so well? Things do change after hundreds of years. Landslides, high snow seasons, fallen trees—anything could have blocked the way, and yet Tex walked you straight to Donovan's Wall. Didn't he?"

"He had a special affinity for knowing which direction would be the best to travel."

"That's true, but didn't you ever wonder about how he always found the perfect place to stop for the night?"

"No," Pira said with a sigh.

"Tex made a pilgrimage to the wall twice each year and camped in the same places along the way."

"Why?"

"He's been waiting to escort me home." She rubbed at the scarred skin beneath her collar. "For nearly two decades he waited. I never made it back, and now I never will."

"Who are you?" Pira asked, trying again and failing to place Críquete's face.

"No one of importance. Except to Sapo," she said with a shrug. "To him I'm a trophy, his first success with the collar, and a sign of his intelligence. He's been planning to take over Santarem for a long, long time, but it took him a long, long time to get all the pieces into play."

"Have you heard his plan? He's going to pull down the wall."

"Not if you intercede."

Pira touched the collar around her own throat. "I can't. Vibora knows every time I plan to do something. She knows I want to kill her."

"So don't kill her." Críquete patted the hammer's handle. "Incapacitate her."

"Even if I could, then what? I can't get this thing off," she said, gripping the collar roughly. "She'll torture me until I come running to her to make it stop."

"Haven't you learned anything about magic on this side of the wall? Anything about its nature?"

"Obviously not."

"When the opportunity presents itself," Críquete said, her voice a hair above a whisper, "make sure you run hard and far."

Chapter 43

Jacaré

Elma stood outside the Council House and waved for Rafi and Johanna to enter ahead of her. "Just a moment, Jacaré, I'd like a word with you."

Johanna shot a dark look at the pair of them before allowing the doors to swing closed behind her.

Jacaré tilted back his head and blew out a long breath, waiting for the hedgewitch to speak.

"You aren't going to be strong enough to reestablish the bond between Johanna and the barrier by yourself. You simply don't have the *essência* to do it."

"I can—"

"Be honest with me and with yourself. You need Leão's power to make it possible, but now the boy's gone. That was the real reason you brought him with you, wasn't it?"

He didn't answer.

"Do you have a new plan?"

"I do." One he didn't intend to share. With anyone.

She snorted. "Do you think I can't feel it? That I didn't notice the change? I've spent the last five hundred years surrounded by people with a trickle of *essência*. I notice when power grows and wanes, Jacaré. It's been part of my survival."

His fingers curled into tight fists, trying to hide a slight tremble. "I don't know what you're talking about." Oh, but he did.

"As the barrier grows weaker, you grow stronger." She thumped her staff on the wooden deck under their feet. "It's an itch now, a hint of what could be, and you're tempted to pull it all down to take back what was yours."

"Never." The word was a growl and a threat. "Every action I've taken has been for the good of Olinda."

Jacaré hadn't noticed a significant difference in his *essência* until he tried to heal Johanna's hand. He'd long ago learned his limits and usually stopped himself before he reached them. At first he was confused by the amount of power that was left in his reservoir. Then the reason became clear. As the wall unraveled, his power returned to him.

"Was this the reason the Mage Council didn't want to send you? Because they knew you were a destroyer disguised as a savior?"

"Oh, come now," he said, forcing himself to relax his fingers one at a time. "I'm the least of their worries."

He turned for the doors, afraid that if he didn't move, she'd see the temptation in his eyes. It was a truth he'd barely admitted to himself. A truth that hinged on one word, one peculiar adjective.

In his last fight with the Mage Council, the one that forced Jacaré to take matters into his own hands, Amelia had called Johanna the *chave*—the key. It wasn't until the barrier began to unravel that he understood what Amelia had meant, the thing she must have known all along but never revealed.

Johanna's link to the barrier could allow him to unlock the portion of his *essência* that was tied into the wall. It was risky, but it was possible. If he pulled too much, the entire thing might collapse. The spell had gone awry in the first place, leaving him in his current state, and there was a chance it could happen again.

No. It was better that he carefully avoided thoughts of what could be, of the Mage he'd once been. There was no point in going back. He'd lived three centuries without the power; he'd live the rest of his life, no matter how long, without it.

"Take me with you," she commanded, and he felt the hum as she gathered her power, making a threat of her own. "I can renew the bond and save you from the temptation."

"No." He opened the doors. "You're old and you move too slowly." It wasn't a lie, she would hinder their pace, but he could see that her offer had value. The old woman might be of assistance or a burden.

He'd rather not take the chance.

"It wasn't a request, Jacaré. I will be joining you," she said as he walked away. "You have your people to care for and I have mine."

Inside the Council House, Johanna stood on one side of the room with Didsbury nearby, both perusing the books that filled the two-story bookshelf on one of the rear walls. Whispering, and occasionally reaching out to touch a binding with hesitant fingers.

Rafi stood as far from Johanna as possible, with his back against one of the pillars that supported the building, arms folded across his chest, chin down a little, but his head was turned toward the girl who held his heart.

Jacaré felt something—not quite sympathy, more an understanding—as he watched the young man. He remembered too well watching a girl across a room as she spoke so easily with someone else, wishing for that simple camaraderie, that shared history.

Young lords—*And young upstart Mages,* he thought with a hint of sorrow—shouldn't always get what they want. There was more to learn from loss than from gain. And Jacaré guessed that before this was all over, Rafi would know that lesson far too well.

Chapter 44

Dom

Dom lay awake staring at the canopy of his bed and worrying about all the things he should be doing. When his bedroom door opened and then closed with a barely audible click, he stayed still, waiting for someone to speak or leave.

The thick carpet on the floor muffled the sound of anyone coming closer, but Dom sensed that someone was there, watching him.

The person's shape was indistinct. It could be his mother, he supposed, checking to see if her wayward son was in his bed.

He held his breath, hoping that if the intruder saw he was asleep, whoever it was would leave him alone. Peering under his lashes, he watched the shadow move closer. A hand raised, trying to feel its way forward.

Not a servant, then, or his mother. It was someone unfamiliar with his room.

Say something, do something, he mentally commanded, but the prowler didn't call out, continuing to ease forward in the darkness.

Dom's fingers slid across the cool linen of his sheets till they brushed against the dagger that had become his constant bedfellow.

Bursting from the bedcovers, he snatched the extended arm

and yanked it forward. The body fell against him, and he used the momentum to roll on top of it. His feet were on the floor; his arm was across the assailant's chest; his knife plunged down where he thought the throat should be.

Her throat.

The knife bit deep, shearing through hair and sinking into the bed. He gasped and the body beneath him giggled.

She giggled.

"There are easier ways to get me into your bed, Dominic," Maribelle said, making no effort to shove him away. "You could have *asked*."

He responded with a string of the vilest curse words he could think of, which only made her laugh harder.

"I almost killed you," he said, pushing off the bed and pacing a few steps away. His heart pounded and his hands shook. He had to lean against the wall to stop from falling.

How in Mother Lua's name would he have explained Maribelle dead? In his bed?

"I don't think you understand how close that was." He fumbled for the window coverings, sliding them open to let the moonlight into his room.

She didn't move, lying stretched out on his bed, her legs dangling off the edge. Instead of voluminous skirts and layers of lace, she wore slim-fitting pants and flat-soled boots laced to the knee.

"Maribelle?"

"My hair is stuck. I'm quite literally pinned to your bed." Her voice turned to a husky whisper. "Was that your plan?"

"Light, Maribelle. You are worse than I am, and I didn't think that was possible." Stomping back to the bed, angry now instead of shaken, he yanked the knife out of the bed and pulled a yard of severed hair with it. The piece was about two fingers thick and inky as midnight silk. "Here."

Her mouth dropped open, and she reached for the side of her neck where the hair had been cut a knuckle's distance from her skin. "Oh."

"Exactly."

"I definitely didn't anticipate that sort of reaction."

A growl rose from deep in Dom's chest.

"Are you always this grouchy when you wake up?" She took the hair from him and divided it into six pieces.

"I wasn't sleeping, but I'd like to. How did you get in here?" He watched as she carefully knotted the strips, fingers moving in a memorized pattern, braiding the hair. "I have guards posted outside my door and my mother's." And at both ends of the hallway that led to her room, but he wasn't going to say that aloud.

Maribelle looked up from her task, her expression condescending. "What guard turns a beautiful lady away from his lord's room in the middle of the night? Especially when that lord is you and that lady is me."

"I've never had a lady in my room."

"Lady, maid, whoever."

"Maribelle—"

"I don't really care. It worked. Your guard believed you had asked for me, and let me in."

"That's something I'll have to change."

She smiled. "Do you really want to?"

He made an inarticulate noise and her grin widened.

"Why are you here? Honestly? I know you wouldn't come dressed in pants and a . . ." He shook his head, trying to figure out what she was wearing.

"It's a cape," she said, swirling the floor-length material. "It makes it easy to blend in with the shadows."

"I noticed. It's one of the reasons I *almost killed you*." He wiped the corners of his mouth with his fingers. "Do I want to know why you're wearing that?"

"You'll want to know that three of the five people I identified as potential spies are outside your estate right now."

"Did they get locked out after curfew?" Since his last discussion with Maribelle, Dom had encouraged his mother and Raul—who would soon be named captain—to set a strict time for all guards and members of the household staff to be back on the estate. They'd agreed, saying that it was a good idea, but hadn't extended the curfew to the rest of the township because many of the pubs and inns relied on their after-dark customers for the majority of their profits.

Later, in private, Lady DeSilva had cautioned Dom not to put too much faith in the curfew's ability to stop the spies. "As much evil is done in the light as in the darkness," she had reminded him. "If someone needs to get a message out, they'll find a way."

He'd felt naive. Maribelle had obviously been passing and receiving messages despite the people Lady DeSilva had assigned to watch their guest. It made sense that others were sneaking around without garnering much notice.

"It doesn't matter *why* they're out. These three are the only remaining suspects. And they are all outside your estate now. At the same time. Doesn't that seem an unlikely coincidence?"

It did. And he hoped that it meant they were closer to finding the traitor. "I'm coming with you."

"I hoped you would." She pulled a string from the torn sheets and expertly wrapped it around the woven hair, turning it into a bracelet of sorts, and dropped it on his bedside table. "You'll draw too much attention like that. You have to change."

He'd gone to bed in a pair of loose cotton pants. They hung low on his hips, baring every square inch of skin from shoulder to hip bone. He almost felt embarrassed, until he realized she'd already seen him half-dressed.

"Do you really want me to?" He echoed what she'd said earlier. It was a joke . . . for the most part. There was something developing between them, though he wasn't sure if he'd call it friendship as much as sociable antagonism.

Leaning back on her elbows, her cape a dark smear against his white bed linens, she studied him. "No, but then we certainly wouldn't get anything *productive* done tonight."

Their first stop—tracking down the stable boy Maribelle had identified—was a bust. The poor boy had been called home to help with his three younger siblings while his mother was ill.

"That makes it simple," Maribelle said, checking a slim slip of paper in her pocket.

It was dark, but Dom could make out the scratch of letters across the page. "Where are we going?" He hugged close behind her, trying to read the square script, but she tucked it into a pocket of her cloak and moved on without a question of direction.

They slipped between houses on a street that featured moderately prosperous businesses with living quarters above. Everything was closed for the evening, but lights burned in many of the upstairs windows. Laborers toiling late into the night, or families gathered before bed. Either way, Dom doubted anyone would notice them.

Which was saying something, considering that normally Maribelle drew attention with her bright, scandalously cut dresses.

This other Maribelle—dressed in black, moving like a huntress, quiet and unseen—made him wonder which side was closer to her true self. When she stepped onto a garden fence that abutted the back side of a house and used it to propel herself onto a second-floor windowsill, he had a fairly good guess.

"I know you have your own spies moving around Santiago. I want to know how many are on my own staff," he said as he followed her onto the slate roof.

"Shh," she hissed, dropping to her belly and shimmying up the sharp pitch. "I'm not telling you my secrets."

He lay beside her and looked at the home directly across the street. A baker was preparing dough for his morning wares, his work area lit by a few lamps and a fire glowing in the oven.

"That baker doesn't work for me. We only have Cook and a few assistants. Is he one of your relays?"

"Next house up."

Dom squinted but couldn't make out the sign above the door.

Light seeped from between a gap in the curtains, but he had no sense of what was going on beyond.

"Who's in there?"

"If there's no movement in five minutes, we'll move closer."

She was excellent at deflecting his questions, and had he not been on a roof, on a quiet street, late at night, he would have pushed for better answers. Instead he lay silently waiting for something to happen.

The side door of the house opened onto the alley, and Dom went rigid. Two people, male and female by their shapes, stepped outside.

They stood close, talking. The man rubbed his hands up and down the woman's arms as if trying to keep her warm. She leaned in, their chests pressed together.

"Let's get close enough to hear what they're saying." Maribelle slid off the roof.

"I don't think they're doing anything that will interest us," he said, but Maribelle was already gone.

He slid off the roof, feeling clumsy in comparison with this privileged duke's daughter. Ridiculous.

Maribelle hopped over the adjoining fence, crossed through the next yard, and slipped into the alley directly across from the couple. Dom followed. Crouching low, they crept forward till they were in earshot.

"Are you sure you'll be all right? I'll walk you back," the man said, his hands continuing to chafe her arms. "I don't like the idea of you being out here alone."

"It's one block over," the woman said, sweet impatience in her voice.

Dom knew that voice too well.

"I can make it on my own," Brynn said. "I'm staying at my aunt's place for the night."

"I should have walked you to the estate before the gates closed. It wasn't very polite of me."

Dom nudged Maribelle with his boot, but she didn't budge. He didn't want to hear any more.

"You don't need to worry about being polite," Brynn continued. "Polite goes out the window once people are married, right?"

"Married? Does that mean . . ."

Brynn must have nodded or made some sound too soft to be heard across the street, because the butcher's son whooped.

A stone plunged into Dom's stomach. "Let's go," he said, pressing his face close to Maribelle's ear.

"We should follow her."

"Brynn is not the spy."

"You don't know that."

Dom ignored Maribelle, walking away from the sound of amorous kissing. *Sloppy, wet, loud kissing. No one can enjoy a kiss that's so messy.*

Unbidden, the sweet kiss he'd shared with Brynn in the meadow came to mind. It had been so innocent, simple and true.

It had meant something to him.

He wasn't sure at what point Maribelle had caught up with him; she said nothing as he paced away in furious silence.

Finally, after they'd passed three blocks of homes, she said, "If we're going to try to catch the third person—"

"Stop."

"We passed the turnoff—"

"You did that on purpose." Dom swung them into the nearest alley. "You knew she'd be there. That she'd be with *him* tonight."

"She was on my list. She was at the Duke's Dagger the night the information was leaked. She has access to everything—"

"Stop!" he yelled, this time loud enough to make Maribelle cower. Guilt fluttered across his mind on hesitant wings. At some point she'd come to trust him enough not to cringe when he was angry. "Why? What's your plan in all of this? Are you like your father and choose to hurt people for the fun of it?"

"Dom," she said, using his nickname for the first time. "Dominic, no. You need to open your eyes. Someone in your house is giving away your defense plans, and it's likely someone you know. Someone you care about. You can't afford to rule anyone out."

"It's not Brynn. You and I both know it's not her."

"I don't know that, and I'm not too close to pretend it couldn't be."

"Did it look like she was selling secrets?" His voice dropped to a low snarl. "Did that look like anything dangerous to you?"

She didn't answer, wrapping her arms around her middle.

"I'm going home. Find your own way into the estate," Dom said as he walked away.

"Wait, don't go."

He ignored her, his steps heavy with anger and heartache.

"It's Raul," she yelled as he reached the end of the alley.

Two more steps while the words sank in. He stopped, back still turned.

"The last person on my list is Raul," she said again, her quiet tread drawing closer. "He's at the Duke's Dagger again tonight. I saved him for last, hoping that we'd catch our spy before we got to his name. I want him to be trustworthy, but . . ."

"Fine," Dom said when her silence dragged on. "Let's go."

"Do you have a plan for getting into the pub unnoticed?" Dom's tone was angry. The slurping sounds of Brynn kissing the butcher's son played over and over in his head like the chorus of a drinking song, too loud and irritating to ignore.

"I do, actually."

They'd stopped a street short of the Duke's Dagger, near the edge of the day market. It was empty of life; nothing moved except the moonlit awnings flapping in the breeze.

Maribelle was searching through her cloak, and Dom realized that there were pockets sewn into the lining, similar to the cloak Johanna wore when she was Storyspinning. Maribelle expertly dusted her hair with some white powder and wrapped the material around her waist so that it resembled a long, ragged-edged skirt.

"Tie this for me. There are places to cinch it all the way down."

He obliged, while she completed the outfit with a pair of oversize false teeth.

"How do I look?" she asked, the teeth giving her an exaggerated overbite.

If he hadn't been so angry, he would have laughed. "Too pretty not to draw attention."

She frowned at him, and one of the buckteeth stuck out over her bottom lip. "It works in Maringa. No one ever notices me."

"So you do this a lot, then?"

"What I do in Maringa is none of your business."

He eyed her, then took a handful of dirt and rubbed it on her cheeks. "Perfect," he said with a gloating smirk. "Lady Maribelle, daughter of Santarem's richest duke, would never walk around town covered in mud. No one would guess your identity now."

"Go find some place to wait," she said, waving in the general vicinity of a barn. "Spying is as much watching as it is doing."

And sometimes it was just doing.

As he walked away, he fingered the slip of paper he'd lifted from Maribelle's pocket. He knew it must have directions to each of the potential spies' locations, but he hoped the note would give him some other clues.

Stopping midstride in the shadows of the barn, Dom realized he'd gotten that and much, much more.

Maribelle spat her false teeth into her palm and wiped them on the edge of her cloak. "Raul has a gambling problem."

She twisted her skirt around and untied the knots that held it in place. "I thought maybe it was some complicated code—intentionally throwing hands or making poor choices to alert a relay—and I'm fairly good at spotting those types of things, but no. Raul is simply the worst card player I've ever seen."

Dom had followed her instructions choosing the stable as a safe, quiet place to wait. He'd created a little nook for himself in one of the empty stalls, pulling a lantern and a blanket down, and angling himself against the back wall of the building.

Instead of responding to her statement, he spread out the torn paper he'd been carrying in his pocket for weeks and the strip he'd lifted from Maribelle. "You *are* good at codes," he agreed, pulling back the edge of the blanket, revealing his scribbles on the barn's wood floor. "But they aren't that difficult when you can relate them to something you already know."

The directions, the name of the pub—he'd been able to identify those on the coded list, and from there he'd worked backward, figuring out the cipher and applying it to what had been the love letter.

Her lips moved as she read the words he'd written. She paled, but said, "It's not what you think."

"That you've betrayed me?" The charcoal he'd used to decipher her notes crumbled in his clenched fist. "That you've betrayed us all?"

"No, Dominic. You don't understand."

"What don't I understand? Twenty-six cannons, four ballistae, one hundred and twenty-four longbows, a series of directions that make no sense." He advanced on Maribelle with every word, backing her into the corner. "Did another copy of this message get sent?"

"Yes," she whispered, raising her hands defensively between them. "Yes, I sent another copy, but it's not what . . ."

Anger was an acquaintance, something that visited Dom from time to time and left no lasting mark, but this feeling . . . this was rage. It was as black and gritty as the charcoal on his palms. It was murder in the making.

Dom had fought with Rafi a time or two, and gone a few rounds with an underlord's son, but he'd never wanted to *kill* someone before. Leaving Maribelle crumpled in the corner of this horse stall was an apt punishment for her treachery.

Her eyes flicked to the stall door, but Dom wasn't going to let her go. He gripped her arms above the elbows, holding her in place, forcing her to face him.

"Was tonight part of your game? Running around the township. Climbing buildings. Were you trying to make me distrust the people I care about most?"

She grasped his forearms, but she didn't try to pull away. "I am *trying* to help you, but there are more elements at play. More people I'm responsible to."

"Like your father?"

"No." She closed her eyes, her lashes trembling in perfect crescents against her cheeks. "Think. What information did I give away?"

"The exact details of our armory."

"Nothing Belem's army wouldn't have seen when they approached the walls."

"Now they know how to defend against what we've prepared."

"I gave them inconsequential information and got crucial information in return. I found a real spy in your household. One who is sharing much more significant details."

Now he gave her a little shake. Her eyes opened and a tear ran down her cheek.

"Please," she whispered. "I want you to succeed. I need you to succeed and Belem to fail grandly. My father can have no allies."

"Why?" he asked through gritted teeth.

"Because . . . because my rebellion is growing, but it won't survive if Belem can come to my father's aid."

Chapter 45

Leão

As a child Leão had had horrific nightmares—as many children with a strong Spirit affinity often did. To help him sleep, his grandmother had once given him a handful of acorns. Her voice was soft, her hands tender as she pressed them into his palm.

"Can you keep a secret, Leão?"

Still shaking from his most recent dream, he blinked away his tears and frowned at the fistful of nuts.

"Do you know how we light the streets of Olinda?"

"No."

She harrumphed and pressed her finger to one of the acorns. "Certain items—naturally occurring things like pebbles and pinecones, things that haven't been changed by our hands—can hold a small amount of *essência*."

With a tap of her finger, an acorn began to glow a dull red.

"H-how did you do that?"

Her face creased with a smile—one of the warm ones she reserved for moments when they were alone. Then she taught him the complicated and secret process of imbuing the acorn with the proper amounts of Fire, for light, and Air, to keep the magic from expanding beyond the shell.

Johanna's necklace must have been created through a much more difficult sort of spell to be able to transmit images to the glass. And the collars . . . the metal was heated and shaped, taken from its natural form and turned into something else. According to his grandmother, that should have made it impossible for the beryllium to hold *essência*, let alone drain and transfer it. He guessed it was some property peculiar to the metal.

For two days he stayed far away from the pulsing sense of power, and anyone else whose *essência* he could feel, by sticking to the poorest parts of town and the very edges of the city. Many homes on the farthest northern border of Cruzamento, the ones closest to Roraima, were abandoned. It was considered bad luck to live so close to what had once been the kingdom's seat, and many people complained about the snakes that seemed to find a way into the homes and businesses, closets and beds.

During those days he poured every ounce of his *essência* into small, unnoticeable items and let his energy recover overnight.

On the third day he snuck into the city—creeping past the dozens of soldiers who tried to mix with the merchants and salespeople—drawing closer to the center of the power. He blended in, another fighting man visiting one of the pubs during his off-duty hours. And he hoped that with all the flitting notes of *essência* from the Keepers and slaves, the addition of his would go unnoticed.

It was part luck and part miracle that he saw Pira, stumbling and dirty, leave the blacksmith's shop at dawn. His first impulse was to rush to her side, but he kept his distance, watching from an upper room of an inn as she staggered to the well and dumped a bucket of water over her head. She dropped to the well's edge, head down in an unfamiliar posture of exhaustion and despair. Even at a distance he could see the soot that stained her apron and blackened her hands, and he almost abandoned his plan.

She's right there! His heart railed against his rib cage, demanding he take action. *Go! Get her now and run.*

Instead he forced himself to rely on his training. He could hear Jacaré saying the words to the youngest cadets: *Slow down, study your surroundings, don't deviate from the strategy.* Rushing to Pira's aid without considering the consequences would end in disaster.

He gripped the windowsill till it cracked, and even though a sliver sank into his thumb, he didn't let go. It was the only thing stopping him from breaking the window and racing into the blacksmith's shop after her.

A few moments later, black smoke rose from the chimney, and he could hear the distinct thump of a hammer against metal.

He watched the street for a while longer, trying to gauge the number of people who possessed the least bit of *essência*. There were a dozen or so with Keeper levels of power, and perhaps two dozen more who had significantly less.

Once he was sure he had a good estimate of what he was facing, Leão crept down to the street and laid his traps.

It was, perhaps, twenty minutes till full dark. The sky to the east purpled like a bruise, the color fading as it spread to the west.

Leão had returned to his room at the inn, waiting for Pira to step outside the shop. The stream of smoke never stopped pouring out of the chimney, and he'd listened to her hammer fall most of the day. Two different women entered the barn, one collared and carrying a basket, and the other moving like she was in charge. For a moment he considered blasting the second woman, but her *essência* was weaker than his. Killing her would draw the attention of the person with the real power that much faster.

Checking the long dagger at his hip, and hoping he wouldn't need to use it, Leão crept to the alley directly across from the blacksmith's shop.

One acorn, glowing slightly blue with the *essência* he'd packed into it, was clenched in his fist.

Slowly, forcing itself behind the horizon, the sun set. One minute before full dark Leão threw the nut toward the pulsing sense of power. It rolled, coming to a stop against the front stairs of a grand inn.

A moment later the sun disappeared, and the acorn exploded with something more significant than light. The entire porch erupted with a blast of searing flame. The few people on the street scattered and screamed. Leão kept moving, knowing that the burning building would have everyone's attention.

As he entered the blacksmith's shop, his second acorn blew. His time was ticking away—perhaps five minutes before the Keeper realized the explosions, lightning bolts, and wind tunnels were distractions.

The firelit forge illuminated his path. Pira lay on the ground, far too still given the disturbance outside.

"Pira," he croaked her name. His heart crawled into his throat, choking off his breath.

Not wasting another moment to consider her condition, Leão scooped her body into his arms, balancing her weight against his knees. She was alive but exhausted. Deep smudges colored the hollows under her eyes and blended with streaks of coal dust.

Carrying her was not an option. They had to move fast, putting distance between themselves and the Keeper with all the power. Despite the risk that he'd alert their enemies to his real location, he had to heal her.

Timing his use of power with the third acorn, he flooded her with as much energy as he dared.

Her eyes snapped open, healthy pink color rushing into her cheeks. She blinked several times, then raised a hand to his face.

"This can't be real," she said, tracing his bottom lip with one finger. "You're not real."

"They'll be after us any second," he said, gripping her collar.

"How did you . . ."

His fingers slid off the metal like it was coated in grease. "What do I do?"

"You can't open it," she said, directing his fingers to the back. "I've tried that a million times."

"Can we pry it or . . ."

She showed him a deep gash on the side of her neck where she'd tried, and failed, to do just that.

Thunder rumbled as his fourth acorn detonated. The explosion was so big it would have knocked anyone nearby to the ground.

"We've got to go now." Holding Pira's hand, he ducked out of the shop and joined the chaos in the street. She didn't question him, keeping pace at his side.

A few more blocks, a twisting warren of streets, and they'd be free. Once on the horses, they'd be safe. They were so close.

Leão tripped, something catching him in the ankle, and he went down on one knee. He bounced to his feet, expecting Pira to be several paces ahead.

Instead she was leaning against the alley wall. Her fingers digging into the bricks, pain twisting her features.

"Run." Her voice was strangled, her arms shaking.

"Yes." He reached for her hand, but she snapped it away from him, smashing her elbow into the bricks.

"Run," she said, ignoring the blood that dripped off her fingertips. She groaned, her warrior's face contorting with anguish, tears pooling in her pale blue eyes.

He grabbed her arms, but her body was rigid, her muscles locked in place. "Pira . . ." He tried to force her away from the wall, but she punched him solidly in the jaw.

"Run from *me*!" she managed, then kicked him in the knee, and he tumbled to the ground in front of her.

"No." The word was horror and disbelief.

She growled and raised his knife. "I can't . . . I'm not . . . please."

He hadn't even felt her disarm him. She must have taken the weapon when he tripped—when *she tripped him*. "You're under their control," he realized with sudden dread.

The knife cut down in a sharp arc and he rolled, barely avoiding a killing blow. It sliced across the top of his shoulder, skipping along his collarbone. The metal bit deep. Pain lanced through the muscle.

Pira sobbed, her chest rising and falling. "Go!" she said, stepping over him, poised to finish him off.

Pushing himself onto his side, he knocked the blade from her fist, but she was on him instantly. All her training, all her skill, rained down on him.

Her fists and feet dropped onto his back and stomach, precise perfect blows. A kick to his jaw snapped his head back, forcing his teeth to clack together. She followed it with a knee to his sternum, and an elbow strike to the face. Dizzy and wounded, blood dripping from his shoulder, Leão tried to wrap his left arm over his head, to protect it from her abuse, while his right arm reached for the blade.

Instead of fear for his life, he felt a wrenching sadness. He was going to have to hurt Pira to save her. If only he could reach the knife, he could incapacitate her, and then they could go.

"I . . . I'm . . . sorry," she said as she stomped on his forearm. "I . . . have to kill you . . . now."

CHAPTER 46

PIRA

Pira wished for the rats.

She prayed they'd come swarming up the alley, stepping on one another in their haste to feed on her flesh. Their wicked teeth, gleaming and sharp, would have been a welcome improvement over witnessing Leão's death by her own hand.

Her thoughts twisted in her head, trying to buck free of Vibora's control. But like a well-trained rider, the cursed Keeper didn't give up the reins.

As if watching from a distance, Pira saw her foot kick his arm away from the blade. He didn't seem to notice, nearly unconscious from the blood loss and the beating he'd already taken. She bent at the knees rather than the waist—the collar used the best of Pira's training against her—and her too-steady hand reached for the blade.

The voice in her head screamed, begged, and pleaded. *Turn it on yourself. Get control. Fall on it. Something. You can't kill* him*!* But the words were unheeded. Her fingers wrapped around the hilt in a perfect stabbing grip. Not too tight and not too loose, thumb pressed against the crosspiece for maximum control.

The toe of her boot lodged under Leão's side, and with a strong push she rolled him onto his back.

"No," she whispered, her tongue the only thing to heed her thoughts. "Get up," she managed, before the magic stripped her of that ability as well.

He didn't move. His left eye was already swollen shut, blood trickling from the corner of his mouth, his breathing uneven. Weak and submissive, he waited silently for the blow that would end it all.

There was simple acceptance on his beautiful, broken face. No thrashing or crying or pleading as she plummeted onto his stomach, forcing the remaining air out of his lungs.

"Leão." The word was a razor slicing open her heart, yet the traitorous organ continued fueling her actions.

She tried to plead with her eyes, begging him to understand that the hand that raised the blade didn't really belong to her.

His lips twitched, and she thought he was trying to say her name.

Then she drove the knife into his heart.

Chapter 47

Johanna

Rafi stood in the Council House's far corner like an outsider.

Johanna had hoped that Performers' Camp, and its lighthearted atmosphere, would help him shake off his worries even for a few moments. And if she was being honest with herself, she'd wanted to impress him with her home. Obviously, they weren't a rich people, but they had wealth in kindness and custom.

Both Jacaré and Rafi wore Performer-style clothes—simple white shirts that laced up at the collar, and sleeves that could be tied at the wrists or the elbows, and dark trousers tucked into their boots. It was almost painful to see Rafi dressed as a Performer, to think of him ducking low to enter a wagon. He didn't belong here, but that didn't stop her from wishing he'd stay.

"There's nothing for us to discuss," Jacaré said as he lowered himself into one of the Council chairs. "If you can spare us a place to sleep for the night and a few provisions, we'll be on our way tomorrow."

"All in due time," Elma said as she relaxed into her seat, leaning her staff against her leg. "Didsbury, I've got people working on accommodations and provisions for their travels, but would you mind making sure that everything is arranged for the trip to the wall?"

Instead of sitting, Didsbury stood at Elma's side, focused on Jacaré and Rafi. "I can. But as head of the guard, I need to know if I should expect any threats."

"Nothing tonight," Elma said quietly. "You will need to appoint someone to take command in your stead. You'll be accompanying Johanna and me tomorrow."

"I will?"

"These men will not come through Performers' Camp again, and Johanna and I will need assistance returning."

A slight gasp escaped through Johanna's lips. *Is that a prophecy or a command?*

"All right." Didsbury nodded to Elma and smiled briefly at Johanna. "I'll make sure everything is ready."

Once he'd left the room, Elma directed Johanna to the bookshelf. "I'd like you to bring me the last volume in the third row. You might recognize it."

Books were expensive, bulky, and not particularly travel-friendly, so the volumes the Performers kept in the Council House were precious. They ranged in size and shape and material, but they all contained the same thing. Each of the books held a master Storyspinner's collection of stories, the things he or she had learned from teachers and parents, with a bit of personal history mixed in. Shelf space was dedicated to only the premiere Storyspinners of each generation, though every person with even the slightest storytelling skill kept a journal, in case one was privy to an incredible event—or made up a tale that everyone, everywhere, would want to hear over and over.

Some of the tomes were so old they were rarely taken off their shelves, and only with special permission, the pages fragile in their antiquity. The book that Elma directed Johanna to wasn't ancient, but she hesitated before pulling it off the shelf.

The handwriting on the spine was so familiar it felt scrawled on her heart. The sting of the nib throbbing with fresh pain.

"Arlo Von Arlo," she whispered, her finger tracing the letter *L* as it looped into the *O*. "I didn't know this was here."

Elma nodded. "We made your mother leave it behind when your family was expelled."

Johanna felt yanked between anger and relief. At least the manuscript hadn't burned with the wagons, but the wagons wouldn't have burned if her family hadn't been expelled. There was no right way to feel in that moment, so she tried to settle on gratitude that this book of stories and memories had survived.

"All right, dear, I need you to turn to the story of King Wilhelm and his bride."

Instead of following the hedgewitch's command, Johanna hugged the book close. "I already know who I am, Elma."

"Do you *really*, Johanna? I think your father knew something that perhaps even Jacaré hasn't figured out yet, and something you've never guessed." She held out her hand for the book, then turned to the page she wanted before handing it back. "Start here. You read it. Your voice is much more suited to this than mine."

Johanna exchanged a look with Jacaré, whose forehead was furrowed. She supposed he was confused or perhaps interested, but his face always seemed distant no matter what he was feeling.

Rafi raised his eyebrows at her, a simple *Go ahead*, or maybe an *I don't care.*

She began to read from the paragraph Elma had indicated, though she could have recited it from memory. "'Many years passed, but the king had not found a suitable bride. His people were concerned, and they sent girls and women, young and old, from every state and from the isles to gain the king's hand, but none could earn his fancy.

"'Then, one night, a knock sounded at the Citadel's gate.'" Johanna stopped. The words in her mind didn't match the ones on the page. "'A girl slumped against the age-old wood, begging for assistance. The sentries hadn't seen her approach, but everyone who heard her voice hurried to find the king, begging him to open the door and let her in. The halls outside Wilhelm's personal chambers were clogged with servants and soldiers, all pleading with him to give the girl admittance.

"'But the king closed his ears to her voice, certain there was madness afoot. Finally, on the third day, she began to sing. The sound was beautiful and eerie, the melody completely unfamiliar, and after five minutes the king could resist no more. He pushed through the people who'd lined up near the gate to listen and broke the lock open—'"

"This doesn't make any sense. Why would the gate be locked? King Wilhelm would never have kept it shut for three days," Rafi said, sitting up straight in his chair. "It must be a tale that Arlo tried to make more . . . interesting."

"Oh, this is certainly interesting." Elma smiled slyly, then nodded to Johanna. "Continue."

Arlo had added to stories all the time, so it wasn't as if what she'd read was all that surprising. Some stories were embellished and changed, while others were always true to one version. "'Her clothes were torn and filthy. Long gouges marred her skin, and her cloak and dress, which had once been fine, were blood-soaked,'" Johanna read on. "'And finger-length thorns were snared in her braid. She trembled from fatigue and hunger, but her beauty was undeniable. King Wilhelm took one look at her and said, "I've been waiting for you."'"

"That's enough," Elma said, her grin tilted and smug.

Rafi ran his hands through his curly hair, tugging at the knots. "It's obviously false. It sounds like she'd come through the hedge on the back side of the Citadel. On the Keepers' side of the barrier."

"That's because she did." It was Johanna who spoke, her voice soft. "Queen Christiana was from Olinda—she was a Keeper."

Chapter 48

Rafi

The book fell out of Johanna's hands and dropped with a thump that Rafi felt through the floor. He could see that the truth had stunned Johanna, and he supposed he should have helped her to a chair. But the realization rocked him so much that he could barely move from his own. It just made so much sense. "When you sang at the prison, the prisoners rioted. They took a guard hostage."

Elma nodded and Rafi continued, "And the way people respond to you when you tell a story, they stop what they're doing to listen."

"Of course they do. I'm a good Storyspinner," Johanna said, defensive. "Audiences are supposed to pay attention to me."

"I've seen a *lot* of Performers, Johanna. Even your parents, who were arguably the best at what they did. They never affected me the way you do." He ran a hand over his mouth, remembering his inability to look away as Johanna performed. He hadn't even been able to applaud, he'd been so drawn in by her song. "The night you sang at my estate, I felt . . . I don't know . . . *bound* to you by the music. Like every word you sang was specifically for me."

He looked up then and saw the effect his words had on Johanna. Her eyes were unblinking, but her chin trembled.

"That's because I was *trying* to impress you, Rafi. I was desperate for your approval. And I didn't even know why. . . ."

She spun and ran out of the building, slamming the doors so hard that they bounced back open.

Rafi sat frozen, watching Johanna disappear into the maze of wagons and tents.

You don't understand. I didn't mean . . . what did I mean? The story makes it sound like the queen bewitched the king with her voice, but I didn't mean that Jo had done the same to me.

Had she?

"That wasn't supposed to happen," Rafi said breathlessly. "She misunderstood."

"It doesn't matter," Elma answered. "Mother Lua used magic to snare the huntsman. Queen Christiana used her voice to coerce King Wilhelm to open the gate. And Johanna used the same power, however unwittingly, on you."

Rafi didn't care. He had hurt Johanna, and he needed to go after her. He stood, hoping he could find her in the confusing morass of tents and wagons.

Jacaré blocked the doors, arms pressed against the frame. "Apologizing now will only make letting her go later that much harder."

There was triumph in his tone, as if this had been the final blow of a battle Rafi didn't even realize he was fighting. He tried to sidestep the Keeper, but something wrapped around Rafi from behind. He couldn't move, his limbs frozen, his feet floating a couple of inches above the ground.

"Rest tonight, young lord. Write your family a letter. Let them know where you are." Elma spun Rafi to face her, then lowered her arm so he dropped to the floor. "Johanna will need some time to process this revelation. Give it to her."

The day dawned gray, casting pools of watery light through the Council House windows. The letter marked with his mother's name leaned against the glass. Elma had promised someone would send it via bird later that day.

After he'd written the short, carefully worded message, he'd climbed into the bed the Performers provided, but he hadn't managed to sleep.

He'd tossed and turned on the feather mattress. Even though he'd wanted to sleep, needed to sleep, he couldn't wipe out the image of Johanna's face the moment before she ran out of the room.

Instead of fighting his thoughts, he'd lit the small taper a Performer had left behind and sought out some reading material. He'd picked journals off the shelves at random, reading a few paragraphs, getting a sense for the different styles of Storyspinning and how the skill had developed and changed through the years. It had compounded his guilt when he realized how good Johanna was at her craft. Instead of using heavy symbolism and complicated vocabulary, Johanna chose the simplest way to tell a story, letting the plot and characters carry the tale.

When footsteps echoed from the loft above, Rafi closed the most recent in a long line of books and prepared for the journey, sorting through the clothes the Performers had given him, adding a vest and a jacket, both too short. It had grown cold during the night, and another storm loomed on the horizon.

"Ready?" Jacaré asked as he stopped at the bottom of the stairs and waited, with obvious impatience, for Rafi to nod. "Then, let's go."

Outside a crowd had gathered, lining the path that would lead them out of the valley. The people—whose noise and laughter during the night had added to Rafi's inability to sleep—stood abnormally silent and motionless, watching.

He saw movement at the far end of the line. Johanna walked between the columns of Performers. Some stepped forward, exchanging a few words, kissing her on the cheeks, or pressing some small item into her hands.

A blond-headed little girl, probably close to Joshua's age, brought a crown of flowers. Johanna hesitated, but bent and let the child place the garland on her head.

Rafi held in a growl. "I guess the word is out, then? They know who Johanna really is?"

Jacaré agreed with a grunt, and while it wasn't words, the sound spoke volumes of displeasure.

Johanna was dressed in jacket and pants, cut close to the skin. The material looked thick and sturdy, but supple as it hugged her shape like an acrobat's costume. Her short hair was braided around her head, and the crown of flowers nestled inside of it.

He'd seen her in gowns and day dresses, hunting leathers and trousers, but he'd never seen her look so beautiful and regal. And terrified. He took a step toward her and lifted his hand—wanting to assure her she wasn't alone. She caught his gaze and held it for a moment before turning her back to him completely.

CHAPTER 49

JOHANNA

Once they were out of the valley, the hike from Performers' Camp to Donovan's Wall was all uphill. Didsbury led, with Jacaré behind, Johanna in the middle, and Elma and Rafi bringing up the rear.

The old woman tired frequently, and powerful Keeper or not, she needed to rest her aged limbs. The pace was slow and laborious, and Jacaré practically buzzed with the energy to move faster, yet he didn't say anything. No cutting remarks, no cruel looks. The end was in sight, and though they could have made the wall by nightfall without Elma, everyone agreed it would be better to face whatever happened next in the daylight.

"We'll stop here," Didsbury said when the clouds overhead had grown heavy with rain. "Might as well put up the tents and get some rest before that storm hits."

Jacaré and Didsbury got to work, and Rafi disappeared off into the distance. Not that Johanna was watching. She could simply *feel* the lack of his presence. Maybe it was that little bit of Keeper power she was supposed to have, but she'd never been so conscious of his location until now. Knowing he was behind her as they walked, near enough to touch but still so far out of reach, was almost a physical pain.

She used this new awareness to ignore him when he got close, horrified that there was actually something in her voice, something that she didn't know how to control, that could bewitch him. So instead she remained mute and distant, keeping Rafi as far away as possible.

The truth hurt on so many levels: that her skill wasn't really something she'd gained through hard work and practice, that she was unable to influence an audience the way her father had, and most horribly, that she'd somehow managed to make Rafi feel something for her that he would never have felt on his own.

"Where'd the lordling go?" Didsbury asked as he threaded one of the small foldaway poles through the roof of the tent. "Does he think I'm going to serve him because he's some spoiled noble?"

Johanna opened her mouth to defend Rafi, but Elma called to her.

"Bring me something to eat, won't you?" she asked as she rested on one of the boulders that speckled the landscape. The lumps of stone, the same slate gray as those that made up the smear of Donovan's Wall in the distance, looked like blocks scattered by a giant child. Their rough edges poked through knee-high weeds and scrubby trees.

Johanna unwrapped their day's rations and set to work making dinner out of soft scones, dried fruit, and a sausage. Jacaré directed her to build a small fire between two of the largest stones, which would block the light and provide them some cover from unseen observers.

A throat cleared behind her, and Johanna found Rafi holding out a mangled bunch of purple flowers with bright yellow centers.

"What . . ."

He offered them to her, hesitantly. His eyes dark and earnest. "Would you join me for a walk? I'd be honored."

A hand fell on Johanna's shoulder. "It's not really a good time or place for a stroll, is it, Johanna?" Didsbury's voice was cloying, full of arrogance and a hint of possession. "It'll be dark soon, and we really should stick together."

Rafi ignored him, but a muscle in his jaw feathered from the effort. "Please."

"Now is not the time," Jacaré agreed, dropping an armful of dry grass near the shallow fire pit.

Elma didn't say anything, her head tipped to one side, staring off into the distance. "I don't think—"

"Please, Jo. I have one thing to say and then"—he took a deep, ragged breath—"and then you won't hear anything else from me. I'll make sure you get to the wall, as I promised, then I'll return to Santiago without another word."

Didsbury's fingers tightened as if he wanted to restrain Johanna, and that action, almost as much as Rafi's expression, made her step away.

"All right. Lead the way."

"Don't take the flowers," Didsbury cautioned, a sneer turning his lips. "They're mountain nightshade. Terribly poisonous."

Rafi's arm dropped to his side, and a few blossoms fell from the bouquet and scattered across the ground.

"I didn't intend to lick them," Johanna said tartly, then snatched the bouquet out of Rafi's hand. "Come on, then."

She led, not because she knew where she was going, but because she didn't want to walk beside Rafi, afraid that her face would expose the emotions she was trying so hard to mask. The Performer in her, the one trained to play dozens of different roles, had a difficult time competing with the girl who felt lost, confused, and overwhelmed.

Giving up her life was hard enough, but now the few talents she'd been proud of weren't really her own to claim. There was very little of Johanna Von Arlo left.

She walked until she found an irregular ring of stones, and hoped that it was far enough from camp that no one would overhear.

"I have something for you," he said softly. "I know Performers bring gifts when they're courting—"

Johanna whirled around to face him, anger welling, to tell him that they were not *courting* and that under no circumstances could they or should they proceed with their betrothal, but when she saw what he held in his hand, the words died on her lips. "Is that . . . did you *steal* my father's book?"

"I borrowed it," he said, color flooding his face. "I stayed up last night reading it, and I think that you should too."

Her resolve softened. "Rafi—"

"'King Wilhelm picked up the girl and carried her to the far west wing of the Citadel,'" Rafi read aloud, tilting the book toward the horizon, catching the last rays of sunlight. "'He stayed away from her, afraid that the sound of her voice would affect him as it had his people. Once she was well, he received a daily report of her activities. It seemed that she never stopped moving, looking for good to do. She visited the hospital, talking to the sick and singing to the elderly. Everyone remarked that she seemed to glow, and King Wilhelm was certain it was because of the magic she carried.

"'Until one day, he saw her in the township playing a game with a group of orphans. No words were used, but the children obviously adored her, and it had nothing to do with her beautiful voice. So Wilhelm spent a few minutes—'"

"Rafi," Johanna whispered, both afraid to use her voice and too saddened by her parents'—her *real* parents'—love story to speak at a louder volume. "Why are you reading this?"

He lowered the book slowly, one long finger marking the page. "Because you need to know."

"Know what, exactly?" she asked, leaning against the boulder behind her, needing its solid support. "That my life is a series of lies, piled up in layers? That even when I think I know who I am, I don't actually know anything?"

"That's not what I meant. That's not what I was trying to do." He raked a hand through his tangled curls. "Your father loved your mother. It had nothing to do with her voice or any mystical, magical power."

He was advancing, and Johanna had given herself nowhere to go. She wanted to turn and run from the look on his face, from the hurt and hunger in his eyes.

"I should have told you. . . ." He closed the book and tucked it into a pocket. "Yes, Johanna, when you sang at my estate, I felt drawn to you. If the table hadn't kept us apart, I don't know what I would have done. Kissed you? Right there in the middle of everyone?" He laughed, but the sound lacked humor. "But you stopped singing and went back to being this cold, aloof girl who took jabs at all my good intentions.

"Then I saw you with your brothers, the way you loved and protected them. And I respected you. I saw you teaching them, and struggling and working to make their lives better, and I admired you. I tromped across my state, dodged Keepers, and fought man-eating lizards. I held you in a tree as you mourned for your family, and my heart hurt for you."

His hand cupped her chin. "I lay in a prison cell, certain I was going to die, and all I could think about was kissing you good-bye." He was close. His body only a hand's breadth from hers, his dark eyes drawing her in.

"Johanna." He whispered her name, and the word spread across her skin like a fine layer of ash, coating everything it touched with an unmistakable heat. "Somewhere in all of that, I fell for you. Don't you see that?"

Lips brushed her temple, her cheekbone, the corner of her mouth. "Your voice has nothing to do with how I feel. It didn't take magic to make me fall in love with you."

"Rafi," she murmured, tipping her head back to look into his face. "I . . . I . . ." The touch of palms sliding down her shoulders, reaching around her waist, made her ache to be closer. She wanted this moment, to believe his words, to accept the sweet gestures, to feel his lips on hers, but she couldn't let it happen. It would hurt so much more when she went back to Performers' Camp and he to Santiago. "I can't."

"Why?" It was a breath of a question.

"There is no place where we can be together."

"So we'll make one. I heard what Jacaré said in the forest, and he was *wrong*. I can come to you, and I'm sure that once in a while—"

"No." She shook her head. "No. We want different things, Rafi. You want to change Santarem—and that is a beautiful, worthy goal—but I can't help you." The sizzle where their bodies touched turned cold. "How many people have died trying to protect me? How many more would die to put me on the throne?"

She slid out from between Rafi and the rock, steeling herself against the chill in the air and the ice in her heart. "Jacaré's right in this one thing: It will be safer for everyone if I disappear after the barrier is fixed."

"Johanna, please." His voice quavered and something inside her splintered.

"Being with me puts your people in danger," she said as she backed toward camp, leaving him standing in the ring of stones. "Don't allow them to suffer for my sake."

The first drop of rain fell from the storm clouds above, but Johanna didn't notice. Her face was already wet with tears.

Chapter 50

Dom

The bedroom door opened, but this time Dom didn't move. He was too tired, too exhausted, too angry, confused, intrigued, disappointed, frustrated . . . there weren't enough words to describe how he felt toward Maribelle and all her secrets.

"Go away," he mumbled into his pillow. "I know you're there. Go away."

"Lord Dom," Michael said, his voice hesitant. "Your mother sent me. She wants you to come to her room right away."

Dom had been in bed for only an hour, but his mother and her minions certainly knew that. Still he didn't move.

A small, warm hand fell on Dom's shoulder. "She said it's important that I make you come now."

"Fine." He pushed himself upright, but his attention snagged on the black streaks that marred his white sheets, just as his handprints had marked Maribelle's arms.

Killing her might have been easier, cleaner, safer, but her explanation had almost made sense. She'd become an integral part of a movement to pull her father down. At first it had been simple things—organizing a disturbance among the mine workers, encouraging riots in the marketplaces. Leaking information about where her father would be, in hopes that one of his many enemies from inside the state would take the opportunity to kill him.

Inimigo had survived too many attacks with Vibora at his side—the woman was his bodyguard as much as his steward—but despite the civil discord, the duke had made no changes. The poor died in the street, while his favored underlords and merchants reaped the benefits and closed their eyes to the truth.

Then the leaders of the rebellion began disappearing. Some bodies turned up, disgustingly mutilated, holes chewed in their flesh. Others became servants in Inimigo's household, wearing collars like those Dom had seen.

"My father is an evil, repulsive man," she'd said, wiping the charcoal from her skin. "But Vibora and Sapo and Barrata—"

"*What* are they?"

"I don't know. They've served my father for as long as I can remember, always taking care of the things my father didn't want on his hands." She choked up then, turning away for a few moments, before she gained control of herself. "There is something about them that is completely unnatural. They're too smart and too strong, and they can make strange things happen. Your limbs feel frozen and your lungs impossible to fill. I watched Sapo tell a boy to stop breathing, and he did. He suffocated, clawing at his own throat, turning purple, lying on the floor in my father's throne room and dying while everyone else laughed.

"Some of my father's underlords call them Keeper-blessed, as if this power is something given to them by Mother Lua." She shivered, and hugged her arms tight around her body. "It's wrong. It's an abomination, but they have followers. Their cult grows every day, and these followers obey every command. They spy. Kill indiscriminately. And they were watching me.

"It was almost impossible to get anything done while under my father's thumb. I hoped coming to Santiago would allow me to cause problems from a distance."

"You've caused problems here, too."

She shrugged. "I know it looks that way, but I swear on Mother Lua's holy name that we're on the same side."

"No. We're not," Dom said, pushing through the stall's door. He wasn't sure whether or not he wanted her to follow him home or head out into the dark night and disappear forever. "I don't know what side you're on, but it's not mine."

Maribelle stayed close, even jogging a few steps to keep up with Dom's pace, but she didn't speak another word. It gave Dom time to consider his next steps. Should he tell his mother? Should he have Maribelle sent home? What if she was telling the truth? The questions had plagued him throughout the short night, but he hadn't uncovered any clear-cut answers.

"Lord Dom?" The little boy prodded him in the side, pulling him out of the memory.

"I'm coming, Michael."

"You might want to put a shirt on. Lady Maribelle is in there with her."

"Fantastic."

Maribelle looked as fresh and lovely as a spring flower, no hint of their long night except a smudge of darkness under her eyes. Her gown was low cut but had long sleeves, and Dom wondered with a pang of guilt if he was responsible for new bruises on her skin.

"Drink this," his mother said, offering Dom a cup of potent-smelling tea. "You're going to need it."

She was angry, her actions quick and clipped as she pushed the cup into his hands.

If you're upset over a rumor about me and Maribelle, it's your own fault, he thought as he dropped into a chair, stretching his bare feet out in front of him. He'd dressed, but he hadn't bothered to wet his hair or put on his boots.

"Raul is dead."

Tea spluttered out of Dom's mouth, streaking his formerly white shirt.

"Raul is dead and someone has soaked our cannon powder with salt water." Lady DeSilva bumped the teapot with her elbow, uncharacteristically shaken. "Raul's death appears unrelated to his position, and there's a chance the powder will dry."

Dom exploded from his seat, covering the distance to Maribelle's chair. "You did this."

"No. You know where I was last night." She shot a sidewards glance at his mother and managed a blush. "Raul was stabbed when a fight broke out among gamblers."

Lady DeSilva agreed. "Everyone at the pub agreed it was an argument that turned violent."

"I don't believe it. You're involved in this somehow."

"I swear I'm not," Maribelle said, her voice certain. "But there are bigger concerns. Belem is marching. His troops will approach Santiago from the west. They'll be here in three days."

CHAPTER 51

PIRA

A voice commanded Pira to move and take the knife with her. It slid out of Leão's body with a wet hiss. Blood followed, pouring down his torso.

What have I done?

"She wasn't supposed to kill him, Vibora!"

The voice rang in Pira's ears, but the words meant nothing.

"I tried to stop her, but she's faster than I anticipated."

A hand pushed Pira to the side, and she fell over limply, lying in the alley with her knees curled to her middle. Her shins rested against Leão's outstretched forearm. She imagined his flesh going cold and stiff at the point where their bodies touched.

For that moment, with her captor's attention diverted, Pira's body was under her control. She wanted to find the knife, to drive it hilt-deep into her own heart, and let her blood mingle with Leão's. They'd never be together in life. At least they'd have death.

Her fingers swept along the ground in a half arc. Instead of the knife, the back of her hand brushed the side of Leão's face, slipping down his cheek. A hint of stubble, the sharp corner of his jaw, a weak pulse at his neck.

It grew stronger under her fingers. Pira raised her head but couldn't seem to manage its weight, and the dizziness pulled her back down to the ground.

Sapo knelt over Leão, hands pressed against the young Keeper's chest. Vibora stood over them all, mouth twisted in a grimace.

"You're healing him," Pira said aloud, forcing through the wave of light-headedness to sit up. She pressed her back against the building's wall, watching the wound shrink.

Sapo glanced up for one instant before resuming his task.

Leão's chest rose and fell, air wheezing out of his freshly repaired lung.

Pira raised her bloodstained hand to cover her mouth. Sapo—their enemy—had brought Leão back from the cusp of death. "Why?" she breathed. "Why did you help him?"

"Help him?" Sapo's grin was self-satisfied as he held an open hand out to Vibora. She placed a collar onto his palm. "I helped myself. I couldn't possibly let power like his go to waste. He'll be the most powerful weapon in my arsenal. Stronger than you and Vibora and Barrata put together." He studied the smooth lines of the collar before looking at Pira. "I'll never have to beg Inimigo for his hidden stash of beryllium again."

The collar gleamed dimly under the night sky. Its sides were perfectly polished, its latch a neat rectangle that slid into an empty housing. Vibora had made a sample collar for Pira to use as a pattern, but this was significantly neater than her master's work.

Pira lunged at Sapo but smashed into an invisible wall. She flailed against the obstacle, kicking and shrieking and crying, as he waved the perfect piece of evil in front of her.

"Such a violent reaction." Sapo dragged one finger down the glasslike barricade, as if he were stroking Pira's face. "Must be love. Don't you think, Vibora?"

"I suppose." Vibora fidgeted with her sleeve, ignoring her slave's antics.

"I think Pira should do the honors." Sapo held out the collar between two fingers. "I find it vastly poetic that you—who love him so powerfully—be the one to strip him of his power."

She looked at Vibora, begging her for help, and saw something akin to remorse on the other woman's face. Still, Pira's arm rose, passing through the barrier with a pop. Blood had dripped down her arm and puddled on her palm.

Sapo pressed the collar into the gore. "You will always be the thing that made him weak."

Chapter 52

Jacaré

At dawn Jacaré led the group up the narrow, treacherous incline, drawing ever nearer to the solid gray line of Donovan's Wall.

Behind him a few paces he felt the merest brush of Johanna's *essência.* It wasn't constant, like the power of a full Keeper; it flared one moment and guttered out the next. Once he realized it was there, he forced himself to pay attention to it.

Of course. Of course she was half Keeper. A decades-old mystery finally began to unravel; dark secrets came to light. Her mother's real name had been Veado—a girl Jacaré had heard of but never met.

When a new face had appeared in the glass, Jacaré had been selfishly relieved that King Wilhelm had taken an interest in someone. It meant Jacaré's job would stay easy, that there'd be an heir to carry on the royal line. He never questioned the queen's identity or its potential ramifications.

Whatever *essência* Johanna had inherited from her mother had been tied up in the barrier because of her father. Until the wall began to crumble in earnest, her power had been latent. The riot in Camaçari had likely been the first time she'd ever been able to draw on her Spirit affinity. He didn't point that out to Rafi or Johanna.

Their relationship was showing a few fractures, and while it tweaked at Jacaré's conscience a little, it also served his purposes.

Every step was one nearer the end of this mission, but it also brought him closer to the place his power had been stored for the past three centuries. The familiarity of it, the sweet temptation to pluck one thread out of the tapestry that made up the barrier. Would anyone notice? Could he do it without tearing the whole thing apart?

Why are you even considering it?

The desire made him nervous, and made him determined to keep Elma with him. If he couldn't trust himself, he wanted to know that someone else would keep him in check.

The boys switched positions without any spoken agreement. Didsbury slung Elma's free arm around his neck, and Rafi steadied her. It was almost comical how well they worked together, even while exchanging dark looks over the old woman's head.

"Stop!" Elma yelled suddenly, swinging away from Didsbury.

Jacaré expected some admonishment, some reminder that they were all on the same side, but Elma turned and faced downhill.

"We can rest when we get to the top." Jacaré pushed forward a few steps, climbing over a slick rock face.

He turned to offer Johanna a hand up a steep incline but found her watching Elma, who was leaning heavily on her staff, struggling to catch her breath. Didsbury stood close to her, a hand centered on the old woman's back. Rafi hovered at the other side, as if expecting her to fall.

Elma raised a palsied finger to point into the distance. "Look. There. Those are my people."

Brightly colored cloaks and skirts fluttered as they moved forward in an uneven formation. Perhaps thirty people in all crawled over the landscape in a halting, jerking fashion, some surmounting boulders and others disappearing into ravines before resurfacing.

It wasn't the way any person would *choose* to cross the landscape.

Collars glittered around every throat, catching the scattered bands of sunlight that broke through the clouds.

"Oh Mother Lua," Elma said, both a prayer and a curse. "My children. My poor children."

"What do we do?" Didsbury asked, looking from face to face for guidance, then turning back to the lurching horde. He reached for the bow on his back.

"No." Elma knocked it aside and it clattered to stones at their feet. "Your family, your *mother*, might be down there."

Johanna picked up the weapon, her face twisted with anguish. "That must be part of the plan. They know we won't hurt our own."

The Performers, driven by an unseen Keeper, moved at a tremendous pace, passing the tents Didsbury had left standing in the valley. They'd been certain they would return to sleep in them after they'd finished at the wall.

They would be lucky to leave this mountain at all.

"Move!" Jacaré yelled. "We need to move faster."

Too late. A crackling blue film stretched across the horizon. Elma's arms were flung wide, as if physically holding in place the magical barricade she'd created. A bolt of electricity smashed into her shield, and the impact knocked Didsbury from his feet.

Rafi's arms were tight around Johanna's waist, trying to guide her uphill, while she struggled to take the quiver of arrows from Didsbury's shoulder.

"Johanna, now!" Cold sweat dampened Jacaré's shirt. That lightning bolt had been much too close, and there was no guarantee that the next wouldn't punch through the shield.

"I'll slow them down," Elma promised, and the first line of attackers collapsed.

He couldn't see what the old woman had done to knock down so many people, but it didn't affect the ones behind. They rushed past, stepping on their fallen compatriots.

"Jacaré, I trust you to do the right thing," Elma shouted as her white hair whipped around her face, her arms trembling in the gusts. "Don't let the power sway you."

Jacaré had a twisting moment of insecurity that maybe, by himself, he was too weak to accomplish his task. He'd never intended to repair the barrier without his crew, but if he didn't succeed, the deaths of his friends would be in vain.

A blast of power hit Elma's shield directly, the boom forcing Jacaré into motion.

"Defend Elma!" he yelled to Didsbury. The Firesword hesitated for only a moment, then nodded, drew his weapon, and turned bravely to face their attackers.

The air around them crackled with the bitter scent of ozone. The barrier above Donovan's Wall hummed against Jacaré's mind, though the buzz was interspersed with an occasional snap. It was so close to falling. A day, perhaps two, and there would be nothing for Jacaré to fix and his *essência* would simply return to him. He could only guess at what might happen if it collapsed completely. If the drought and the snakes were a result of the power leaking away, the full release of power into Santarem would be devastating.

You could let it fall. The elements have a way of righting themselves over time. No one would blame you for taking back what is rightfully yours. The thoughts were a plague, filling his mind with their infection and spreading to contaminate other parts of his body. His heart, which had always been true to the Keepers and Olinda, thrashed in his chest. His lungs heaved and his muscles trembled—all a physical reminder that he was not as strong as he'd once been.

"How close do we have to be?" Johanna yelled, clambering over the rocks with all the agility of an acrobat.

"You have to touch it."

"The wall?" she asked, breaking into a shambling jog where the path smoothed out.

"Ye—" The ground flew upward, knocking all three of them off their feet. Jacaré heard the clatter as Rafi hit, the gear in his bag flying free, scattering across the landscape. A flash to his left as Johanna rolled over a rock and disappeared.

A disembodied voice rumbled above them with the volume of a vengeful god. "Give me the girl and I'll let all of you go."

"Release my people." Elma sounded like a whisper in comparison. With a pop, she raised her shield again, though Jacaré could see it fraying at the edges. She wouldn't be able to protect them for long.

Jacaré hefted Johanna to her feet by the quiver's strap. Rafi rose unsteadily, clutching a hand to his jaw, where blood streamed between his fingers.

"Run!" Jacaré commanded.

The wall stretched as far as his eye could see in either direction, the barrier a glowing net of blue electricity following its sinuous path.

From below shouts rose. Didsbury's voice pleaded for his friends to stop. Thumps of ground-rocking explosions were muffled by Elma's shield.

They climbed one last behemoth rock, and the wall was there. The square blocks were too even, too perfect, to have been quarried from the surrounding stone. Jacaré guessed that Donovan, whoever he was, had built the wall with some magical ability, just as the barrier stretching high above it had been. The wall had been at least a thousand years old when Jacaré was born, if the tales he'd heard about it were true.

A curve in the landscape offered them shelter, the wall cupping around them, partially obscuring the view from below.

"Quickly, Rafi, Johanna, each of you put one hand against the stones."

Johanna did as she was told, her hand covering a crisscrossing net of lines that she couldn't see. She snatched her hand back as if stung. "I can feel it."

Rafi hesitated, studying the rough surface next to Johanna's hand. "Why do I need to touch the wall? Johanna is the heir."

"Do what I say."

"What are you doing, Jacaré?" Johanna's eyes narrowed in suspicion.

"We don't have time—" His words cut off as a blast of flame landed a few paces short of them. "I'm going to split the bond. In case anything ever happens to you or your line . . ."

"Rafi's will carry it on." Johanna's expression shifted to angry betrayal. "You manipulative *monster*. You've been planning this from the beginning! You've been trying to divide us because you want to be sure the barrier will always be strong."

"You make that sound like it's a bad thing," Jacaré said, ignoring the guilt that sat heavily on his spine. "In my travels I've found no one who is as devoted to the safety of Santarem as Lord Rafael. Take it as a compliment. He is the only other person I can trust with the task of protecting both of our peoples."

Chapter 53

Rafi

Hope gave its death shudder. Heartbreak slipped into its place, a cold and static substitute for the warmth of courage and pulse of anticipation.

Rafi turned to Johanna, her gray eyes reflecting his emotions. He'd let her walk away the night before, but he hadn't let her go. Not really. Once things were settled, once Jacaré had returned to his people, Rafi thought he and Johanna would work out their differences, find some way to be together.

But with thunder rolling in their ears and stone grinding under their feet, the time for figuring had passed. This was Rafi's future whether he liked it or not.

"For the good of Santarem," Johanna said, with a tremulous smile.

"For the good of Santarem," he echoed, placing his palm on the wall. The stone was cold and lifeless, and certainly as heavy as his heart. He mourned silently for the loss of something that could never be.

Jacaré didn't wait for them to change their minds, but clapped a hand on each of their shoulders. His eyes drifted shut, his face lined with concentration.

And Rafi stood, feeling useless, watching as sweat beaded Jacaré's head. Johanna leaned against the wall, relaxing her grip on Didsbury's bow till it rested on the ground beside her.

Yet he felt nothing. Not a tingle, not an ache, but the other two were certainly feeling the effects.

Jacaré began to sway. Johanna's face contorted with pain, and Rafi almost broke away, but a faint blue glow seemed to emanate from Johanna's fingers. As he watched, it spread, tracing the line of her arm, widening as it crossed her chest, blotting out Jacaré's hand where it rested on her shoulder. The light grew more brilliant, more intense, as it tracked across the Keeper's body, moving through his outstretched arm.

Mouth dry with fear, Rafi watched as the glow spread from Jacaré's wrist, into his hand, into his fingers, then . . .

Voices. Hundreds of voices, all layered on top of one another, filled Rafi's head. They sang and laughed and whispered and shouted. All of them saying different things, in a hundred different tones. High and low, ringing like wind chimes, scratching like rocks, grinding into his mind.

The pressure. The weight inside his head. The pain.

It all came with an encompassing sense of heat as power rushed in through one arm and out the other. He wanted to raise his hand, to cover his ears, to blot out the noise, but somewhere deep in the recesses of his mind he knew that he couldn't stop now.

Somehow this had to happen. This was the right choice, and no matter how much it hurt or how easy it would have been to quit, he held on, waiting for the moment when it would all stop.

Chapter 54

Johanna

A cacophony of sound filled Johanna's head, making her sick and dizzy with its noise. It was too much, too many, too overwhelming, and she wondered how her first ancestor—the king or queen who'd first agreed to protect the barrier—had managed to stand the flood of words and voices without going insane.

It hurt, and yet the pain was welcome. It was the burn of a stretched muscle, agony and relief all at the same time.

Her *essência*, the power she'd inherited from her mother, was knotted into this flood, tied by the strands of her father's lineage. A part of her she never even knew existed snapped into place. She smelled the moss growing along the base of the rock, heard the weeds shivering with the breeze, and tasted Rafi's uneasiness as if it were a flavor to be sampled.

Johanna looked beyond the precipice to the trail below. The blue light around Elma winked out and the old woman collapsed. Didsbury raised his sword, only to have a man wearing a Firesword's sash impale himself on the blade. Then her friend disappeared, rats climbing up his legs and torso, and onto his face, then he, too, crumpled. A dozen other Performers, their expressions oddly bereft of emotion, pressed past, closing on her location.

"Jacaré! Rafi!" Neither responded, both caught in the swirling thrall of voices and power. Rafi sank to the ground, hand flush against the wall. Jacaré followed, kneeling to maintain the connection, oblivious to the flood of death that rushed toward them.

Above their heads, perhaps twice the height of a man, hung a lacy confection of blue lines spanning the sky. The barrier stood solid, and Johanna hoped that whatever Jacaré was doing was almost done.

Their attackers were upon them.

With her free hand Johanna reached for the bow. It was longer then she was accustomed to and built for a stronger pull, but with both Jacaré and Rafi incapacitated, she had to stand in their defense.

She waited until the first face appeared at the edge of the alcove, hoping that Jacaré would suddenly release her and turn to fight, but his eyes stayed closed as he rocked from side to side.

A blond head peeked over the precipice. Yara—an acrobat Johanna had known since childhood—heaved herself up onto the level ground, and Johanna had no other option.

She broke the connection, nocked an arrow, and shot.

It hit the acrobat in the shoulder. Yara tumbled backward and was instantly replaced by a Skylighter from another troupe. Johanna aimed a flank shot and watched the man drop.

They came, one after another, teachers, mentors, friends, sometimes climbing over one another in the frantic push to reach the level spot where Johanna waited.

And she shot them all, hoping to stop them without killing, but they wouldn't stay down unless incapacitated. Blood spattered, painting the rock's edge and making it slick, but the attacking Performers didn't notice what they were slogging through.

More than a dozen down and Johanna's arm was exhausted, and her quiver was nearly empty. She'd always been good with a bow, better than her brothers and even her father. Despite the new power purring under her skin, she didn't have the strength to keep it up for much longer.

"Johanna." The voice was grim, unfamiliar, and she spun around, assuming that someone had managed to get behind her. It was Jacaré. He'd collapsed at some point, falling next to Rafi. "What did you do?" He raised a shaking arm, pointing.

Slumped against the wall, blood pouring from an open wound on his chin, Rafi looked dead, but what was worse—a million times worse—was the blaring blue light that surrounded his entire body. The lacy pattern that had once made up the magical barrier encased Rafi from head to foot.

And the lines that had stretched along and above the wall . . . they were gone.

Chapter 55

Dom

Once in the library, Dom walked to the desk, where his father's journal lay. He gripped the worn leather binding and threw the book against the wall. Notes, papers, diagrams, scattered across the room.

With a sweep of one arm he cleared away all the tactical manuals and battle reports. They hit the floor with a dozen uneven thumps.

He wanted to tear down the whole library, throw books through the windows, stomp and scream. His brother, his father, his mother, had forced him into a position where he was responsible for so much. Belem's approach was a problem he couldn't ignore or joke his way out of. And what scared him the most was that he didn't want to. He loved Santiago and the people he'd come to know as he worked alongside them. He loved his estate and its stained-glass windows and white balconies.

This was his home and these were his people, and he didn't know how to save them.

Leaning his weight on his knuckles, he closed his eyes and breathed deeply through his nose.

What options were left? What was in the pile of his father's papers and in his mother's imagination that could save them now?

"Dom?"

It was Brynn, her voice soft, her feet careful as she picked her way through the mess he'd made. In her hands she had a silver tray, which held a bottle of clear liquid, a small glass, and a basket of fresh rolls.

She set the tray down on the table, then uncorked the bottle and handed it directly to Dom, bypassing the glass. "I heard about Raul. And thought, maybe, you could use this."

Dom snorted when he saw the label: *Álcool Fogo*. The name couldn't have been more accurate. The clear liquid tasted like citrus but burned like live coals all the way to the bottom of your stomach. Apparently, only a half glass could make a heavy drinker drunk, and the estate's physician used it to clean wounds and sedate difficult patients. Dom had drunk it only once, two years ago, after his fifteenth birthday party, and vowed never to consume the vile beverage again.

Even though he knew its effects, the clear bottle, cool against his palms from chilling in the cellar, was tempting. He could take a few swigs—enough to avoid the hangover—and it would soften the dread that was taking up all the room in his chest.

"It was very thoughtful of you." He tilted the bottle to her in a half toast. "Perhaps I should pour you a glass, and we can celebrate your impending nuptials?"

As he'd expected, she blushed.

Dom raised the bottle to his lips, trying not to relive the awful night, the mounds of failure, the layers of betrayal. The fumes of the alcohol singed his nostrils.

Singed.

"How many bottles of this do we have?" he asked, taking a long sniff that made his eyes water.

"Enough that no one will notice if you drink the whole thing." She covered the mouth of the bottle with her hand. "I'm not suggesting that you should."

An idea was bubbling in his mind. "This is the most flammable alcohol we own."

"Probably." Her brow wrinkled, waiting for him to complete his thought. "Do you intend to light it on fire? I'm sure that would be entertaining, but—"

"How much do we have?"

"You don't need more than this."

He huffed impatiently. "Give me a number, Brynn."

"I don't know. Maybe six or seven."

The brief burst of hope faded, and Dom lowered the bottle to his side. "Belem didn't bring any when he visited?"

"Of course he did. The man doesn't go anywhere without his own personal brewery. There are new cases in the cellar."

"Cases? We have six or seven *cases*?"

She eyed him with concern, then pulled the bottle from his grasp. "Didn't I just say that?"

Without thinking, Dom kissed her firmly on the lips. She startled, spilling a few drops of the liquid on the floor.

Dom snatched it away. "Don't waste it—"

"You can't do that!" she spluttered, raising fingers to her mouth.

"I'm sorry. It was a reaction." He grabbed the cork off the table and tamped it into the bottle. "No, it wasn't a reaction," he corrected, his fear of *everything* evaporating in the light of this brilliant idea.

"What? Dom, I'm betrothed—"

"Break it off." He set the *Álcool Fogo* on the table hard enough that the glass tipped over, clanking against the tray. "Break it off, Brynn."

She shook her head. "No, you can't say something like that."

"Yes, I can. Because you don't love him. You love me."

Her face flushed to the deepest red he'd ever seen, and she shook her head.

"It's true, Brynn. You always know exactly what I need when I need it." He waved to the bottle and the basket of rolls. "You know where I go when I'm upset. You know the stupid mistakes I make. You know all my stories and my jokes. You know me better than I know myself."

His hands were steady, his fingers sure, as he touched her arms. "What I didn't realize was how much I needed someone who knows me, even when I'm trying to be someone else."

She shook her head. Tears pooled in her green eyes.

"I love that about you." He slid one arm around her back, holding her close. "I love your wild hair, and the way your face turns red every time we're in the same room. I love that you never let me charm you, and that you never believe my lies."

"Dom, please." He felt a shiver run through her body, but she stayed inside the circle of his arms.

"I love you, Brynn," he whispered. The words were an oath, a promise he intended to keep. "I love everything about you, and it wasn't until I was certain that I was going to lose you that I realized how much."

She closed her eyes and the tears leaked onto her cheeks. Dom wanted to believe they were happy tears, that she'd say the same words back to him, but her face was too pale. No pink stained her cheeks.

"It's too late," she said softly.

"Of course it's not," Dom said, wiping the tears away with his thumb. "You're not married yet."

Her face changed, resentment replacing sorrow. "You've only decided you care about me because you like having my attention all to yourself."

He couldn't lie; he probably wouldn't have admitted his feelings if he hadn't been forced to.

"There were always other girls—girls of your class, rich merchants' daughters—that I had to watch you sneak off with to the barn and the garden and the meadows. Because of my station I got the pleasure of packing the snacks you'd take to your little romantic entanglements." The side of her fist pressed against his chest. "You've never looked at me as something other than a servant, never considered the way *I* felt, until I showed interest in someone else."

"I know and I'm sorry. That was thoughtless and immature." With a roiling sense of self-loathing, Dom realized that those words weren't true. He hadn't acted thoughtlessly; he'd known exactly what he was doing—playing a foolish little game with Brynn's affections simply because he could. "Can't we—"

"No." Pushing him away, she stood tall, the tears on her face long forgotten. "Don't say you're sorry. Don't pretend you see me as something more than a servant now. I'll always be lower than you, and I'll never be worthy of your notice."

She was breathing hard and so was he. The words racing out of them and stealing all the air. Dom sought for something to say, some way to fix this. Should he take it all back, pretending that it had been an effort to charm her? No, he'd be someone different, someone more like Rafi.

"I apologize for any pain I may have caused you," he said, stepping away and giving her free access to leave, which seemed like the right thing to do, even if it felt wrong. "Please pass my congratulations on to your aunt and brother."

"See? This is what I'm talking about. You don't know anything about me. My aunt died six months ago, but you didn't notice, even when I took a few days off to handle her funeral arrangements without even my brother to help. You don't notice anything until it's about to be taken from you." With that she turned and fled down the hall.

Dom righted the goblet on the tray, his finger sliding across the smooth lip without any conscious thought.

The glass was fine, so clear it almost disappeared into the tray's gleaming silver surface. It was right there, obvious but almost invisible.

Like so many other things.

Chapter 56

Pira

An Elite Guard was trained to sleep lightly and maintain a sense of time and location. As the cart bounced over a hole in the road, jolting Pira awake, she realized she'd done none of those things. She had no idea how or where she'd passed the night, but from the cramp in her neck and the gray light of the sky overhead she guessed she'd been in the cart for a long while.

Bodies were pressed close to her. She was lodged between a white-haired man and a middle-aged woman. Both were small boned like Performers, and both were blank eyed. She didn't remember them from among the original dozen Sapo had brought with him to Cruzamento, and one look at the collars around their necks confirmed her suspicions. These were new captures, wearing collars she'd made with her own hands.

Made by my hands.

Leão.

With dreadful clarity she remembered. Centering the knife on Leão's chest. Plunging it deep into his body. Sapo healing the ghastly wound and then forcing her shaking hands to lock the collar around Leão's throat.

But Leão didn't wake up. He didn't move, didn't shift. His chest rose and fell, his pulse thundered in the hollow of his throat, but his eyes didn't open.

Essência usually helped Keepers recover quickly, but Leão's was being diverted to Sapo. Pira had heard of cases like Leão's, of times when a Keeper had gone to the very precipice of death, and although the physical body recovered, the soul escaped into Mother Lua's embace. Then it was only a matter of time. The body might last for a few days longer, until it withered away from dehydration or starvation.

It was against Keeper law to heal a body in Leão's state, continually prolonging its life, until even magic couldn't keep the heart beating.

But Sapo followed no such law. Keeping Leão drained of his power and sedated served Sapo's purposes. He'd have one less slave to worry about feeding, training, keeping on task. Leão had become a well, something for Sapo to use and drain and use again.

Leão tried to save me, and one way or another I've killed him.

Unless she could figure out some way to defeat Sapo.

A hysterical laugh bubbled to her lips. She clamped her hand over her mouth and felt tears drip onto her fingers.

No one could defeat Sapo.

She'd made fifty collars in the time she'd worked in the blacksmith's shop. As she looked down the line of carts, seeing heads bob in each one, she guessed Sapo had used half. Beyond that were two long lines of armed and mounted soldiers.

"Where are we going?" she asked the man, but he stared at her listlessly.

The woman answered, raising a quaking hand to her collar. "Performers' Camp." She cleared her throat and started again. "My grandmother was a Performer. I heard one of the drivers say we were going to Performers' Camp to rally the rest of the army. I always wanted to see the valley."

"What army—"

Her words were drowned out by a guttural scream. It arose from the carriage near the middle of the train. Pira moved to her knees to get a better look but was nearly knocked over when a blast of *essência* rent the air. The people in her cart went rigid. Their eyes rolled back in their heads, while their heels drummed against the cart's bed and their fingers scraped against the wood convulsively.

The door to the carriage swung open and Sapo tumbled out, clutching his hair in his hands.

Vibora followed close behind, yelling after him as he ran to the top of one of the rolling hills that hugged the east side of the trail. The wagons following the carriage jarred to a halt, a trumpet blew, and the entire line of soldiers stopped. Every head turned toward Sapo.

"No!" he screamed again, dropping to his knees. Horizontal lightning tore across the sky, dividing their position from that of the Citadel.

"Stop! Don't waste your power!" Vibora fell to the ground behind him, wrapping her arms around his middle, her face pressed into the curve of his neck.

"The barrier is falling! Can't you feel it?"

The barrier is falling. Pira lurched to the far side of the cart, trying to get a better look at whatever had drawn Sapo's interest. *If the barrier is falling, then Jacaré failed. If Jacaré failed, then this line of carts, all those unused collars . . . this is the beginning. Without the barrier for protection, who can stop him from recruiting new members of the Nata from Olinda and using them to destroy Santarem?*

"It doesn't matter! You have enough power now, and when we get to Performers' Camp, you'll have so much more." Vibora tried to smooth down his rumpled hair, but he smacked her hand away.

"This wouldn't have happened if you'd found the heir." He threw an elbow to break her grip around his stomach, and stood up. For once, he towered over her. "This is your fault."

"Sapo, I tried—"

He struck her across the face with the back of his hand, and she tumbled to the ground at his feet.

Vibora pressed her palm to her cheek, her expression wounded. "Sapo," she whimpered.

He held up a hand, silencing her. "Miserable wench. No wonder Jacaré left you to die—" He cut off suddenly and pointed into the distance, somewhere northeast of their position. "What . . . what is that?"

Pira's attention was torn between the scene on the hill and the sustained column of lightning glowing in the distance. The beacon of blue stretched from the sky to touch the mountain's feet. It reminded her of the time when Leão had touched the glass that was connected with Johanna's pendant. A blue glow had emanated from his fingers. This lightning was precisely the same color.

"Oh! Oh!" Sapo beat his fists against his temples in a sudden fit of childlike glee. "It's so *perfect*!"

"What is that?"

He seized Vibora's wrists and hauled her to her feet, hugging her close, oblivious to her rigid posture.

"The barrier didn't fall," Sapo continued. "The lines of power didn't collapse and disperse. They condensed. It has all been absorbed by someone."

"Barrata? Did he succeed?" Vibora asked, arching away from his grip.

"Barrata, the heir. It doesn't particularly matter," he said, kissing her soundly. "Once that person is collared, I'll control it all."

Vibora nodded but didn't speak. Her gaze caught Pira's for a moment, and the woman's composure broke. A flicker of despair passed over her features.

Pira turned away, unwilling to share in her captor's desperation.

Chapter 57

Dom

The window opened easily under Dom's palm. He wasn't surprised; it wasn't the first time he'd climbed from the roof into this particular room, just the first time that the room was occupied by this particular lady.

Raindrops dripped onto the desk that hugged the wall under the window, splattering the letters stacked neatly in the center.

He didn't bother to rifle through them. All Maribelle's correspondences were undoubtedly in code, and he didn't have time to decipher anything now. The meeting with his mother and the soldiers had run late, and the rest of the house had gone to dinner without them. Maribelle and her attendants would return in less than ten minutes, and he didn't know what he was looking for exactly.

Something incriminating. Something that would put her firmly on his list of enemies. Maribelle had ulterior motives. Even if she was leading a rebellion against her father—and Dom was sure there was more to that story than she was letting on—it didn't mean her loyalties lay with Santiago.

If he failed on all those counts, maybe he could find a code book, a list of names, or a map that would help him infiltrate her spy ring.

All the guest rooms in the north wing had the same layout: a small sitting room with two adjoining bedrooms, one for nobility and one for attendants. Dom crossed the plush carpet between the desk and the door on quiet feet, pausing to listen for voices on the other side.

Silence. Perfect.

He started under the bed—it seemed like a good place to hide things—and he was right. A half dozen daggers were driven into the bed frame within easy reach of Maribelle's pillow. She could slip her arm between the mattress and the headboard, snag one, and take out an intruder without worrying about stabbing herself in her sleep.

It was a good idea, he admitted grudgingly.

The chest of drawers held only silken underthings, which he felt guilty pawing through. It was one thing to imagine her wearing them, and something entirely different to touch them without her consent.

Her box of jewelry held an enormous amount of baubles, but no secrets. And the only thing under the rug was dust.

Frustrated, but not surprised, Dom moved to the closet. The smell was noteworthy. Instead of the powerful fragrance of lavender that scented the rest of the room, the confined space had a musty, almost animal aroma. It reminded him of the rabbit he and Rafi had kept as children.

Would Maribelle hide a rabbit in her closet?

The space was overrun with dresses and skirts, but there was a careful sense of order. Blues next to purples, pinks and reds side by side. All hung from a series of hooks on the wall, with matching slippers below. There was an obscene number of boots and shoes, sometimes three or four pairs in the same exact color and style, which didn't seem at all logical. Maribelle wasn't the kind of person to wear the same dress twice, let alone enough times to warrant an extra pair of matching shoes.

A large trunk, perhaps waist-high and as wide as Dom's arms outstretched, was pressed against the rear wall of the closet. Leather bands, held in place with nailheads, wrapped around the frame, and a large iron lock held it shut.

The back of the closet was dark. He wouldn't be able to pry open the lock without a candle or at least a bit more light. So he opened the door wide, letting the dim moonlight and fire illuminate the space. It also brought the sound of whispering voices. Someone was in the sitting room.

Low and hurried, the tone was significantly less giddy than Dom was used to hearing from Maribelle's attendants. He couldn't catch every word that was being said through the wall, but gathered that it had something to do with the man who'd been selected as the new captain.

A third voice added to the mix. Maribelle was back from wherever she'd gone. Dom cursed silently and closed the closet door partway. The lock on the room's outer door clicked open, and Maribelle came in, still carrying on a conversation with the women in the sitting room.

"As far as I can tell, the water in the well is fine," Maribelle said, undressing as she moved. "There are too many access points, and the soldiers are stretched too thin to guard all the wells in the township."

"Could it be something else? Something other than the wells?" one woman asked. "The message was unclear, and I think it's a key word instead of a code."

"Why are we doing this, anyway?" The voice was softer than the previous one but had a similar cadence. "We should go home. We're wasting time here while our friends die in ill-planned attacks against your father's troops. If Sapo's away from Maringa, then we're missing an opportunity to take over while your father's greatest weapon is elsewhere."

Dom pressed himself into the first row of dresses, watching through the narrow gap. Maribelle had shared a few tidbits about the strange people who worked for her father, but it wasn't enough. She was, obviously, keeping him in the dark about some things.

"You're too attached to Lord Dom," the first voice said. At least, Dom thought it was the first voice; Maribelle's attendants all sounded alike to him. "You aren't looking at this objectively anymore. You've forgotten our goal."

"Don't you dare," Maribelle said as she stepped out of her skirt. She wadded up the material and tossed it toward the closet. "This has been my plan, my goal, since the very beginning. I've fought for this. I've *suffered* for this."

Standing in nothing but a blouse that clung to her damply, Maribelle shouldn't have been intimidating, but her tone shut the other women's mouths.

"I know what I'm doing," she continued. "We need the united powers of Impreza and Santiago to help us defeat my father's troops. We can't expect Duke Fernando's and the DeSilvas' help if they're waging a war against Belem."

"What about Sapo?"

"What about him?" Maribelle snapped. "He's got goals of his own, and all the recent reports suggest he's hunting this lost princess.

While he's busy, we will destroy Belem, unite with Impreza and Santiago, and take Maringa. Sapo will never stand a chance against all four states. And he'll never, ever help my father hurt us again."

Her chest was rising and falling rapidly, her hands clenched at her sides. Maribelle played the beautiful coquette perfectly, but she was every bit as deadly and devious as her father. Dom wanted to be suspicious of her. He'd come to her room hoping to find proof of her duplicity, and instead he'd caught her in an unguarded moment, speaking without restraint to her closest confidants, and showing all the colors of an ally.

The varying facets of her personality were both confusing and interesting. What had turned a pampered duke's daughter into a scheming rebel? It was one thing to harbor hatred toward an abusive parent, and something entirely different to work toward that parent's destruction. What were her motivations? Power, greed, or maybe vengeance? He didn't know, but he was determined to find out. Until he understood her, he wasn't positive he should trust her.

"Was there anything else?" Maribelle asked as she shrugged out of her blouse, leaving her in nothing but a thin, thigh-length camisole.

Dom looked away and then looked back, afraid of missing something important in her body language.

"The stable hand is out again tonight. Cintia is on him."

Maribelle nodded. "And Brynn?"

"In her room with Michael."

"Who has been following the boy?" Maribelle asked, rubbing her temple.

There was silence except for the shifting of material.

"Michael loves Dom," piped up one of the attendants.

"And he's eight."

Michael? Dom held his breath.

"Age means nothing. Children are perfect spies. They're often overlooked and forgotten. He may not even know he's providing information to the other side." Maribelle took a deep breath. "Eva, please follow him tomorrow."

"If you insist."

"I do." Maribelle shooed them out of the room. "Get some rest. We won't have any downtime till this is all over." The door clicked shut after them, and she let out a deep sigh.

Cintia and Eva . . . wait.

Dom mentally replayed the conversation. Two ladies were with Maribelle, and another was out watching the stable hand.

Three attendants? But Maribelle had brought only two with her. Both attractive, one was a half head taller than Maribelle, and the other was closer to Maribelle's size but with lighter hair and fairer skin. Who was the third?

Footsteps came closer, and Dom had to make a decision to try to hide or be noticed or . . .

The closet door swung open completely and Dom lunged at Maribelle, clamping a hand over her mouth and stifling her gasp of surprise. He looped an arm across her body, trapping her arms at her sides, and pinned her face-first against the door's frame. She struggled, bringing her heel up and nearly catching him in the groin. He shifted, and the blow landed on his thigh instead.

"Stop," he whispered. "I'm not here to hurt you."

He felt her teeth against his palm, but she couldn't get much skin. "If you quit trying to bite me and promise not to yell, I'll take away my hand." She gave a sharp nod in acquiescence.

As soon as his hand moved, she started talking. "I don't know why I assumed you had a hint of that DeSilva honor, but no one who lurks in my closet, watching me undress, has any integrity at all."

"Don't pretend you're upset about that."

"Of course I am," she said, writhing against his grip.

"No. You're more upset that I listened to your conversation and stumbled onto some of your secrets."

She froze.

"How many of my servants are working for you?"

No answer.

"Was everything you said to your ladies true? What's this about the wells?"

"Release me," she said, stomping on his foot. "I think you enjoy interrogating me far too much. I still have bruises from the last time."

He had to give her credit: She knew exactly what to say to make him feel like a horrible person, and he released her. "Maribelle, I am sorry—" His words cut off when he caught a sharp elbow to the gut and grunted.

"I thought I made it clear," she said, hurrying to the bedroom door and locking them in. "I'm on your side. I said as much."

"*But*," he said, giving up on his apology. "You gave Belem an exact report of my weapons stash, and my weaponsmaster died an hour after you last saw him alive. Why would I believe you're telling me the truth about anything?"

"What has telling the truth brought me? You attacking me in a barn and now in my bedroom?" She put her hands on her hips, and the already short camisole pulled up even higher, revealing more of her legs.

Dom couldn't help but notice.

"Do I meet your approval?"

"I've never complained about the way you look." That was putting it lightly. Her dresses never left much to his imagination, but he couldn't have imagined her like this.

Which is why Brynn is marrying the butcher's son, you heartless bastard. You can't keep your thoughts focused on one girl even when you're trying.

He gave himself a mental slap. "What's your endgame? You want to bring down your father, but then what?"

She shook her head, eyeing him in stony silence.

"You've got to give me a reason to trust you."

"You heard what I just said. I was protecting your water supply." She pointed to the wet skirt piled near his feet. "Why would I do that—in a downpour, I might add—if I wasn't trying to save your state?"

He didn't have an answer to that. "You think someone was trying to poison the wells?"

"That might be the goal, but if so, no one has taken action yet."

If it wouldn't have brought her attendants running, he would have screamed in frustration. Instead he said, "I'll have everyone lay out extra barrels to catch rainwater. It will provide a small backup."

"It's always good to think ahead."

A smile forced its way onto his mouth. "I'll never outdistance you."

"You'll never even catch up."

They stood for a moment, battling with their gazes, her expression giving nothing away. Not embarrassment from standing there in her underclothes, not anger from his intrusion, not annoyance at his constant mistrust.

Light, she was tough, and he respected her for it.

He gave in first, offering a mocking bow. "Good night, Maribelle." He walked past her, heading for the door, but she reached out and touched his arm.

"Birds."

"What?" He looked down at her hand, against his forearm.

"I want you to trust me, Dominic. So I'm telling you that I keep birds in my closet." Her fingers glided down his sleeve till they rested on the back of his hand. "You forbade me from using the pigeons on the roof, so I bought two ravens. They aren't as reliable over long distances, but they ferry notes to a contact in town, and he sends the messages on."

"Who in the township?"

She tilted her head to one side. "I told you that your brother was in Camaçari. I helped you narrow down the list of possible spies in your household. You don't expect me to give up all my secrets, do you?"

Dom's eyes traced down her body, making his perusal obvious. "I don't think you have that much left to hide."

Leaning forward, she pressed a lingering kiss against his cheek. "Haven't you learned anything yet?" Her whisper made the hairs on his neck rise. "I've always got something to hide."

Chapter 58

Dom

Dom left Maribelle's room via the window and clambered onto the slick tile roof. The rain had turned from a sprinkle to a deluge, and he lost his footing more times than he dared to count. Once, a tile crumbled under his boot, sending him careening into a stone-sided chimney. He clung to it for a moment, catching his breath and cursing Maribelle under it.

The rocks that ringed the chimney were dry. Raindrops fell but evaporated quickly.

It gave him an idea—a crazy, dangerous idea.

Instead of heading back to his room, Dom climbed to a lower part of the roof and dropped to the ground, startling the guard standing near the kitchen's outer door.

"Get four men and meet me at the washhouse," Dom said as the young soldier slid his sword back into its scabbard.

"The washhouse, sir? But why?"

"If I wanted you to know, I'd tell you," Dom said, a hint of DeSilva temper lacing his tone.

The washhouse was a small, separate building tucked behind the main house. It had a large cement floor, an enormous fireplace, two huge brick basins for wash and rinse water, and underground access to the cellars.

It was perfect for Dom's plan.

Whoever had poured salt water into the cannon powder had known exactly what they were doing. No one would have noticed that the powder was wet if the influx of supplies hadn't overrun the cellar. If the servants hadn't been forced to stack boxes and crates of food in the tunnels where the powder had been stored, the soldiers would have carried up a few barrels the night before the battle and been shocked when it wouldn't ignite.

It would have been a disaster.

Or a bigger disaster, Dom thought as he studied the first cask's stopper. Marks marred the cork. It hadn't been some kind of fluke or accident. Each cask had been opened, soaked, and sealed.

Giving information to the enemy was treason, but secrets shared between servants and then whispered to an untrustworthy friend or bedfellow were an unfortunate risk of running a large house. Sabotage, however, was an entirely different level of betrayal. And this particular act was something that would have resulted in the death of people that the spy knew.

The cannon powder came out of the caskets in wet clumps, sticking to Dom's fingers and coating his hand with a sulfurous muck. He was certain the stench would stay with him for the rest of his life, but if they didn't defeat Belem, there was a very good chance that the DeSilva line would be extinct by the week's end. The duke could—and likely would—have Dom and his mother hanged from the estate's gates, and Rafi, too, if he was ever found.

Careful not to flick it into the fire, Dom smoothed the powder in a thin layer on top of bedsheets he'd torn from the drying line. He prayed the exposure to the air and heat might dry the powder enough to make it usable.

It took hours, even with the fire built up high, but it was working. At least some of the powder would be ready as early as the next morning. Hopefully, by then the barrels would have also dried out enough to reuse.

Dom rolled into one of the washbasins full of soaking clothes, and let the citrus-scented water close over his head. He didn't know if it was particularly clean, and he didn't care. It washed some of the stinging grit away. Then he found himself a set of unused sheets, curled up in a relatively powder-free corner, and went to sleep.

Dom couldn't say what exactly it was that woke him. He was dozing in a giant powder keg, so he certainly wasn't sleeping deeply. But like so many times over the last few weeks, he had a sense that something was amiss.

He sat up slowly, eyeing the rows of sheets that hung from the drying lines like hammocks, weighted with the nearly dry powder. The only light in the too-warm room came from the fire in the hearth, which had burned down significantly while he slept. He wished he'd taken the risk of having a lantern nearby.

The rain fell steadily on the tile roof outside. One of the soldiers, standing protected under the eaves, called to his counterpart on the opposite corner. The next voice responded and passed the call to the next soldier, till all four had answered. Whatever had startled Dom wasn't outside the building. Fingers of dread tickled up his spine.

Could the sound have come from inside?

The hanging pouches of powder swayed lightly, as if stirred by the wind or a gentle touch. Dom scanned the windows, but all were shut tight, keeping out the rainwater that would have destroyed his efforts.

Had the sheets been swinging on their own earlier or . . .

Sand through a sieve, salt spilling from a jar, something hissed across the floor with the tumbling of a thousand grains. He knew that sound.

Bolting to the trapdoor, Dom found it open wide, a trail of cannon powder trickling down the stairs in an unbroken line.

Oh Light.

He scuffed out the line, breaking it up, but he'd seen the powder in action and knew that one spark would light every speck. One firefly-size ember would land, and the entire thing would go, racing up the stairs and turning the washhouse and everything around it into a ball of flame.

Dom couldn't let that happen. Afraid to yell and startle the culprit into lighting the powder, he sprinted after the sound of the footsteps and the hiss of powder as it trickled out of a sheet.

Whoever it was knew the way through the tunnel system and into the cellars, moving toward the stairs that would lead up to the kitchen. Before he turned the corner, Dom heard a sharp *shtick* of flint against steel.

The smell of the powder hung in the air. Could it burn, too?

"No!" Dom screamed as he dove around the corner and into the body holding a knife and flint.

His shoulder sank into the intruder's stomach, and they tumbled to the floor. A slashing pain burned across Dom's chest—a knife wound, he was sure—but he ignored it and used his weight to keep the weapon pinned between their bodies. A glancing blow crossed Dom's head, but he managed to raise an elbow and block the second attempt.

The blade grazed Dom's ribs again, but he used his toes to propel himself up the intruder's body and slam the heel of his hand into a jutting jaw.

A bobbing light appeared over Dom's head, then a booted foot materialized out of the darkness and kicked the traitor in the ear.

Once, twice, and the body went still.

Dom rolled to his side, pressing his hand against the gashes on his chest, and looked into the face of his savior.

"Maribelle."

She dropped to the ground at his side, lowering the lantern to cast its light on his wounded chest.

"Don't set it down," he said, raising his hand to stop her. "We're surrounded by cannon powder."

A puddle of powder spilled out of the torn sheet and coated the ground around the intruder's body.

"Is it *dry*?" Maribelle asked, holding the glass-entrapped flame high over her head.

"It is now." Dom had hoped to be able to keep the secret a little longer, and announce it with more fanfare. It had been a brilliant, dangerous idea, and he was proud. Instead of celebrating, he was lying on the cellar floor bleeding with . . . "Who is it?"

Maribelle swung the light over the traitor's face. "It's the butcher."

"You mean his son, Renato?"

She shook her head. "Not unless all his hair fell out and he doubled in girth overnight."

Something in Dom's chest loosened, relief rattling. The butcher had come with his son a few days earlier to deliver a large shipment of salted meat. Dom wagered that if he checked, he'd find the meat stored in the same passage where the powder had been. They were trusted members of the community, and with Brynn's engagement, Renato had been visiting the estate more often.

Poor Brynn. Plied with love for information. Dom could imagine her sharing gossip with the man she thought would be her husband, only to have it passed to Belem.

This would hurt her, and no matter what had happened between them, he never wanted that. But he felt a guilty thrill that this also meant she could go back to being *his* Brynn.

Maribelle set the lantern on the stairs, then hastily tore strips from the sheet and bound the butcher's hands together. "How bad are your wounds? Honestly?"

"It's just a scratch," he said, rolling to his feet. From one of his pockets he pulled a mostly clean square of linen and pressed against the worst spot.

"You're sure?" she asked, peeling his hand away from his sternum.

"A few stitches, maybe, but I won't die from it."

Her fingers floated over the gash that crossed his heart. "You're lucky."

"It was a little knife."

The smile that had curved her lips failed. "Sometimes the little wounds hurt the worst," she said, and turned away from the kitchen stairs. "There's something else you need to see."

Dom wasn't surprised that Maribelle knew her way around the cellar, its passages and storerooms. There weren't many access points—the kitchen pantry, the washhouse, the barracks' armory, and the barn—but it was certainly possible that she and her attendants had been using them to get around unseen.

"We have very little time before Belem arrives," Maribelle said as she led the way. "His spies have ramped up their efforts to destroy us from the inside. I, in turn, have redoubled my efforts to find the traitor by splitting my attendants—"

"All three of them?"

She ignored him and pressed on. "I've worked on breaking the cipher his spies are using. I thought Belem was going to try to poison the wells, but the message we intercepted today said to 'destroy all supplies.' I thought maybe it meant they were trying to destroy your food stores, and I stationed a *couple* of people near the pantry and in the tunnel to watch for intruders."

Maribelle stopped, shifting her weight nervously, before pointing to the gratelike door that led to the winery. Only a few people had keys—Dom had never been trusted with one—but the heavy lock on the door hung open.

A breath stuck in Dom's lungs, burning like he'd inhaled something toxic.

"Careful," Maribelle cautioned. "The floor's wet."

Of course it is.

The smell in the air wasn't just noxious, it was slightly citrusy, but mostly it stank of potent alcohol.

Two lanterns hung from hooks on the wall, illuminating three people. One was Maribelle's attendant; the second had her hood up, pulled forward to disguise her face, but Dom knew this was Maribelle's secret weapon—another attendant, likely a twin to the first.

But it was the third person who drew Dom's attention. She wore a tight-fitting tunic and black pants that hugged her body in a way she'd once said was inappropriate. A bruise marred her fair skin, and blood crusted one corner of her mouth. Her hair, bright and untamable, was hidden beneath a black scarf.

She struggled against her captors' grip, and broke free to run straight into Dom's arms.

"Help me," Brynn said, resting her cheek against his clavicle, ignoring the blood on his skin.

He thought she'd feel warm and soft in his arms, but her face was cold and she smelled like the worst sort of pub.

The crates to his right were open; ten empty bottles and corks littered the floor.

"What did you do?" he whispered into her hair.

"It's not what you think," she responded as softly.

Closing his eyes, he ignored the sharp pain in his chest that had nothing to do with the knife wounds. "Then tell me what I should think."

"I caught them down here—"

"Please don't lie, Brynn. Not now." Grabbing her elbows, he pushed her back a step. "You brought me the *Álcool Fogo*. We discussed how flammable it was. *You* were the only person who could have guessed that I had plans to use it."

Tears welled in her eyes. "You don't understand—"

"That you've turned traitor to Santiago. To my family. To *me*?" The last word was a shout. Dom took a shaky breath and moderated his tone. "I understand that completely."

"Dom . . ."

He turned his back to her and faced Maribelle. "Can you watch over her while I get the guards?"

Maribelle opened her mouth, and Dom thought she was going to argue, but instead she said, "Yes, of course. And find someone to stitch up your wounds as well."

Halfway to the stairs Dom stopped and rested his hands on his knees.

He was tired. He was injured. He was facing a battle that, even with all his plans in play, he might very well lose. At least, that's what Dom told himself as he tried to catch his breath.

A sinkhole expanded inside his chest, sucking at his heart and lungs, crushing them in a black void.

This is not panic, or fear, or heartbreak, Dom coached himself. *This is not heartbreak.*

Chapter 59

Jacaré

The soft sound of weeping replaced the thunderous pressure of a hundred voices. The booming pain inside Jacaré's head disappeared, but it left behind a raw, gaping hole of sorrow. For a few moments, while he channeled the power of the wall through Johanna and Rafi, Jacaré had felt the presence of his friends and family long dead.

Their souls weren't trapped inside the barrier, but their *essência* had left an echo of the people he'd known and loved and watched sacrifice themselves. He'd relived a dozen lifetimes in that brief moment, feeling his mother's lips feather across his cheek and his best friend's hand on his shoulder. He'd heard snatches of battle songs and the booming laughter of a former crewmate.

He opened his eyes and saw Johanna supporting Rafi's head. She brushed his curly locks away from his brow, tears dripping onto the boy's face. "I'm sorry. I'm sorry for all of this. I'm sorry for last night. . . ."

Her apology stretched on as Jacaré watched with a sick sort of realization. "Johanna," he said, rising slowly. His legs were shaky from the strain on his *essência* and from a sense of grief that couldn't be ignored. "What did you do?"

Her eyes went as flinty as the stone wall that stood behind her. "What did *you* do?" She gestured to Rafi's prone form. "He's *glowing*."

Jacaré tilted his head back, searching the sky for any hint of the perfect tapestry of light that had hung for centuries above Donovan's Wall. It was gone.

I failed.

His hands gripped the sides of his head, fingers spread over his shorn scalp. The leather *cadarço* he wore around his head pressed against his palms. He tore it free and threw it against the wall. He didn't deserve to wear it.

I've failed them all.

His second attempt at saving the barrier had been as futile as his first. He'd tried to donate his *essência* to the wall then, and had been left with a fraction of the power he'd had. And now, even though he'd battled the temptation to take it all back, he'd failed to repair it. All that power, all the swirling light that had been sucked out of his friends, was useless now, stored in a lifeless teenage boy.

"Fix this," Johanna said, her voice cutting through the miasma of Jacaré's emotions. "Whatever you did, undo it."

"I can't!" Jacaré shouted. "You broke the connection with the wall. I pulled all the power through you and pushed it through him. It was supposed to be an unbroken circle, binding all three of us to the wall, but when you broke the connection, everything poured into him. There's nothing I can do to change it now."

A pain, fresh and vicious, shot through Jacaré's calf. He looked down, wondering if he'd managed to fall onto one of his own weapons—and at this low point he could almost believe it—but he found a rat the size of a *capivara* tearing through the leather of his boot.

The animal raised its head, brandishing two yellow teeth marked with his blood. "What in the . . ." He grabbed the animal by the back of the neck and cocked his arm to throw it off the cliff, when something worse peeked over the edge.

Johanna gasped at the sight. Its face resembled a candle half-melted. An eye socket dripped down onto a cheek, puddling into the corner of a ruined mouth.

"Don't," it gurgled. And as a backup to the threat in the half-masticated word, it encased Jacaré's arm in ice.

The rat fell limply from Jacaré's frozen fingers and scurried across the rocky ground to its master. Jacaré forced his arm to straighten, and the ice shattered. He pulled on his weak *essência* and reached for his weapon simultaneously, but the steel was too cold to draw. Instead he created a small field of electricity, a thin mesh that flickered weakly around his friends.

A high laugh dribbled from the man's twisted lips. "Even now," their attacker said as he pulled himself onto the shelf of land. "Even without any extra power. I'm stronger than you."

Jacaré couldn't divert his *essência* to take the chill from his sword without weakening the already-dwindling strength of his shield.

"Oh, come now. Don't you recognize me?" The man ran a hand over the ragged clumps of brown hair on his head. "I looked a bit different before your little friend hit me with a fireball. Sadly for everyone, it wasn't a direct hit. And he's lying somewhere under a pile of prison rubble."

"Leão?" Johanna asked, her voice soft.

"Was that his name?" their attacker asked, then giggled. "I didn't stop to shake hands and introduce myself. I can only imagine how that would have gone: 'Hello, you melted my *face*. Let me do you the favor of crushing you with tons of stone.'"

The ice makes him a Water affinity. Member of the Nata. That voice.

There was something there, prickling the back of Jacaré's mind, but he couldn't find the name.

The rat skittered up its master's body and perched on his shoulder.

"This is embarrassing," he said, with a pout that stretched his skin into a swirl of pink, red, and white—puckers of skin and oozing blisters. "I've been holding a grudge for all these years, and you can't even remember the nickname you gave me."

"If it's me you want," Johanna said, edging out from underneath Rafi's head, laying it down as gently as possible, "then fine. I'm all yours."

Jacaré held up a hand, stopping her from brushing against his shield, which was rapidly losing power.

"Yes, yes. I'll take you, and the boy, too, since he'll be the one Sapo wants now." The stranger rubbed his palms together in expectation. "But what I want, right this moment, is for Jacaré to *say my name*."

A dozen rats, smaller than the first, ran up the slope and hurtled into Jacaré's shield. A few died instantly, their singed fur filling the air with an awful stench. Small as they were, they took a toll. The ones that didn't die shook off the shock and tried again.

No collars or bracelets were visible on the rodents; they were controlled by the other Keeper's mind.

Animal control. Animal control. Animal control.

"Barrata?" Jacaré asked, his voice low and disgusted.

"Yes!" Barrata squealed, clapping his hands together excitedly. "Vibora's little cockroach. Do you remember me now?"

"Always hiding in darkness, watching her from the shadows, and fleeing as soon as you were exposed. I could never understand why she could stomach your company."

"And yet I've spent the last three hundred years with her and Sapo—"

"A Mage stabbed her in the stomach. I watched her bleed out." *Gasping and crying, and me too far away to do anything about it.* Jacaré had gone back for her body later, sneaking across enemy lines, only to be caught by his own crew and dragged back to face Tex's rage.

Barrata clicked his tongue, but it sounded like someone slurping soup. "Sapo's an excellent healer. He'll be able to fix this," he said, running a hand over his face. "He can bring someone back from the gates of death."

Jacaré reached for the dagger tucked in the top of his boot. The chill of the steel drew him out of his most painful memories.

"Funny, how easily your affections can be swayed by someone when they save you. Especially when you're abandoned by the one person you trusted more than any other." Barrata gave a gleeful laugh. "Such a pretty, pretty turn. I'm so glad I've lived long enough to witness the fall of the untouchable Jacaré. After all those years of your teasing and torture, I have the chance to return the favor."

From the corner of his eye Jacaré spotted movement. Rafi, lying prone at the foot of the wall, shifted slightly. Jacaré could see the strain on Johanna's face, knowing she wanted to rush to Rafi's side, but instead she positioned herself in front of Barrata.

Jacaré felt a sudden surge of pride at her courage. No matter the odds, she'd always stand in danger's path if it meant protecting someone she loved.

Shutting his mind to Barrata's taunts, Jacaré figured the trajectory the dagger would have to follow and what it might encounter. His shield dissolved and the knife flew at its target, but a stinging blast of frozen hail blinded both him and Johanna. They fell backward, raising their hands to protect their faces. Jacaré reached for Johanna's bow, knowing the weapon would do nothing against a magical attack.

But the attack never came, and after a moment the hail stopped.

"Rafi?" Johanna's voice trembled.

Jacaré wiped blood from his eyes—the hail had opened a gash at his hairline. When his vision cleared, he realized Rafi was sitting up, though he seemed to be leaning heavily against Johanna.

"What did I do?" he asked, looking at his hand. "He was there, and then . . ."

Jacaré picked himself up and walked toward the cliff's edge, but stopped a few feet short. Where Barrata had stood, a pile of white ash stirred in the wind. A still-twitching rat's tail writhed alongside it.

"You vaporized him," a breathless voice said from behind them.

Turning slowly, Jacaré raised his eyes to the hill beyond the wall. Four figures, two dressed in long robes and two in too-familiar uniforms, stood on the rocky hillside beyond Donovan's Wall.

Amelia—head of the Mage Council and Leão's grandmother—wiped beads of sweat off her forehead with an irritated flick. She was not the kind of woman to sweat. Ever. But a wet patch stained the front of her long robe. Beside her, two of Jacaré's own soldiers panted under the heavy packs they carried. They must have run a great distance to be so winded.

"You," Amelia said, pointing to Rafi, "will now return the power to where it belongs."

Rafi stood slowly and Johanna tucked herself under his arm, becoming his crutch. "Actually," he said, something new and hard lining his mouth, "I think I'll keep it for a while."

Chapter 60

Rafi

Rafi had been forced to accept that the Keepers, an entire clan of magic-wielding *people,* not demigods, lived somewhere over the mountains. But seeing them beyond Donovan's Wall—in rough, travel-stained clothes, breathing hard—seemed like an abomination.

What was more distressing was the blue halos that surrounded them. Bright as moonlight around the old woman, fainter around a man who looked to be near Rafi's mother's age, and a glimmer around the two men who wore matching uniforms and carried large canvas packs.

The same shade surrounded Jacaré, but it was muted, like light through stained glass. Johanna had it too, but it flickered and faded, one moment there and the next gone.

He leaned against her for a moment while the buzzing in his head subsided. Without an explanation, without a word from anyone, Rafi understood exactly what had happened. He could see it out of the corner of his eye; the glow that surrounded everyone else was nothing compared with the light pouring off his own skin.

I'm one of them now, he thought, raising his hand and watching the blue undulate over his skin. *I have magic.*

The woman was talking, saying something about returning the power to where it belonged.

Rafi wasn't really listening, trying to decide if he should be disgusted that he'd snuffed out a life so easily or horrified that he wasn't at all upset. Killing Barrata had been effortless, mindless, a reaction. This new, terrible power gave Rafi the ability to control the outcome of . . . *everything.*

He could walk to Belem's estate—*Wait, if I'm a Keeper now, can I fly?*—and force the fat duke to call off his troops and swear fealty to the DeSilvas. Then, on to Maringa to do the same with Inimigo.

The power rushed into Rafi's fingertips as he imagined pulling Inimigo's castle down and crushing the duke into a mangled pulp, pulverizing his bones, and using the remnants to paint the walls of the city with a warning against anyone who wanted to rise up in rebellion.

From a distance he heard a muffled cry of pain, and he shook off the haze in his mind. Johanna was on the ground at his feet, her eyes startled; Jacaré had his weapon at the ready, his eyebrows set in a tight line. The other Keepers had come down from the hillside and were scurrying over the wall.

"What happened?" Rafi asked, reaching for Johanna, but she scuttled away, a look of fear on her face.

"You shocked me when I tried to touch you."

"I—I—what?" He looked from Johanna to the glint of Jacaré's blade.

"You were pulling on the *essência*," the old woman said as she leaped down from the top of the wall, moving with more grace than he anticipated. "You were preparing to use it."

"I wasn't," he said hastily. He had been thinking about it, surely, but he wasn't actually intending to kill the other dukes in a dozen different ways. Destroying them without considering the consequences—the political upheaval, finding replacements—that would be . . . wrong.

But as he looked down at his glowing arm, he realized it might make things so much easier.

"You can't possibly control that much *essência*." The man in the robe stood one step behind the woman, as if in deference, but condescension was clear on his face. "You're not even one of us."

Rafi felt the power flare in response to the insult.

"Cristoval. Enough." The woman lifted her hand, stopping the man from taking another step. "This young fellow is going to return the power to where it belongs. I'll increase the strength of the barrier's tie to this young woman. Everything will return to normal, as it's been for the past three hundred years, with one change."

She waved, and the two soldiers accompanying her stepped close to Jacaré, each taking one of his arms. They forced him to his knees, though the Keeper didn't seem to need much encouragement. "Since you've been ineffective and unable to follow simple orders, you will be a permanent fixture on this side of the wall. You will serve as a bodyguard to this heir, and her heir, and every heir after, until Mother Lua sees fit to break this curse and you *die*."

Rafi would never have considered Jacaré a friend, but he respected the Keeper's single-mindedness and determination to achieve his goal, damn the consequences. It was something Rafi recognized in himself.

"You, like your predecessor, will remain forever an exile. Forbidden to return to Olinda on pain of death," she continued, her blue eyes flashing, but she said the words with a cool, simple certainty. "Cristoval," she said, turning to her robed companion. "As we are away from the Council, will you support this motion?"

The arrogant set of the man's mouth turned to a sneer. "Without question, Amelia."

Jacaré made no sound, his posture remained the same, kneeling and stoic, but the blood drained out of his face.

"Hold my hand, boy." Amelia offered her hand, palm up, to Rafi. "Perhaps between the two of us we can fix this mess once and for all."

CHAPTER 61

JOHANNA

"Don't touch her, Rafi," Johanna said, rushing to her feet. "Jacaré, how many people died when they gave their power to the wall?"

The Keeper's mouth opened and shut.

"Was it all of them? Everyone but you?" she asked, stepping closer to Rafi, wishing she could somehow protect him from all of this. "If he puts the *essência* back into the barrier now, he's going to die. Isn't he?"

No one answered. The younger of the two soldiers shifted, eyes flicking to his elders as they waited for a response, but he didn't release his grip on Jacaré's arm.

"I already said I wasn't going to return the power." Rafi gave a cool smile, and his fingers twitched at his side.

"Yes, you will," Cristoval said. He was about Rafi's height, but his narrow shoulders and long neck made him seem taller. "You will return it because, though I love my people, when others learn what this Sapo person attempted, they may want to follow his—"

"I, too, love my people and will not allow a madman, a rogue Keeper bent on control and domination, to run free across Santarem. I will not give up the only opportunity I have to bring him down," Rafi countered.

Johanna saw his Adam's apple rise and fall as he struggled to gain control of his anger. After a moment the glow around Rafi winked out, and he continued speaking. "I will keep this power until the threats are eliminated and my people are safe. When it's done, and only then, will I rebuild the barrier as you ask."

Cristoval's face was gray enough to match Jacaré's, but he wasn't ready to let the argument drop. "You don't know how to appropriately wield *essência*. How can it possibly do you any good?"

In response the blue light flared around Rafi again, glowing so brightly that Johanna had to turn away and Cristoval raised his arm to protect his eyes.

There was something frightening in the tense lines of Rafi's back and the sweat curling the hair at his neck. "You can help me, or I'll figure it out on my own."

"And watch you burn the world?" Cristoval bent his knees, as if preparing to attack. "I don't—"

"Peace. All of you." The woman made a calming motion with her hands. "A compromise, perhaps? Keepers should not venture into your land. During the Mage Wars my people split down the middle. I fear that many, especially the younger generation, would be tempted to join this other faction."

"They would be the Nata reborn," Jacaré said in a low voice.

Amelia made a soft noise of disgust and agreement. "You have until the full moon rises to destroy Sapo and his minions, and solidify this kingdom. If you can't defeat him in that time, you will face the united power of all the Keepers, and *we* will eliminate Sapo, his followers, and the rest of the people on this side of the wall. Then there will be no temptation for the Keepers to face. Ever again." She nodded, and her soldiers came to her side, releasing Jacaré. "I will leave Jacaré with a command to teach this young man everything he knows. And believe me when I say he was *once* the very best we had."

Johanna's mind spun, searching for a different solution, a better compromise. She looked to Rafi, expecting him to have some rebuttal.

He stood tall, staring down the Keepers' leader. "It will be done."

"No." The word was torn out of Johanna's mouth. "Rafi, *no*. Don't you understand? You'll die. You won't survive."

"If that's what it takes to protect Santarem, then so be it."

She grabbed his arms, forcing him to see that the words were hurting her more than the shock caused by his power. "There's not enough time—"

The woman interrupted Johanna. "I'm sure you'll prefer this over the alternative. We will meet at the Citadel at the full moon, and one way or another we will finish this."

Chapter 62

Dom

Prisoners were usually held in the township's jail, but because of her crime and the pending attack, Brynn was confined in a barrack basement. It was a dark, dank, windowless hole—a short-term holding place for the worst sort of criminals. The murderers. The rapists. The traitors. The people who didn't deserve a comfortable place to stay, and wouldn't live long enough to suffer from the lack of accommodations.

Dom stood on the last stair from the bottom, out of sight of the guards he knew were waiting around the corner, and pressed two fingers to the gash that trailed from above his heart to the middle of his sternum. It hurt, the new stitches protesting their rough treatment, but he needed to feel the pain to remember his anger.

Brynn's crimes could have far-reaching consequences, he reminded himself. *If the estate is overrun, innocent people will die, the soldiers from Belem will likely rape and pillage, burn and destroy. Those atrocities could, in part, be laid at Brynn's feet.*

He forced down the disbelief, focusing on the sharp sting of righteous fury till his feet took the last step.

"Lord Dom." The soldier outside the cell door gave a brief salute.

"Your mother and her guard are inside." He knocked twice before opening the lock.

"Thank you," Dom said as he squeezed through the narrow entryway.

Brynn was curled in the cell's farthest corner, elbows on her knees, head resting on her arms. Lady DeSilva sat in a small chair near the door, and the guard split the distance between the two women. A lantern hung from a bracket above his head, casting a small circle of light around him and shadows on Lady DeSilva's cold expression. There was nothing sympathetic in her eyes, and the corners of her mouth were pinched.

"She won't speak to me," Lady DeSilva said, standing and smoothing down the wrinkles in her skirt. "I thought, perhaps, she'd offer some explanation of her actions, but she just sits there. Mute. Refusing to look at me." Her voice cracked, and Dom saw that underneath his mother's stony facade she, too, was struggling with Brynn's treachery.

"And so," she continued, carefully articulating each word. "I turn her over to you, the highest-ranking member of our household, to interrogate as you see fit."

Instead of moving toward the door, Lady DeSilva ignored her guard's outstretched arm and squatted next to Brynn. Dom's mother studied the wild red curls that hung loose, then reached out with gentle fingers and raised Brynn's chin.

"You held my hand when Camilio died." Her lips trembled, but she continued. "I trusted you. I cared for you. I would have gladly claimed you as my own."

At that Brynn turned her face away, pressing her forehead against the wall.

Lady DeSilva stood, regaining her perfect posture. "You are the worst sort of traitor, Brynn Cavalcanti. You manipulated the very people who would have sacrificed themselves to save you. May that thought haunt you for the rest of your very short life."

She whisked out of the room, her guard hesitating between following her or staying with Dom.

"Go," Dom commanded, certain he wouldn't need anyone to protect him from Brynn.

Dom grabbed the chair, dragged it under the lantern, and sat, his toes a few inches from Brynn's thigh. She didn't acknowledge him, keeping her face turned to the wall.

"I don't want to do this," he said, fatigue instead of fury lacing his words. "So please, for both our sakes, tell me anything you may know of Belem's plans."

He waited, till the silence stretched thin enough to snap. Brynn said nothing. Not a sniffle, not a whimper, not a sigh.

"Tell me who your contacts are. Tell me who you were passing messages to. Tell me who recruited you." Dom stood then, pacing anxiously behind the chair. If she didn't say something, he'd have to find someone who could *force* answers out of her. And that, even more than the looming battle, terrified him. "Please, for the love of all that's holy, give me an explanation."

Nothing.

"Damn it, Brynn! Answer me." He grabbed the back of the chair and threw it across the small space. It cracked against the door and one of the legs snapped off. She cringed but didn't move otherwise.

Dom dropped to his knees at her side and took hold of her shoulders. "Please, say something. Give me an excuse to pardon you. *Lie* to me!"

She looked at him then, her eyes wide and tear filled. "I can't."

"Because you don't know anything? Because you're so devoted to Belem? Because . . ." His voice trailed off, and he saw something else in her face. Certainty. Acceptance. "Because you're protecting someone."

Jealousy bit with vicious ardor. "The butcher's son? Renato? Are you sacrificing yourself for your *beloved* fiancé?"

"No," she said quickly. "Renato had nothing to do with this. He's just a nice boy who got caught in the middle."

"And I'm sure his father will say the same when he wakes up."

Brynn closed her eyes and shook her head, not bothering to argue. Even after all the lies and deception, he believed her in this. "If not Renato, then who? Cook isn't involved, your aunt's dead, your brother . . ." Dom's voice trailed off. "Gavin was due back last week, wasn't he?"

"Shh." She clamped a hand over Dom's mouth. "They'll know."

He yanked her hand away. "No one is down here. No one will hear us."

"They'll kill Gavin, if they haven't already."

"Belem has—" Dom stopped, realizing that something didn't quite make sense. "Your brother sails with Guildmaster Tolapia, but they didn't go south, Brynn. They went *north*."

Her breath caught, and she went unnaturally still. And then he knew. He *knew* the truth.

"They were sailing to Camaçari, like they do every fall. Belem doesn't have your brother." His heart faltered. "Ceara does."

"Yes," she whispered, dropping her head back onto her knees.

"Maribelle had her attendants checking on our supplies, but it wasn't food she should have been worrying about. It was the cannon powder. You did all of this to save your brother."

She nodded, her hair falling over her face like a veil.

"The butcher was your contact. You worked with him and his son—"

"Renato was just a ploy. Seeing him gave me an excuse to pass messages to his father when I couldn't get them out any other way."

Dom wanted to feel relieved, to hang on to the naive hope that this girl had betrayed him only for her brother's sake, but he had a sick sense that there was something missing from her story. "How long has Ceara had your brother?" When she didn't answer, the gashes over his heart began to throb in time with his pulse. "How long, Brynn?"

"Two weeks," she said weakly.

"Maribelle said she intercepted the first message almost a month ago, just after Belem returned to his estate." Dom's breath rushed out in a harsh rattle. "You were spying for Belem *before* Ceara captured your brother." He saw her standing next to Belem's chair, keeping the duke's cup filled, smiling prettily. How long had it been going on? Months? *Years?*

"It was never supposed to go this far. I was just sharing gossip—rumors I heard in the kitchen, who visited, who left, which nobles fought, and which snuck away together." She twisted her fingers together. "Little things, innocuous trivia. It was never supposed to hurt anyone. He promised me enough money to join one of the upper classes—"

"So you betrayed me for money? I would have *given* you money." He lurched to his feet, towering over her.

"I never wanted your money."

"Then what, Brynn? What did you want?"

"You!" She stood and grabbed the front of his shirt. "I wanted to be the girl you couldn't toss aside."

"You already were!"

"No, Dom. I was a *challenge*. You only ever saw me as the one maid who wouldn't give in to your charm."

"You're wrong. You were the only girl I imagined was my friend." Dom broke her grip and stepped away, backing toward the door. "I see you now, Brynn. I see you for *exactly* what you are."

Belem's forward scouts had been spotted. They were approaching from the west, heading for the bridges that spanned the ravine between the two states. Dom had one final task to complete before he left for battle.

Opening the nursery door, he found Michael asleep on the floor, stretched out in front of the fire that warded off the chill brought by the seasonal rains. He looked sweet and unhindered, one arm thrown over the back of Rafi's big red hunting hound, and the other folded under his head.

The animal snorted as Dom entered the room but didn't shift. Perhaps it sensed how badly the child needed his rest.

"Michael," Dom said, shaking the boy gently. "I have a special job for you."

"For me?" The boy rubbed his red-rimmed eyes. He'd been crying since he heard about Brynn's arrest.

"Yes." Dom pressed the heavy key into the child's hand and explained how it was to be used. "If something happens, if Belem's troops get over the walls or if I . . . I don't come back, then you do what I asked. Can you promise?"

Michael's lips puckered, but he nodded his head solemnly. "I promise, Lord Dom."

"Thank you. I knew I could trust you with this."

The boy's small fist clenched the key, and he pressed it over his heart in a salute. "I won't fail you."

Dom dropped to his knees and crushed the child to his chest in a tight hug.

If Santiago fell, being trapped in the barracks would be a fate worse than death. Brynn didn't deserve *that.* At least in this one thing Dom's conscience would be clear.

CHAPTER 63

PIRA

Leão was being kept in a box—a coffin, really, but without a lid.

The simple casket of wood was slightly too short for his long frame. His knees were bent, the soles of his feet pressed against the bottom. Keepers didn't bury their dead. They were cremated; the smoke supposedly carried their souls into Mother Lua's embrace. But it was much too easy for Pira to imagine Sapo's intentions. Keep the body alive for as long as possible, drain Leão's wealth of *essência*, and then drop him in a hole somewhere convenient.

Sapo forced her down beside the box and said, "Water it."

As if Leão were a useful garden herb. Water it. Feed it.

Her fingers gripped her thighs to stop from taking a swing at someone who could blast her instantly.

"You care about him," Sapo said, nodding to the silent servant who stalked close at his heels. The slave set a bowl of water and a strip of linen next to Pira. "You'll see that he gets the water he needs, because even now, even defeated, you hold on to hope like I hold on to *essência*."

She hated that he was right. That she would smooth water over Leão's cracked lips and dribble what she could into his too-still mouth. Even as she hated it, she planned to find some broth so she could give him something more substantial than water.

Sapo leaned close, his breath moist against her ear. "I'll tell you a little secret. You won't need to nourish him for too much longer. My Seer has promised that should the heir gain the power—and you saw the light as well as I—she will become my slave, and there will be no Mage on either side of the wall who can stop me."

"I wouldn't put much faith in anything Críquete has to say. Or haven't you learned that lesson already?"

"You love to taunt." He ran his fingers across the top of her head, looping one around her ear. She couldn't help but cringe away from his touch. "Remember that when all this is over, you will still be mine."

"I'd rather die."

"That can be arranged."

Pira held her arms out wide, which drew a long, loud laugh from Sapo. "Perhaps if Jacaré and the rest of the Keepers had as much fire as you do, they would have defeated the Nata cleanly."

"There's nothing clean in war."

"Too true." He toed the bowl, spilling some of the water on the ground. "Keep him alive."

"Or what? You'll kill him?"

"No," Sapo said, taking a few backward steps, smiling as he moved. "I'll make you do it. Then I'll heal him again and have you kill him again, over and over until you learn the price of disobedience."

She held his gaze till he turned and walked deeper into their camp, then she dipped the corner of the cloth into the water and trickled it across Leão's lips.

"I don't know if you can hear me, but I really need you to . . ." She paused, wiping a speckle of blood off his chin. "I really need *you*."

Críquete found Pira the next afternoon when the battle train stopped for lunch. The Seer knelt next to Pira as she tried to force water into Leão's mouth. His bottom lip was bleeding from a crack in the middle, and despite her efforts, he was obviously dehydrated.

Críquete reached into the coffin and raised Leão's head a bit, tipping it back so his mouth hung open. "If you rub his throat, his body will swallow on its own. That might help."

Pira didn't say anything but did as the Seer suggested. Sure enough, the water she'd managed to get into his mouth disappeared down his throat.

"He seems like a nice boy," Críquete said, looking into Leão's face. "I would have chosen someone like this for my daughter. Alas, it was not meant to be."

"Your daughter? You have a daughter?"

"Of course. You've met her."

Pira looked around the camp, wondering if she was one of the many captured girls with dead eyes and listless movements. "Where is she?"

"Not so far now." Críquete settled Leão's head back into the box. She pointed to the east, over the hills pockmarked by open-faced mines. "You'll see her. Soon. A few days."

"If you say so."

Críquete nodded, looking into the afternoon sunlight, her gaze blank. "Or I will. One way or another."

Pira snorted. "Do you ever say anything clear enough to be helpful?"

"I told you to run fast when the opportunity presented itself. But that warning wasn't enough." She reached under her skirt and withdrew the long hammer handle. "You forgot this."

Pira wished her temper and her pride had allowed her to listen to Críquete's previous warning. She took the handle; one end was cracked, probably why it had been discarded.

"When will I need it?" she asked, gripping it harder, feeling the wood bite through her calluses.

"I don't know, but you'll have to keep it hidden."

"I will." She placed it into the box next to Leão. No one would search him for a weapon.

Chapter 64

Johanna

Rain turned the trail between the wall and Performers' Camp treacherous. The few surviving Performers, weak after Jacaré's and Rafi's efforts at healing them, stumbled over loose gravel and damp stone.

Yara leaned against Johanna for support. She'd always been a vibrant woman, an eye-catching entertainer, but with her voice broken and her face somber, she seemed a faded version of herself.

"I was making dinner and watching my children try to train our new puppy." She paused, wiping the tears out of her eyes. "I looked up and saw someone unfamiliar standing at the back of the wagon, and wondered if he was from another troupe or . . . I don't know.

"I've always trusted other Performers without question. Isn't that silly of me, knowing what I know about the rest of Santarem?" Yara raised her fingers to her throat. "Were we delusional to think that because we were isolated and didn't involve ourselves in politics, we were safe?"

Johanna didn't answer that question. Arlo had been steeped in the kingdom's turmoil, but maybe he'd chosen to spy for King Wilhelm—and to save Johanna's life—in an effort to keep the gritty fingers of war from reaching into their perfect little valley.

The conversation broiled in her mind and left her stomach bubbling with a sick sense of responsibility. Her fathers, both Arlo and King Wilhelm, had given their lives to protect the things they loved. And now Rafi . . .

She checked the line of Performers following her, and saw Rafi swing the arm of an injured Skylighter over his shoulder. Her heart swooped at the simple, thoughtful action, then plunged to her feet when he caught her looking. His mouth opened as if he was going to call to her, but she couldn't bear to hear anything he had to say.

Seven days and Rafi would be another body cooling in the ground.

She couldn't acknowledge him. If she opened her mouth now, she wouldn't be able to say anything coherent—she'd either rail on him for thinking he could so calmly plan to sacrifice his life, or burst into hysterical tears because he was exactly the kind of person who would give up everything for those he loved.

His eyes were on her back; she could feel the warmth of his stare, trying to thaw the chill that had penetrated to her very soul. Ignoring him, ignoring the comfort he'd try to offer, she marched on.

Two wagons blocked the trail that led into Performers' Camp. Four Fireswords stood behind the barricade, weapons dangling from their sashes, and the short bows they used for hunting slung across their backs.

"Stop!" a voice shouted from a small gap between the axles. "Don't come any farther."

"James, it's me, Johanna."

"Prove it."

"You can see me," she said, edging closer to the wagons with her hands held out to her sides. She heard Rafi's voice from somewhere behind her, calling her to stop, but ignored him. "Isn't that enough?"

"Not after what happened the other night. We let six of our own into camp, and the next morning those six plus twenty others went missing."

Yara cleared her throat, raising her head to meet James's grim visage. "James? We're back. Well . . . some of us."

James leaped onto one of the driver's seats, bow pointed at Yara. "I see four . . . five Performers, plus Johanna and two strangers. Where's Elma? Where's Didsbury? Wh-where's . . ." He swallowed and started again. "Where's Julia?"

Julia. Johanna wiped her hands on her pants, as if she could wipe away the blood that stained them. Julia was one whose shot Johanna had missed horribly, one that Rafi and Jacaré had tried and failed to save. James had been in love with the young contortionist since they were both in swaddling.

"She's . . . we're the only survivors," Johanna said, struggling with the words.

The arrow swung to point at her. "They're all *dead*?"

"Yes."

A flickering, iridescent bubble suddenly surrounded Johanna, and the Fireswords shouted in fear and surprise. James released the arrow and it stuck in the shield at Johanna's knee level. She hopped back from the point and exchanged a surprised look with James.

Rafi strode through the crowd, blue fire licking up his arms. "We're not here to hurt you. We're here to save you. Move aside and let us in."

Murmurs of "Keeper" and "demon" rolled among the Fireswords.

"Please, Rafi. Stop. Can't you see they are frightened?" Johanna stepped in front of him, blocking his way. "James! James!" She had to shout to be heard over the men's frantic arguments. "James, when you were six, you ate a tree frog and it made you sick for days. If it weren't for that dreadful medicine Elma gave you, you would have died."

Except now I know the truth. That medicine was a ruse.

The arguing stopped, and the light around Rafi and the shield he'd created to protect Johanna winked out. The wagons rolled aside and James stepped through. "You can come in, Jo. And the rest of the Performers, but everyone else stays out." His fingers twitched nervously on his sword's hilt.

"They've stayed in Performers' Camp before."

"That was *before*, Jo." James snatched his spent arrow from the ground in front of her feet. "We don't let anyone in. Not anymore."

"Go," Rafi said, nodding toward the camp. "We need their help. You have to convince them to stand against Sapo."

She knew he was right, but she also knew that recruiting these people might mean leading them to their death.

So much loss, and more to face.

With the death of her brothers, with the invasion of the valley, with the collapse of the barrier, someone had to take on the mantle.

Elma's prophecy seemed well on its way to becoming true.

Chapter 65

Dom

Dom crouched in the weeds, watching a man unwind a length of braided fuse. He couldn't see Belem's troops through the crush of the forest beyond, but he could hear the tromp of hooves as they approached through the trees.

The salvaged powder had served its purpose. The bridges had collapsed to their foundations, leaving a wrecked mass of wood and stone. Belem's troops had only two remaining options if they intended to invade: turn north, pass through Cruzamento and enter Santiago by way of Camaçari, or cross the ravine and ford the river, leaving their wagons, siege engines, and ballistae on the far side.

"Lord Dom," said the breathless fuse man. "It's ready. I'll light it on your order."

"Wait till the first line of horses are in the ravine, but before they start to come up the far side," Dom commanded.

Belem's soldiers would be forced to overwhelm Santiago's with sheer numbers now that they had neither surprise nor superior weapons to their advantage. The newest reports from Maribelle's relay suggested that the attacking army outnumbered Santiago's by nearly six to one—significantly more than the original estimate.

The odds wouldn't have been so alarming if Fernando's troops hadn't been mired on the South Road. Even at the horses' fastest gallop, they wouldn't reach Santiago before Belem did.

The newly appointed Captain Demian lowered his spyglass. "Two minutes."

Dom's heart hammered with the deliberate blows of a blacksmith at his anvil, but he gave a sharp nod. "Go to, Captain."

"On my mark," Demian yelled, raising his arm.

A row of infantry, each specially selected for this duty, raised slings overhead. The next row of soldiers loaded half-full wine bottles into the pockets.

Mother Lua, Dom prayed. *I know I've never deserved your blessings, but today I'm begging you to spare my people. Please, Goddess, let this work.*

"Hold," Demian yelled.

The first line of Belem's troops broke through the trees. Longbowmen, as Dom had suspected, with cavalry pressing between the ranks. The bowmen nocked their arrows and pointed them skyward, to use loft to get distance from their shots.

"Shields!"

Santiago's infantry created a wall of steel and wood, protecting their bowmens' torsos and legs, but leaving their heads and arms exposed so they could get a clear return shot.

Terror mixed with the stench of sweat and alcohol. Dom licked his lips, tasting salt on his skin, took a breath, and licked them again, but he didn't turn or break, eyes focused over the top of his shield.

With a twang and hiss, Belem's bowmen released their second

volley, and the cavalry charged. Shields shifted, blocking most of the arrows, but a voice shrieked in pain somewhere down the line.

"Bows, fire at will," Demian commanded.

Horses screamed as Belem's men fell from their mounts. Dom counted the seconds in his head, waiting for the first row of horsemen to disappear into the gully, the second row following close behind. His fingers twitched, wanting to give the sign, but he waited . . . waited . . . waited.

"Now!"

The fuse man dropped his torch onto the pitch-soaked rope, and a speck of flame raced across the wet field.

The first line of cavalry started their ascent up the ravine's steep side.

Demian looked to Dom before giving the order, "Slings, light! Slings, fire!"

The bottles ranged in color from glistening gold to deep maroon, each with a burning length of bandage trapped under the cork. On another day it might have been a beautiful sight as the glass caught and reflected the light from the sun and their flaming fuses.

Instead it was raining death.

Glass shattered, and the burning *Álcool Fogo* splashed over men and horses. Their cries rent the air, blotting out the crash of breaking glass as the bottles exploded, shards sinking deep into unprotected flesh.

Then the cannon powder went. It hadn't been enough to fill two barrels, so Dom had spread it out. Four small casks had been packed halfway with powder and filled the rest of the way with metal filings, bits of broken blades, and all the nails the township could spare.

Three lines of Belem's cavalry were decimated. Only four riders of the first one hundred who tried to pass through the ravine survived, and they were easily picked off by Santiago's arrows. Horses reared as blood blossomed on their coats, and riders tumbled from their saddles.

The wind shifted, and instead of fear and sweat Dom smelled burning meat. He clenched his jaw shut to stop from heaving all over his troops.

The men around him cheered, almost drowning out a voice calling his name from somewhere deep inside their ranks.

"Dominic!"

Maribelle jumped off her horse and pushed her way to the line of commanders. She waved a piece of paper as she ran.

He broke away from the group and rushed to her. "What are you doing—"

"Camaçari," she panted. Her black hair was slicked down with sweat. "Small group coming from the north. Already here."

"What?"

"They were in hiding. On this side of the ravine. Not more than fifty."

Understanding exploded in Dom's mind like one of his liquor-filled bottles. "Demian! They're going to flank us."

From the corner of his eye Dom spotted the arrows arching through the blue sky, whistling toward them.

"Shields!" Multiple voices took up the shout, but it was too late. The north end of Santiago's line collapsed, and the screaming started anew.

"Get down!" Dom yelled, hauling Maribelle to the ground beside him. He rolled on top of her, protecting her with his body.

Their faces were a breath apart. Maribelle's dark eyes widened as her skin went gray with terror.

"Your horse. Where did you leave it?"

Her long lashes fluttered, and she raised her hand as if to touch his face. "D-Dom." Her tawny skin was stained dark with blood. He sat back, holding Maribelle close. Her other arm was wrapped around her stomach, half covering the arrowhead that protruded from above her right hip.

He froze. He couldn't think, couldn't understand, couldn't *breathe*. The call to fall back sounded, and he didn't move, staring with a sick fascination at the arrow that had pierced all the way through her body.

"I—I think," she said, stumbling over the words. "That we could have been good together."

"Shh. You're fine, Maribelle." He wasn't sure if that was the truth, but it felt like the right thing to say. "It's not that bad of an injury."

"Lord Dom!" Someone jostled him, trying to pull him upright. "We must move now."

Dom slipped his arms under Maribelle's knees and shoulders and stood. She felt too light in his arms.

"Not the only reason I came . . ." She shook her head as if to clear her thoughts. "Fernando is bringing help."

"I know." He ran over the uneven ground and heard her cry out as he threw her across his saddle.

She blacked out long before he reached the estate, and he wasn't able to make sense of the rest of her message until much later.

Chapter 66

Johanna

The balcony that wrapped around the upper floor of the Council House was packed with Performers. They stood shoulder to shoulder, faces grim. The air in the building was close, full of woodsmoke, spices, and fear.

Johanna stood in the center of the floor and told the story simply, without pomp or pageantry. It wasn't the kind of tale that required an ornate delivery or tricks to evoke an emotion from the audience. No one spoke, no one moved, all were focused on her in the center of the floor as she relayed the truth about Elma, about Keepers, about *essência*. In the grim lines of their faces, the pallor of their skin, and the way they leaned toward one another for support, she knew they believed her. But believing her and fighting beside her were two different things.

"Yesterday we lost twenty-one of our own. They were your friends. Your parents. Your siblings, and your loves." She saw the words take their toll. Poor James hunched over the railing, his head in his hands, his face hidden. "Their deaths will mean nothing if we refuse to take action. We've hidden in our valley for too long, pretending to have no part, no sway, no power to affect the goings-on of Santarem."

She raised her eyes, connecting with the people, before leveling her gaze on the four remaining elders. Elma's chair had been draped with a swath of gray cloth. Johanna ran her fingers over the funeral embroidery before continuing. "If you want to become a puppet, to have your free will stripped away by a power-hungry madman, then sit here in your wagons and wait. Wait for the fireballs to crash among the tents and burn them to cinders. Wait for the lightning to strike down your children. Wait to have a collar strapped around your throat and become a mindless slave.

"But if you want the sacrifices of Elma, and Didsbury, and Sergio, and Olivia, and Julia, and all the others to mean something, then join me. Follow Lord DeSilva and me. Together, with his power and our help, we have a chance to save Performers' Camp and ultimately all of Santarem."

There was a moment of silence, of breath held in anticipation, then with a gasp, sound returned in a cacophony of discussion, arguments, and sobs.

Guilherme, one of the oldest men in Performers' Camp, raised an age-spotted hand. The volume decreased, though the voices didn't silence entirely.

"Johanna, you're saying we have two choices: We stay here and become slaves, or we fight. Are there no other options?"

"What about the Keepers? Would they accept us?" said another.

"Could we go to the Wisp Islands?" shouted a third.

"Is there any way to convince them to leave us alone?"

Johanna shook her head, sickened and disappointed that her people were so blind to the dangers facing them.

Then she felt a hand take hers. It was small, with a callus across the thumb and pad of the palm. "I know what it feels like to lose my will to another," Yara said. "And I will die before letting it happen again. I will fight."

Enzo, another one of the survivors, took Yara's other hand. "I will fight."

Those who had been captured formed a line, faces brave and determined.

The younger members, those nearest Johanna's age who barely had any memory of the Ten Years' War, were the next to join them. The line continued up the stairs, around the curve of the balcony.

The voices quieted, the arguments ceased. All heads turned to the four elders. The woman nearest Johanna, a white-haired grandmother, placed her palsied fingers over the point where Yara's and Johanna's hands met. "I will fight," she said, her words thin and reedy.

Guilherme's age-clouded eyes followed the linked hands. His bottom lip protruded, his face a mask of deliberation. "Well then." He raised his hand and reached for Johanna's. "We will all fight."

Chapter 67

Jacaré

Rafi was strategizing, using sticks, rocks, and shallow trenches in the ground to map out routes and describe defenses. "We can't stay in the valley," he said as he placed a rock over a squiggle in the dirt that was meant to illustrate the narrow road that led into Performers' Camp. "The trail itself is defensible, but there are ways through the trees. Then we'd be at a disadvantage. They'd have the high ground and we'd have nowhere left to run."

He drew a line that represented the coast, the inlet that formed Santiago's harbor, and described how they'd be forced into the ocean or to move a long line of people along the beach. His voice and actions were passionate, so certain that his side would find a way to prevail because they were fighting for freedom and equality—as if fighting for the goodness guaranteed victory.

Watching Rafi work made Jacaré sick with anger. Rafi was young and in love, and so thoroughly soaked in *essência* that it rolled off him in waves, but Jacaré knew too well how this story was going to end.

"Stop, Rafi." Jacaré leaned against the log—the very log Tex had rested against a handful of weeks ago—and folded his arms across his chest. "Even if Jo is successful in recruiting a fighting group from these Performers, we cannot go to Santiago along the coast. We'll be strung out and easy targets. If we head due south, we'll have to pass through Camaçari. We won't have the men to hold off Ceara's troops. And in the end none of it will matter. The fight will come to you."

Rafi looked up; his dark eyes reflected the flames from the fire. He wiped his eyebrow with the back of his fist, cleaning away the smudge of dirt there. "Aren't you some sort of military commander? Don't you have some strategy to suggest? Don't you *want* me to destroy the Nata?"

Jacaré didn't answer. Amelia wouldn't have let Rafi leave the wall alive unless it served her purposes.

"I know your leader intends me to fight this battle for her," Rafi said, snapping the stick he'd been drawing with. "If I win, she gets what she wants. If I lose, then I'll have weakened her enemy."

The little kernel of respect Jacaré felt for Rafi grew roots. "And you've given her a week to marshal her troops."

"That too." Rafi nodded and rose from his crouch. "I learned battle strategy from my father, but nothing about magical battles. I need you to tell me what I'm going to face and the best ways to take down a mage."

Jacaré wanted to laugh. "I had a decade of training, and even then I was unprepared. A few days . . ." He made a vague hand gesture. "Even with the power of every Keeper in existence, you won't stand against someone like Sapo."

"So you're saying I'm destined to fail?"

"Yes."

The fist crossing Jacaré's jaw came out of nowhere. His head bounced off the log, and he raised his forearm barely in time to block the second shot. Rafi knelt over him, one hand gripping Jacaré's shirt, the other raining blows on his head and arms. Jacaré rolled to the side, throwing an elbow that caught Rafi's ear. They rolled again, coming close to the fire.

"Stop!" a voice shouted. "What are you—Rafi, stop!"

Jacaré wasn't sure how Rafi had managed to get on top of him again, but he dimly recognized a few other people in the clearing, all working together to break up the fight. Johanna had her arms tight around Rafi's middle, looking tiny and angry as she tried to pull him away. Another man, a Firesword maybe, held Rafi's right arm with both of his own.

Rafi looked nothing like a Keeper, not with his curly black hair and dark eyes, but he moved like one. Jacaré couldn't remember the last time someone had bested him in a fight. The boy moved faster than anyone Jacaré had *ever* seen—maybe the power from the barrier had enacted more than a magical change on the boy. Maybe it had been a physical one as well.

And maybe that meant they had a chance.

CHAPTER 68

RAFI

Light, it felt good to smash that smug Keeper's words down his throat. The carefully composed arrogance, the constant expression of discontent, disappeared the instant Rafi's fist cracked against Jacaré's jaw. For a moment he showed a real emotion—shocked disbelief.

As if from a distance, Rafi felt Johanna's hands on his chest, shoving him step by step to the edge of the campsite.

"What are you doing? What is wrong with you?"

He barely heard her, still immersed in the heat of his anger and wanting to stay that way. Anger was an easier emotion for Rafi to face than paralyzing fear. It was sweat and adrenaline, action and release—all a welcome change to the chilled dread that had dribbled into his bone marrow.

"What did that prove?" Jo asked, giving him one last push, which left him standing in the darkness around the campsite and her still in the light.

"That Keepers aren't unbeatable." Rafi smiled, and felt a sharp tinge of pain in his bottom lip. He didn't remember Jacaré landing a single punch, but the metallic taste in his mouth suggested he was wrong.

It didn't matter. "That I'm stronger than he thinks. That he underestimated me, and that if he can be beaten, then Sapo can be as well."

"So you punched him in the face to prove that point?"

"Yes." One of his knuckles was bleeding, but the sting of the gash and the pull of the muscles made him feel alive. He wasn't stupid and he wasn't blind. Death was on the horizon, either in a magical battle or when he returned the *essência* to the barrier, and he refused to live the rest of his life under the shadow of dread. "He needed to know I wasn't going to lie down and let these Keepers trample over me and my land. I intend to put up the best fight possible."

"Like when Beta stood against the Horde."

Fear was a feather in the back of his throat, and he swallowed to force it away. "I hope the odds aren't that impossible, but yes."

"You plan to die in the end." Her voice was too flat, void of emotion.

He had known this conversation was coming, but he'd hoped to put it off till after they'd beaten Sapo. "I'd like to live. I'd like to take down Belem and Inimigo and establish peace. I'd like to go home to Santiago and apologize to my mother for all my stupid mistakes and give my brother a hug. I'd like to see the docks rebuilt and the sewers of Santiago running smoothly. I'd like to do a dozen other things that seemed mundane and irritating when I was going to be duke. But most of all"—he stepped forward quickly, using the same speed he had with Jacaré, and wrapped his arms tight around her—"I want to hear your stories. Not the ones you memorized, but the funny, embarrassing, heart-wrenching tales about Johanna Von Arlo. I want you to sing me to sleep every night. I want to spend an eternity kissing your lips and memorizing the texture of your skin."

"You're not going to die," she said, her elbows digging into his ribs, trying to break free. "You'll have plenty of time to do all those things *after*."

After. After. If only after were a possibility.

"Johanna?" James approached. "We want to go over the plans."

Rafi raised his eyebrows at Johanna.

"I came up here to tell you that the Performers agreed," she said, backing away from him. "You've got your army. They'll be ready to march tomorrow afternoon."

The Performers moved faster than any army in any of the books that Rafi had studied. It was the nature of their society to be ready to change locations, without stopping for supplies, at a moment's notice.

At noon the next day the youngest, fittest, and most powerful members of each troupe cracked their whips over their horses' heads and began the climb to the valley's lip. Jacaré had spent the rest of the night walking throughout the camp identifying which members had a strong *essência*, and through that Rafi learned to sense both the presence and strength of it in those around him.

Birds were sent to each of the states, seeking reports from Performers' friends, and Rafi took the opportunity to send another letter home. It was difficult to compose, knowing that these few lines would be the last he could offer to his brother, mother, and country. But they were not to know any of that. The letter had to remain on point.

He named Dom heir, with Lady DeSilva serving as his regent until he came of age, should Rafi be killed in the ensuing battle. Rafi also confirmed Johanna's true identity and stipulated she be cared for as royalty, and finally, that if Johanna wished, Santiago would help her regain and rebuild her ancestral home.

There wasn't room for apologies and good-byes, but he hoped his actions would serve as testimony enough if he didn't get a chance to tell them himself.

As the brightly colored army made its way toward Cruzamento, Rafi rode knee to knee with Jacaré.

Neither had said a word about the brawl the night before, and Rafi wasn't going to acknowledge the nick of guilt he felt about the bruises on Jacaré's face. As if by some unspoken agreement, they chose to focus on the other challenges ahead.

"Strictly by numbers, I'm more powerful than Sapo. Can't I just blast him with fire or lightning or something?"

Jacaré actually laughed. It was a cold sound, devoid of humor. "Do you want to lose the battle in the first five minutes?"

The blue light of *essência* flared up around Rafi with the unexpected rush of his anger. Johanna whipped around in her saddle, eyes narrowed with concern. No one else seemed to notice, and Jacaré didn't comment.

"Relax," Jacaré snapped. "You may have the power of a hundred Keepers, but Sapo's had hundreds of years to hone his skill. If I gave a child an excellent sword but put him up to fight against a master, who would win?"

Rafi exhaled and tried to release his grip on the power. He'd always had a quick temper, but he'd trained himself to hide his anger until he could release it on the training yard. Since the incident at the wall, rage had boiled just below the surface. When it started to bubble over, blue light burst through his skin. He struggled to rein it in, to tamp it down, but his first inclination was to blow something up.

When the glow began to fade, Jacaré continued his analogy. "Even with a stick a master would win because he knows how to defend himself against the worst or wildest attacks. Sapo may not be as powerful as you are, but he's sure to be crafty.

"The battle will focus on ambushes over field maneuvers. Sapo wants the power you have, which means he'll try to incapacitate rather than kill you." He gave Rafi a significant look. "You can always tap the Performers if you're running low."

"Don't we have to collar people to use their power?"

"No." Jacaré touched his eyebrow absently, brushing against the scab that Rafi had not offered to heal. "The barrier was built without collars. To some extent, *essência* can be shared by touch. We lined up along Donovan's Wall and funneled it all into one person. You can use the strongest of these people if things get bad . . . and maybe you noticed, but those with the most *essência* are the most athletic. They'll be the best fighters anyway."

Jacaré followed Rafi's gaze, looking up the line of wagons. "How many of them are you willing to sacrifice as fodder?"

"None," Rafi said quickly.

"Then we'll need to be devious in the ways we use them."

Chapter 69

Dom

The short-lived battle in the meadow had given the townspeople enough time to get inside the estate's walls. All the preparations Dom had made—building the palisade, strengthening the walls, stockpiling food, drying out the powder—weren't enough. Belem had come ready to bypass the palisades, tear down the walls, or, if necessary, starve them out. The blown bridges were only a slight inconvenience. Belem's engineers were working on ways to get their cannons and ballistae across the ravine and until then he had other methods of destroying Santiago.

The central market was the first thing to go, with the docks a close second. Belem's men burned everything on the east side of the river that bisected the township, and cut off any escape Dom's people hoped to make by water.

There wasn't enough room inside the DeSilvas' manor to fit the whole township, and all those crowded in the courtyard were affected by the billowing smoke from Santiago's flames. Men, women, and children hung wet cloths over their faces just so they could breathe.

Once night fell, Belem's troops stopped shooting flaming arrows onto the estate's roofs, but Captain Demian reported that there were . . . things . . . floating in the well water. Belem had camped between the central aquifer and the estate, and had his soldiers dump feces and animal carcasses into the wells and the river south of his base. The water that came into the estate was full of that filth and completely undrinkable. Even with the rain barrels and strict rationing there wouldn't be enough clean water to keep the entire township alive for more than a few days.

Frustrated and angry, Dom paced the halls of the estate, until he found himself at Maribelle's room. He wasn't quite sure what he was doing there; she'd been unconscious since their frantic ride back to the township. While the arrow hadn't struck anything vital, she had lost a significant amount of blood.

"I'm sorry," he said, apologizing to her attendants. "I don't know why I'm here. I guess . . . I just hoped that maybe . . ." He trailed off, trying to put into words what he was thinking. That he could glean inspiration from Maribelle's sleeping body? That he could absorb some of her resourcefulness by sitting nearby? That he could apologize for having treated her so poorly?

He shook his head in embarrassment and despair.

They seemed to understand. One of the shorter ones, he wasn't sure which, patted his shoulder as if she guessed at what he wasn't saying.

"I know you are sworn to keep her secrets, but if there's anything you know that could help us . . . ," he begged, looking them each in the eye. "Please."

They exchanged a look he couldn't quite read.

"Lord Dom, her trust is hard to earn, and for good reason," she said. "We've been with her since the beginning, and she keeps secrets even from us. But if we knew anything that would help, we'd tell you now."

They knew what he had only grudgingly admitted. The estate walls weren't going to keep any of them safe for very much longer.

"There are the wells," the dark-haired one—he thought she'd been introduced as Eva—said, biting her bottom lip.

"They're unsafe to use—"

"Not to drink from, Lord Dom, but to travel through. The wells of Santiago are interconnected with horizontal tunnels running to one another and the central aquifer. Someone might have . . . *liberated* . . . a copy of Lord Rafi's sewage maps and found the connection."

Dom's mouth opened in shock. He knew that before Rafi had gone after Johanna, he'd been planning to add new sewer lines but wanted to make sure they didn't come near the groundwater reserves. "Have you been in these tunnels?" he asked, adrenaline making his fingers twitch. "Are they passable?"

The ladies exchanged a glance. "Yes," Eva said, nodding. "A person who was, say, my size or a little bigger could fit through most of the passages."

"Would someone my size fit through the tunnels?" He held his breath, knowing that even if the answer was no, he was going to use this information to his advantage.

"Yes."

Dom called Lady DeSilva, Captain Demian, and a grizzled veteran named Gesias to help him work out a plan. Townspeople looked on while Gesias and Eva climbed down the courtyard's central well and came up at the one just beyond the kitchen door.

The water was only knee deep, and although it was moving, if they hugged the walls, it wasn't strong enough to sweep them off their feet.

"I know what you're thinking, Dominic," Lady DeSilva whispered as Dom marked the locations of the wells nearest the enormous tent topped by Belem's pennant. "And I'm telling you no. You're the highest-ranking member—"

"Yes, I know, Mother. You reminded me of that before I interrogated Brynn." He winced at the bitterness in his own voice. He didn't mean to be so sharp, but the memory still cut. "It also means that you cannot command me to stay. I'm leaving the state in your hands, and it will be in better care than it would be if you left it in mine."

Lady DeSilva grabbed his collar and forced him to look away from the map. "If something happens to you, I will . . ."

"I'm sure you won't be able to think of a punishment harsh enough."

She fidgeted with the crease in his shirt, smoothing her hands down his sleeves, trying to hide the tears glistening in her eyes. "I'm proud of you," she said finally. "You've honored the DeSilva name."

Pride filled his chest. It felt good to have done something right, but Dom simply couldn't accept the praise. "I sincerely hope that you will never, ever expect this much from me again. I have every intention of handing this responsibility to Rafi as soon as he returns."

"I'm sure," Lady DeSilva said with a laugh, then pressed a goodbye kiss to her son's cheek.

Four teams of two, eight of the DeSilvas' best soldiers, climbed into the wells and split off to four separate segments of Santiago. Three of the teams would provide a distraction, killing as many soldiers as possible, creating confusion, destroying food and weapons stores, and returning to the wells without getting caught.

Dom had joined Gesias and one other guard; they would come up closest to the ornate silk tent that sheltered the duke. The time for diplomacy had passed, and they would convince Belem to leave Santiago or die. It was a desperate plan. They all knew it.

Gesias led them through the tunnels, then free-climbed up the brick-sided well and disappeared over the lip. Dom waited, tense and impatient, staring up at the bucket and crank, and wishing he could see beyond.

A shadow appeared at the well's mouth and waved for Dom to move to the side. He exchanged a quick look with the other member of their team, then pressed himself against the wall an instant before a body fell over the side, sinking to the bottom and disappearing under the weight of weapons and light armor.

Dom knew that his decisions had killed men, he'd heard them scream and watched them burn, but seeing it from a distance and feeling a dead man's leg pressed against his own were two different things. Guilt and sorrow warred for a place in Dom's mind, but they lost to the sudden, overpowering awareness that he was alive. He stood for too long, staring at the lifeless hand that floated on the water's surface.

The other soldier jostled Dom, and for a moment he really *thought* about what he was doing.

Sneaking into the enemy camp in the middle of the night? This is crazy.

It is, but you can stay in the well with the dead man, or go face the men who are destroying your home. Choose.

Dom gripped the rope and hauled himself skyward.

They came up on the far side of the well and sheltered in its shadow. Gesias gave a quick rundown of their situation. They were deep into enemy territory, and the camp was quiet save for the snoring of men, exhausted after a day of battle and certain the dawn would hold victory for their duke.

Security was lax. Only the camp's perimeter was ringed with sentries, and two guards stood watch on the duke's tent. Gesias would take care of the guard in the back, and they'd enter through the rear door and eliminate whoever waited inside.

Moving on silent feet, they paused in the shadow of the tent closest to Belem's while Gesias loaded a small crossbow and yanked back the crank.

This was the moment everything depended on—Gesias's ability to take down the guard silently.

Dom took a breath and held it, eyes focused on the guard, on the dim light from the tent beyond. Wild energy danced in his fingertips as he eased his dagger out of its sheath. It took every ounce of his self-control to wait, wait, wait. . . .

The arrow flew and Dom dashed forward. If it missed, he would follow it up with a killing blow.

He didn't need to worry. The bolt punched through the man's throat, eliminating the possibility of a shout, but his armor would make a clatter as he fell. Dom caught the guard and eased him to the ground.

Gesias nodded his approval and then followed the other soldier under the tent's flap.

The interior was divided into a large center room and two smaller sleeping chambers on either side. Both were dark, but the distinct growl of sleep rumbled from the room on the right. Gesias signaled for their other crewmate to keep a lookout. Dom didn't wait for the command to follow.

His dagger was cool against his palm, but he felt a desperate need to warm the blade in Belem's blood. Moving silently, with Gesias hard on his heels, Dom entered the sleeping chamber. It, like the rest of the tent, didn't lack for comforts. Two braziers of glowing coals warmed the air around a long, low bed topped with silky furs and heaps of pillows. Bedside tables were littered with half-eaten food and melted candles, and an open chest showed an assortment of weapons.

Sleeping heavily in the middle of the bed was Belem, his chest bare save for King Wilhelm's crystal signet.

It would have been easy to kill him and flee, but it was too simple a death for the man who'd ripped that necklace off Johanna's throat and marched a foreign army onto DeSilva soil.

No. This man was going to suffer and then retreat with his tail between his legs.

Dom dropped onto the side of the bed and covered Belem's face with a hard hand. The duke woke with a jolt.

"I dare you to scream," Dom said, wedging his dagger under Belem's jowls. "Let's see how long you live after that."

Panic rolled off Belem, as potent as the bottle of wine that had spilled at his bedside. His eyes were wide, flitting from Dom's face to the weapon's hilt.

"If you raise your voice, it will be the last noise you ever make." Dom let the knife's edge bite into Belem's flesh, illustrating his point. The duke didn't blink, but Dom sensed his agreement and removed his hand from the duke's mouth.

"A DeSilva. A man of honor." Belem's breath was toxic with alcohol fumes. He tried to sound confident, but Dom could see the pulse hammering at the duke's temple. "Are you going to kill a defenseless man?"

"Do you think I care that you're unarmed? Do you think it will stop me from slicing through that fat gizzard? I am not my father. I am not my brother. I will not hesitate to cut you apart to prove my point." Dom leaned closer, his face almost touching Belem's. His hand shook with rage, and it nicked the duke's neck afresh. "You will leave my land tomorrow. You will issue an apology. You will agree never to attack Santiago again."

"Or?" Belem choked out, spittle collecting at the corners of his mouth.

"Or I slit your throat now and then come after every member of your family." And in that moment Dom meant it. He'd burn Belem's estate to embers if that meant Santiago went casualty-free.

"Listen," Belem said, eyes shifting to Gesias, who stood guarding Dom's back. "You have Princess Adriana. I want to see her on the throne and the distribution of power to remain the same. We keep our states, trade agreements—"

"You fool! We don't *have* her." Dom eased up enough to snap the green pendant's chain and tuck it into one of his pockets. "Didn't your spy tell you as much?"

"My spies didn't know where the princess was, but that didn't mean you hadn't secreted her away somewhere." Belem's throat undulated with a heavy swallow, and his eyes flickered to the side, held, and then back to Dom. "If I'd known what I had that day in the forest . . ."

It was the pause that made Dom check over his shoulder as a sword burst through Gesias's abdomen. Belem reared up with all the force of a mad bull, tipping the bed. Dom dropped to a defensive crouch, positioning himself between the naked duke and . . .

"Ceara." Dom took an extra step back as the underlord from Camaçari kicked Gesias's body off the end of his sword.

"Lord Dom, so pleasant to see you," Ceara said, wiping his blade on Gesias's back. Even as blood pooled around his feet, Ceara acted like finding enemy soldiers in the command tent was a minor irritation. "You look better than your brother."

"Thank you." Dom didn't rise to the bait, but whirled his blade casually, a trick Johanna had taught him, to draw an enemy's focus. "I suppose I should take that as a compliment." Then he spun the dagger around his finger, hoping it disguised his desperate need to hear about Rafi.

"Blood poisoning." Ceara wrinkled his nose as if he could smell the rank wounds that would result in such a condition. "He refused my assistance. You DeSilvas have such a problem with pride. You were aware of that, no?"

Dom raised his eyebrows at Belem's naked posterior as the

dimpled duke scrambled to his weapon stash. "It's difficult to be humble when no one else can compare."

"Why don't you stop playing with your little knife and prove it." Ceara stepped over Gesias's body, swinging his sword in a full arc. Dom stepped into the blow and the blades clashed. Metal screeched as Ceara's blade slid down and caught on the hilt of Dom's weapon. With leverage in Ceara's favor, Dom kicked out, catching Ceara in the groin.

"Guards!" Belem screamed as he located a sword. "Intruder! Intruder!" He moved to block the door, eyes darting between the still-hunched Ceara and the opening beyond.

"I think this is where the DeSilva line ends." Ceara straightened slowly, all his arrogance replaced by cold fury. "I'll share the details of your death with your mother right before I break her neck."

"Good luck with that," Dom said as he spun the dagger again. "You're going to need it." He looked bored, idly whipping his knife around, but his palms were damp and sweat prickled along his ribs. He needed to get out of this tent alive, to get back to the estate and stand with his people.

Shouts were raised outside the tent; soldiers were approaching.

"Maybe I'll take a sampling of all Santiago has to offer." Ceara raised his sword to engage, and Dom flipped the dagger so it landed blade-first in his palm. "I'll start with that little maid—"

Ceara's words cut off as Dom's blade thudded into his stomach. He looked down, conceit melting into a look of surprise. His blade fell from his hand and he tumbled after it.

A soldier stepped into the tent at Belem's side and raised a crossbow. Dom dove to the ground, sheltering behind the bed as the bolt flew over his head. His breath came in erratic pants as he drew his small knife, sliced a gap in the tent wall, and scrambled through the hole. A burning line cut across his hip, but he rolled forward, sliding in leaf debris.

The camp had come alive, men dashing from their tents, voices raised, and then a bugle sounded from the south side. The soldier who followed Dom out straightened and looked toward the sound. A second bugle, and then a new call. A sound Dom would have recognized anywhere—the deep ring of a shell horn.

The soldier stared down at Dom, raised his weapon, and then disappeared as a cannonball blasted into his legs.

Dom froze, watching as the ball bounced, pummeling through the tent wall, and then exploded. Shouts turned to screams of terror, men rushed toward the tent and away, a second volley of cannonballs burst through the camp, and Dom lay on the ground, unable to move.

He blinked once, twice. His heart kicked in his chest and his brain registered what it was hearing.

Shell horns. Cannons. Surprise attack.

Uncle Fernando.

Ignoring the burn across his side, Dom scrambled to a crouch, took a half dozen stumbling steps, and fell headfirst into the well.

Chapter 70

Johanna

An army had been sighted; a battalion of Inimigo's soldiers, sixteen wagons carrying collared slaves and supplies, and two carriages, all moving east from Cruzamento.

"We're outnumbered," whispered James. The young Firesword had been quiet since learning of Julia's death, but he was taking the role as the captain of their small squad seriously.

"And overmatched," Yara added. "We've got one hundred people with no fighting experience and no magic."

"We have Rafi." Johanna met Rafi's stare across the fire. He looked so young and vulnerable, the perfect hero contemplating his last night in Santarem. Perhaps his last night ever. Her heart thudded a broken rhythm in her chest, limping along with a dozen wounds. She pressed the heel of her hand against the sore spot, as if she could ease the ache.

Rafi's expression shifted to concern and he mimicked her pose. The action made her pain ten times worse. She closed her eyes to break the connection, to blot out the worry on his face, and tried to listen to what Jacaré had to say.

"The odds aren't as bad as they seem," he explained. He took a stick and drew the road ahead of them, adding some circles to either side of the trail. "To the south is the village of Vicente, and off the road are some open-faced copper mines. They're abandoned, falling into ruin, but we can use them like foxholes, hiding and popping out when they least expect us."

He laid out his plan, and Johanna heard the words, but they washed over her without sinking in. She felt separated from the group, a distant observer, and no matter how she tried to engage herself in conversation, her mind kept dashing to other places.

Rafi sat next to Jacaré—they'd been plotting as they traveled. Throughout the journey the clouds had swirled, the wind had picked up, a boulder had rolled across their path. Rafi had been practicing, and while Johanna doubted Jacaré was the kind of teacher to offer much praise, his mouth had looked a little less angry as the day passed.

Unlike the rest of the group, and despite using magic all day, Rafi seemed energetic and refreshed. His long fingers drew lines that represented their defenses and offensive tactics. She nodded at all the right places, but her thoughts drifted to something else: Joshua and Michael.

They'd always been mischievous and usually silly, but a few times they'd come close to real trouble. Like when they'd played with the Skylighters' powders and tried to sneak into the animal cages in Performers' Camp. Her own troupe didn't have animals. Her father didn't trust that the big cats and monkeys wouldn't follow their natural instincts—he'd seen too many accidents during his time—but maybe the best animal trainers among the Performers were like Barrata to some small degree. Their gift with animals was really some unconscious use of their *essência*.

Like her own gift with Storyspinning.

She got up and left the fireside in the middle of the conversation, her thoughts spinning like a wagon wheel in a mudhole.

Fireswords were one obvious weapon. Jacaré had already talked to the Skylighters about ways to use their powders to blow things up. The animal trainers' mountain cats and jaguars would be messy but were a possibility. What could the rest of them do?

Too bad I can't talk our enemies into submission. She almost laughed at the thought. *Or maybe I could distract them. I'm good at that. I...*

She hurried back to the campfire. "I have an idea," she said to Jacaré, her voice breathless. "A way for Storyspinners to help in the foxholes."

Chapter 71

Rafi

Battles were supposed to be fought on wide-open plains, with careful lines of infantry and cavalry. Flags were raised, representatives from each group rode to the center of the field, and a last effort to broker peace was made. Or final insults were hurled.

There should have been shouts rising from both armies as the men rallied themselves into a frenzy. He should have known the face of his enemy, been able to identify where the leader stood behind his lines, and sent a specially trained group of men to flank his adversary's position.

Instead Rafi squatted in an open pit mine with twenty soberly dressed Performers. The mine was like a well, a gaping vertical shaft with a bottom far enough from the surface to be cloaked in utter darkness. The terraced walls were pockmarked at irregular intervals where horizontal tunnels connected one mine to another.

Johanna had disappeared into one of those holes a few moments before dawn with half a dozen Storyspinners and a handful of Fireswords at her back. He'd wished for a chance to hold her close before her plans were set into motion.

He swallowed against the sudden dryness of his throat. *That's all right,* he tried to convince himself. *I will see her again, and hold her close, and tell her—*

A whistle sounded, the note high and shrill, mimicking the call of the red-bellied macaw. The enemy had been sighted.

"Lord DeSilva?" The Performer at his side, a small man named Ursu, who had the largest capacity for *essência*, touched Rafi's arm softly. "That's the signal."

"Thank you." Rafi reached for the power and it fell easily into his hands. In his mind's eye he saw it as a glowing rope that he could manipulate into any shape. He wove the power around himself, forming a bright barrier of electricity beyond his position. It stretched across the road in a crescent shape, encompassing the two nearest mines and their hidden occupants.

Pressing his hands against the gritty gray-black stone around the top of the mine, Rafi lifted himself over the edge. Alone, a glowing figure on the horizon, he walked to the center of the road and held out both arms.

It was time to put a face to the enemy.

Chapter 72

Pira

Pira had been given the "privilege" of riding inside the carriage with Sapo and Vibora. She sat on the bench across from the Keepers, eyes half closed, head resting on the joint between the walls.

Her captors sat side by side throughout the journey from Cruzamento, but Vibora turned her entire body toward the window, watching the passing terrain. Sapo alternated between looking out his window and staring at Vibora's back in a way that made Pira's skin crawl.

Soldiers rode in half-armor—breastplates, helmets, and gauntlets—as if waiting for an ambush over each of the hills or in the scrubby forest that patched the landscape. Pira hoped whoever stood against them knew that these men weren't the worst things they would be facing.

A captain, Pira guessed by his plumed helmet, rode up and trotted alongside the carriage window. "Sir? I think we've found them, or they've found us. There's one man standing on top of the next rise, blocking the trail."

"One man?" Sapo said as he pushed open the door, with Vibora close behind him. Pira followed tight on their heels. She hadn't been commanded to stay, so she didn't. Sapo called the line to a halt and took the spyglass the captain offered.

"Who is it?" Vibora asked, stepping close to Sapo. Pira hung back a few steps, as a good servant might, out of the way but not out of earshot.

"I don't know, but he's the one who absorbed the *essência*." A hint of worry entered Sapo's voice. "He's not one of us, that's for sure."

Vibora took the glass out of Sapo's hand. "That's Rafael DeSilva. Interesting that he ended up with the power."

"It doesn't matter. He can't possibly know how to use it." Sapo yelled down the line for Críquete. The waiflike Keeper approached, her shawl, as always, pulled tightly around her. "This boy, what have you seen that involves him?"

"Many things." She jolted, her face twitching as Sapo shocked her through the collar.

"Specifics, Críquete."

She exhaled; her eyes drifted over Vibora and Pira before focusing on Sapo once again. "He'll call on power from both the Earth and the Sky, but this battle will be a thing from his nightmares."

Sapo gave a deep, vibrant laugh and pulled Vibora close. "His nightmares will be our dreams come true." He kissed her sloppily on the lips, though she didn't return his affection with much ardor. "Chill a bottle of wine, Críquete. I expect this battle to be quick."

He raised one hand as if to stroke Vibora's cheek, but opened his fingers with a sudden flick. Vines shot up from the ground. Thick, twisting creepers, bright green and studded with thorns, snapped around Vibora's legs.

With a scream she fell backward and tried to scramble away, but her feet were hobbled by the vines. "What are you doing?"

Pira felt her *essência* drain as Vibora used it to counter Sapo's attack. Flames licked up the vines, but they didn't burn. Then ice crystals glazed the dirt around Vibora's feet and whitened the stalk of the growing plant. With a snap of Sapo's fingers, a flash of heat melted the ice, turning the dirt into a puddle of mud.

Vibora couldn't compete; she didn't have control of enough slaves or *essência*. Vines wrapped around her hips and spread across her ribs, forcing her upright, encasing her like a bug in its shell.

The air around Vibora crackled with a sudden burst of purple-red light—a lightning blast that Sapo absorbed before it could hit him. Leaves exploded from the vines, twining around Vibora's head in a helmet of greenery.

"This," Sapo said, pointing toward the hill, "is the result of your failure." Without a word, a slave from one of the nearest wagons climbed over the side and stumbled to his master, dragging a bag that clinked as it hit the ground.

"If you had only found the princess, if Barrata had been able to accomplish *one* task . . ."

"No, Sapo, please." Vibora flailed against her living cage, blood splattering as she tore her skin on the extended thorns.

Sapo drew out the moment, opening the bag's mouth, sorting through its contents slowly, ignoring Vibora's pleas. Finally he selected one shining collar and held it up to the sunlight. The perfectly smooth surface reflected the light like a well-polished blade.

A blade would be better, Pira thought, struggling to stay on her feet. *Dead would be better than being under Sapo's inflluence.*

For as awful as Vibora was, Sapo was infinitely worse. Pira stumbled closer, for the moment under her own control, fueled only by pity and fear. Was there anything she could do to help?

A small hand fell on her arm. "No," Críquete whispered. "Not yet."

The seer must have read the disbelief on Pira's face, because she added, "Your chance will come, but this is not it."

Sapo spun the collar around his finger a few times, watching Vibora's frantic struggles.

"You need me," she shrieked, flinging her head from side to side. A thorn grazed her cheek, opening a slash across her face, and blood dripped down her throat, splattering the leaves like red rain. "You don't know all the secrets of the beryllium, of how the collars work."

"In a few hours it won't matter." He parted the leaves with a gentle hand, holding the collar wide. "You can be my head slave, still in charge of your own little cadre of followers. And with you and the boy, no one will be able to stand against me."

Vibora screamed one last time, and then the collar clicked shut.

CHAPTER 73

JOHANNA

The whistle sounded, and Johanna edged toward the tunnel's mouth. A few passageways connected the pits beneath the road, but most of them had collapsed with disuse.

The mine Johanna had been assigned was the smallest, perhaps eight feet across at its widest point and five times as deep. Terraces supported by half-rotten framework disappeared into the darkness. The openings were unstable, the edges overgrown with long meadow grasses and crumbling inward under too much weight.

So far Inimigo's cavalry had kept clear of the holes. One wrong step, and the horses and their riders would tumble over the side.

The sparkling light of a shield glowed behind Johanna's position, barricading the road that led into Performers' Camp and blocking access to the valley. Johanna and the people hiding in the mines were beyond its protection. Rafi couldn't extend the shield that far, and hold it for long, without draining his strength.

She pressed her back against the mine wall and tried to get an angle so she could see over its edge. Rafi was too far away to see clearly, but he stood tall and brave at the center of the road, midway up the hill; it was the perfect opening to the epic she was already composing in her head.

Like a beacon, young Rafael faced the approaching horde. Solitary and brave, blue light dancing off his fingers, he repelled the evil armies of the Nata.

Her teeth sank deep into her bottom lip. Everyone she loved had been taken from her in one way or another. Telling him how much she cared in a voice laced with *essência* seemed the fastest way to curse herself, turning a sweet love story into a heartbreaking lament.

It was better to keep silent than to speak their story aloud.

The soldiers in glittering armor, silver except for the golden fist emblazoned on the center of their chests, trotted past her position. They spread across the field in uneven clumps, avoiding the mine openings that speckled the ground like oversize anthills. The ends of the line curved in an effort to stop another group from flanking them. They were prepared for an attack, but no one would be ready for the trickery Johanna had planned.

Rafi yelled, warning Inimigo's soldiers to stand down or they would be killed. They rode forward anyway. On the trumpet's call they raised their bows and released their arrows with a musical twang.

Johanna closed her eyes, too terrified to watch. She knew the shield was there to protect Rafi, but it seemed a flimsy thing compared with the razor tips of hundreds of soaring arrows.

They struck the glowing barrier with the wet thunk of a knife sinking into a ripe avocado. Her pulse raced in her ears as she waited for one of the Performers to tell her that it was over, that one of the arrows had struck home, that Rafi was gone. Instead she heard the muffled surprise of the soldiers and dared to peek over the mine's lip.

The arrows hung in the air, frozen in the sky. Rafi was safe. Johanna sagged against the mine wall, sending a prayer of thanks skyward.

Despite the result of the first attempt, the second group of soldiers approached, their pikes leveled at the shield.

Their leader raised his hand, but before he could lower it, Johanna nodded to her friends and they angled long ironwood tubes toward the line of soldiers. "Now!" They each stomped on the end of a bulb attached to the tubes, and clouds of Storyspinners' smoke blasted onto the field from all the open mines. The powder itself wasn't harmful, but it hung in the air, a dense fog, blotting out the horses and their riders.

Now, Rafi.

A blast of lightning stabbed into the haze, setting the entire thing aflame. It became a hail of sparks, landing on skin and coat, armor and saddle. Horses reared and screamed; riders fell in a clatter of shields and crunching bones.

Johanna and her small crew waited, anxious and impatient, for the last of the sparks to fall, then dashed over the edges of the mines and into the smoking fray. Groups of Performers swarmed out of their holes, fading in and out of the miasma like specters in a nightmare. Each was supposed to take down one rider and return to the safety of the mine.

The Firesword nearest Johanna lit his sword, and a steady flame licked along its length. He held it out to her, and she lit the tip of her tar-soaked arrow. "Go!" he shouted, slashing the nearest animal along the hamstring. Johanna's arrow found its target, puncturing through layers of steel and into the man's belly.

Her crew crept forward, running, leaping, tumbling across the field, using their agility to avoid contact with the disoriented soldiers. They dropped into a mine before the smoke cleared and their enemies could follow.

She prepared the next round of powder and prayed her diversion gave Jacaré the time he needed.

Chapter 74

Jacaré

Jacaré always called it battle fever. It struck him moments, sometimes hours, before a fight was expected to happen. His heart thumped, blood rushing to his extremities, fueling the muscles that would hack and slice and destroy.

For some soldiers battle fever became battle frenzy, an uncontrolled fury that turned their vision red and made them susceptible to mistakes.

But Jacaré didn't make mistakes in battle. The fever pulsed out of his veins before the fighting began and was replaced by something colder and infinitely more honed, dedicated to sharp, precise actions. His emotions, his anger, his horror, were buried under layers of crystalline ice. He could see what he was doing—cutting cleanly across one man's midsection, continuing a spin to block a sword, snapping his elbow into an unprotected nose as he hurried across the field—but it was all part of a well-rehearsed dance. It was something he *did.* Not something he thought about.

He focused on his objectives: get behind enemy lines and find the Nata's source of power. They had to weaken Sapo enough to defeat him. It would likely mean killing innocent people if Jacaré couldn't remove the collars by himself, but it was the only way.

Across the field he saw Johanna drop into an open mine and disappear. The next blast of powder would come soon, and Jacaré had to be well on his way to the edge of Sapo's shield.

Sticking close to the ground, he scurried through the trampled meadow and past the indentations of closed mines, heading northwest, cloaked in a twisted bit of light. It reflected the weeds around him, turning him into one more patch of windblown grass. The ruins of Roraima were on his right, the Citadel looming behind it. Sapo's shield was centralized at the middle of his line of soldiers. The leader was hiding there somewhere, but he wasn't visible.

Jacaré choked down the rush of heat, the need to cut off the head of the monster. But that wasn't Jacaré's assignment. At least not yet.

Chapter 75

Rafi

Rafi didn't know what he was doing. He knew how to make a shield. He knew how to throw a lightning bolt and a fireball. He knew how to make the wind blow from the east, if it suited his purposes. Jacaré assured him he was doing well with so little training, but Rafi knew it wasn't good enough.

It was just as Jacaré had said. Rafi was holding an impeccably crafted sword and had only the barest knowledge of what could be done with it. He could stab and block, but there was a significant difference between knowing those things were possible and mastering the best way to do them.

Sapo was a master.

Every single bolt of lightning, ball of flame, and harpoon of ice was pinpointed, smashing directly into Rafi's shield or at its ever-shrinking edges. A blast of wind had blown away the smoke from Johanna's second powder trick, and though the enemy's numbers had been cut down by a third, they continued to advance.

Rafi had magical might, but his might couldn't stand against Sapo's mind.

"Lord DeSilva." It was Ursu again. He pointed to one of the open mines. "Look."

A group of bowmen had dismounted and formed a tight circle around the pits and fired their arrows into its mouth.

It was the mine Johanna and her friends had slipped into. Rafi tried to divide his power to maintain his shield and send a bolt of lightning toward the bowmen, but his control slid through his fingers. He shook out the tension in his hands, as if he'd actually held the power in his palms instead of in his mind, and flexed his knuckles before trying again.

As the soldiers planted a flag into the ground, Rafi managed to direct one more blast of lightning without dropping his shield. Four men fell to the field, smoke rising from their bodies, but it was too late. The purple banner flapped in an unnatural breeze; a trumpet blared. The bowmen all rushed away from the mine's edge, dove to the ground, and covered their heads. An instant later the pit slammed shut, closing like a mouth, swallowing the Performers who were inside. And burying Rafi's heart with it.

"Johanna." He breathed her name. Frantic, his eyes scanning the field, he sought a specific Performer dressed in black.

Was she in there? Was she trapped?

Reaching a hand toward the pit, he tried to force the mine to reopen. A geyser of rock shot into the air, pelting the nearby soldiers, but the effort to move that much earth was grueling.

"Ursu!"

A hand landed on his back, then another and another. Rafi felt a small burst of energy, and he opened the mine's mouth to half its earlier circumference.

An earthquake rolled, men and horses falling. Like a whip cracking, it followed the line of the road, smacking into Rafi's shield and knocking him and his helpers off their feet.

The bright blue light wavered, but Rafi managed to regain control of the shield before it fell completely.

His hands shook. His heart thudded in his chest, but it was a slow, heavy beat, like the footsteps of an exhausted man.

Where was Johanna?

CHAPTER 76

PIRA

Six guards. Two at the tent door. One at each corner. Pira stepped over the bodies of the half-conscious slaves. They barely fluttered an eyelid at her passing, except for Críquete, who shifted to pillow her head more comfortably on her arm.

All the slaves were exhausted, their power being drained to fuel the battle raging beyond the tent doors. All of them except Pira. Her mind was unencumbered by Vibora's—or worse, Sapo's—presence. Her body and power were hers to control.

In the last moments, when Vibora could have used the dregs of her slaves' power to make one last attempt to fight off Sapo, she had let Pira go. The other slaves who were connected to Vibora lay on the tent's floor, sometimes thrashing as if against a bad dream, their eyes shut and their breathing shallow.

But Pira was free.

It's some twisted sort of self-preservation, Pira convinced herself as she crawled to the edge of the tent. *Vibora's a slave now, and if she expects me to free her after everything she's done, she's dead wrong.*

Ignoring the flash of guilt, she surveyed the soldiers' shadows against the tent walls and tried to determine the fastest way to get past them.

"Good luck," Críquete whispered. "Did you bring the hammer handle?"

Stricken by a sudden sense of dread, Pira froze, her hands trembling on the canvas's edge. "I left it with Leão."

"Oh, Pira." The Seer gave an exhausted sigh. "Go to him. Now. Retrieve it. You'll need it."

Pira knew she was a good fighter, but she'd be pitting herself against very uneven odds. Perhaps it was weakness to give in to her fear; still, she asked, "Will we survive the day?"

"I know this," Críquete answered, her voice small and tremulous. "If you go into battle with fear in your heart, you've already given the enemy an advantage."

A sense of calm washed over Pira at the familiar words. "Jacaré used to say that."

"He learned it from Tex." Críquete's eyes closed. "He was a wise man."

Reaching back, she touched the Seer's arm. "I'll come back for you."

"Yes," she whispered. "Yes, I hope you will."

"I *will*." Pira took a deep breath, forcing the tension out of her limbs, finding the clearheadedness she'd lacked under Vibora's control.

A guard stood with his feet spread wide and his back almost flush against the canvas. Pira slipped under the material, coming up directly behind him, and looped her arms around his neck. He was dead before he even registered her presence. She took one step back under the man's sudden weight and brushed the tent wall.

The vibrating material alerted the guard at the next corner. "Hey!" He stepped toward her and whisked his weapon out of its sheath. "Stop!"

Pira slipped a dagger from the dead guard's belt and threw it into the space between the approaching man's breastplate and chin strap. He grasped the blade and tumbled forward.

A ball of condensed lightning slammed into the shield that stretched across the camp's length. The sudden brightness nearly blinded Pira to the next soldier's attack, but her affinity had returned. She ducked under the sword raised to run her through and came up inside her assailant's guard. Her right elbow obliterated his nose, and her left fist knocked his teeth down his throat.

She shook the blood off her fist and smiled. Light, it felt good to be free.

Six fireballs smashed into Sapo's shield, revealing for a moment its careful meshlike design and leaving it unaffected.

Lord Rafi's attacks would never succeed while Sapo's shield held, and Pira knew the quickest way to tear it down.

She turned toward the wagons and ran.

Chapter 77

Jacaré

The armor was sticky, the breastplate too short for his torso, but Jacaré hoped that the blood that marred the golden emblem on his chest and the arrow shaft stuck in the metal would help him sneak past the last lines of defense.

Sapo had built his shield so that people and things could press through it without injury, but it stopped anything of magical means. Reserve soldiers and medical teams waited in anxious groups for a signal that would send them out to face the battle's results. Jacaré headed due north, cutting far beyond the shield before stumbling into Sapo's camp.

He was spotted by a medic, a balding man in a spotless gray tunic, who rushed to Jacaré's side. "How bad is it?"

Jacaré hunched over, causing his stolen helmet to slip farther over his face. "Just a flesh wound." He held his bloodstained fingers around the arrow's shaft, completing his performance.

"It's a miracle, friend. You must be Keeper-blessed."

Jacaré managed a nod, but his eyes darted around the line, searching for the person responsible for all this disaster and madness.

The bald medic escorted him through the camp, and no one paid him a second glance.

The plan was simple, and so far succeeding. Find someone with no *essência* that he could force to free the slaves. Then locate Sapo. Blast him in the head. Battle over.

Jacaré kept his perusal of the camp secretive. Tents, soldiers, piles of extra weapons, then something caught his eye. Something that froze his feet to the ground.

The medic caught Jacaré's elbow. "I should have called for a stretcher."

The man's words floated across the surface of Jacaré's mind like leaves in a cyclone, small and inconsequential. Nothing compared with the storm of Jacaré's emotions. Standing on a wagon's seat, her hair hanging long and thick over her shoulders, was the only woman Jacaré had ever loved.

Vibora.

He'd watched her die, hundreds of years ago. Stabbed by a Mage while they were on an assignment. An assignment Jacaré had convinced her to take. Her death was blood he'd never been able to wash from his hands—hands that were continually being bloodied in an effort to stop innocent deaths like hers from happening again.

And now he could feel power emanating from her as she worked to support the opposition. He'd known for weeks that Vibora had become the enemy, but until that moment, he hadn't really *felt* it.

Clutching the arrow's shaft, he ripped it from the armor. It had been part of his disguise, but her duplicity hurt worse than any real arrow wound.

"Vibora!" he shouted, his *essência* rushing to the surface. People turned, some faces white with surprise and furrowed in concern, others flushed with anger. But Jacaré saw none of them. He was swept away from the battle, away from his duty, like a stick in an unconquerable current, and propelled toward her.

The upward slant of her cheekbones matched the angle of her eyes; the rose-colored lips formed his name as he approached. She'd changed, more than he had, but there was no question. This was his Vibora.

She raised a hand, as if she could stop his progress, her face set in the same lines of panic that had been stamped in his nightmares. "Jacaré, no."

Two soldiers stepped to block his path. He cut them down with no compunction, striding forward, taking down the next two who stepped in his way. He'd lived for her. He'd killed for her. He'd devoted his whole life to honor her memory.

A barrier snapped into place around them, blocking out the rest of the soldiers rushing to her aid, like an invisible hand had shoved them all away. It was a neat piece of magic; something he wouldn't have been able to do even at full strength—something Vibora should *never* have been able to do.

She vaulted over the wagon's side, moving in jerks and starts, one arm wrapped around her body, her other hand gripping her throat.

Despite three hundred years of heartache and the fresher wounds of betrayal, he rushed to her, catching her as she fell against him, their bodies connecting from sternum to thigh.

"Jacaré." She said his name again, and it shuddered through him, curdling the blood in his veins. "You . . . shouldn't have come. Not now. You have to run."

His mouth opened to ask what had happened, what she was doing, what was *wrong* with her, but he couldn't pluck the right words free.

"You have to go." Her hand dropped, revealing the silver-white collar.

The band around her throat filled him with a sort of sick relief—a trembling hope that some of her actions could be explained away. He wanted to believe that this Vibora was the same person who had once fought at his side and could never be his enemy. "I've just found you," he said, reaching for the collar and knowing he wouldn't be able to remove it. "I will not let you go again."

"We're in agreement, then." The voice was familiar, musical, and nearly as painful to hear as Vibora's. "I have no intention of letting her go anywhere. Ever."

Jacaré had been so focused on Vibora that he hadn't noticed her companion. The bench was small, the seat narrow. Sapo must have been pressed right up against her for them both to fit. That knowledge, more than anything else, broke through the wall of ice.

Battle fever rushed in, making Jacaré forget that he was outnumbered and overmatched. He stepped in front of Vibora, his sword and *essência* ready to bring Sapo down.

"Ah, the great Jacaré. Alive after all these years," Sapo said as he jumped off the wagon's seat with leisurely grace. "After all these *centuries*, and I never even suspected that she held on to that little love affair you shared at the academy." He gave a slow round of applause, as if showing appreciation at the end of a show. "I suppose the Performers have it right. Acting *is* in our blood."

Jacaré let a bolt of lightning fly, but it rebounded off Sapo's small personal shield, making the air around him shudder.

"I heard that you were weak, but that's embarrassing." Sapo gave an enormous, gloating grin. "It must have been hard to live all these years with only a remnant of the power you once had. We should put you out of your misery. Vibora, love, why don't you start?"

Her arm rose stiffly before flexing, her wrist bent at an awkward angle, like a disjointed marionette. One finger uncurled, bending so far that it bowed in the middle, and stopped to point at Jacaré's heart.

"That's fitting," Sapo agreed, as if he hadn't manipulated her actions. "He certainly broke *your* heart. Time to destroy his."

Vibora's mouth twisted with silent horror as fire blasted out of her extended arm. Jacaré dove to the right, fetching up against the barrier that separated them from the rest of the army.

"You missed." Sapo gave an irritated grunt. "Let me show you how it's done." With a flick of his hand he tossed Jacaré to the enclosure's far side. The invisible wall absorbed his weight and he bounced off of it, landing on his feet. Sapo hurled attack after attack—fire, ice, air, fire, earth. Jacaré managed to avoid them by raising his magical shield at precise moments, but he knew it was only a matter of time before his efforts fell short and one of Sapo's blows landed.

His eyes darted to Vibora. Her body was visibly quaking in its efforts to fight off Sapo's control, but otherwise she was out of harm's way.

"While this is quite enjoyable," Sapo said, yawning dramatically, "I have some important matters to attend to."

A sudden rush of *essência* made Jacaré's hair stand on end. Sapo's next attack would not fail.

Jacaré raised his shield, expecting it to collapse under the force of the blow, but what bore him to the ground was something solid and soft. Under the scent of smoke and sweat were the sweet fragrance of summer gardenias and the memory of a body sleeping against his side. His sword fell somewhere to his right, but he didn't reach for it. Instead his hand sought out the valley of a waist, where it used to rest so naturally.

"Vibora," he whispered, fingers trailing up her back, reaching for her shoulder, and sliding off the wet pulp where it should have been. He sat up quickly, cradling her body as it tumbled limply across his lap.

"Jacaré." She said his name with a weak smile, blood marring her white teeth. "Why didn't you come for me?"

"I did, of course I did! But by the time I made it, your body . . . you were already gone."

"I'm sorry."

"As am I. . . ."

Her head lolled back, her eyes drifted shut, her lashes stilled against her cheeks.

Jacaré had convinced himself that there was nothing crueler than losing her the first time.

He was wrong.

Chapter 78

Rafi

Rafi volleyed six rounds of fireballs into the enemy's shield, only to see it shimmer under his assault. It should have felt like a victory, knowing his attacks were making some difference, but his attention was split between the approaching soldiers and the collapsed mine. Ursu's hand was on Rafi's right shoulder and Yara's on his left. They lent him whatever strength they had; it didn't feel like very much against what they were facing.

Layer after layer of dirt fountained into the air, and so far they'd recovered two bodies, both dressed in close-fitting Performers' gear. Neither moved.

He wouldn't be able to keep searching for survivors without putting the rest of the Performers at risk. Nausea struck, making sweat bead across his upper lip, when he thought of leaving people, leaving Johanna, buried alive.

A boy appeared at Rafi's side, shouting something about another army approaching. Rafi heard the words but couldn't afford to split his attention.

Then he heard Belem's name.

"Wait," he said, trying to process the information and continue his magical efforts. "What did you say about Duke Belem?"

The boy was an apprentice Firesword, wearing a yellow sash around his waist, with a spyglass instead of a sword slung through it. He was breathing heavily, having run from one of the lookout points near the shield's farthest edge. "An army is approaching behind Sapo's troops. They're carrying Lord Belem's banner."

The strands of power slipped through Rafi's fingers. His shield started to crumple, but he caught it at the last possible moment. "They came from the south?"

"Yes, Lord Rafi. There aren't many of them, but they've got more than a dozen cannons on wheels."

Yara gave Rafi an encouraging squeeze, but it didn't do anything to stop the fear winding tight around his stomach. Had Belem's troops blown through Santiago? Was his homeland in ruins? Were Dom and his mother safe? "Are they headed toward us?"

"No, sir," the boy said, cringing when a sudden lightning bolt crackled over their heads. "They're moving west, toward Sapo's left flank."

"What?" Ursu asked, as confused as Rafi. "That doesn't make any sense. You're sure they aren't moving toward *our* flank?"

"Yes, sir."

"Maybe they're reinforcements," Yara suggested.

Rafi shook his head, trying to guess what Belem had in mind. "Send the signal."

"But, Lord DeSilva—"

"We need to give Performers' Camp as much time as possible. Tell them to stick to the coast, but have them bypass Santiago." The words tasted of ash and failure. "Tell them to head for Impreza. Fernando won't turn them away."

CHAPTER 79

JACARÉ

Vibora's lips were lightly parted, her cheeks still pink. Jacaré shifted her body in his arms so the side of her head rested against his shoulder. If he closed his eyes, he could almost pretend she was sleeping. He'd lie down and stay beside her for however much time Mother Lua gave him.

A high-pitched whistle rose, followed by another round of applause. The sounds punctured holes in Jacaré's despair, which drained away, leaving a viscous layer of fury behind.

"By the look on your face, Jacaré, I feel like I'd be doing you a favor to put you out of your misery." Sapo took a step closer and folded his arms behind his back. "But that's not my plan, you see. I'm going to collar you, like the rest of the Keepers I've captured, and then I'll use your power to continue fueling mine. You'll help destroy all the people you've worked so hard to save."

Jacaré pressed a kiss to Vibora's cooling brow and lowered her body to the ground.

"You can stay on your knees," Sapo said, reaching for a shining collar that hung from his belt. "It will make this so much easier to snap on. And let's be honest—with Belem sworn to me, his troops on his way here to clean up the rest of the Performers, Inimigo foolish enough to think I need him, and the princess cowering on the other side of that shield—it's over. The battle has been won."

Before Sapo could turn and call to one of the awestruck guards waiting beyond their little bubble of air, Jacaré shot a narrow tunnel of ice into Sapo's side. It bounced off the thin personal shield Sapo maintained around his body, but he staggered. The congenial smile fell from his face, replaced by something chillingly dark. "And here I thought you'd given up."

"I haven't changed that much since the academy, Sapo." Jacaré kicked his sword into the air and caught the hilt with practiced skill. "Let's see if you've learned anything."

"You really think I'm going to fight you?" Sapo snorted. "I'm going to destroy you."

"You're welcome to try." Jacaré could feel his pulse in his fingertips; his breath was coming in rapid puffs. He'd never be able to win, but Sapo was supporting three shields: the giant barrier spanning the length of the camp, the bubble that kept the other soldiers away, and the small shield around his body. If Jacaré could draw Sapo's attention for a while, it would give Rafi and the other Performers a chance to retreat from the soldiers on the field.

Sapo cracked his neck before reaching for the two-handed sword slung over his back. "Your *essência* will be useful, even if you are handless, and footless, and tongueless. Your sister has become very adept at keeping invalids alive."

The last word hadn't left his lips when Jacaré struck, raining concussive blows of fire in counterpoint to the slashes of his blade. Each time they came in contact with Sapo's shield, the air shimmered like a heat mirage.

Sapo's attacks were slower, almost unwieldy in their power, but each hit that landed on Jacaré's shield nearly knocked him to the ground. It was only a matter of time before his shield vanished and Sapo's blows landed on Jacaré's unprotected flesh.

He managed to dodge a blast of fire by falling to his knees. The ball hit above his head, making the barrier shudder.

Sapo growled at his failure, and then sudden surprise crossed his face. He dropped one hand from his sword's hilt and pressed it against his bicep. Jacaré hadn't scored a hit, but Sapo reeled as if wounded.

The shield protecting the camp flickered like summer lightning, then dissolved, and the small barricade that kept their fight separate from the rest of the camp winked out. Cannon fire rang in the distance, and a ball bounced through the camp before smashing into the wagon Sapo and Vibora had been sitting in. Soldiers scattered, others crouched, unsure if they should be more afraid of the cannon fire or the Keeper who commanded them.

"What is Belem doing?" Sapo looked behind him, confusion shifting to anger.

Jacaré pressed the small advantage, throwing himself into a forward roll, coming to one knee at Sapo's side, and slashing diagonally. The blade hissed across the invisible wall that protected Sapo's body. He stumbled off balance and Jacaré followed. His second cut would have amputated Sapo's arm, but only the barest edge of Jacaré's sword made contact.

They both looked at the line of blood that marred the sleeve of Sapo's shirt.

"Congratulations," Sapo said, eyeing the spreading stain with a grin. "You've scored first blood. Enjoy that small victory."

A sizzling heat bit into Jacaré's back. A dagger skipped off his shoulder blade and sank into the muscle below. He expected to see a man looming behind him with his sword positioned to run him through. Instead there was a surprised soldier squatting several feet away, pawing at his empty belt.

"Metal affinity." Sapo took slow, deliberate steps toward Jacaré, the tip of his sword dragging across the ground. "I have learned a few things since the academy."

Jacaré coughed, and blood splattered across his chin. He wiped it away with the back of his hand and struggled to his feet.

"Surrender, Jacaré."

"Never."

Sapo raised his hand, and Jacaré fumbled to raise his shield. It was the first defensive skill he'd ever learned, but it melted away like dew on a hot morning. His power was spent, his energy with it. He wavered, dizziness making balance difficult. Two stumbling steps backward brought him to Vibora's corpse. If he was going to die, he was going to do it at her side.

The men ringing Sapo and Jacaré broke formation, retreating for cover as another cannon shell exploded close by. A hole appeared in their ranks, revealing a clear path through camp.

It was no escape for Jacaré. He wouldn't run from Sapo and he wouldn't leave Vibora behind. Not again.

"Lay down your weapon."

Jacaré shook his head, ignoring the coppery taste in the back of his throat and the fact that he couldn't lift his arm. "Take it from me."

With a sigh, Sapo stepped closer. "If I must." He raised his sword over his head, but the weapon flew from his hands.

"What?" Sapo looked at his empty palms, then turned to see where his blade had gone.

And stepped directly into Pira's blow.

With a surge of pride and relief, Jacaré watched as his sister cracked Sapo across the face with a short staff of wood. The leader of the Nata fell to his knees, and Pira smashed him in the side of the head, spittle flying from his mouth.

Flame shot from Sapo's fingertips, but it rebounded on him in a cloud of steam. He screamed, raising his arms to protect his face. A hole in the ground opened under his feet, sucking him into a muddy morass.

Jacaré's thoughts were disconnected; he couldn't quite understand what he was seeing. Pira was collared, but she wasn't responding to Sapo's attempts to control her. And she didn't have affinity for Water. *How . . .*

Leão, alive and whole, stepped into the circle. A red mark ringed his neck, and his cheeks were hollow, but he held Sapo's sword with a certain grip.

"Today," Leão said, grabbing a fistful of Sapo's hair. "Justice outweighs mercy."

Sapo's scream cut off as the blade dropped across his neck.

Chapter 80

Rafi

Rafi sat at the center of a web of bodies. He'd called all the surviving Performers close; they shared their *essência*, but their mutual strength was fading. Exhausted and mentally bruised, Rafi did his best to protect the survivors by shrinking the shield blocking the road.

"Lord Rafi!" the lookout shouted. "Sapo's troops are running."

"Is it a trick?" Rafi asked, afraid to move and break the tentative hold he still had on the power.

"No, sir! They've turned directly west, heading straight toward Maringa."

"What are Belem's troops doing?" Rafi asked, unsure what it meant that his enemy had come to his rescue.

"Most are pursuing, but there's a group of ten or so riding this way."

"Friend or foe?" Rafi asked, unwilling to hope.

"Sir . . ." The apprentice Firesword hesitated, lowering the spyglass. "The approaching group. They've dropped Belem's banner. They're raising yours."

If this was some trick, if Belem was here to deal the final blow . . .

Before Rafi made a move, he looked to Ursu and Yara, the two Performers closest to him. Deep shadows marred their eyes, and Yara's hand quaked where it rested on Rafi's back. They both nodded.

Rafi let the shield fall. The sudden release was an astounding relief. He hurried to his feet and fumbled for the sword provided for him by the Performers. The small band followed, ready for an attack, and unwilling to admit they were probably too worn out to defend against one.

A black horse with a white blaze on its nose cantered at the center of the approaching men. The rider took off his helmet, shaking out black hair not quite as curly as Rafi's.

"That's my brother," Rafi said in awe, dropping his weapon to the ground.

Breaker trotted forward, the line of guards and standard-bearers falling back.

A cocky smile creased Dom's face as he leaped out of the horse's saddle, but there was something cautious behind the bravado. "No one expected *me* to save the day, probably you least of all."

"Santiago's safe?" Rafi asked, the words rushing out of his mouth.

"It is. We defeated Belem's troops at the estate." Dom paused for a moment and kicked the dirt between his feet. Rafi recognized the nervous habit. "I didn't get your letter until after Belem's attack, and came as quickly as I could."

Relief was one more drop in a too-full barrel. Rafi gathered his brother in hug, pounding him on the back. "I want to know how you ended up with Inimigo's cannons, but I don't know where Johanna is. The mine collapsed and—"

"Then we better find the princess." Dom whistled for his men to follow. "We'll help wherever we can."

"Make sure none of Inimigo's troops double back and try to surprise us."

"Already on it." Dom dropped Breaker's reins and jogged away.

Rafi wished he had time to say more, to thank Dom for coming, but he settled for a quick pat to Breaker's flank and rushed to the last spot where he'd seen Johanna.

Despite his earlier efforts to excavate, the terraces of the mine had collapsed and the tunnels were blocked. Tons of dirt and stone filled the places where people had stood, and he could see a piece of black fabric trapped among the rubble.

"Has anyone seen Johanna?" he shouted.

Performers were emerging from the other mines, wounded and dirty. They fell into the arms of their loved ones and hurried across the field to seek out others who'd been caught in the melee.

Johanna wasn't among them.

"The tunnels collapsed behind us," an old man said as he stumbled closer to Rafi. "A few were trapped."

"Was Johanna with you? How many are unaccounted for?" Desperate, Rafi slipped over the lip of the mine and tried to work his way deeper into the wreckage. Exhaustion made him clumsy, and he slipped, barking his knees on a stone.

"I don't know," the old Performer said, his voice soaked in sorrow. "I didn't see her after."

For a moment Rafi felt nothing, not the uneven dirt beneath his feet, not the sweat that dotted his brow, not the weariness that made his arms heavy. He was a void, an empty hole, as still and emotionless as the mine he knelt in.

I'm supposed to be the most powerful person in the world, and there is nothing I can do against all of this.

"Check the field," the Performer advised. "Maybe she was among the inj—"

"Rafi?" A voice cut over all the others. It was shaky and weak, but he'd recognize it with or without the tang of power it carried.

He spun toward the sound and saw Johanna's silhouette weaving toward the mine's mouth. Scrambling over the boulders, he met her before she came too close to the edge.

There was blood on her forehead and down the side of her face, and she limped as she approached, but otherwise she was whole and alive.

Before he could put his relief into words, she was in his arms. Her cheek pressed against his chest, her arms tight around his waist.

"You have to help them. The tunnels. Some of them are trapped." She took his hand, trying to tow him back into the mine. "We have to get them out."

Chapter 81

Johanna

Tears were clogging her throat and making it hard to talk, but Johanna hurried on. "Please." She climbed down into the hole, frantic to get her friends out. "James was behind me."

Johanna pushed against a boulder that was three feet tall and partially buried, and was surprised that it wouldn't move. She was a Performer. She was part Keeper. Shouldn't she be able to do something? The tunnel was at least fifteen feet farther down. If Rafi could move all this stone . . .

She turned, expecting him to be hard at work, but instead he was standing a few feet behind her with his head down and his hands on his hips.

"What are you doing?" she yelled, grabbing a stone that was about the size of her head and trying to roll it aside. "They could be suffocating. We need to . . . we need to *save* them."

"Jo." There was a plea in his voice, but she ignored it. Pushing on. Digging at the stone. Bloodying her fingers.

"Someone get shovels and—"

"Jo." He touched her arm lightly.

She swatted him away. "Help me!"

"Stop."

"No. Not till they're out."

Rafi's arms wrapped around her, gently pinning hers down. "We already found James."

Found. Found, not saved. Her breath came in jagged gasps, tearing at her lungs, but she couldn't seem to slow it down. "I sent them to their deaths. The mines were my idea. I should have done something different. I should have . . ."

The world swirled inside her skull, and her legs turned to jelly. Rafi kept her from falling against the stones, but he sat down hard, jarring her back, and her thoughts.

She could feel his heart racing against her spine. The tendons in his hands stood out in sharp relief. He had already tried to save them, she realized, and was so weak from the attempt that he couldn't hold her up.

Joshua, Thomas, Mama, Captain Alouette, Snout, Pira, Leão, Elma, Didsbury, Sergio, Olivia, Julia, James . . .

All dead. All killed before their time.

He squeezed her hard, as if he could force the remorse out of her. "You did what any good leader should do. You gave your people a chance at survival. You strategized to protect as many as possible. You put yourself in danger to protect them. No one would ever ask more."

"No one would ask for more, but you *expect* more." She felt his breath catch and knew that she'd surprised him. "You expect to live your life like this, constantly putting lives of individuals aside for the greater good. Even if that means sacrificing them—or sacrificing yourself."

The pause in their conversation was long, long enough for her breathing to calm and her head to stop spinning.

"I have no intentions of dying this week or this year," he said, guessing at the deeper meaning of her words. "Have a little faith, Johanna. We survived this battle when no one thought it was possible. I think chances are good we can survive anything else."

It wasn't the promise she wanted to hear. She wanted him to say, *Since I have you to live for, then I simply won't die.* But she knew the truth. Rafi, the honorable lordling, would be a martyr for his people. He'd be venerated in song and story. His face would be painted on city walls. People would leave flowers at the feet of his statues. He'd be the hero every child looked up to and pretended to be.

But he'd never be hers.

A voice rose from across the smoking field. "Lord Rafi! Johanna! People are coming!"

They broke apart, struggling to their feet, preparing for another wave of attacks. Johanna fumbled for the dagger at her belt but found her sheath empty.

"It's okay, Jo. Look." Rafi pointed, and a small breeze blew the smoke away. Three familiar shapes were limping toward them. Two supporting a taller one in the middle. "They'll be our allies," he said with more optimism than she felt. "If anyone can help us figure out what needs to be done now, it's those three."

Rafi gave her hand a gentle squeeze, ratcheting the vice around her heart a little tighter.

Following Jacaré, Leão, and Pira were a straggling bunch of people. The haze of the battlefield hid their faces, but every now and then a beam of sunlight would catch the metal around their necks.

"Help us get these damn collars off!" Pira shouted.

Dom's troops rushed forward, offering supporting hands. The former slaves fell to their knees, begging to have the collars removed. The DeSilva soldiers hurried, fingers fumbling against the smooth metal, seeking out the clasps. One by one the bands fell free, dropping from scarred throats.

"Thank you." The words were repeated as embraces were exchanged between strangers.

"Thank you for saving us."

Chapter 82

Dom

Dom sat on the ground with his back against one of the poles that supported the Performers' tent. The peaked roof had a small hole that let the smoke from the fire escape without letting the rain in. It was comfortable, as tents went, and the heat from the fire, combined with his sore muscles, made him drowsy.

A sad bit of music rose from outside—nearly drowning out Rafi and Johanna's argument at the tent's far side. Drinks were being passed around; soldiers and Performers huddled together, remembering their dead.

It was a victory, but for Dom it felt hollow. He wouldn't be returning to his normal life no matter how things worked out. He could accept the responsibility of being duke, but facing it alone was something else. Brynn was lost to him, and soon Rafi would be as well.

His brother had given him the barest details, fantastical as they were, about Keepers and magical barriers. They'd had an ugly quarrel over true honor, duty, and sheer stupidity, but nothing Dom said could sway Rafi. Johanna was taking another shot, but Rafi kept changing the subject.

Time for some of that alcohol the Performers are sharing.

He rose slowly, favoring the hip that had been grazed by the crossbow bolt, but his movement caught Rafi's attention.

"Don't leave," Rafi said, cutting off whatever Johanna had been saying. "Jacaré's gathering the Performers' representatives. We've got important things to address."

Dom did as his brother asked, and lowered himself to the ground with a groan. He didn't want to listen to any more of Rafi and Jo's fight or watch the way they revolved around each other, finding excuses to touch. Her words were angry, but her eyes betrayed her sadness. Rafi responded with sharpness that was at counterpoint to his desperate need to be close to her.

Knowing that the connection between Rafi and Jo could be severed in the next few days made Dom hurt for things that were gone and things that would never be. Tears sprang to his eyes, and he rested his head back against the tent pole to keep them from falling.

Don't be ridiculous. DeSilvas don't cry, he reminded himself, but this short period of rest, these few moments of calm, gave him too much time to really examine the last few weeks at length. Brynn's betrayal, Belem's attack, and the miracle that had saved Santiago.

He knew better than to call it a miracle. Their safety hadn't been assured by some benevolent god; it was all Maribelle's doing.

Fernando's arrival and cannon barrage had forced Belem's troops against Santiago's walls. The enemy rushed the main gates, hurriedly laying planks across the palisade.

It was a close thing, the gate buckling under their harried attempts, but with continued cannon fire and heavy losses—especially in the upper echelons of their command—Belem's troops surrendered.

Dom's hair was still wet with well water when his enemy raised a white flag.

Fernando confirmed Dom's guess once he made it into the estate. "That 'package' Lady Maribelle requested I transport from the Wisp Islands? Three dozen of the finest cannons I've ever seen." He called one of the artillery crews forward. "Brand new, freshly cast from lightweight metal, and all of them marked with Inimigo's clenched fist."

Lady DeSilva was equally amazed. "How did she manage something like this? Without telling anyone?"

The duke shook his head. "Is that girl promised to anyone?"

"No," Dom said too quickly. His uncle noticed, raising eyebrows at Dom's reaction. "I mean, why? Are you in the market for a new wife?"

Fernando's eyes shifted to his sister and back, and he smiled in a way that made Dom feel exposed. "If you don't take her hand, someone with close ties to you should. A woman that crafty is better as a friend than an enemy."

Dom doubted, even now, that Maribelle would give her loyalty to someone simply because they shared a name.

She hadn't woken before Dom rode north, and thoughts of her courage plagued him. She'd done so much for Santiago, for the freedom of his people, and he'd repaid her only with suspicion and unkindness. When he returned to Santiago, Dom swore, he'd find a way to make it up to her.

DeSilvas don't break their promises.

Jacaré swept open the tent doors, and the stiff breeze that followed him shifted Dom's attention to the present.

Two Performers entered in quick succession, and Johanna stepped away from the table to greet them.

"Is something wrong?" she asked quickly as they ringed the small table.

Rafi signaled Dom over, and he joined them at the far end.

"Inimigo's troops are well on their way to Maringa. A few bands of stragglers have been dealt with," the older man said. "We'll keep watching for more. The freed slaves are resting. One of them keeps asking for you, Johanna, but she's exhausted and difficult to understand."

"All right," Jo said with a nod. "I'll try to see her when we're finished here."

"She'd appreciate that, my lady."

"Please don't call me that," she said, her bearing stiff.

Rafi pressed a hand to her lower back and whispered a few words into her ear, and Dom saw it again—the intensity, the focus, the affection.

"Let's discuss the future of Santarem," Rafi said, taking control. He faced Dom, something deceitful in his smile. "You're going to want to pay attention."

Chapter 83

Leão

The Performers had circled their wagons in the meadow east of the battlefield. Tents had been pitched inside the ring, with small fires burning within the perimeter.

Leão sat on a log near the fire with a blanket draped around him. He felt the cold all the way to his bones, like a flu he couldn't shake and that no one could heal. Pira sat next to him, close enough that their shoulders brushed when she stirred her bowlful of *feijoada*.

She'd positioned herself in front of the tent's door, turning away anyone who came close with nothing more than a scowl. In the morning they would pool their power to destroy the collars, because none of them had recovered enough energy to do it now.

The sound of someone sobbing softly reached Leão's sensitive ears, and Pira's as well. She shifted, checking behind her every few minutes, conflict clear on her face. He knew Pira well enough to know that the former slave's crying penetrated the armor she wore around her heart. Leão hoped that it wasn't the only thing to get through to her tonight.

"Tell me again," he said, feeling parched though he'd drunk all the water his stomach could handle. "How many soldiers did you have to get through to free me?"

There was a hint of a dimple in her cheek that appeared only when she was trying not to smile, but she didn't respond to his query.

"Was it six? Seven?" He placed a hand on her knee. "Don't be humble."

"It was eleven, if you're counting the one that I forced to take off your collar," she said, brushing his hand away.

Leão forced a small laugh, though the truth terrified him. "Eleven. The mighty Pira. I should never underestimate you."

"A lesson you should have learned much earlier."

"That is the truth."

They exchanged a look, holding gazes for a moment too long for friendly conversation. She broke it by returning her attention to her food.

"Even with all that bravery you're still afraid of your feelings for me," Leão said as he studied her profile.

The spoon fell out of her hand. "What?"

Leão took her bowl and set it on the ground. "You fought through a camp full of armed soldiers to get to me. You found a way to save me when no one else could have done it. And please don't say that night at Performers' Camp meant nothing to you, because I've relived that kiss a hundred times, praying—"

"No, Leão. No." She stood, moving a step away. "That night was a mistake. I'm your superior officer. I could be stripped of my rank. I could be forced out of the Elite Guard."

"That's not going to happen. If we succeed and the barrier is restored, we will be honored," he said, looking up at her, wishing she were still sitting beside him. Her proximity had made him feel daring. "You may even be advanced in rank."

"*You* may be. You're a full Mage and the grandson of the head of the Mage Council. You have hundreds of options, but I am not one of them."

He stood slowly, letting the blanket tumble down behind him. "Why not? Because you're afraid of what other people would think of us being together?" Grabbing her arms, he jerked her closer with all the strength he had. Her hands shot up between them, palms resting on his chest. "Are you *afraid* of what people would think?"

Her lips fell open in a little O of surprise; she blinked rapidly as she tried to formulate a response. Leão didn't give her the option, covering her mouth with his.

She melted against him for a few of Leão's too-fast heartbeats, and then just as quickly she wrenched away. He took a stumbling step backward at the sudden loss of connection.

"I made a decision long ago that I was an Elite Guard," Pira said. "I don't want to be another soldier. I want to be High Captain, and that will never happen if I let myself be distracted by a pretty boy who is fun to kiss." She stepped into the space she'd forced between them, and looked directly into his eyes, driving her point home. "And that is all you'll ever be to me, Leão. A pretty boy who is fun to kiss."

"I know what you're trying to do, and it won't work." He swallowed, nervous, doubting himself for a moment. Then he remembered the gentle brush of her fingers on his face when he nearly died in the alley. "You feel guilty for what Vibora made you do, but that wasn't your fault."

"You don't know what you're talking about."

"Yes, I do. Don't you think I've put the pieces together, Pira? You're following in your brother's footsteps too closely. You can't push away everyone you love simply because you're afraid to get hurt."

She spun away, heading toward the perimeter.

"Go ahead and run," he said with certainty. "I'll be right here waiting when you get back."

CHAPTER 84

PIRA

"You're relieved of duty."

The sentry jumped to his feet, looking at Pira with nervous eyes. "I sat down for just a minute, and the view from the top of the boulder is really good," he said as he rubbed the sleep from his face.

"You're not in trouble." If he were one of her men, she'd have him lashed, but he was a Performer—not even a Firesword—and he was exhausted. "Go back to camp."

He edged around her, as if trying to keep a wild animal at bay.

Pira didn't care what he thought, so long as he went. Emotion boiled in her chest; hurt, sadness, loss, filled her to bursting, and she didn't want anyone to see it spill over. She dropped onto the boulder, clenching her arms tightly around the dreadful roiling in her middle, and tried to contain the tears.

The pain was real, as bright and wicked as an unexpected punch to the stomach, but it was something she wanted to feel. It was something she'd earned.

"He's not wrong, you know," Jacaré said, startling a half sob out of her.

She wiped away the evidence on her forearm before she spoke.

"How did the meeting go with Rafi and Jo? Are we leaving for the wall tom—"

"There were a lot of lessons I intended you to learn." He climbed onto the boulder and sat down beside her. "You excel at weapons. You're a good leader, and make careful decisions when the consequences affect others."

He paused, and she felt his eyes on her, but she couldn't meet them. Instead she focused on the darkness, staring at the scrub forest and boulder-littered hills that stretched to the south.

"But I failed to teach you your own worth."

She did turn then, seeking his gaze under the night sky. "What are you talking about? I know what I'm worth."

"You might know your worth as a soldier, your worth in a fight, but I doubt you know your worth as a person." Jacaré touched her shoulder, giving it a brotherly shake. "You don't recognize that you are *worthy* of another person's affection. You blame yourself for what happened to Leão, what happened with the slaves, but none of it was your fault. You didn't choose to hurt those people, and in the end you saved them."

It had been a long time since they'd talked like siblings, like people who knew each other outside the structure of command, and she realized how much she'd missed it. Her upbringing had been quiet, her memories full of Jacaré, the glint of the sun on weapons, hearty meals, and the smell of steel, leather, and sweat. It wasn't a soft childhood, but it had turned her into an Elite Guard. She was proud of that, and she was proud of him. But even so, she had to admit to herself that despite his attention, his devotion to her and to the Guard, he'd never seemed fully happy.

"Are you preaching to me about love, Jacaré? You're not exactly the prime example."

He gave an irritated grunt. "What was the first thing I taught you in weapons training?"

"How to defend myself."

"Did I smack you with a sword and make you learn from your mistakes?"

"Of course not."

"Precisely. I tried to show you what I knew from experience, Pira. I'm asking you to trust that experience now." He thumbed behind him, toward the fire where Leão sat. "You are worthy of every happiness. If that boy makes you happy, then don't let some self-inflicted torture keep you from what you deserve."

The emotions welled again, and she tried to slam a wall of self-control in place. "But I almost killed him," she said, her voice watery. "I'll never forget what it felt like to stab him. To feel *his* blood on my skin."

"So don't forget," Jacaré said with a simple shrug. "Use that memory. Let it remind you how grateful you are that he survived. If you don't, you might as well have died. Living without love isn't really living at all."

Her heart throbbed with a shared pain. She lowered her voice to a whisper. "I'm sorry about Vibora. I know she must have been . . . different once, for you to have felt her loss so keenly for such a long time."

"She was." His lips compressed, not quite a smile. "You might have liked her. Or hated her. In some ways she was a lot like you."

Pira couldn't quite believe that, but she nodded anyway. "She did save me in the end."

"She did," he said, his voice hoarse.

There was more that Pira wanted to say, more questions she wanted to ask. She wanted to spend more time with Jacaré—the brother she remembered—but neither of them was any good at sharing their feelings. The little exchange was a nice start. The rest would have to wait for another day.

"While I'm sure you appreciate my advice"—there was a hint of humor in his voice, but Pira knew him well enough to recognize that it was forced—"I actually came to talk to you about a project I need some help with."

Chapter 85

Johanna

Johanna lay still for a few moments, her head resting in the crook of Rafi's arm. There was nothing particularly romantic about their sleeping arrangements. Dom snored rather loudly a pace away, and Jacaré and Leão were asleep somewhere near the door. All the extra blankets had been sent to the tent the former slaves occupied, and it made sense for the rest of them to curl up together.

She couldn't complain. Sleeping close to Rafi, sharing his warmth, feeling the stubble on his chin catch in her hair, were all things that she longed to continue. Nights lying next to Rafi, even on rock-ridden ground with too many other bedfellows, were precious.

Her stomach wrung like a wet rag, twisting with misery. They'd argued politics and plans till they were both hoarse, and had come to a loose agreement about her future and the future of Santarem. She'd convinced Rafi that with the imminent threat gone, a council made up of dukes and their underlords would help nurture the peace of Santarem, and at his insistence she'd been persuaded to accept a new title: Grand Arbiter.

Her presence on the council would give the Performers representation, and she'd already received backing from Vicente and

Cruzamento—both had pledged to serve King Wilhelm's heir once she could prove her claim.

And thanks to Dom, she had the necklace that had once been her father's. She also had a letter from Rafi's father asserting her identity, the testimony of dozens of Performers, and at least one Keeper. Rafi felt certain it would be enough.

Part of her longed for the simple life of a Performer. She'd buy a wagon of her own and join a troupe, and she and Michael would live out their lives far distant from intrigue and violence. But as she watched the rise and fall of Rafi's chest and felt his breath feather across her brow, she knew that this was her destiny. He'd accepted the lot he'd drawn, and she would take control of hers.

A shadow passed across the tent's outer wall and then moved closer to the door. A hand parted the flaps, and Jacaré was instantly on his feet, weapon drawn. Besides the whisk of his sword, Johanna heard no other noise. He held out one hand toward Johanna, motioning for her to stay still.

A pale face peeked between the tent flaps. Jacaré straightened from his defensive crouch, eyeing the woman with openmouthed confusion. They didn't exchange any words, but he pressed his palm over his heart and gave a half bow. The woman hesitated, then gave a nod in response. She backed out of the tent, and Jacaré waved for Johanna to follow.

What in Mother Lua's name was going on?

Johanna slid out from Rafi's arms and he slept on, undisturbed. She stepped carefully over the sleeping bodies and out of the tent.

"Jacaré?"

The Keeper emerged from the darkness along the tent's side. "Johanna, she went toward the northern perimeter." He pointed toward the line of mountains in the distance. "She wants to talk to you."

"Who is she?"

"I'll stay here and keep watch," he said, not answering her question. "You'll be fine."

She wasn't worried about her safety, but new concerns rushed in. This was a precipice. She could feel herself standing on the crumbling edge, unsure if she should take a step backward toward comfort and safety, or if she should leap into the void.

"Go," Jacaré said, giving her a little push.

Beyond the ring of the wagons the woman had stopped next to one of the boulders, her posture impatient and expectant.

"Adri—Johanna," the woman called to her, her voice laced with recognizable power, though it resounded with tenderness instead of compulsion.

The woman was tall, Johanna realized as she edged closer. Not quite as tall as Pira, but at least four fingers taller than Johanna, and thin in a way that suggested illness. Starlight spilled onto her face, highlighting eyes of an indiscernible color, a narrow nose, and a full mouth. The skin on her face was drawn tightly, highlighting the hollows beneath her cheekbones and the small cleft in her chin. She might have been beautiful once.

"Do I know you?" Johanna asked before she noticed the scarf tied artfully around the woman's neck. "Were you one of Sapo's captives? Were you the one who wanted to speak with me?"

"Yes." The word trembled somewhere between a laugh and a sob. "I am . . . I am a Seer."

Johanna hesitated, measuring her words. "Forgive me, but I knew one other Seer, and everything she foresaw was bleak and miserable. If my future only holds darkness, please, I'd rather not know."

"Oh, no. Not for you, my darling girl!" The woman reached for Johanna's hand, and after a moment's indecision Johanna slipped her fingers into the stranger's. They fit together, similar in their size and shape, small and thin. Johanna was surprised to find comfort and familiarity in the contact.

"Your past has prepared you for a glorious future," the Seer explained. "For you I see a home full of music and laughter. You will have many great friends, and friends destined for greatness."

Breath rushed out of Johanna's lungs, replaced by relief.

"But all of this will come at the price of sacrifice—of yourself and others close to you. Your life will be devoted to service, your decisions will always be made with others in mind, but you will be assured in this choice. It is a life to be proud of."

A tear dropped onto Johanna's hand. She wasn't sure if it was her own or if it belonged to the Seer. They were both crying freely, but Johanna couldn't quite explain why. She felt sadness for all that had happened, for all those she'd lost, but these were tears of connection, of finding a soul that echoed her own.

"What about Rafi? Will he survive? Will we . . ." She couldn't finish.

The Seer cupped Johanna's chin, smoothing away the tears with her thumbs. "I have done all I could to protect you, but there are decisions to be made," she said, as if that were clarification. "Happiness will be yours to *make*."

"What does that even mean?" Johanna asked with a half laugh. These prospects were much better than what Elma had revealed, but they still weren't particularly clear.

The woman smiled sadly, and Johanna allowed her to draw in close. "Happiness is a decision. Every day, even on the bad ones, you must decide to seek the good in the world."

"I will try."

"You *will*." The Seer pressed her lips against Johanna's forehead, sealing her benediction.

Fog had risen, obscuring the field and tents, and Johanna got the sense that it was drawing the Seer away. "Must you go?" Johanna said hastily, gripping the woman's hand.

"I'd love to stay, but I simply don't belong here. My purposes have been fulfilled," she said in a near whisper. "Never fear. I will always be watching out for you."

She took a few steps backward, fading into the evening mist, before disappearing. Shapes drifted, shadows twisted and merged, then the fog cleared with a sudden snap, in a way that was completely unnatural.

"Is she gone?" Jacaré asked, startling Johanna with his appearance.

Shivering, Johanna rubbed at the goose bumps pebbling her arms. "I don't know. She walked away."

"Did she say anything to you? Anything helpful?"

"She said that there will be sacrifices ahead, but that in the end I'll make my own happiness."

Jacaré put a gentle hand on Johanna's back. There had been times in the weeks that she'd known him when she would have shoved him away, but now his touch felt protective and solid. His comfort was welcome. "It's good advice. We're never happier than when we make a conscious decision to be."

The words rang true, and she hoped that no matter what the next few days held, she would choose to be happy.

"Who was she, Jacaré? You seemed to know her."

"I'd never met her, Johanna. But you and I both know who she was."

Gulping against the tightness in her throat, Johanna whispered, "She was my mother."

Chapter 86

Rafi

If despair could be forced into a shape, it would be the Citadel. The gray stone towers hunched beneath the Keepers' Mountains like careworn shoulders, the dark windows were bereft of light and life, and the gaping, groaning gate gave Rafi the impression of abject hopelessness.

"Welcome home," Johanna said aloud, earning a laugh from Dom.

Rafi smiled at them both, glad to know that his brother and Johanna were friends. Maybe the castle wouldn't be so bad if it was filled with the right kind of people.

Jacaré had been commanded by the Mage Council to stay with Jo, and while he didn't have a particularly pleasant personality, he'd protect her and offer her some companionship. Half of the troops Dom had brought to the battle would stay as her Guard, led by Captain Demian.

Demian was a good man, and though it flooded Rafi with a hot wave of jealousy, he'd be a good fit for Johanna if . . .

Rafi wiped the rest of that thought away. He wasn't giving up hope. At least not yet.

"It's sturdy," Leão offered, studying the battlements. "It won't take much to make it livable."

He raised a hand and water rushed out the open gate, carrying mice and other detritus past the group.

"If you ever get tired of being a soldier, I'm sure my mother would hire you to mop our floors," Dom said, his mouth twitching.

Leão caught the sarcasm. "I'll consider that offer."

Pira grunted. "I didn't see any snakes as we passed through the township, so taking down the barrier has reversed some of the negative side effects," she said, not able to hide a little shiver. "That is a definite improvement."

The land was returning to normal. Little shoots of green covered the road that stretched from the Roraima township to the Citadel, and a fuzz of moss coated all the fallen buildings. There were signs of recovery that the Keepers insisted weren't there before.

All good things, apparently, but Rafi couldn't shake off the feeling that this building, large as it was, would become Johanna's prison more than her home.

They'd stretched the journey to the Citadel over two days, moving slowly so that those who were wounded or recovering wouldn't be overtaxed, and the line of Performers' wagons could find a clear path over the broken road. It also gave time for word of their victory to spread. Riders from Cruzamento and Vicente brought letters confirming the rumors about Duke Belem's escape, and about the various underlords vying for his title. Maringa wasn't in much better shape. A quarter of the state had sided with the rebels—Maribelle's rebels—but Inimigo held the capital and the mines.

Rafi could see the DeSilva honor hanging heavy around his brother's neck. The DeSilvas owed Maribelle, and Dom would fulfill that debt.

Peace wasn't something that would happen overnight, but perhaps they were closer.

The tie to the barrier would be split between Johanna and Dom, instead of Rafi. It had been Jacaré's suggestion, and they'd all agreed, though the reasoning wrung Rafi's stomach.

"Shall we go in?" Johanna said, taking his hand.

Rafi nodded and let her lead him through the gate.

Everyone split off in different directions. Leão magically repaired things as he went, and Performers carried in supplies, some of the older ones pointing out different features they remembered from times when they'd entertained the king and his underlords.

"Do you want to stay and listen?" Rafi asked as Johanna led him past the group and to the base of a twisting staircase.

"I'll live here forever. I'll have plenty of time to figure out where the kitchens are." She nibbled her bottom lip. "Would you like to explore with me instead?"

His heart galloped, his face flushing hot. "Yes."

They stayed on the stairs, ignoring the landings that branched off into hallways that had once been private quarters and meeting rooms, until they stepped through an open door and onto the roof.

The ruins of Roraima stretched in front of them, the rubble sprouting with the first signs of rebirth. The city disappeared into a fold in the land and reappeared in the sprawling outskirts of Cruzamento. Beyond that everything was lushly green and vibrant. "It was probably a beautiful view, once," she said. But Rafi saw none of it; he was focused solely on Johanna.

She caught him staring and smiled shyly. "Now would be the perfect opportunity to kiss me."

"No."

The smile dropped from her mouth. "Why not?"

Rafi shook his head, trying to ignore the knot twisting beneath his ribs. "Kissing you now would feel too much like a good-bye." He motioned to the moon, nearly full and dangling over the horizon. "Tomorrow after the power is returned, we can come back up here, and I'll kiss you in full sight of anyone who cares to watch." He stepped close, putting his hands low on her waist and drawing her in. "Tomorrow I will kiss you, and you will never forget it."

"Rafi . . ." Her hands slid up his sides, winding deep into his hair.

The feel of her hands on his skin, of her lips on his throat and on the new scar on the underside of his chin, was almost enough to break his resolve. Instead he reached for her wrists and gently unwound her grip.

"I don't want a soldier's send-off, Johanna. You know those never turn out well in the stories," he said, and she dropped her face against his chest. "This is a promise. And you know I don't break my word."

She sighed, her breath a warm spot over his heart. "Then I better not tell you that I'm in love with you either."

"Probably not." He raised her chin. "I'll wait till after all this is over with to express the deepest wishes of my heart."

"The deepest wishes of your heart?" she asked with a small, playful smile. "That sounds like something worth waiting for."

"It is. I promise—"

She stiffened in his arms, her eyes focused beyond his shoulder.

"What's wrong?"

"Look," she breathed, pointing over the rampart.

Rafi followed the line of her finger and saw lanterns bobbing in the distance.

The lights were too white to have been flame-lit and too steady in the breeze that rolled out of the mountain pass. The procession made its way down the steep mountainside, moving too fast and disturbing too little shale.

"Well," he said, the moment of joviality whisked away. "It seems they keep their word too."

Johanna shivered, and Rafi pulled her close.

They stood together watching the Keepers take up a position beyond Donovan's Wall.

Chapter 87

Johanna

The day dawned bright and clear. One of those perfect, fall mornings that wiped away the previous night's chill and erased the mud puddles that littered the steep incline between the Citadel's foundation and Donovan's Wall. Keepers lined the mountain's feet, standing eerily still. Their faces were expressionless, staring straight into Santarem. Johanna couldn't see any weapons, but the threat was clear. The barrier would be reestablished today or there would be consequences.

The sun's cheery warmth didn't reach Johanna. She'd once fallen into a river swollen with icy winter rain. Soaked to the skin, she'd had to hike back to her parents' wagon, trembling with every step. Walking through the back hall of the Citadel to the small gate that led out to the Keepers' Mountains was a similarly bone-rattling experience.

Performers had crowded into the narrow space, lining the walls. They were subdued, and came to attention as they caught sight of her, fists clenched over their hearts. Their bodies were unmoving, but their faces betrayed a wide mix of emotions: sorrow, pride, fear, and hope.

Rafi managed a smile and a head nod for all of them, putting on a braver face than Johanna could accomplish. The calm was an act, though. He gripped Johanna's hand so hard that it hurt, crushing her knuckles together. She didn't complain. It was the only part of her body that was warm.

Ahead of her, Jacaré swung open the Citadel's rear gate. Brambles pressed into the space, nearly filling the doorway with twisting limbs and finger-long thorns. It was amazing her mother had once fought her way through the tangle.

Jacaré stepped forward and the branches curled back on themselves, clearing a path, and the Keeper strode forward unharmed. Pira and Leão followed, maintaining their rigid soldier's posture and the measured distance between them. Their expressions might not have been easily readable, but the camaraderie they'd once shared was clearly missing.

The thicket opened to accommodate the rest of their small group, with enough space for Rafi to slide next to Johanna and for Dom to stand on her other side. It was cramped, but as she scanned the faces of her companions, she was grateful to be in close company with these five.

"Pira," Jacaré said, nodding to her. "Do you want to . . ."

She gave her brother a long, hard look before reaching for the satchel over her shoulder. Fumbling, she extracted two silver chains with faceted metal pendants hanging at their centers. "This is the best I could do on such short notice," she said, holding one out to Johanna. "It isn't fancy and it won't send images beyond the wall, but Leão worked some *essência* into them so we'll know if you're ever in trouble. I hope that you'll never be in trouble, because I don't want to come to Santarem again. Ever."

The necklace settled around Johanna's neck, the pendant disappearing down the front of her shirt. "Thank you."

Pira hesitated, looking down at Johanna, indecision making her lips twitch. "Well . . ." She gave Johanna a quick embrace before shoving the other necklace into Dom's outstretched hand.

"No hug for me?" Dom asked, drawing a startled laugh from Leão and a frown from Pira. "If you do come back, you're welcome to rescue me any—" Rafi released Johanna's hand long enough to cuff his brother on the back of the head.

Leão's smile held as he shook hands with Rafi and Dom. Then he dropped a kiss onto Johanna's forehead. "Make your own happiness, my friend."

His words, an echo of her mother's, stole her breath. She managed a strangled, "You too."

He stopped in front of Jacaré, offering a formal salute, and Pira snapped to attention.

"Stop, please," Jacaré said in a gruff whisper. He snatched Pira, crushing her to him, in the bruising sort of hug reserved for older brothers. She squeezed him hard in return, unwilling to say goodbye.

Johanna closed her eyes against the scene, remembering too well all the times she had wrestled out of Thomas's embrace. Light, what she wouldn't give to feel that again.

Rafi swayed closer, and she leaned into his side, looking up as her friends turned toward their homeland. Pira's hand sought out

Leão's. He stopped on the trail, studying their interlocked fingers, then placed a quick kiss on Pira's knuckles.

Warmth surged through Johanna, and she couldn't help herself. She stood on her toes and brushed her lips against the corner of Rafi's mouth.

"Jo . . ." His eyes searched hers.

"A reminder of what's waiting for you when this is over."

His arms snaked around her. "It won't be a long wait—" Suddenly he straightened, so quickly that he sent her stumbling into Dom. Dom took a step backward, and two thorn-covered branches whipped forward and wrapped tightly around him.

There was a metallic click, and Rafi's hands flew to his throat. A collar, bright and shiny, pressed tight into his flesh.

"Jacaré!" Horror made Johanna's voice shrill. "What are you doing?"

Rafi lunged toward the Keeper but came up short, as if he'd run into a solid wall.

"Kneel," Jacaré commanded, and smiled as Rafi dropped heavily to his knees. "I wasn't sure if this was going to work." He rolled up his sleeve, revealing three black bands, as dark and flat as the silver collar was bright and shining, ringing his wrist. "I couldn't figure how Vibora could drain and transfer the *essência*. If that fire bolt hadn't hit her precisely in the shoulder, I would never have noticed she was wearing these around her upper arm. Pira realized that each collar was linked to a bracelet."

"Oh, Jacaré," Johanna said, sick with sudden realization. He'd prepared for this moment all along.

Dom thrashed against his constraints, and Rafi railed on a barrier as smooth and solid as glass, both brothers believing the Keeper had betrayed them.

But Johanna knew the truth.

"You don't have to . . . please . . ." Johanna trailed off. This was Jacaré, determined, stubborn, resolute.

"For sixteen years you were an assignment, a duty. I fulfilled my task to care for you physically, but I failed to protect you from sorrow." He ran a thumb over the bracelets with a lover's caress. "I can't promise this will work. I don't know if this will save Rafi's life. But please, Johanna, let me try to save you from this one heartache."

"Jacaré," she said, her voice falling to a choked whisper. "You won't survive."

He offered her a smile, beatific and bright, happier then she'd ever seen. "If that's the case, then so be it. I'll finally rest."

Her mother's warning rang clear. This was the first sacrifice of many to come, but there was sweetness with this bitter. Jacaré was leaving this decision in her hands, and the weight of it would stay with her forever.

Behind her, Rafi beat his fists against the barricade, his voice muffled. She could only imagine what he was saying, but she could remember clearly the voices of those people whose power had been trapped in the wall. All of them Jacaré's friends and family. And if it was their goddess's will, he'd finally join them.

"Please, Princess. Let me try."

She nodded slowly, her head heavy with her blessing. "It will be a rest well earned."

He gave her shoulder a gentle squeeze, then pressed one hand against the Citadel's foundation. Rafi groaned, raising his fists to his head, then he crumbled to the ground. A band of blue light stretched from the collar to the bracelets at Jacaré's wrist.

Jacaré threw open his arms and the light intensified, blotting out everything in Johanna's vision. She could hear Dom shouting in confusion and fear, and Rafi's pained cries.

The silver pendant flashed hot, and arrows of agony stabbed into her chest. She cried out, cursing Mother Lua's name, and then the light winked out, replaced by total darkness.

Chapter 88

Johanna

A hand shook her shoulder; a voice called her name; blood and roses flavored the air. She ignored it all, waiting for the cocoon of sleep to wrap tightly around her and cradle her to a place where dreams of love and hope lived on.

The hard slap of a palm against her cheek forced her eyes open, and she looked into the glowing ball of the sun.

"Johanna, you've got to wake up. I don't think Rafi's breathing." Dom's words came out in a hurried rush.

She sat up too quickly; the thornbushes around her wavered at the edges of her vision. "Where is . . ." She answered her own unfinished question, scuttling across the ground to Rafi's side. He lay on his back, one arm thrown out across the rocky ground.

Her hands shook as she reached out, afraid to feel the chill of death on his skin. "Rafi?" she whispered, brushing one of his wild curls off his forehead.

He didn't respond.

She'd already done this once—thinking Rafi was dead—but this time there was no heat in his skin and his chest was still. His face was cold.

With a rattling breath, her tears broke free. "You promised." She reached for the pulse at his throat but found blistered skin and the solid metal of the collar. "You said this wouldn't be good-bye."

Dom found the collar's latch and the band fell free.

"You liar," she cried, falling across Rafi's chest. "You promised. You never break your promises. You have no honor!"

A hand touched her back, a few inches too low to be proper.

"What will it take to get it back?" Rafi asked with a wheeze. "You are so difficult to please."

She didn't have a chance to answer. His lips found hers, warm and sure and certain.

And as he'd promised, it was a kiss she'd never forget.

Chapter 89

Rafi

Rafi stood at the top of the tower, looking over the craggy mountains and twisted trees that stretched beyond Donovan's Wall. The Keepers, more than two hundred of them, had disappeared, leaving nothing—not a broken branch or a disturbed patch of shale—to show that they'd ever poured through the pass.

The thorn hedge was another matter. In every story Rafi had ever heard, the brambles stretched the entire length of the Citadel in an unbroken line of gray brown. Now a narrow trail snaked from the castle's rear gate to the mountain's feet. It didn't look like a comfortable way to pass, what with the sharp thorns and twisted branches, but for the first time in anyone's memory bright blossoms speckled the hedge.

"Do you see the rabbit?" Johanna asked, shifting in Rafi's arms to point at something his eyes couldn't pick out. She'd retained whatever Keeper powers should have been hers, and Rafi was adjusting to the idea that she could see and hear things he couldn't. Including the bright lines of the magical barrier that stretched toward the cloudy sky. "It's nestled right along the path's edge."

Rafi placed a kiss on the curve of Johanna's neck instead of responding. In a few weeks, when all was settled in Santiago and his mother and Michael reached the Citadel, they planned to complete the betrothal contract their fathers had drawn up so many years before. He smiled against her warm skin, knowing that soon there would be plenty of other places to kiss.

"The hedge will always remind me of him," Johanna said, unaware of Rafi's thoughts—or maybe ignoring them. "It's forbidding and impossible. It looks like something that will tear you to pieces, and it probably could, but it's also offering protection to so many things we can't see."

"Is that how you'll spin the epic of Jacaré?"

The Keeper's body had been found a few paces farther into the bramble hedge. The hardness that had traced lines on his brow and around his mouth had softened in death, and Rafi hoped that Jacaré had finally found peace.

"No," Johanna said, her voice dropping low, the tingle of *essência* brushing across Rafi's skin. "His story will be sacred. He will be revered for his sacrifice, and children who bear his name will be expected to give it honor."

Rafi nodded, a hint of sadness pinching in his chest. Jacaré's sacrifice had been personal, giving up his own life, sealing the barrier with the last residues of his *essência*. Rafi would have tried to stop him. Jacaré had known that and had prepared for every eventuality.

He would never have admitted it, but Jacaré had wanted Rafi to have the future that he'd been denied.

It was an honor debt Rafi could never repay, but he'd live the rest of his life trying.

Feet pounded up the steps to the tower and a throat cleared. "May I join you, or is this *another* private moment?" Dom asked as he peeked around the corner.

"We'll never have a private moment with you around," Rafi said with a sigh.

"Keeping you honorable, brother." Dom's grin was bright, but something in his bearing had changed. He'd never lacked in confidence, but he seemed slightly more conscious about his actions.

"What's in that letter that's made you so happy?" Johanna asked, waving to the small scroll in Dom's hands.

"It's from Lady Maribelle, formerly of Maringa. She asked me to speak to you and the Council of Lords about supporting her rebellion against her father." Dom reread the short missive to himself, and his eyebrows rose. "She makes some interesting promises."

"To you or to the Council?" Rafi asked drily.

Dom didn't have to answer. His shrug insinuated enough.

Johanna punched him playfully on the shoulder. "Go. Respond to her letter. Tell her you have the Council's ear."

"And keep the rest of it appropriate." Rafi raised his eyebrows at his brother. "You never know whose hands it will fall into."

"You take the fun out of everything," Dom said, and retreated toward the stairs.

Once the footsteps had disappeared, Rafi turned Johanna to face him. "I suppose this is a new beginning for Santarem. Councils of dukes and underlords, representatives from every township and Performers' Camp."

She nodded. "Someday it will an incredible tale about how a duke and a princess changed Santarem."

He nuzzled the soft skin below her ear. "And how will it end?"

"Exactly how we want it to," she said, shivering at his touch. "Happily."

Acknowledgments

There's a reason authors thank their editors first: editors' names aren't on book covers, but their hearts and souls are on every page. If you love a book, remember a great editor was behind it. They pick at the flaws, the logic, the very word choice, and encourage and inspire authors to find better, smarter, cleaner ways to craft a story. Thank you, Annie Nybo, for picking up this orphaned manuscript and loving it enough to make it shine.

That gratitude extends to the entire team at Margaret K. McElderry Books and Simon & Schuster for all their work on this book and on *The Storyspinner*. Thank you Justin Chanda, Bridget Madsen, Erica Stahler, and Michael McCartney. Treats and smoosh hugs for all of you!

My Super Agent, Jennifer Laughran, is quite literally made of magic. I love her supportive snark and sharp mind. I owe her a dozen dinners, and maybe a cape that she can swoosh every time a deal gets done.

When I met my publicist, Audrey Gibbons, for the first time, I said, "With a name like Audrey, you have to be super classy." She is. And savvy. And persistent. And incredibly kind. Thanks for all your hard work on my behalf!

By the time this book prints, I'll have known Nicole Castroman for nearly five years, talked to her on the phone almost every day, hashed out dozens of plot and character problems, laughed over millions of stupid things, and never met in person. I hope we can fix that very, very soon. Expect a hug.

To my other fantastic critique partners and the people I'm grateful to call friends—Jess Lawson, Lynne Matson, Diana Wariner, Katie Marie Stout, Kristin Rae, Trisha Leaver, Lindsay Currie, and Mary Waibel—thank you, thank you for the supportive, helpful, insightful emails and phone calls. I really couldn't do this without you. Like really. For reals. You ladies make my writing and my life so much better.

Stacy Sorensen and Kara McCoy are the kind of real-life friends that can never be replaced. We all live in different states now, but still manage to exchange hundreds of slightly inappropriate text messages every week and get together a couple of times every year. I can't even think about you ladies without getting teary. I would be a lot less sane (and stylish) without you two. Love you forever.

And then there's Jen Wegner (aka Perfect Friend), who is the most optimistic, positive, thoughtful person I know. You live up to your nickname every day.

Authors wouldn't stay authors for very long without an army of booksellers and book bloggers who support and recommend their novels. Thanks particularly to: Blue Willow Books (Houston), Brilliant Books (Traverse City), The King's English (Salt Lake City), Mundie Moms, My Friends Are Fiction, Icey Books, There Were Books Involved, Fiction Freak, and Reader of Fictions. You make the world a better place!

Librarians and teachers who work so tirelessly to give the right stories to the right readers deserve my undying gratitude. Thank you, thank you!

Without my parents, Dave and Ardy Vallett, this book would never have gotten finished. They give my children so much love and attention while I write that it almost eliminates my mommy guilt. Thank you for a clear conscience, a place to stay every summer, and home that was always full of laughter and books. Love you guys.

The rest of my family is pretty darn amazing too. Thank you Grandma Edie, Lizzy, Joel, MeMe, Travis, Amanda, Brandt, Brandon, Looli, Jarod, Brianne, and of course, Warden (Olivia) and Ricketts (Rick) for supporting this crazy dream, telling your friends about my book, and bailing me out from time to time. Families are forever, and I'm so glad you're mine.

Then there's my own little quadsquad: Gavin, Laynie, Audrey, and Adelynn. Knowing that you are proud of me is the most rewarding part of this entire process. I love hearing you tell friends and strangers all about my book. It makes my heart melt. I believe cupcakes, snuggles, and a movie are in order.

And to my husband, Jamie: you have been incredible this year. Thanks for picking up the slack, sitting up with me on so many late nights, and for helping me figure out fight scenes. I couldn't have done it all without you.

Last but not least, thank you reader! Thanks for going on this crazy adventure with me, letting me pull at your heart strings, and blow up so much stuff. You've given me the greatest job in the world!